The Nightingale's Tooth

a novel

Sally McBride

Milton, Ontario

This is a work of fiction. All of the characters, events, and organizations portrayed in this novel are either products of the author's imagination or are used fictitiously.

Brain Lag Publishing
Milton, Ontario
http://www.brain-lag.com/

Copyright © 2023 Sally McBride. All rights reserved. This material may not be reproduced, displayed, modified or distributed without the express prior written permission of the copyright holder. For permission, contact publishing@brain-lag.com.

Library and Archives Canada Cataloguing in Publication

The nightingale once had teeth as sharp as a shark's, but she traded them for the ability to sing more sweetly than any other bird. She has regretted it ever since.

PART ONE

Chapter One
THE DUST

The boy walked along an unfamiliar road. His feet were bare. Each step raised a little puff of the road's soft tan dust, which laid itself upon his skin and vanished into it.

He looked around, hoping to spy a landmark, but it was too foggy, though the air did not feel chill or damp. It felt like nothing, it sounded empty. A road of nothing, leading nowhere. But the dust that rose to his nostrils was full of shreds of everything—dung, sweat, metal, worms. Clay, piss, bones, blood.

The boy looked down at his toes. Brown and limber, they burrowed into the dust like sparrows taking a dirt bath. He stretched out his thin arms and looked at them. They had no hands at their ends. That was wrong.

I know what to do, he thought. The dust flew up around him in a small whirlwind, seeking a home in his skin. In a moment hands grew, like sea-stars crawling.

He turned them palms-up before his face, seeing the dirt-darkened seams that were the life-lines and the heart-lines, and the small pink pads of his fingertips.

He licked one fingertip and tasted nothing, but he could smell the dust. It made him dizzy, and he almost fell.

The boy jerked upright at a sharp noise. A rhythmic squeaking, as from a wheel. Was there a farm nearby? A woman raising a bucket from a well, turning her winch and peering down into the darkness for the gleam of water? The boy felt that he must be thirsty. He had been walking this dusty road for... hours? Days?

But the squeaking grew closer, and soon resolved into an old woman pushing a top-heavy wheelbarrow out of the fog, looking as if, instead of getting closer, she and her cart were getting bigger. She stopped in front of him.

"Boy," she said, her voice somehow familiar, "are you lost?"

She had white hair in two long braids tied together across her sagging bosom, and bright blue eyes set deep among many wrinkles. Her wheelbarrow held the implements of a knife-sharpener. It looked too heavy for such an old crone, yet she stood straight, her wrists as hard and sinewy as olive branches.

He nodded, wanting to make a proper and polite greeting to the old woman, but finding that he could not take a breath. In fact, he was not breathing at all. He made an effort to inflate his lungs, but stopped as the woman scowled down at him.

"Boy! Are you looking for someone?"

He began to cry.

"Hush! What do you have to cry about?"

"I..." The act of forming the smallest of words made them all come back.

He had words. He had breath. He had memories. He had horror and pain and regret.

He knew why he was crying.

The old woman bent and took him in her arms, and it was like being embraced by a tree that had troubled itself to pity him. He thought he could hear wind in her hair, but that was impossible.

This isn't right, he thought. *This isn't how it is meant to be.*

The dust reached up and pulled him down into its soft relentless bed.

I found myself clinging to the Minotaur fountain's edge, the sculpture's huge stone eyes staring blankly into mine. Wind still sounded somewhere overhead, whining and eerie. An old woman had been holding me. I could still feel her arms.

My fingers trailed, limp and shaking, in the tepid water of the fountain. I drew them out and ran the blessed wetness over my sweating face.

Wetness where there should be dust.

No. I was not a boy trudging aimlessly on a road. I was in the city, and I was most definitely a girl. The wind died away to nothing, vanishing into the heat and clamour of the market.

The damned visions. This one was The Boy on the Dusty Road. The next would be The Moorish Woman, then The Falling Bird. Were all three to happen right here, one after the other, in the middle of Perpignan's market? By now, excuses for my strange behaviour came as easily as the slide of honey on a spoon. The heat, the filthy merchants hawking their wares, even my menses if it came to that. Though I had used that once too often, perhaps. Sigrun wouldn't fall for it again. So, the heat. I'd fainted in the hot sun.

Sigrun sneered, fed up with waiting for me to revive. "You didn't faint, Vara. You raved and cried like a lunatic. What's wrong with you?" She hastened to straighten my robes and snarl at the gawkers. I'd embarrassed her.

I shook Sigrun's silk-draped arm off. Even as companion she was lacking; as friend, impossible. Yet I needed someone to accompany me on a clandestine exit from the villa, and I had little choice. Next time, I'd take a servant and pay her for a closed mouth.

"Nothing is wrong with me. Can't I test your attention now and then? You'd better learn the difference between a noblewoman receiving the subtle wisdom of the Gods, and a mere lunatic." I admit I spoke harshly, but she provoked me. Had I really cried and raved? Sigrun, lesser than I in the social scheme, bowed her head, gritting her teeth at the nonsense she had to swallow.

Of course there was something wrong with me. I suffered from fits, didn't I? Sigrun never believed me when I tried to tell her what I'd seen in the visions; I gave up after the first couple of times, and suspected her of spreading the rumour that I was touched in the head. It had been stupid of me to confide in anyone.

Relenting, I took her hand, and after a moment's tension she gave me a smile. We walked on, arm in arm as companions did.

Sigrun took a ripe apricot from a fruit-seller's cart and bit into it, walking on as the shopkeeper watched her resentfully. It was the sort of thing she did frequently, and I'm not sure she understood that she was stealing. I found a coin in my sleeve and tossed it to him without Sigrun seeing. This is how our friendship progressed, up and down, in fits and starts—so bereft of companionship was I.

I should be thankful that I was blessed with extra coins.

Sigrun spat the apricot pit into the gutter and began to eye the next cart. I tightened my grip on her arm and swung her toward a rug seller. When would the next vision start? The one about the Moorish woman. I hated that one. As Boy, I wailed and lamented like a child, but as Woman I collapsed in a sodden heap of looming horror. Very hard to explain. What had I, Vara Svobodová bint Jameel, a wealthy and loved girl, to be woeful about? Boy and Woman knew, though. *Loss.* Terrible, impenetrable loss that gnawed like a rat at my innards.

"It's getting too hot," I said. "Let's go home."

"But I want to see the god."

Some street boys had captured one earlier that day and were displaying it for money, at least until someone larger and more ruthless came to relieve them of their prize, which wouldn't be long. The little god would soon vanish in one way or another. But I needed to get home before the next vision came. For come it would.

I tested my body's signals. Was I indeed hot? No more than usual. Hungry? Someone of my station did not go hungry. My head was clear again, my guts calm and my curiosity rampant. The next vision would not come for a while.

"Very well. Let's go see it—but then we leave."

Sigrun emitted a squeal of glee and dragged me past the throngs of market-goers poking among the piles of pomegranates and apricots, cheeses and loaves, chickens and butchered goats. The whole market had the rank, greasy smell of unshorn sheep.

More people than usual filled the streets, for it was the Festival of the Sisters. I hadn't imagined so many hereabouts kept to the old ways of worship, but here they were, strolling about like the country bumpkins they were. And I was one of them. Our family had settled on the Sisters to represent our public faith, as Mother and Father would not compromise on their own separate faiths. It was humiliating to belong to that old religion, when a new one—Sarafism, the particular obsession of Petru Dominus—was sweeping the land.

My father, Jameel, had loud arguments about religion and politics with my grandfather. Josef, Count Svobodá, was my mother's father, and lived with us. I called him Pada, and I loved him very much. He had a suite of rooms on the second level overlooking the central fountain, but mostly he inhabited his vast, cluttered workroom in the attics. I wasn't allowed to go there, but of course I did all the time. Pada Josef kept quiet about it, for he liked the company.

"There are the ordinary, everyday gods," Jameel-my-father would say in his logical, even way, "and there are the Great Gods. No praying? No true belief within your deepest heart? Then blame yourself if you get boils on your buttocks, or your best milk cow dies." He would take up his mint tea, and wait for the reaction. It always came.

"No, no!" Pada Josef would shout, waving his arms and spilling tea on his robes. "You're missing the point! We are our own worst enemies. Our own gods!"

My father would smile. "The lesser gods mean nothing—but do you think the Great Gods will ever leave us alone? Look what's happening to that poor bastard Petru."

"Don't pity him!" Pada would holler. "Bloody Hun!"

Ragna Svobodová constantly warned them both to keep their big mouths shut. "Don't talk about Petru! What's wrong with you two?"

I cared as much about Petru Dominus as I did a lighthouse. Something big and stony that did its job. But it was true that Petru, who had been sent to oversee our district by Emperor Ludvik in the spring of 1232, seemed to be going mad. A dour, ginger-haired man, fervent about drainage and irrigation, he'd suddenly embraced Sarafism, a religion that everyone had thought was defunct a thousand years ago. He'd overflowed with manhood, begun to drive himself and his men mercilessly in military exercises, and started stockpiling gold and grain. Now and then he would seem to grow tired, and abandon these efforts to return to his ledgers and plans. Things would be quiet for a while, but then he would once again immerse himself in frantic activity. Including, of course, religious rituals. Influential families were bowing to Saraf and his snake symbol, probably to curry favour.

Sigrun and I shoved our way through the crowd of wine-salesmen, herders in from the flocks to spend their coins on salt and cider, families idling along hand in hand, chattering loudly in their native tongues. We were going to ogle a little god, one weak enough to get itself captured.

Sigrun, blonde and wearing a studied haughty expression, drew looks from grown men as well as boys. She didn't care about the danger in this—I was sure she relished it. "Oh, Vara," Sigrun would say, "you're so slim and lovely, and your hair! Like a black waterfall. See how that Saxon boy gazes at you." She knew she was better looking than I. Most folk who saw us assumed she was the mistress, I the servant. It was difficult to hold my head up with the assurance to which I was entitled. I was my father's daughter, with his dark skin, and little to show of a bosom or hips. Male eyes slid past me to my plump and preening friend.

I was safe from the next vision for a while, but I could feel it in the base of my spine like an insect crawling. When that dread crept to my neck, down I would go, right here in the middle of the town plaza. Unthinkable. But I did want to see the captured god...

We elbowed our way forward.

Shouting and exclamations in several languages, many of which I'd studied. *Look at that horrid thing! Stop shoving! Ugh—it stinks!*

Pigeons flew in a ragged circle above the throng. A skinny beggar boy grabbed me by the arm and demanded money. I snarled at him, and he darted away for easier pickings.

The crowd shifted, and there it was, held tight in a net of wire. Trapped and squawking. I'd never seen anything like it.

It was small as a she-goat, and seemed to be made of both fur and feathers, tawny brown, here and there slashed with white and black in no particular pattern. Entangled in its cage, it screamed and fought like a Saracen. The over-sweet stink of honey wafted out as it struggled. We drew our shawls up against the smell, too strong to be pleasant, and gawked along with everyone else.

Three filthy, hooting street boys poked at it, making it hiss. Its yellow beak clacked, and its eyes, a strange shade of blue, flashed around. The boys wanted to sell the thing and were yelling for bids. In a strange lisping squawk it cried, "'et me go, you pig-'uckers, you 'ornicators!"

"Is it really a god? Can't they turn to smoke and vanish?" I shouted over the din.

"I can't see—what's happening?" We clung together, alert for pickpockets and groping hands.

A wave of angry jeering swept down the street, and a squad of Lord Petru's men, Saraf's snake-symbol freshly hammered into their breastplates, strode in and took over from the street urchins, dispersing them easily with shouts and kicks, and a single coin tossed to the ground. The boys scrambled for it as it hopped into a crack between the paving stones.

I felt a sudden throb in my chest. The little god would suffer much worse at the hands of Petru than if left to the tender mercies of street boys. Its cries lost their menace and became pitiful, the begging of a helpless creature. But why should I care? I didn't know, but I suddenly regretted its captivity. If not for people like me wanting to see it, the boys might have let it alone. It might indeed vanish to wherever small, suffering gods went.

"Poor thing," I muttered, pulling Sigrun away.

But then I saw one of the soldiers draw his knife. Long and silver, it flashed red as blood in the lowering sun. My eyes were caught by it. A shiver convulsed my skin.

My surroundings began to blacken and close in. The sounds of shrieking metal and crashing boots filled my ears. The sliding, meaty crunch of a sword hitting bone.

I clapped my hands over my ears. Closing my eyes never stopped a vision, for that's what this was, but not the usual one. Something new was flooding my brain. I fought against it, knowing it was hopeless.

With the last of my dimming consciousness, I spotted a dark, shadowed space under a fruit bin nearby. The clean, plain scent of pears pulled me down to hide. My next vision, the one about the Moorish woman, shouldn't be until the sun touched the base of the south minaret. And it always started the same way—on a sunny mountain road.

This was different. A God had invaded my mind. A Great God. The little captive god tore uselessly at the wire with claws like a cat's, shedding feathers, fur, and honey-scented dust. The soldiers slung it onto a pole, hoisted it up and marched away into a stinging, wavering black silence. There had been no sword chunking into bone. It was just a damned vision.

Silence! Cool darkness. I thought I'd got off easily. Night air, sweet and cool, flowed across my skin like balm. I must have fainted and been brought home... The heat and crowds of the market were gone, quickly fading into a memory that meant nothing—a tiny speck of light gulped down by the darkness around me.

I suddenly realized that there really was *nothing* around me. The insistent pull of the earth below me had vanished. I was floating in the air. A pulse of fear started in my gut. Had I died? Was this the afterlife? I wanted to flail my way to something solid and hang on.

"You're not dead and you're not going to fall," I muttered to myself. "It's but a vision, and you will learn from it."

My eyes soon adjusted to the dimness, and I saw, below me, what appeared to be my own bed. With someone who looked very much like me in it. A man bent over the sleeping girl. I could hear his gasping breath through the dark air as my heart jammed against my ribs.

"Vara...Vara, forgive me," the man whispered. My floating self let out a breath. It was only my Pada Josef, his voice faint and choked.

Forgive him? For what? Was he drunk? Demented? I tried to speak, tried to tell him it wasn't me in bed—I was up here in the rafters, but my voice was dismayingly weak and small.

I could see the top of his bald head with its wispy grey fringe of hair. And I could see that behind his back he gripped a long silver knife.

Frantically I pinched my arm, but all the pinching I'd ever done never stopped a vision. I had to let it run its course. I hovered like a puff of smoke high among the rafters—not even in my own familiar bedroom next to my parents. I had no idea how or why.

The girl—the other Vara Svobodová bint Jameel—slept on, unaware of our grandfather crouched over her like a desperately weeping vulture. Her legs were bare, her coverlet tossed back. I did the same thing in the hot nights, to free my feet. But unlike me, she had the rounded hips and breasts of a woman, showing in dim waves through the thin muslin of her nightdress.

The rubies on my gold Blindeye glinted on the chain lying in the hollow of her throat. It was the Blindeye my mother gave me two years ago, when I turned thirteen, to replace the plain silver one I'd always worn. The girl *must* be me, an older me, for I would never give up that eye, nor the silver owl coin on the chain with it.

But there was a third thing on the necklace. Triangular, black. Blurred like a dream within this dream. It gave me a sick feeling of something about to happen, like a storm rolling down from the mountains. Something lost and dead nearby. The air around me shuddered and rippled, as if heat were rising through it. There was a boy, somewhere at the edge of my vision. A sideways shape, dancing erratically like a candle flame. When I tried to focus on him, he flickered away.

The air smelled of chalk and lightning.

I shivered like a dog as I floated under the ceiling. It was a vision of the future that I watched, happening down there in my bed.

I felt someone tug on my arm, and let out a stifled shriek. For a moment hot sunlight and the babble of voices penetrated the vision, and I struggled toward it. I wanted out of this nightmare. The sound of men shouting, the whir of pigeon's wings—but the dark story continued its telling...

I saw my sleeping self awaken. I saw her look up at Josef, saw her eyes grow huge and her mouth gape open. She didn't see me. Did I want her to? I don't know, even now. For a moment it looked as if she was about to say something, but then she seemed to reconsider. Her mouth snapped shut.

Crashing noises. The sound of boots on tile, coming closer. With a jerk of his arm my Pada Josef pressed his knife to her throat. His hand shook and the blade bit into her skin. He wept harder. She flinched, and I could hear her panting, her eyes locked on his.

Why didn't she fight? What was wrong with her?

Then, in a deliberate motion, she leaned her head back and bared her neck to him. She closed her eyes and whispered, *I love you*.

Again he begged, "Forgive me," and with one quick, brutal motion slit her throat.

Slit *my* throat. He killed *me*.

I watched myself choke helplessly, blood spraying everywhere. Very soon I stopped moving. My fingers, clutching at my bloody neck, were the last to go limp. My eyes and mouth—and the new-cut mouth in my neck—gaped upward, wide and lifeless.

Pada Josef collapsed to the floor, howling like a dog.

I told the story to my mother, after the villa had settled down and the servants had gone to bed. She had never been so quiet in her life as she was while listening to my tale.

We huddled together on her bed, whispering. I had been carried home from the market, raving and fighting, by two of Petru's Monitors, Sigrun trotting behind weeping with outrage and humiliation. The men had released me to the care of the startled

Eli, our gentle old doorman, who sent for my mother. Ragna Svobodová had to swallow a lecture on the proper behaviour of girls and women, and pay a fine in the amount of two drachmas.

"One for each Monitor," grumbled my mother. "Money-grubbing thieves."

My teeth chattered as I sipped sweetened wine. "I wasn't in my room. I was somewhere else. It had a high ceiling with rafters, and a small glazed window."

"It could be one of the store-rooms at the back of the third floor. We can find out later. Tell me what happened next."

"Pada was crying. I was dead. Then I heard boot-steps coming up the stairs, and I clung to a rafter. I thought I might suddenly fall. Pada... he started to laugh as if... as if he were happy, then he coughed the way he does when things get too exciting."

Ragna Svobodová nodded.

"A soldier burst in. He had a helmet with white plumes. Pada yelled that he was too late, and shook his fist. The soldier kicked him."

Mother's lips thinned. "Petru's men. So, he wants you. But—" She shook her head, as if telling herself to stop talking and let me continue.

"Two more soldiers came. They were angry. They must have wanted me alive." I found myself gnawing at a thumbnail, and quickly put my hands out of sight. "I cowered up there in the shadows, praying I wouldn't become solid and fall among them. Mother, why did they want me?"

She didn't answer. Perhaps Petru had been captivated by my beauty and desired me for his own. At that I actually started to laugh, which became sobbing until my mother shook me.

The men had thundered around, turning over furniture and slashing the tapestries with their swords. Purely spiteful.

"The first soldier grabbed Pada Josef by the neck and hauled him up. Pada dropped his knife. It... spun on the floor." Silver, black, and blood-red. I took a breath. "Pada was so brave! He snarled like a lion at that soldier!"

My mother had turned very pale, and I could see she was biting back tears. She would never display weakness. "So. You will die, at some time to come. Can you guess how long that time might be, Vara?"

"By the way I looked... maybe... maybe two years? Three?" Oh, let it be more!

"And what of Josef-my-father? What will happen to him?"

I bowed my head. "The men didn't know what to do with him. At first they wanted to take him to Lord Petru. For... for questioning. But..."

"But what?"

"They killed him." I could barely get out a whisper. "The first soldier. At first I hoped he might show mercy. But he put his sword through Pada's heart." I couldn't go on.

"Vara, remember this has not happened."

"Yet."

"It may never happen! And it *was* mercy, Vara. Think of this: that your grandfather will die—if he does—quickly by a sword to the heart, rather than slowly at Petru's hands."

I hadn't thought of that. But Petru wouldn't torture an old man, would he?

My mother stroked my hair. "Have you had any other visions?"

I hadn't told her about the boy on the road, or the Moorish woman, or the little bird. All three of them had plagued me for weeks now, but I had been too stubborn and frightened to tell anyone. What if it meant I was crazy, and needed to be sent away to an asylum for a cure? I had heard of the cures at such places: ice water baths, starvation, whippings. Sometimes, for girls, the cutting away of one's private parts.

But this vision involved not just me, but Josef Svobodá, a scientist and nobleman. It was important. Still, I wanted to keep my other visions to myself for a while. I shook my head.

She let me stay with her that night, and I was glad of her softly snoring presence keeping me company as I stared into the darkness.

Chapter Two
GHOST BLOOD

O n the low table in the main dining room lay a circle of red flowers: the Eye of Sister Uzma. Within it, a smaller circle of candles flickered in the late afternoon breeze that filtered through the doors and windows. Red symbolizes the blood shed from Uzma's own eyes when her Sister Afra's eyes were put out, shortly before she was flogged to death. Something you have to ignore to keep your food down.

Sigrun and I had been confined to the villa, no great hardship, and had commandeered a bright window in this breezy room to work. Mother had been so incensed at the loutishness of the men who'd brought me home that she'd ignored their instructions to give both of us a sound thrashing.

"It doesn't matter where cicadas come from," I informed Sigrun as I squinted at my square of fine linen and jabbed with the needle. I'd already pricked a finger. She was barely listening. "It's where they go. If you want a long life, you must collect their cast-off shells and boil them into broth, then drink it under a full moon." The insects lived underground more years than I had been alive, then burst forth for their few days in the sun. So I'd overheard from old Kai, who'd been gossiping with another woman. "Then at a great age, you can pass through the Eye of Uzma and be free of the Gods."

Sigrun shrugged, busy counting out her complicated pattern. She had suffered no consequences from our market adventure, perhaps from being a good liar.

She said, "The next full moon isn't for days." She looked up at me. "And I'm not drinking cicada broth. You Uzmites need to change your foolish ways."

I reached under my tunic to touch the small tokens around my neck, but it made me think of the bloody gash my own Pada had cut there. I grabbed my throat as if to deflect another death.

Wasn't I done with that damned dream? The vision had shown me my future—why did I have to keep seeing it? If this was going to keep happening, I would have a short, sad, and pitiable life.

Sigrun stared at me. "What's the matter? Are you all right?"

"Nothing. A mosquito on my neck."

Carefully and slowly I returned my hand to my lap and picked up my needle. If Sigrun noticed my panic, she'd never let go until she had learned the whole story. I didn't want to tell it.

I had come up with a theory as to why I, of all people, had had such a terrifying and detailed vision.

First, let me say that since my mother was always distracted and busy, my servant Kai was elderly and deaf, and I was an only child, I had spare time on my hands. I can't say I spent it wisely.

Closed doors were meant to have ears pressed against them. I didn't hesitate to press. People talked, in whispers, about the *da resu* folk. "They're devils," hissed some. "No," assured others. "They're valuable! If I had one I'd make it work for me." Then they made warding signs just in case a God was listening.

No one I encountered had ever met one—as far as they knew—so anything I learned was most likely exaggerated or outright false. But I didn't care. The *da resu* were special beings, destined for a life after death beyond what simple mortals would ever know.

"Sigrun... do you know anything about the *da resu*, or the *resura*?"

"The resurrected? There are no such things," she said immediately. "My father says so." She looked doubtful, though, and traced the curved sign of Saraf on her chest with a thumb. She wanted me to get rid of my Blindeye and get the proper token instead, but I wouldn't. I hated snakes, and I disdained Petru. "Everybody dies except for gods," she said. "It's a tale for children." Her blue eyes narrowed. "Do you believe in them?"

"I... I guess not."

But really, I did. I believed in *da resu*, and thought it might be a reason for my vision, as well as the ridiculous amount of studying I had to do. *Da resu* folk died and were resurrected, to become valuable *resura*. They got special training, and were guarded jealously. Or so it was said.

It was an enticing thought, but it was most likely just wishful thinking, something that would make me important, and not merely a girl being groomed for a safe and boring marriage one day.

I gave up questioning Sigrun. If I could design my own perfect friend, it would not be her, though for a long time it had been. But she was changing, and so was I. She was drawing closer to the flame of religion, and I was feeling its heat start to crisp my skin.

Three centuries ago my mother's family had migrated south from the Khazar city of Balanjar on the far-away Volga River. That wild, ignorant tribe had been blurred and softened by many generations of wandering. And marrying tamer people. Her father Josef, Count von Svobodá, was so intellectual that it was dangerous, while she still clung stubbornly to her old barbaric ways, and was notoriously backward in her knowledge of true civilization.

She had told me to think hard about my death vision. "You must hear what it tells you, Vara. What it said to you."

What it *said*? What did that mean? Except that Pada and I would die. And our house would be invaded by Petru's men.

Mother had sent me to bed to do some thinking, obviously fed up with my moaning. Choking back sobs of self-pity and anger, I buried my face in the pillow to try to smother the noise. It worked too well; I began to gasp for air, and sat up quickly.

Could a person smell ghost blood? I really thought I could, seeping from the bedclothes into my brain.

I tossed the pillow across the room and flopped backwards. It felt good to be flat on my back, with the weight of the world pulling me down. It was my Pada's gravity, which he told me meant that the world was filled with molten gold, way down deep. Its weight pulled us all down.

Think.

When I had watched myself die, I saw images at the corners of my eyes, among them the shadowy boy. He had wavered like a candle flame. It might have been two boys, dancing in and out of the shadows. I saw a cat, long and lithe, slinking close. Next a big yellow-eyed bird wheeling over the cat. I heard the sound of steel clashing, and smelled the stink of wildfire.

Mentally I toured our home, which sprawled around a spacious atrium, searching for that death room, and found it upstairs, next to my parents' suite. It's used for nothing but storing out-of-season clothes, linens, a locked chest full of old jewellery and hairpieces that are out of fashion, and so on. It's a rough-walled, drafty room with a barred window and no balcony, no way in or out except via the stairs. In my vision it was different, lined with tapestries to keep out drafts, and cluttered with familiar furniture.

Will I be relocated there to protect me, or to contain me?

Another thing: my Blindeye had shifted as my spirit-fingers touched it, as if it too was a spirit. There are so many stories of Uzma's Eye and what it saw. My Pada Josef says they are all hogwash.

Nervously I pulled the chain from under my shirt and looked at my treasures, Eye and Owl. Safe and sound. What had the difference been?

The memory shifted and sank like sand in water.

What would happen to these things after I died? Would someone keep or wear them, or would they be buried with my body? And would my body rot in the marble box among all the other marble boxes in the crypt under our family chapel?

I'd asked my grandfather these very questions.

He had not been helpful. "Everyone rots eventually, child. Your Blindeye?" He had shrugged. "I'll take it if you like. And the Owl too."

But he would die right after me. I began to weep again.

When we came here from Massalia, before I was born, we brought our family bones along and placed them in their new crypt, built into some natural caves. In summer I loved the delicious shiver in my skin from being in the dim, chilly place. It stank only a little, and was almost pleasant. But then I would think of all the dead stacked around me, those who'd finished rotting in the marble boxes and were now just empty, painted skulls and long bones bound like firewood. So many bones. Babies and children, the sick and old, warriors cut down in their prime. Gone... but where?

Heaven, it's said, lies somewhere beyond the realm of the Great Gods, who dwell among the clouds. The Gods stand in the way even of the righteous, simply out of spite. It is said.

"Pah!" shouts Pada Josef. "The Great Gods don't give a squirt of toad piss for us."

I wiped my eyes and stared out at the dusk. I was ready to start hating summer.

My father, Jameel ibn Hayyan al-Kindi, travels in summer, stays home in winter. But even when he's home, his mind is somewhere else. Tall and slender, his skin the colour of cinnamon and his hair as black as mine, he was my hero. I wanted him to grab me, lift me to his broad shoulders and spin around till together we fell to the ground shrieking with laughter.

Those days were gone forever. What I wanted now was to talk, really talk with him, about the subjects that men discussed. Politics, religion, trade. War and animals and the seas. Did I only want to show off what I'd learned? I longed for him to see that I was clever.

Just as I was realizing that I shouldn't have skipped dinner, my mother came in.

Chapter Three
THE RAVENOUS MOUTHS

My mother is the kind of woman who, given the chance, would chop off her hair, bind her breasts and take up a sword. She strides about the villa like a man and wears a red-handled Sexsum knife on her belt, beside her big ring of keys, and uses it to spear her meat at the dinner table. My barbarian princess, says father, while stroking her pale arms and playing with her long yellow hair.

She pulled my shutters closed, then took my hand. Together we sat on my bed, and her perfume enveloped me. It was made especially for her, and I always tried to inhale enough of it to keep in my nostrils after she left a room. I can always tell when she's near because her wonderful smell lingers. It's like fruit that's gone a little soft, like spices too long in leather bags, flowers crushed to dust. And yet I love it.

"I talked with your grandfather." She sat straight, ignoring the comfort of pillows. "He experienced the vision as well, or at least some of it. He remembers only the sound of booted footsteps and a burning need to kill you. He said blackness then overtook him, and he wouldn't say any more. I fear it upset him more than his health can bear."

I sent a silent *I'm sorry* to my Pada. All this trouble stemmed from me. What was wrong with me?

My mother is very beautiful in her own way, and likes to dress well. In her own way. Her saffron linen tunic, banded with woven silver and little lapis beads, left her arms bare except for four thin hammered-gold bangles that she always wore, two on each wrist. The sound of their soft clinking went together with her scent in my mind. I possessed bracelets like hers but would not be allowed to wear them until my wedding day, which now looked as if it wouldn't come.

She rose and went to the window. "The Great Gods sent you a vision of what has not yet happened. It must be important."

"But why do they do that? Can't you make it *not* happen? Can't we just—"

"No. What was foretold will happen. And you will be ready."

"I... I don't want to be ready. I don't want to die."

"Vara, my dear girl, I don't want you to die either. Your father and I had planned... a life for you. A long, safe life." She paused, and I could see her throat constricting. This sign of emotion from my mother was more frightening than anything else. "But you *will* be prepared." It was odd how she said this more to herself than to me. As if she knew that such reassurance was not what I wanted.

She left, and after a while a slave entered with a tray of dinner. The food made my stomach lurch. I drank some water because it had honey in it, and lemon slices floating like little suns, and it seemed to take away the ice from my heart.

At moonrise she returned. I had just managed to fall asleep, but she shook me until I sat up, rubbing my eyes.

"Get dressed," she ordered. "You'll need your heavy shawl; it's going to be cool. Then meet me downstairs."

Excitement surging within me, I drew my second-best wool shawl over my hair and wound it tight around my neck. Together we crept downstairs and across the smooth tile floor of the entry hall. We left the villa silently, hurrying along like beggars after a hiding hole, for we had no male accompaniment. It felt deliciously bold.

"Where are we going?"

"Quiet," she hissed. "You'll find out."

Few people were on the streets, for it was almost the hour of curfew. Three young men lounged at a torch-lit corner, murmuring together and eyeing us as we slipped by. My mother showed her knife and they looked away.

Music and talk sounded hollow and mysterious from behind walls. The smells of garlic and frying fish, the grunts and clatter of animals being herded home, and the shuttered yellow gleam of lanterns thickened the night.

The streets looked very different at night. Intriguing. Perpignan is a big city, with more than thirty thousand souls—and more in times of festival. We have two principal avenues, a *plaza major* with a splendid fountain in the old Roman style, and a multitude of small, cramped, twisting lanes, some with names, most relying on the memories of those who have lived here forever. A food market sheltered by swaths of cloth and netting, and another market for everything else. A coliseum, which fills up with farm folk and bonded peasants, landowners and workers from leagues around to see circuses, war games, ceremonies and judgments. We even have a quite decent library, but it's only for men. My Pada had taken me there, when I was young enough to pass for a boy. My hair was hidden by a turban, and my eyes greedily sought out each and every scroll and book and sheaf of curling parchment. How I longed to go back there, seek out the ancient stories, touch and decipher them.

Bats flitted overhead, gobbling up insects in their ugly, ravenous little mouths. Pada had made me dissect a bat once, just to see its innards. "Believe it or not, they are just like ours!" I had almost vomited on his shoes.

We stopped beneath the minaret that floated palely above the abandoned south-side mosque where the wine merchants' union meets now. Dark and quiet at this time of night. A small coin satisfied the building's guard that he could let us pass. Perhaps we planned to fling ourselves from the top, but why should he care?

Puffing from the climb up steep, narrow stairs, we approached the edge of the low rampart ringing the topmost, open level. I have never been afraid of heights, so when she insisted I join her in dangling my legs over the edge of a drop that must have been the height of ten tall men, I didn't hesitate.

From here we could see the River Tet rolling dark between its banks to vanish under the city streets. The river feeds the water and sewer systems, draining to the Mediterranean from the snowy Pyrenees—our mountainous ramparts to the south and west. Askain's lands border the lands of the Spanish Arabs. Their cities, cosmopolitan and sprawling, were legend, and their lust for war, gold, and song even more so.

The night was crisp and clear, the sky packed with close-hanging stars. All the familiar gods and heroes glimmered above us. I could see my breath, and blew it upwards to wisp briefly before the brilliance of the constellations that drew their ancient patterns among the lesser jewels. At times like this I could easily give in to Roman beliefs. There were so many spangled heroes chasing one another through time and darkness...I shivered and tried to rein in my imagination.

There were also the Great Gods. I was afraid to see them. Afraid that I might. Some people could, or so they claimed. Most people could feel them, poking away at our resolve, our strength and goodness, looking for a chink in the armour. That's what they liked to do.

Since my mother wasn't sharing her reasons for being here, and only sat silently staring up, I decided that this was as good a time as any to ask questions. "Mother... am I *da resu*?"

She went completely still. Then she turned to look at me. "What? How could..." A shudder ran through her. "I forget how clever you are, Vara. You are very good at noticing, and perhaps at spinning fanciful tales." She took my chin in her hand and turned my face to hers, as was her habit. "What makes you think such a thing?"

I bit my lip. What, exactly? Suddenly I felt like a fool. "I don't know. Nothing. It's—"

She held up a hand. "Don't move." She took her shawl from her own head and began to wrap it about mine. Before I knew it my eyes were covered in three layers of the fine dark material. Through it I could dimly make out the brightest stars and the glow of street lanterns below. Nothing else.

Dizzy, I stretched my hands out as if to clutch the air for support.

"Sit still! If you can deduce the truth, then so can others."

My heart seemed to fall into my bowels. Was she going to tell me my theory was correct? Suddenly I wanted very much to be wrong.

"To be *da resu*," she whispered, "is to be waiting. Waiting for death. When a *da resu* person dies, she or he passes from being a live human into the realm of the *resura*. The resurrected. Everything will be different, everything will be strange. A *resura* has power, and immortality. This is what I was taught."

I narrowed my eyes. Immortality? "Who taught you? Could I learn too?"

She remained quiet, and I thought about it. Why would someone teach Ragna Svobodová the lore of the *resura*? We mortals should not know these things. I thought some more. "You are *da resu*."

She grunted as if a weight had fallen onto her shoulders. "Yes. I am, though I have experienced no visions. Someday I will tell you of how it was, before you were born. How it was planned to use me."

By now I was ready to scream. I didn't want to think about her life—it was my own I was worried about. My eyes strained uselessly to see through the cloth, my view just as dim as my understanding. "But, when you die, you die. That's what Grandfather Josef says. You are put in the ground, or burned—"

"Quiet! And stop squirming." She pulled away, leaving me feeling utterly alone and precarious on the wall, my feet hanging uselessly. "Now listen."

"Listen to what?" I groped for her arm.

"Vara, control yourself. Stop trying to see. Listen to the night."

I could only obey, though listening to the night—whatever that meant—seemed useless. I wanted information! Nevertheless, my ears strained, compensating for my eyes which blinked and squinted behind the cloth. My own breathing, loud and fast, was all I could hear.

I forced my breath to slow and soon became conscious of many small sounds all around. They became clearer as I focused my attention outward. Normal city sounds, the cry of a night-hunting bird, the hum and shrill of insects, dogs barking, the rush of water in the Tet as it passed under a bridge nearby... I relaxed a little and pictured my ears growing large and pointed like a dog's, able to interpret all the noises of life and understand exactly what they meant.

Footsteps sounded below. A heavy person. A man. Wearing stiff new sandals that scuffed the stones... from my left came the skittering and brief yowl of a cat on a roof, slipping as she dislodged a loose tile.

I found that if I closed my eyes behind the cloth I could hear even better.

The night seemed to blow close around me, like invisible clouds of darkness that I could feel, not see. Suddenly it occurred to me that if I leaned forward and pushed a little I could fall into the air and float there. The idea was very compelling. I could turn and swoop and get a much better vantage for hearing the little whispers and groans, the kisses, the brushing of hair, the pouring of water and the simmering of pots, the liquid slither of silk robes dropped to the floor...

And something else. Something big and as empty as the sky, and yet as stuffed full as a bag of broken bones. *They* were in the night air like vast birds, filling my head and emptying my heart. Their ravenous mouths were open to catch me, as the bats gobbled up insects.

Around me swept a sort of wind, buffeting me with emotions—fear, anger, cruelty, passion, curiosity—all burning and flowing in and out of my head. Love was there too, and it was very tempting. Hot and delicious... I felt a sudden heaviness in my loins. Low, rumbling voices were all around, like an enormous choir of men in the air, and I held my breath to try to understand what they said. *Come, lean forward... Let go...*

I wanted to surrender to the voices. But then my hands flew out, flailing for balance, and I threw myself back from the edge, landing with a thump behind the low stucco barrier. I ripped frantically at the scarf around my head, afraid I was going to vomit.

Mother was beside me in an instant. She freed my face, and I drew in big gasping breaths, though the air smelled of burning trash. Its acrid reek filled my nostrils. The sky was alive with movement. The stars were obscured by shapes that formed and blew like bunched-up curtains. I'd never seen the heavens like this before, a vast storm that made no wind or thunder, just a weird weaving of silver and grey and black that my eyes couldn't quite catch. Clouds that were not clouds.

I pointed upwards, my hand shaking. "S-something, out there! Things in the air!"

She glanced at the sky. "I see them too." There were tears on her cheeks. "You are right, they are up there, and they are in the middle of a war of ages. It is the Great Gods, and they want to snatch us up as if we were mice."

The Great Gods. Not the lesser ones, the pitiful three-headed snakes, horses with useless wings, or bulls that never stopped bleeding from invisible wounds. No one feared those.

"You knew they were there! Watching us! You showed me to them—now they know I'm here!"

How could she do this to her own child? She wanted to scare the piss out of me, didn't she? Well, she had about done it. I ground my teeth and tried to control my urge to hit her and run away screaming. I hated her. Nothing, even her own nasty Pagan gods, could frighten *her*! Of course not. She was brave and defiant.

She ignored my rant, and I thought spitefully that she looked old. But really it was sadness on her face. We were both *da resu*, which meant that we were valuable, according to the lore I'd gleaned. Wasn't that a good thing?

She said, "You feel what is out there, waiting, don't you? And you can see it, if only a little. It is the Nether Realm, of Gods and the dead. And of *resura*."

My sudden anger deflated. The cold stone was hard against my knees as I huddled next to her. Vertigo still had me, and that glimpse of death. Heartsick, I muttered, "You would have let me fall, to be eaten by those things, like... like a mouse."

"Never. I had a good grip on your tunic."

Or would I have simply hit the pavement below, died instantly and avoided having my throat slit? But I would die inevitably, somewhere and somehow. It was the time after death that I feared. I looked up at the sky again, and saw twinkling stars reappear through the ominous clouds. The burning smell was gone.

"The Gods want you, Vara, but not as a morsel of meat to devour and forget. It isn't only humans who covet a *resura*."

Perversely I felt a swell of pride, mingled with the horror and the knowledge that I was terribly small. And terribly ignorant. But I had had seen a little of the Nether Realm and had survived.

Ragna Svobodová said, "*Da resu* folk are born as well as made. The secret knowledge of how to enter the afterlife with spirit intact is in your blood and bones. Only a few are so blessed—or cursed— and many of those die untrained, of all the things folk generally die of, before they can pass into the realm of the *resura*."

I blinked. Only after death are such as I truly alive. Only after death are we truly valued.

She said, her voice catching harshly, "I have always known in my mind what you are. Now I know in my heart."

She wasn't happy about it. Well, neither was I. My childish suspicions had been confirmed, and no longer looked enticing. I looked past her, out into the night. The sky was almost normal again. Where did the clouds go? Were they the Great Gods? Why should things that looked like nothing but shadows rule our lives?

"The vision tells me that your destiny has changed. Our plans for you are gone like smoke." Mother rose to her feet and I followed her.

Our plans. So, Jameel-my-father was in on this too. Of course. He and Ragna-my-mother were as thick in this as two egg-stealing snakes.

"My destiny?"

"We had hoped for a soft and quiet life for you. A good husband. Children. But that is not to be. You need more training," my mother continued, all at once sounding firm and determined. She had the knack of grabbing painful things and forcing them into something manageable. "More languages of course. As many as you can absorb, for without the ability to understand and be understood, you might as well be a deaf-mute. Map-reading, astronomy and astrology, the use of various weapons."

Weapons? That sounded good. Did she mean I could learn to fight, like a boy? My arm tensed in anticipation of taking up a big, shiny, jewel-encrusted sword. But then it fell limp. I didn't want to be anywhere near swords. Swords had one function: to release the lifeblood from helpless, screaming victims.

"The most important thing you can learn, Vara, is the power of observation. There is something to be learned from every tree, every shadow, every animal, every person whether man or woman, freeman or slave. You will learn to burrow into the skin of another, and live there."

I shuddered.

How did she know all this? What exactly was she? A *da resu* who had never crossed over. Who had been *her* teacher?

"We will talk more when your father gets home." And that was all the information I got that night, or for many nights thereafter.

Could I burrow into my mother's skin and learn her courage? *Like a tick, sucking out her knowledge and her strength, drop by drop...* Or—a nicer image—like a babe at the breast. I felt my lip curl.

I remembered how my Pada Josef had crowed with glee when the soldiers arrived to find only my dead body. He seemed to think he had won something.

There must be a way out of the trap. There must.

We returned home in silence, and I don't know if she slept. I know I didn't.

Chapter Four
SCOURGE MARKS

My Pada Josef has many enthusiasms. Science. Teaching. Anything that makes a loud bang, even better if it also stinks.

The Great Library at Alexandria was a pet interest. He wanted to disperse its vast contents to many smaller libraries throughout the known world. "Do you realize how vulnerable it is? Fire! Vandalism! Earthquakes! I tell them to make copies of everything and send them everywhere. But they don't listen!"

"Wouldn't it be awfully expensive?" I loved prompting him to get really worked up.

"Of course it would be expensive! But consider the cost of losing everything!" He started coughing, and I felt a twinge of remorse.

I had been relieved of the usual lessons girls got—thanks to my new, secret status as *da resu*—and was now attending his sporadic lectures. I sat veiled at the back of the room, behind his smelly, arrogant male students who sent me curious glances. History today, which Pada made almost interesting. I loved his stories of ancient Greece, especially when he quoted poetry from hundreds of years ago.

Later, as I clattered down the stairs from his small lecture hall in search of something to eat, Sigrun suddenly glided from a shadowed corner, clutched my arm and whispered, "Vara, you have to come with me, right now."

I was used to her commands, but lately I'd been questioning them. Sigrun often didn't think things through. "Why?"

"Lord Petru is here!" Her voice trembled with excitement. "Here in Perpignan, but just for today. This might be our only chance to see him!"

"See him! Where will he be?" I tried to sound interested. I didn't really want to spend time with Sigrun, who was brilliant at ferreting out information. Mother had made it very clear that my being *da resu* was never to be mentioned, even to my best friend.

"He'll pass through the main square, on his way to the barracks. Say you'll come, Vara!" She gave my arm a hard squeeze.

Sigrun had a father and two brothers, who lived with us. Her mother had died in childbirth, along with the stillborn baby, a few years ago. Her father was our chief accountant. Her older brother was studying with his father, but the younger had run off to the western coast to learn shipbuilding, which was an insane hotbed of development these days. With no mother to watch her, Sigrun had a lot of freedom, and excelled at talking me into doing things that I'd never think of on my own.

Her excitement started to infect me. I nodded, and we made quick plans to meet in an hour at a sweet shop on the square.

A simple plan, but it did not work out as we hoped. We had underestimated just how popular Petru was. Or perhaps we simply didn't understand the undercurrents of life under the rule of such a man.

The sweet-shop's proprietor cast a jaded eye upon us. He knew us well, and our kind: over-privileged females anxious to waste our coins on candy. He was ready to do his part. As he weighed our purchases and doled them into small sacks, he said to me, "One day you'll give up that Owl to buy sweets."

"Never! My Grandmamma Svobodová who is dead now gave it

to me." The silver Athenian coin dangled on a chain around my neck along with my Eye. It had the head of Athena on one side and a sweet, rather silly-looking owl on the other. It was real, not a cheap copy, and was terribly old. A charm, supposed to bring wisdom. I would never use it as currency.

For a moment I felt the slice of steel in my neck, and had to swallow carefully to keep from gasping. It was true that I'd never give up my owl, for I had seen it with me when I died.

The merchant began to shoo us out.

Sigrun protested. "But we want to watch Lord Petru from in here!"

"I need room for customers." He gestured to the crowds gathering on the street. "When the show is over, those people will want to buy my wares. Off with you!"

We shuffled outside, stuffing our faces with marzipan and chewy, pistachio-studded nougat. At least this distracted me from thinking about my neck, until a rhythmic shouting started, and the clop of approaching hooves got louder and louder.

Sigrun and I ran to the nearest corner but soon found ourselves shoved back by the crowds. We couldn't see a thing, but then managed to dodge into an alley and climb up on some barrels. From there we had a narrow view of the street.

The shaded alley framed a hot yellow slash of activity. Men and women of all races and classes jostled for a glimpse of the procession. Children clung to their mothers or nurses and begged to be lifted up to see. The chanting rolled along getting louder and more coordinated by the moment: Pet-ru, Pet-ru, PET-RU!

Despite myself, I felt a shiver of anticipation. The air seemed filled with a tang almost like orange rinds, sweet and harsh, and the sun seemed to waver and darken, casting shadows at strange angles. The Gods were overhead. I didn't dare look up.

Petru had a God on his side, it was certain. One that was goading him into greed for territory and taxes, and the increasing glory of his mundane idol Saraf. It made me feel sick.

A couple of ragged urchins made an attempt to commandeer our position, but we kicked and shouted them off. A roar cascaded along the street. Mounted soldiers, three abreast, went by on prancing horses held in control by cruel metal bits. The men were armoured and helmeted, white plumes in stiff crests above the glinting, polished metal. Many wore the long, drooping moustaches the Huns favoured. Each man stared straight ahead, stern and upright. More and more clattered by, their horses' shod hooves ringing loud on the cobbles.

Sigrun and I clutched each other, on tiptoe on our precarious perches. My heart was racing, I admit it. Did I really want to see him so very badly? My father had met Petru, and had fashioned a word-painting of what he looked like. We craned our necks to try and pick the chieftain out of the men parading by. At last we saw him, unmistakably the centre of attention. He rode slowly by, ignoring everyone.

"Is that him?" Sigrun screamed into my ear.

"Yes!"

"Oh, just look at him! He's magnificent!"

He *was* magnificent, I had to acknowledge it. Lord Petru Aska Tolny, simply known as Petru, was burly and big-headed, his mane of ginger hair loose and flying in the sun. His chin was shaved bare, but his moustache was luxuriant and dangling with pearls at the low-drooping ends. He held his helmet under one bare, muscular arm, reining in his huge grey Andalusian stallion one-handed. He didn't smile, nor even really look at anyone. Either he wanted to seem aloof and regal, or he simply didn't care to acknowledge the seething mass of his Emperor's subjects, many of whom were trying to grab handfuls of his mount's tail, or lay a fingertip on his booted foot, though they couldn't get anywhere near him. He was more popular in these parts than Emperor Ludvik, and he knew it.

The sun, dark gold and hot, shone mostly upon him, as if funnelled like wine into a jar. The crowd of watchers screamed like animals running toward their death, and loving it.

They loved him. They loved the death he promised.

I shuddered, and tried to pull my thoughts away from hot, painful, glorious death.

Two bareheaded men clad in grey robes trotted beside him, each holding a long, barb-tipped whip. Randomly, they slashed these whips around, not seeming to care whom they hit. People pushed and shoved their way forward to get a chance at the touch, whooping gleefully at the sting, proudly displaying a fresh welt or torn skin. I watched, my mouth open, my flesh crawling. Some cheered the newly marked, some jeered at them. Those who jeered or frowned soon shut up, when they saw the avid looks Petru's men gave them.

Petru suddenly started shouting something about loyalty, or maybe it was liberty—I still couldn't hear him over the crowd—and his citizens responded by yelling harder and pumping their fists. Many of the women were tossing bunches of flowers at him, or displaying their bared backs or breasts, apparently in hopes of a whipping. A hot wind seemed to be forcing the crowd to surge back and forth. Fights started to break out. Dust and sun were in my eyes, making it hard to see. I wanted to run away, but I wanted even more to press forward and get close to Petru. I wanted to bare my back to him.

Sigrun jumped and screamed, waving a handkerchief above her head to catch his attention, with no luck. She had pulled the front of her robe down, and I could see her round pink breasts. I think the only thing that stopped us from joining that maddened throng was the certainty that if we left our place in the alley, we'd be trampled to death, or worse.

My eyes snapped back to Petru. I couldn't look away.

With a nudge of one booted foot Petru made his mount rear and wheel around, his sword, his hair, and his horse's gleaming hide shooting bright lances of light around him, as if he were the centre of something marvellous I now saw that Petru wore only a leather harness that crossed over his shoulders and joined his metal-studded belt, leaving most of his broad back bare to the sun. I blinked, dazzled.

Then I blinked again to sharpen my gaze, though what I saw was plainly visible. His scourge marks.

It wasn't only his subjects who loved the whip.

Petru was called the Scorpion—which was the ancient Latin

term for the Roman flagrum. I'd heard that he whipped himself
with it, or had others wield the wickedly painful instrument of
penitence. Now everyone knew it. Like the scorpion, the flagrum
stung hard. In fact, it was said to sting like a snake, another name
for Saraf the Burning. Petru encouraged Sarafites to follow his
example and gain the sinuous lines of the burning snake upon their
backs.

My back itched and the skin crawled as if insects were in my
clothes. Again I felt the urge to run into the street and bend to the
whip.

With a hot, queasy feeling in my stomach I traced with my eyes
the pale lines and puckered welts that decorated his tawny skin.
And the fresh, crusted marks of a recent scourging. What if we all
became Sarafites? Everyone here, now, wanted it. Pada Josef
believed it would happen, and soon. We would all be whipped till
we bled.

Then he moved out of our line of sight. The air thinned and lost
its dusty burning smell. The shouting receded along the street.

At that dizzy, empty moment I became truly frightened of Petru
and what his madness meant for our land. Though I'd heard not a
word he said, and knew little about him really, I knew that he
could squeeze us all into happy submission with the clench of his
fist.

The last of the throng following him roared dazzle-eyed past us
under the watchful gaze of soldiers.

Sigrun stood teetering on her barrel, grinning like a maniac and
fanning herself with one hand, when suddenly she screeched, flung
her arms up and disappeared from view. Her vacated barrel rocked.
She'd been grabbed by the legs and pulled off it, and now lay on
the filthy ground shrieking with pain and fury. Immediately she
jumped up and began to tussle with the boys who had pestered us
before.

This time they had the upper hand. Sigrun and I were
thoroughly kicked and spat upon, and robbed of our purses. And
our remaining candy. With a few final taunts the boys ran off.

"What will I tell my father?" Sigrun howled, wiping her tears and trying to pull her shawl over her head again. At least the sons-of-pigs hadn't stolen our shawls, leaving us to slink home bareheaded.

Since we weren't supposed to be out in the first place, we could hardly tell the truth. Could we? Would Mama punish me less if I claimed public duty? But claiming devotion to Lord Petru would be a mistake. And a dangerous lie to allow inside my head.

Mother came in when I was washing. I had stuffed my soiled and torn clothes into the basket for cleaning and mending, hoping the servants would ask no questions.

"What in the name of Uzma have you been up to?"

"Nothing." I tried in vain to hide my scrapes and bruises with my hands.

Her eyes narrowed and immediately she strode to the basket. It was as if she could read my guilty mind. "Your clothes are ruined!" She marched up to me, grabbed my chin in her hand and raised my face to examine it. "Vara, what has been going on?"

"Nothing! I fell!" Why, oh why, couldn't I be more composed in front of my mother? Soon she had the whole story, even the stolen candy part.

"You stupid child. You went to see Petru, eh? You could have been injured, or killed. Or worse. And all to gawk at that... that..." Her lip curled. I had rarely seen her more angry without beating somebody.

"But... but, I just wanted to see him!"

She pushed me down onto my bed and growled deep in her throat. "See the man who won't rest until every one of us is flattened under his boot-heel? Is that what you wanted?"

I shrank back. "No! I...I..."

She gave my face a hard slap. "You and that little *besom* Sigrun—neither of you has a grain of sense."

I bit my tongue and lowered my eyes. I wouldn't betray Sigrun by insisting it was her idea. That much pride I could hold on to. And I had learned something today: a man sufficiently insane could be more compelling than logic, more enthralling than truth. Petru had ensnared my friend with his madness. I had felt, myself, how easily he could do it.

He was a man to whom the Gods had given a taste of their own power.

He was turning into a God, and Gods demanded to be worshipped.

Chapter Five
THE BLEEDING CARPET

Everyone with eyes could see the Gods meddling in our little human lives. It was easy to perceive the difference between the sickness brought on by a festering wound or bad food, and the tangled horror that a God could gift you with.

A gift even a king could not refuse. Well, too bad for Petru. Now that my lust for a sacred whipping had worn off, I felt no pity for him. There had been flies following the great Petru, sniffing after his blood, and flies were filthy things. If he wanted to worship a stupid little tyrant like Saraf—obviously sent to him by the real Gods, who lay in wait for his soul—then let him.

I wiped my tears and spoke up. "He's proud of his scars. He made sure everyone saw them when he rode by."

My mother shook her head and made a flicking motion with one hand. Flies. Men. Gods. "No one likes him, but you don't have to like a ruler, you just have to agree with him, and pay your taxes. Years ago, my father saw Petru's life laid out like a carpet, tightly woven, even and straight. All the colours clear and balanced."

I felt a shiver down my arms. Pada could go into a trance and see things that others couldn't, as if he'd gone on a lonely journey and returned to show us what he'd found there. Usually it was nothing that interested me, so I'd stopped paying attention. People probably thought he was merely drunk or addled by the fumes in his work-room. But it was true: he could see, he whispered to me once, around the corners of the universe. This might be true, or it might be that he was simply a lot smarter than most people.

"Then," she said, "he saw the carpet begin to go crooked, the colours to bleed. As if someone had been killed on it."

Petru had seemed to be a willing participant in his own destruction. I might be wrong. The Gods were inscrutable. "Why him, and not any other of Emperor Ludvik's princes?"

She spread her hands. "There must be a weakness in his character. Something in him, or something he's done, has called down their interest and now they want to play with him."

On the minaret I'd been tempted to leap to my own death by the Gods. *Things* that had wanted to trick me, to drag my soul on a new course of their own devising. They could make any madness sound sane.

"Is Saraf a Great God?" Should I fear Saraf, instead of despising him?

She shook her head. "I... don't think so. Unless he was once a manifestation of a Great God, who somehow persisted in the world. In people's minds and hearts."

That could happen, I could see it. People loved to worship something. Anything. And worship made a God grow stronger. Saraf, who had been a man a thousand years ago, was after all nothing now but an idea in peoples' minds.

"Do you know what I wish?" Ragna Svobodová was looking out the window now, her arms crossed, making her look more pensive and sad. "I wish we could leave all this behind and sail away to the New Lands."

"Really? You'd leave Askain?"

She squared her shoulders. I could almost smell the salt sea in her hair, almost see her standing at the prow of a stout Vascone ship, staring ahead.

The huge, wild lands across the Aetheopian Sea were divided up among the Persians, the Britons and the Danes, in concert with the more rapacious of the Native peoples, with more nationalities joining the rush all the time. Our Hunnic emperor would love to own more than the wee sliver he had of that territory.

My mother's wishes were not mine. I asked, "Why does Emperor Ludvik tolerate Petru? Doesn't he fear him gaining strength?"

"He should. But Ludvik is a weak, venal man interested in filling his coffers with gold, and Petru knows how to bring in taxes. And he was a clever negotiator politically and economically, Ludvik's favourite when he was a youth, or so I hear. But he became too virtuous. Emperor Ludvik didn't like a young sprout monitoring his every plan and scheme, so he pushed him into obscure positions, even imprisoned him for a while. When he was released, he seemed to have smartened up, so Ludvik gave Petru the title Dominus, and three separate estates on the Mediterranean— including the lands and businesses and people they entailed—that he could tax and rule any way he wanted. One was our own. Now he oversees this entire southern portion of the Hunnic Empire. It got him away from Soissons and out of Ludvik's hair."

My mother slid me a sideways look, and began to rub her hands together as if washing them.

"Your father has had dealings with him over the years. I have met him too," she said. "I found him... compelling. He seemed clever, strong. Practical. I... I was overcome by his presence. How can I explain it?" Her knuckles grew white as one hand fought the other. "You will find out one day, if you have time. A man like that, powerful, big, handsome... he can be hard to resist. A woman can suddenly find herself in his thrall."

I understood what she was talking about, damn her. My lips tightened. I tried to keep my face from expressing my revulsion at the thought of my mother *in thrall* to a man not my father. She saw through me.

"You are right to judge me, Vara. I was foolish... but only for a moment. If he had power over me, I felt also as if I had some power over him, because he found me beautiful. But now, I know my power is gone. His lust is for Saraf, only Saraf."

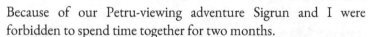

Because of our Petru-viewing adventure Sigrun and I were forbidden to spend time together for two months.

Sigrun insisted that we slip notes back and forth via the servants, but this turned out not to really be worth the anxiety. You never knew who among them could read, who was lazy and forgetful, and who just plain spiteful. And of course there were spies. Spies everywhere. The kind that reported to the marshals if the sign of Saraf wasn't prominently displayed somewhere on your body. I had one now, a silver pin that I wore to hold my shawl when I went out, but my Eye and my Owl still rested hidden at my breast.

Why I clung to the Sisters' cult I didn't know. Perhaps because while the Gods played with us like cats with mice, the Sisters wanted better. There was a One True God above them all, who loved us, they said. No wonder we Uzmites were a dying breed. The Gods loved no one.

Bored and lonely, sick of studying maps and star charts, I found myself trailing around after Pada Josef. He'd given up wearing his antique Egyptian dagger, the one he'd kill me with.

Today, once he noticed my presence, his bright blue eyes focused, crinkling around the corners as he smiled. I wished I'd had a tail to wag.

"You are becoming a young woman, my Vara-Varisha. How are your studies?"

"Fine." I rolled my eyes.

"Got any boyfriends yet?"

"No!"

"Never mind," he said consolingly. "You will have plenty one day."

Then a trapped look suffused his face. He knew that I would die before boyfriends were a problem. I didn't know how that made me feel. Angry at him for forgetting, maybe. Or just sad.

"But who needs boys?" he continued hastily. "Pah! Most of them are idiots. Come with me. I'll show you what I'm doing." He grabbed my hand and hauled me toward the far end of his vast work area.

The attic space was rectangular, bigger than our dining hall, and had several glass-paned windows that could be shuttered for winter. The smooth, curved beams, dark gold with age, were made of whole branching tree-trunks, stripped of their bark but looking as if they had grown by themselves into huge braces for the roof. They were dappled with reflected sunlight from myriad glass vials and polished metal bowls set on several sturdy, slate-topped tables. He had a small stone vessel of quicksilver that I was not allowed to touch, though its strange liquid sheen tempted my fingers.

Pada Josef's workroom was huge and dangerous, with fumes that made me sneeze. I loved it.

He spent his time fiddling with contraptions, peering through lenses, devising complicated experiments or scribbling lines of numbers on every scrap of paper he could lay his hands on. He was like no other adult I had ever met.

Excitedly he dragged me around his big central table to stop before a bubbling cauldron set atop a charcoal fire.

With one foot he began to pound away at a pedal-driven bellows, which turned the coals bright orange. "This—" he waved a hand over the cauldron, "is symbolic, of course. This quest to make gold."

How was making gold symbolic? And how was it supposed to work? In the cauldron bounced what must be an ox heart, among other nasty things. I kept my mouth shut lest he think me stupid, and to keep out the smell.

He pointed skyward as if to invoke the approval of the Gods. "Paracelsus knew it. The ancients all knew it. Alchemy is a spiritual discipline, much more than a physical one. Gold isn't just metal. It can mean many things. It fills a despot's treasure-trove, it's fashioned into beautiful ornaments to the glory of the Gods." He shrugged. I knew what he thought of Gods.

"Do you know what comes back in the ships Petru sends to the new lands? Some gold, but mostly silver. And emeralds and slaves that we buy from the princes there, and so on, of course. When men first got there, they found that smelting ore in the Terra

Torridia was useless, nothing worked the way it did here. But I figured it out!" He rubbed his nose and capered a bit, like a decrepit, aging schoolboy. "Sent a letter to Petru with instructions. All they needed was copper sulphate in the brine of mercury! Ha! It's called magistral, but it's only a chemical compound. What do you think of that?"

I took him at his word, though it seemed unbelievable. If you could make silver from base rock, who needed gold? You would still become wealthy. Perhaps enough wealth could buy us out of our fate.

He said, more soberly, "Perhaps I thought that giving Petru this technique might make him favour us." He grimaced. "Not sure if that was such a good idea. Now he's amassing more wealth than is probably good for him."

I was opening my mouth to ask about emeralds, when Mother's voice wound thin and pungent as smoke up the attic stairs. "Vara! Your father is home!"

Chapter Six
THE COLOBUS MONKEYS

On horseback, I felt higher off the ground than when I'd been on the edge of the old minaret. Perhaps it was the constant surging and snorting of Papa's big leopard-spotted stallion, Amjad, who, according to papa, was born running and now was forever unable to stand still. Amjad means *more glorious*, and I loved that beautiful horse. I also feared him, for he had a temper and would try to bite.

Papa had extended one long brown arm down from Amjad's back to lift me as if I were a parcel of dried apricots, and now I sat before him clinging to Amjad's coarse amber mane, grinning with exhilaration and a desperate desire not to scream. I had ridden with him before, but it had been a very long time. Papa handled the reins expertly, resting them this way or that on Amjad's neck to turn him; no brutal digging with heels or spurs for his high-bred steed.

Two weeks had sped past since Papa had arrived home, early due to favourable winds on the Mediterranean and a quick finish to his trade obligations, and he was to stay for the winter. I wanted him to notice how tall I'd become during his absence, to tell me how pretty I was.

But I saw the look he gave my mother. His eyes were deepest

brown, wide and slightly slanted, giving him a faun-like wildness. The air between them practically crackled. With a kiss on my forehead, and one on each cheek, he had put me from him. "Tomorrow," he promised, "I will unpack my bags... what do you suppose I have brought for you, my Varisha?"

I could only blush and look down. He had told me that Varisha meant lightning-of-the-woman. I liked that. To flash and sear the ground, to call the god of thunder and have him rumble round my feet—power like that would taste sweet.

Late the next morning we shared a breakfast of figs, yogourt and slices of orange drenched in honey and sprinkled with cardamom. Papa's favourite meal. Orange trees have become the fashionable thing to have lately, and many of our friends' villas have orangeries enclosed within their walls, and experts to tend them. We have twelve orange trees, also lemons and limes.

Papa spent the time between bites of food quizzing me about my studies. Mama watched, reclining on her couch like a Roman noble and eating grapes, the extra-sweet ones from the foothills where frost had already come. She popped them in her mouth one by one, crunching the seeds with her strong white teeth.

Finally, after testing my Turkish and Hebrew grammar, he called me close for a hug and a whispered blessing, then sent me off. I found that I *had* hoped for presents, but knew he liked to tantalize me. I wanted Sigrun then, to help me speculate on what he had brought for me. I was desperate for a monkey or a parrot. A man in the market sold talking parrots, which I had begged for and not been allowed to purchase. At last, a really useful reason for studying: the birds had filthy mouths.

The idea of a day trip outside the city walls was Mother's idea, and she let me help prepare. Invitations to some of their close friends and business associates were sent, the servants were directed to get tents, fuel, food and drink ready to go. She swept around the villa pounding her fist on tables and haranguing the staff. They loved her for it, and called her the Golden Queen behind her back.

Papa had brought me a glorious fan of peacock feathers with a bone-and-silver handle. A carved wooden box full to the brim with sweets I had never eaten before (some of which were quite awful but I didn't tell Papa that). A pair of soft leather boots bleached white, lined with squirrel fur and laced with black silk cords, and many other lovely things.

He had got me my longed-for monkey—actually a pair of young colobus monkeys which he told me looked as if they were wearing black-and-white fringed shawls, but they had not survived the trip. Offered a diet of meat, they had sickened and died, shivering in their cage. When he told me this, I wept, and Papa thought I was crying from the loss of a present. But it was for the poor little creatures, frightened, sick and cold, torn from their jungle home simply for my amusement.

Ashamed, I resolved never to ask Papa for a gift again. Certainly not a living one.

Amjad suddenly wheeled under Papa's heels, making me grab his mane with both hands, and we cantered across a small hill to meet the hawk-master and his helpers.

The man was a Seljuq Turk who had recently escaped from an uprising of mercenary soldiers, hired by the city of Byzantium from Russia, and angered by lack of pay. Fires and looting of a city already damaged by Romans wanting their city back from the Huns made the situation there intolerable. The Turk was scrawny but handsome, sporting a black turban, a huge black moustache and a look of the lion in his eyes. He grinned as he handed over a hawk.

Papa took the bird on his wrist, where she clung to the thick leather gauntlet he wore, and removed her hood, holding on to the jesses. She shook her head, spread and fluttered her wings briefly, then gazed alertly around with her evil yellow-rimmed eyes. She looked right at me, then bent to sharpen her beak on the leather, shifting from foot to foot on Papa's arm.

"She's a gyrfalcon," explained Papa. "A big one. Lovely, isn't she?" He crooned at the cream-coloured bird. It was barred brown in a pattern that looked like small sand dunes on its wings and breast, rippling as it preened.

The Turk and Papa exchanged a few joking words, some of

which I could actually understand, then we rode over to show the gyrfalcon to Mama. Three big flapping tents had been set up, plus tables and benches arrayed in a circle. A couple of fire pits were already sending out wonderful aromas. This spur-of-the-moment outing was to take advantage of the last warm gasp of fall. Those who knew, by the aching in their bones, or by their secret, hoarded weather-sense, declared that today and possibly tomorrow would remain mild and sunny. After that would come the chill rains and winds of autumn.

Mama was in the largest tent sheltering her skin from the sun and overseeing the food preparation.

Papa swung down from Amjad and helped me to the ground, the bird complaining and flapping the whole time. A red-haired boy, his skin sunburned as brown as a nut, collected Amjad's reins and led him back and forth to keep him warm, trotting to keep up with the big animal's prancing steps.

"Ragna Svobodová! Come out and see my new prize," Papa shouted.

Soon she was stroking the bird's sleek neck-feathers, crooning to it. "Oh, what a beauty! Look at those eyes, that sharp beak! Oh, such a huntress!"

Papa turned her this way and that, allowing the bird to spread her wings and be impressive. "Varisha wants to come with us on the hunt," he said.

I did? I couldn't contradict my father, nor did I want to seem less than brave and spirited, so I maintained a happy, eager expression... maybe a little glassy-eyed. In theory, I knew how to ride, but unfortunately I was the kind of girl who just didn't take to it. I tended to shriek and fall off. It was embarrassing.

"Wait for me, Jameel my love. We'll all go! Vara, I'm glad we brought your riding clothes." Maybe she was, but I was not. My mother grabbed my hand and we dashed back into the tent to tie our hair back, jam our feet into boots and pull on leather gloves.

A shouted command and the red-haired boy returned with Amjad, and then ran to get Mama's dun mare Saila, and for me a steady bay gelding named Fizan, chosen for his easy gait. The boy pushed me up and I collected the reins and tried to look carefree. Mother flung herself into the saddle and settled her robes modestly as Saila backed and circled eagerly. Ragna Svobodová was a superb horsewoman.

With a pounding of hooves and a warbling yell from Mama, my parents galloped from the picnic site, scattering people and dogs.

Gritting my teeth, I urged Fizan into a trot and then a canter as their happy yells diminished in the distance. We were followed by slave-boys running behind carrying flails, nets, bags, extra quivers full of arrows and so on. Papa's friends and colleagues quickly mounted up and thundered past me, yelling and hooting.

The water and the air were full of birds: herons, ducks, geese, swans; countless small songbirds; sandpipers, gulls, bee-eaters, even a few tardy flamingos that hadn't decamped for Africa yet. Our land was lush, full of life and all its sounds and smells. The air was warm and sweet, thick with moisture and the scent of earth and water. The hunters' arrows found their marks over and over. Our table would be full, and the down and feathers would find their way into beds and pillows and padded winter jackets.

That sunny day, despite the riding, was the most enjoyable I could ever remember. I even managed not to fall off, and felt proud of myself.

In late afternoon we all returned to the camp site, and everyone retired to their tents to nap while our feast was in final preparation.

Mama and Papa lay down separately upon the feather-beds the servants had brought, primly pulling coverlets up and bidding me to sleep well. Obediently I curled in my own little bed and closed my eyes.

Then I cracked them open a tiny slit and watched through my eyelashes. I didn't feel like sleeping—my thighs were aching, and I longed for some of Kai's ointment to soothe them—but I carefully let my breathing slow and my limbs relax, until they were assured I had fallen asleep. Then Papa stealthily crept into Mama's bed and they wrapped their arms around one another. He began to hum a twisting little melody, something he did around her. She had the talent of purring like a cat, and the two of them could produce a duet that was almost musical.

I awakened when I heard Papa say my name. His voice was urgent but low, and I strained my ears to listen.

"So she knows what she is."

Mama paused. "Yes. She deduced it herself, in fact. But she doesn't truly understand, and so feels no fear."

I lay as still as a stone, my heart suddenly lurching. But of course I felt fear. My mother had seen me panic that night on the minaret. Wasn't that fear enough for her?

She continued, whispering. "We are watched so much, it's difficult to find the opportunity to teach her of the beyond."

Papa growled. "You think he suspects?"

He. Petru Dominus, of course.

"No. He thinks so little of females that he dismisses the notion of her power, or mine. It would offend him, and he doesn't like to be offended."

"But...?"

"But he isn't stupid. And he is greedy for a *resura*. Do you know he had a *da resu* under contract last year?"

Papa hissed out a breath. "What happened? Who was it?"

"An Israelite boy whom he bought and put into training. The boy died of fever well before he was ready to be used, and as far as I know has never manifested himself."

"So the great man was cheated of his treasure. I can only imagine his reaction..." After a thoughtful pause, Papa murmured, "It's for the best that the boy never manifested. A half-trained *resura* would be like a devil clinging to your face. It would make Petru more crazy than he already is. But, the boy..."

"Yes. Where, or what, is that boy now?" A pause, then she continued. "Do you think our Vara will be able to do what is necessary?"

"To choose for herself? To learn to kill, do you mean?" My father grunted, *huh.* "Truthfully, I doubt it. She isn't like you and me, my love, hardened by experience and sorrow. Part of me longs for her to stay that way, but..."

"Yes. But. And why should she be different from me? I had my duty and was ready to do it. I still am."

"She's just a child!"

"She is older than I was when your parents bought me!"

Their voices rose, and I couldn't take it anymore. I flung my cover off and sprang to my feet. "Stop it! Stop talking about me!"

They clutched each other, guilty as adulterers.

I wanted to start throwing things. I wanted them to shut up, but I needed to know what they were talking about. "You want me to kill? What do you mean?"

Jameel-my-father made a lunge for me and got me in his arms. I struggled uselessly, my arms clamped to my sides by his grip, trembling with fury and fear.

"Vara, be quiet," he hissed. "People will hear you."

Mother pulled us both down onto their bed. I tried to escape but she grabbed my head in both hands. "Yes! We may—*may*— need you to kill. You will learn how, just in case. You must."

"But, why?"

"Because you are *da resu*. Because one day you will cross over and take up what Jameel and I started. You must be ready."

I tried to jerk free, but they closed over me like the wings of an eagle over a rabbit, two relentless monsters who would use their only child as a weapon of war.

I wanted to run away. Leave all the intrigue and lies and whispers behind. I could beg the indulgence of some priestess-clan in the north. They'd take me in, feed and shelter me. And doom me to a life of celibacy, thin porridge, and service to some nightmare goddess.

Could I leave my home to save my skin? I saw myself alone on a muddy road, freezing, hiding in bushes from marauders and slavers, digging turnips from farmers' fields with my cold hands...

A few deep breaths and I clamped down on my morbid imagination. I might still have years before the time of my vision. In my mind was a chimera of doom that was, really, only words. I wiped away my tears of self-pity.

"We will talk about this at home," said my mother, relaxing her grip.

Chapter Seven
A Curious Barbarian

As predicted, autumn blew in the next day, with chill winds, cold rain and lowering grey clouds. It was as if yesterday had never existed.

Yet my life had changed. For one thing, I was no longer plagued by the recurring visions of the boy, the woman and the bird. Part of me missed them, because I wanted to know what they signified, and they were already fading from my memory.

Weeks passed, cold and dank, and still I got no instruction in the arts of war. The promise to enlighten me was put off with muttered promises of *soon* and *someday*. I knew there were spies and informants everywhere, and that Petru had ways to coerce anyone, but I could be discreet. Why didn't they trust me?

My mother had taken to spending a lot of time out of the house working with the various charities and schools that needed support, and often got home exhausted and filthy. It was more and more necessary these days, for Petru's civic works and ambitious projects meant harsh taxation and even harsher punishment for those incapable of generating money. Father, of course, spent most of his daylight hours involved in business matters, and was constantly conferring with agents and sending packets and messages here and there.

I begrudged every day that passed, for it meant that spring would come and my father would leave, and I knew it was not on a trading trip. He was forging alliances for some plan of his and Mother's. What if Petru suspected him? Interrogated him? If I ruled Askain, I wouldn't trust a man like Jameel al-Kindi, or anyone in his family. And Petru would be a fool not to have spies in our midst.

I could find nothing about *resura* in any of the papers and scrolls I had access to, and had to finally resign myself to my parents' inscrutable timetable. At least it was almost the end of Sigrun's and my punishment. Another two days and I'd have the semblance of a friend again.

I thought I might ask Pada Josef about the strange creature we'd seen at the market. The little god. Such odd animals were seen or captured now and then, and were called lesser gods, but what were they? Did they have souls, like humans? Or were they just devilish animals? Were they immortal? I had almost worked up the nerve to ask him about *resura*, too. If he could see the pattern of a life unravel, as he could with Petru's, surely he could see my pattern. I would dearly love to meet a *resura* in one of its earthly forms, but would I even know it if I did? They'd be the very epitome of stealth.

But when I got to the attic one look told me this was not a good time. Papa and Grandfather were talking in a very serious manner, their voices too low to understand. I could tell what their conference was about, though: gunpowder. I had watched and listened often enough to my Pada instructing his ever-patient and stoical assistant, Saskia Lubodová, and some of his older students, to be familiar with the bowls and vials and packets of special materials they used to make explosive devices. Saltpetre, willow charcoal, sulphur. A sieve stood ready, and vials of ox blood and urine to purify the saltpetre. My father was waving his hands, explaining something in a husky whisper as Pada squinted down at his array of ingredients, frowning hard. They were up to something.

Definitely not a good time. I turned and quickly scuttled down the stairs—to bump into Sigrun on the way up.

We stood teetering on the steps gawping at each other, without speaking. Sigrun, looking paler than usual, giggled nervously.

Then she hugged me close. "I've missed you so! What are you doing here?"

I wanted to ask her the same thing. "Nothing. My father is head-to-head with Pada, and mother's off with Cook shopping for ingredients for Solstice cakes. We'll be safe for a while. Come on!"

Defiantly we joined hands, stifled our pent-up chatter, and ran as lightly as we could to one of the storage rooms below the attic, a chilly little room where we could hide and talk to our hearts' content. But something was wrong.

"Someone's been using this room. It should be empty," I said, looking in.

Though no one was in it now, it was obvious that our hideaway was not being used only for storage. For one thing, it had a bed placed against one wall. It hadn't been there three days ago, when I'd been there retrieving a piece of chamois leather for my grandfather. Curious.

"Go listen, in case anyone's close," I told Sigrun.

She stood at the head of the stairs, head cocked. "Nothing," she whispered. We began to snoop around.

At the foot of the bed was a small pallet of blankets, as if for a servant or slave. Right now a big orange cat, one I hadn't seen before, occupied the spot. It opened its eyes and watched us, paws tucked under, with an attitude of disdain. A basket containing mending, yarn and knitting needles rested beside the bed. A table held a small lantern, tinderbox with flint and firesteel, water pitcher and so on. In a small chest were carefully folded clothes. Very odd clothes. Tiny, close-stitched, mostly made of leather and boiled wool, they looked foreign, the colours drab and the cut unusual. We refolded and replaced the items, and closed the chest.

"Who do you suppose lives here?" Sigrun's voice held the focused excitement of a natural-born sleuth.

"I don't know. A woman, because of the needlework and skirts. Everything is so strange."

Strangest of all were the jars, wooden crates and baskets woven of reed and willow stacked along two walls. Odd smells emanated from them, dusty and thick.

"This isn't my grandfather's stuff," I whispered. "I've never seen it before." On tiptoe, I reached for a small crate at the very top, with what appeared to be a loose top. What could be inside? "Look, they have labels on them." Tied to each crate, box, basket or jar was a small scrap of parchment covered with angular black shapes drawn in ink.

"Can you read these?" I asked Sigrun.

She peered at a couple. "No. Can't you?"

"Some marks look sort of like Latin... I see a few Arabic numerals." I could speak and understand more languages than I could read. "Help me lift this crate down."

I gave it a tug. Sigrun, not much use at all, stood beside me in a posture of anticipation, her hands out tentatively as if to catch it. The crate began to wobble, the whole stack shifted, and I jumped back. "Look out!"

Sigrun dodged as the crate crashed to the floor and burst open, sending crockery containers spinning and shattering. We both shrieked and clung to each other. The cat jumped up, hissed and backed into a corner. A horrible stink filled the air, and thin, putrid liquid began to ooze across the floor. There were things within the liquid. Nasty, twisted *things*...

Gagging, we backed quickly away. The cat sneezed.

"What under God's nose is go on here?" a shrill voice rang out.

Again we screamed, whirling away from the mess in the storage room towards what appeared to be a young boy.

"We didn't do it!"

"Oh yes you did! You dare enter to my quarters, for why?" Said in fairly good Latin, but with a vulgar accent that betrayed this person as a foreigner.

Sigrun and I tried to shove past the tiny, angry presence, but it was remarkably strong. On closer examination, it appeared to be a woman. A small, furious, sharp-featured woman with her hands clenched into fists. She had two deep parallel scars on one cheek, looking as if a lion or bear had clawed her.

I tore my eyes from her scars and gathered my dignity. "I am Vara, daughter of Jameel bin Hayyan al-Kindi and Ragna Uricka Svobodová. This is... my, uh, friend." I didn't want to get Sigrun implicated by providing her name. "We have the right to enter whatever room we wish."

The small woman snorted. "I doubt! You are but childs, and you are pick through my things like apes!" She raised her small, pointed nose into the air.

At that I bridled. How dare she call us apes? "Who are *you*?" I demanded, looking down on her but feeling a creeping sense of guilt.

She narrowed her eyes. They were grey as the winter sea, surrounded by a network of tiny wrinkles. "I? I am Miss Carolina Anne Marsh, lately of the Shire of Oxford in the Kingdom of Wessex. I once be lecturer in biologic at the University of Cambridge. A where-be I sure *you* never have know."

She was right, though I deduced that she might be referring to somewhere in Britannia. I knew of Britannia, but understood it to be a cold, dreary island full of painted savages, speaking a terribly degraded version of vulgar Latin, and who consorted with pigs.

I was about to point this out when Miss Carolina Anne Marsh shoved past us, huffing like a steam-driven pump, and began plucking up the grey, bloated little items scattered among dirty liquid and shards of pottery. Some seemed to have legs, or fins. And eyes. Grasping her half-empty water pitcher, she popped the things into it as fast as she could gather them. She glared at us. "You will to help me!"

"We will not!"

Sigrun, hanging over my shoulder to watch, made retching noises in my ear. "What are those... things?"

"Specimens. It take long to collect, preserve, transport specimens. For shame on meddlesome girls! Thank Mithras it summer-not."

I narrowed my eyes. I had heard of Mithras and his worshippers. A cult that had at one time rivalled those of Saraf and of

Mohammad. Perhaps her scars were part of this barbaric religion.

She saw my look. "Oh forsaken Gods, it just a saying! Really, I thought you civilization here in south." She scrambled to her feet. "You," she said, looking at me with her piercing eyes, "are daughter's daughter of Josef, Count von Svobodá. You will fetch him to me. Tell to bring someone clean-up for mess. And quantity of spirits of alcohol."

Wisps of pale hair were coming loose from the stiff brown bonnet she was wearing, and her cheeks were pink. Her thin lips were made thinner by her obvious anger. Bolstered by Sigrun's presence at my back, I stood my ground. "Why should I do your bidding?"

She stamped her foot. "Insufferable child! You think specimens smell bad now? Wait until an hour in air. Go! Go now!"

Eyeing the little harpy, I whispered to Sigrun, "You had better leave. If we're caught together, it will be even worse for us." All the crashing and shouting was bound to bring someone.

"No! I'm staying with you," she stated loyally.

"Go! I can talk my way out of this."

After a brief glare at me, while Miss Marsh stamped her feet once more, Sigrun gave up and scurried away. The cat strolled back to its blanket and lay like a sphinx, his eyes following Miss Marsh, presumably his owner.

I said, "I will call a servant to request that my grandfather join us here. I assume he has some knowledge of your presence, Miss Marsh?" My diction had improved in response to her broken speech. My smile was sweet, my eyes as cold as I could make them. I turned to glide away regally, only to bump directly into Pada Josef. Close behind him was my father.

Papa steadied my grandfather, and took me firmly by the arm. Vainly I tried to wiggle away. Had he seen Sigrun fleeing the scene of the crime?

"What is going on here?" His words echoed Miss Marsh's, and were accompanied by a wave of his hands before his nose, and watering of his eyes. "What's that stink?"

Miss Carolina Marsh stepped up and began to shout. "This

girl—"

"I didn't—"

"Two of them, in room! Ruining specimens!"

"But we—I mean, I…"

I realized my mistake and closed my mouth. Caught in lies already. I considered bursting into tears but realized that no one would find them convincing.

Papa was steaming, and appeared ready to shake me hard, but Grandfather gazed into my eyes, his expression full of concern, not anger. This made it worse. Despite knowing that my eyes were shifting from side to side like a felon's, I tried to own up. "I… I was curious. I didn't know anyone was living here." Although it had been quite obvious. Another lie, but it seemed small now.

"Curious, eh?" Pada Josef seemed to consider the word, find it pleasing, and recalculate what to do next. He glanced at my father, in whose eyes I saw a gleam of humour. I bit hard on my lip to keep my expression contrite.

Papa let me go and stepped back. He crossed his arms and looked on like a judge. Impartial? I hoped not. As his only child, I should take precedence over some underfed foreigner.

Mildly, my grandfather looked down his thin, cold-reddened nose into the furious grey eyes of Miss Marsh. "The girl was curious. Surely you can understand that tendency, my dear friend."

I managed to raise my eyes to hers, trying to achieve a steady, repentant, yet dignified demeanour Something must have worked, for as I watched, her face went through a series of expressions, starting at righteous indignation, sliding into resentful outrage, thence to resignation and on to acceptance. And then to something unexpected.

She burst out laughing.

In a moment my grandfather had joined her, as if infected. I looked from one to the other. Was I now a laughingstock? What was wrong with them? I heard Papa snort, and my cheeks grew hot.

"Oh," gasped Miss Marsh, "I look so ridiculous, on knees my little treasures to pick up! Ha, ha!" She had a mouthful of large, crooked teeth, and looked younger now, whether from smiling or blushing I didn't know. I started to feel a little better.

"I... I'm very sorry," I tried, but they weren't listening.

Pada Josef wiped his eyes and said, "My dear Carolina, you must show me your 'little treasures' as you call them—and tell me of your adventures in Africa. It's been much too long since I last saw you."

She'd been to Africa! She was an adventuress. She didn't look at all like what I thought an adventuress should be. Except for the scars... How had she got them?

She bowed low to him, flourishing one hand as if she were a courtier. "I like to do that, thank you. Also might some space I get, with large table and, and... magnify lens?" She clasped her hands and gazed at him beseechingly. Was he her patron? He obviously knew her, but from where?

There was more to my grandfather than his skinny old body and dazed manner would lead one to believe. They seemed to have forgotten about me and the mess I'd caused. No mention of Sigrun's complicity in all this. Perhaps we'd both gotten away with it. I began to edge away.

My father shot out an arm and captured my wrist. "Wait just a moment, if you please, daughter."

Miss Marsh crossed her arms and rocked back and forth on her booted feet. She wore a calculating expression. Inwardly I groaned.

Father stared down at me. "What shall be your punishment? Since you were here all by yourself, with no one to share the blame..." He gave me the opportunity to betray my friend, but I didn't take it.

"Hmm. Well then, I suggest that you offer to assist Miss Marsh in her work."

I curled my lip. I'd already apologized, now I must help this barbarian interloper sort her nasty, smelly plunder? Didn't I have enough work and studying to do already?

As I opened my mouth to object, I felt my father's hand tighten on my wrist. He gave me a stern, admonitory look, and I felt myself wither. What choice did I have? I shuddered and turned to Miss

Marsh, who now was beginning to look happy. And perhaps a little eager...

I remembered her laugh, loud, merry and uninhibited. She was so small and strange-looking. Perhaps it would be interesting to see what else was in those crates and baskets... "Miss Marsh, please forgive my intrusion and my clumsiness. I hope you will allow me to assist you in whatever you may wish." I bowed my head. Papa's hand loosened and he smiled thinly. Grandfather grinned like a fool but said nothing.

Miss Carolina Marsh had no such restraint. She leapt forward and flung her arms around me. "Oh! We such fun we have! Not all so smelly things, I swear." She let me go and backed off, rubbing her hands together like a miser.

"Well," said my father, "I suppose I had better officially inform the household that you are here. Obviously the secret of your friend's presence is out, isn't it, my dear and esteemed father-in-law? She will be staying for a while, I presume? The winter, at least?"

"Er, yes. Um," said my Pada, scratching his nose. "That was the plan."

"You are much kindly." Miss Marsh fluttered her eyelashes.

My jaw was aching from clenching my teeth, but it seemed I was off the hook. I could hardly wait to find Sigrun and tell her everything.

The orange cat closed his eyes and began to purr.

Chapter Eight
A BASKET OF TIME

Miss Marsh was a talker. But she had fascinating tales to tell, and I soaked them up along with the rest of the family. Many an evening was spent around the fire in my parents' private living quarters, nestled on pillows with furs tucked around us, listening to her tell of camels, elephants, painted tribesmen, vast waterfalls, daring escapes from death, giant sea creatures, and more. Her command of the language improved fast, and it became easier to follow her quick changes of subject.

Even Papa was enthralled, now and then having to jump up and pace when things got tense. She was a natural storyteller.

I wanted to ask her about those scars, and about the *da resu*, but never worked up the nerve. Her scars were her own, and anything she knew of the ways of the *resura* were best inquired of by my mother. But my mother seemed strangely reluctant to challenge this little Briton.

Three months passed. Miss Marsh got rid of her camels, except for one female, named Jasmine, whom she couldn't bear to lose. It joined our stables and began to eat everything in sight and annoy the other animals. The other camels were either sent north to Soissons laden with specimen boxes, or sold. Miss Marsh had contracts to fulfill and bills to pay.

The vision of my bloody death faded, and my future fate lost urgency. I began to make better progress with languages, partly because of tutoring Miss Marsh, who appreciated the help. Also with map reading, of the earth and of the sky.

So many countries, cities, roads, rivers and mountain ranges. So many stars in the Heavens—and just to make things more difficult some of them moved along tracks of their own devising. But the tracks were in patterns that could be learned; something else Grandfather found interesting, the way some stars moved and others didn't, the way stars sometimes fell to Earth but were never found. Surely their light should make them easy to locate and collect, like the rarest of jewels?

It was all like a tale from The One Thousand and One Nights, a collection of stories my papa had bought last year from a Jewish bookseller in Cairo. Full of tales of handsome princes finding emeralds and rubies the size of roc's eggs, menaced by ghouls and talking serpents, tricked by wily genies, it was a world tantalizingly more glamorous than our own.

After I got over my revulsion, I enjoyed helping Miss Marsh sort her specimens, and became fascinated by learning how and where she'd found them. She didn't need to embellish her stories as she did at our evening sessions. She had been all over—Europe, Africa, Asia, even the new western lands. "The world," she told me, "is much larger than it seems."

Unlikely. Everyone knew that the world was huge, and as round as an orange. A sphere, as Grandfather called it. Explorers seeking spices and other treasure had proved this a hundred years ago, though as yet none had managed to circumnavigate the ball of the Earth. But one could head west, turn around and return, holds crammed with money-making goods. Established Oriental traders ground their teeth at how their prices were falling.

Vascone sailors returned from the Western lands laden with furs, mineral ores and nuggets of gold, exotic plants and a few oddly-garbed, sharp-eyed emissaries from the new world. My own father had backed an expedition that he'd thought lost for three years, only to have the two ships return with soft, thick beaver and fox pelts, tobacco, amethyst crystals and the shells called wampum, used in trade with many new-world tribes. The explorers constantly begged for more backing in their efforts to colonize the new lands, but had pretty much given up trying to reach Serendib the short way.

I loved listening to Miss Marsh and Pada Josef argue and try to outdo one another in knowledge, as I wrote up neat little labels for all her collected things. My mother rarely joined in, and after a while I came to the realization that she couldn't read. Or only enough to aid in her perusal of household records. She certainly spent no time immersed in poetry as I did. She had managed to hide this deficiency very well, and perhaps it explained why she seemed lacking in knowledge of the *da resu*. Had her training been curtailed by the inability to decipher ancient texts? Had her teachers given up on a girl they'd thought stupid?

I had to admit that it changed the way I thought of her. She wasn't perfect after all. I needed to gain information from Miss Marsh, not from my mother.

One day, on the way to tackling Miss Marsh about *resura*, I worked up the courage to ask her what decided her to become an adventuress.

"It seems a hard and dangerous life. Why would you pursue it?"

"Very simple. I was betrothed to a man I hated," she told me, her voice clipped and brisk.

Seeing my blank look, she expanded on this. "A scoundrel he was, so I ran away. I was fourteen years. Stole my mother's jewellery and purchased passage on a ship southward heading. The thought of marriage to that debaucher was intolerated."

"Intolerable," I corrected.

She shrugged. "It was easy to run away."

Easy? "But, you were promised in marriage. How could you…"

"How could I defy my parents? How could I steal?" She tossed her head, and got up to retrieve a tray of shells from its box and place it on the table where we worked. The cat nodded on his blanket, ears pricked and twitching, his green eyes half-closed, then suddenly stood, stretched and sauntered off. Perhaps he would start to earn his keep by catching a mouse.

I loved the shells, some delicately pink and spiny, some smooth and white, some black as a burnt bun. She also had trays of stone shells, which she called fossils.

"Simply because," she continued, "I valued myself more than I valued... allegiance?" I nodded. "Allegiance to parents who thought me chattel. More than blind adherence to a rule I did not make."

I opened my mouth, and closed it again. Her thin face had taken on a dark look. A rule one did not make? Surely that was every rule?

A thousand questions filled me, but she held up a hand. "My dear Miss Svobodová, you are young and innocent too much and not require details from me. At least for now. It is that I made decision right for me, though there were times when doubtful overcame me. Oh yes, not all my adventures were enjoyful."

My eyes went immediately to the two deep parallel lines on her cheek. Her mouth turned down wryly, and she ran her fingers over the scars. Affectionately, it seemed to me. I longed to know how she'd got them, but she had never revealed it. "I have plan to write accounting of my travels from the very many notes I have made, and I will have copy prepared for you. I was much surprised you can read and write. Most women cannot."

Tantalized, I was about to ask her about the University at Cambridge. A school set up by a group of the Kingdom of Wessex's scientists, lawyers and mathematicians to rival the great College of Science and Mathematics at Byzantium, it gained prestige when internal disputes and lack of funding starved most of the greatest teachers out of Byzantium's school and into Cambridge's. Did she still lecture there, between her travels? Pada Josef had told me all about it, rubbing his hands together at the thought of all that brain power concentrated in one huge school.

Her servant came in just then and began to stack and replace the various boxes and satchels we had opened, working nimbly despite a withered arm. Apparently she had acquired him somewhere in Africa. Appearing about twenty, he had curly brown hair and skin as dark as mine, also a long, bumpy nose and a pair of startlingly light eyes, almost golden, which made him look like a wild creature.

His name was Akil, he barely spoke, and tended to look at me with disapproval. His big ears, pocked skin and uneven teeth made him homely, so I ignored him, as Miss Marsh generally did.

For several days I felt exhilarated but uncomfortable in her presence. She was an iconoclast. A rebel. She was a daughter who disobeyed her father, stole from her mother. Thinking of the moment when she made her decision to run away made me remember how I had felt sitting on the minaret, deciding to let myself fall off it and fly.

And here she was, small, alive and loaded with exotic curiosities.

How had she avoided the snares and dangers of humanity? Never mind those of monsters and devils, of hungry Gods whispering in the air. I know what I felt and saw in that moment of desire on the minaret, my head swathed in cloth. They wanted everyone, not only *da resu*, to fall into their arms.

Petru Dominus eventually caught wind of Miss Marsh, her scholarly leanings and unwomanly exploits, and demanded her appearance at his local headquarters in Perpignan.

This could not be good.

Miss Marsh had once made the hard decision to run away from an intolerable situation. But also from home, from family, and from security. She had found a safe haven here. Would she run away again? It would take reckless courage rather than cowardice, for if Petru wanted her, he would have her no matter what disguise she attempted.

Yet she was strong and lucky enough to have met many devils and defeated them, perhaps even used them in her travels. Perhaps, from hints she had dropped, even loved them.

Could one actually use a devil, instead of being used by it? The devilish Petru Aska Tolny, for example. This was up to her. I knew Miss Marsh quite well by then, or so I thought; I knew Petru only by reputation. Would he test her, taunt her and let her go? Or would he keep her and drain her dry?

"Don't worry," she said to me. The day had come for her audience, and she was picking out what to wear, contemplating one of her dowdy boiled-wool tunics versus the local robe and loose trousers she'd bought in the market. "I can handle your Lord Petru."

She had already received plenty of advice from Josef and my mother, and, oddly, from Saskia Lubodová. All agreed that an air of subdued, pious dimness would be the best. She would do best to keep her brilliant intellect under wraps.

She held her head high. But I saw that her face was pale and drawn, and her thin lips were even thinner. "I shall be the... *epitome* of foolish stupidity. He will believe I only travel for fortune, not that I spying am."

Spying? I hadn't thought of that, and felt stupid. Of course he'd suspect her, a reportedly clever woman with no husband, father or brother minding her.

She left her servant boy Akil at home with us, instead being escorted to Petru's headquarters by two of our guardsmen and by a hired female bodyguard whose bulk served to emphasize Miss Marsh's child-like slenderness.

The women vanished into a litter, flanked by the men who would walk alongside, and I ran back into the villa and up the stairs to a window from which one could glimpse the top of Petru's sprawling palace, with its towers and its deep windows black as eyes at midday. But unless my gaze could penetrate rock, it was pointless to watch. I stayed there anyway, sending waves of courage from deep inside my body.

After a while I noticed a big bird circling over the city, swooping and soaring here and there, but always about the palace. *Oh Sisters.* What if it was a vulture attracted by the scent of a kill?

The sun sank as I waited and watched.

She returned just before the evening meal. She looked tired, but her back was straight as she strode in to the main reception room and its hot fire, stripping off her gloves.

"Well," she stated calmly, "I am very glad that is over."

I hung back, letting my parents and Pada Josef help her remove her heavy wrap and sit her down before the blaze. My father stood, arms crossed, glaring down at her. He wasn't angry with her, he was furious at a guest of his being treated rudely.

"What happened?" Mama asked, her voice low.

Miss Marsh gave her a significant look and gently tapped her lips with a finger as a servant brought hot drinks. "Oh, it go very well I think," she said brightly. "What an imposing man is Lord Petru. I was dazzled much by his knowledge. He must thinking me quite the fool!" She simpered and hid her mouth behind her hand, giggling.

She sat back and smiled guilelessly up at my father, whose lips were curled in a silent snarl. It was quite a performance. The servant shuffled out at last. Petru had his people everywhere, and if they were not precisely *his*, they were kept as such by threats and bribery.

"You are all right?" asked my father. "He didn't..." He waved a hand expressively. *Hurt you.*

"I am quite well. Lord Petru was perfect host. We drinking spiced coffee and discussing New Western World. He had heard, somehow," and at this Mama snorted, "that I have visit the Terra Torridia. I entertain him with tales of the very odd animals and men I encountered."

Mama sat beside her on the padded bench, and took her hand. "How... delightful."

"Hmm, yes. He say certainly that I must, *must* stay as an honoured guest in his city and think no more of travelling So welcoming, he put arms around me and gave me a very... affectionate squeeze." She rubbed her shoulders as if they ached.

At this both Grandfather and Mama sucked in their breath. Papa's nostrils flared. It was obvious what had happened. Petru had threatened her with violence if she attempted to escape Perpignan.

Fortunately she didn't seem to want to leave anyway, though it must be galling to know you were essentially under arrest.

Miss Marsh had had a close call. We ordered fresh tea brought in, and talked loudly for a while about the magnificence of Lord Petru. Then we all went to bed.

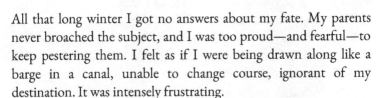

All that long winter I got no answers about my fate. My parents never broached the subject, and I was too proud—and fearful—to keep pestering them. I felt as if I were being drawn along like a barge in a canal, unable to change course, ignorant of my destination. It was intensely frustrating.

However, some of my studies were less boring than others. The scroll Mother handed me on poisons, for instance. How to make them, detect them, and use them. Very interesting. For a while I went about sniffing everything suspiciously. Also, the talk she gave me on what men and women do together under the sheets. It is not always just to start a baby. She kept on relentlessly, showing me drawings she'd got from who-knows-where, as I blushed and squirmed and couldn't keep from looking.

One very strange evening was spent with a woman, a Theravedan entrepreneur born on the island of Serendib, who travelled the world, she informed us, teaching the art of Deception Fighting which she had developed. It stemmed from her knowledge of Silat, an ancient fighting style based upon the movements of animals. Deception Fighting was mostly for women or delicate boys and men, and involved intense observation, training, and the ability to set aside squeamishness. I spent the evening marvelling at the grace and strength the woman exhibited. I was never told her name. She travelled with an entourage of other women whom she had trained, and who served as a buffer between herself and those who would wish to challenge her.

After her ritual movements and chants, she beckoned me to join her on the layer of thick rugs that had been laid on the floor of an empty storeroom. We circled for a moment, then I was suddenly flat on my back gasping for air. This happened over and over, until I was dizzy and humiliated. The one truly useful thing she taught me was very basic and not really part of Silat: how to kick a man in his most tender parts. I'd known these parts were there, of course, for every male animal had them—and mother's drawings showed them—but I hadn't understood their pitiful vulnerability.

I also knew that learning anything useful from her would involve many months or years of study, and that there was no chance I'd be afforded any such thing. So I merely marvelled, and bowed and gasped at her ability to disarm and vanquish men two times her size. In parting, she said, "Much strength can be gained merely by remembering what you have seen tonight. Think upon the moves and techniques I displayed, my child—practice them alone in the darkness of night if you must. Any training is better than not knowing such arts even exist."

I bowed once more as she and her fighting women left.

In spring, as soon as the ruts in the roads had dried up and been smoothed by crews of workers, my father set off once more, north to Alemania and Germania and some of the prosperous merchant cities there. Perhaps even across the northern channel to Britannia if weather permitted. Now that the Viking raids seemed to be no more—the Vikings having decided to loot and pillage the New World instead of the old—travel was much safer. Grandfather had said more than once that we were in the middle of a Golden Age.

Which he would follow up by muttering, "If Petru doesn't send us all to hell."

Papa quietly asked Miss Carolina Marsh if she would like to take the opportunity to escape the city and return to her homeland under the protection of his caravan, defying Petru's order.

She bit her lip, considering. Then, remembering perhaps that it would not be she alone who was punished for disobedience, she politely declined, in her best Latin, which was becoming very good. "I will stay here, as commanded. I do not mind at all, my dear Jameel ibn Hayyan al-Kindi. I fear that should I return to the cold and damp of Wessex, I would very soon sicken and die." She looked down demurely. Papa didn't even blink at this transparent falsehood. Everyone knew she had the constitution of a donkey.

I think he was disappointed at her decision, perhaps hoping to become embroiled in a thrilling adventure. But it wouldn't have ended well.

Chapter Nine
THE HOT SPRINGS OF LUCHON

As spring turned to summer, rumours of plague started up: a believable excuse to get out of town for a while. Mother had to petition Petru to be allowed to leave the city, but after some tense negotiations—and a lot of guarantee money—her request was granted.

We were going northwest to Luchon, where there was an ancient but still popular spa. Pompey and Tiberius once stayed there, and called it Ilixion. Hunnic generals and nobles took over once the Romans were driven back eastward—finally handing over, at bargain rates, several provinces including our own to the Huns to pay down their debts to Egypt and Persia.

According to legend, a Nazarene prophet called Jesus and his wife, Mary of Magdalen, settled there for a few years, along with Jesus' mother Mary.

The prophet lost heart when he was accused of instigating unrest or blasphemy or something crucifix-worthy, only to be pardoned. Disgruntled at the lack of respect, he refused to preach any more, or was prevented by his wife and mother lest he get in more trouble. I had read some of his writings, and thought the fellow had some good things to say. But he'd been dead for twelve hundred years.

Mother started packing and organizing for departure; no matter what her motives for leaving, plague was not something to ignore. Sigrun's father, bowing low, asked that his daughter accompany us. Begged, really. For a long time Mother resisted answering him either yes or no. I pleaded and whined for my friend to come along, until finally she sat me down.

"Vara Svobodová bint Jameel, you must stop this. It's not just the plague that takes us away from here—it's something more imperative. You need more training, and Petru has eyes and ears everywhere in the city. You know he is here more often than not."

"But he's busy with his new Communica. Sigrun told me he's there all the time, ordering the architects and clerics about."

"True, but..." She sighed. "Vara, I don't trust your friend. If Sigrun learns something she shouldn't..."

"But she'd never betray us!"

"Of course she wouldn't. Not willingly."

She let that soak in for a minute. I felt my heart thud painfully. Could Petru or his men actually torture information out of poor silly Sigrun? Petru, though he had a vicious streak, was such a pious leader. Some of his ideas seemed harsh, but he was admired everywhere. He was above such squalid acts as torture.

I got the job of trying to talk Grandfather Josef into accompanying us.

We were leaving in three days, so I got right to it. "You know, hot springs are very good for the health," I remarked casually, leaning both elbows upon his big stone desk. He didn't bother to look up. He was scribbling down line after line of numbers and shapes onto a large sheet of yellowish paper, the ever-present orange cat dabbing at the quill with one paw.

"There's nothing wrong with my health."

"But Pada, your hands... they get so stiff and painful, don't they? The waters will cure them. And what of the plague?"

"Pah! The only people who get sick are peasants who sleep with their dogs and pigs! Does your Papa allow pigs anywhere?"

"Well, no, but—"

"I'm too busy to traipse off into the wilderness, and I certainly don't want to waste my time wallowing in a sulphurous pool with a lot of ignoramuses." He waved his arms, spraying ink, indicating the array of experiments he had going on here and there in his vast attic. Besides the experiments, he had students too. My Pada had a reputation as a scholar, and paying clients would shove their sons forward to be educated. The attic was usually cluttered with several of the smelly louts, kept from sloth and pilfering only by Saskia Lubodová's watchful eye and willingness to tattle. There weren't any right now, but he waved a hand at their imaginary presence. "How can I leave all this?"

"Everything will still be here when you get back. I don't want you to die."

He hooted, which I thought was a rude reaction, and a wheezy echo came from Madame Saskia, in her usual corner. I couldn't see her, as she was surrounded by draped lengths of soft fabric that seemed to have festooned the huge room like the nest of a giant spider. I went over to see what she was doing.

Obligingly, Saskia Lubodová held up a length of pale, sand-coloured silk. "We are sewing all these bolts together in a special way—to form a huge bag." She had three women with her, each wielding needle and thread, squinting down at their neatly stitched double seams. Judging by the amount of fabric, it looked as though they would be at it for months.

"Ah. Grandfather and his balloons. But isn't there an awful lot of this?" I took a slippery handful of silk and was amazed at its fineness. It must have cost a fortune.

I'd seen some of his miniature balloons floating here and there at night, charming paper or silk lanterns drifting slowly up and down. They were mere experiments, he said, and told me the theory behind this power to lift and float: it was light rays from the candle impacting the silk and bouncing off it, causing a force he called "thrust" that urged the little bag skyward. So they wouldn't operate in daylight, due to the opposite effect of the sun's light rays pressing them down. He hadn't actually tried this, as everyone preferred to see the "lanterns" float in the dark.

Grandfather rocked back and forth on his feet. "I have calculated that a bag of silk, properly close-woven and made tight with oil and wax, needs to have a circumference of eighty cubits to lift a basket with a small furnace and a man inside."

Lift a man? This sounded like a terrible idea. "Perhaps you should send a mouse up first, in a smaller one?" The cat, I swear it, began to purr.

"Clever girl! Exactly what I deduced, and have done! With a frog, though."

"What?" I stared at him, feigning outrage while truly feeling quite clever. "No, you didn't tell me!"

He blinked and looked guilty. "I'm sorry, Vara. Forgive me."

The words sent a slice of heat across my neck. I could barely restrain myself from screaming and clutching myself. But I wouldn't, couldn't, spoil this moment. "Oh, Pada, of course I forgive you." I hugged him, my chin quivering.

"Thank you, my dear. And don't worry, I have it all worked out. It isn't the light that does it, it's the heat! All along the candle at the base was putting out heat as well as light. Hot air inside the balloon tries to regain the skies, where I have deduced that nighttime temperatures are much higher than on the ground, due to the influence of the stars."

I prayed to the Sisters that he wouldn't die of plague while we were gone. Then I remembered that he wasn't destined to die that way.

But, whispered my selfish heart, if he dies of plague he won't be there to kill me. But then the soldiers will get me. So, I might live a day longer, but at what price?

Anyway, visions did not lie.

I left him, and told Mama that he wouldn't leave the city.

She sighed. "As I expected."

Chapter Ten
THE MIDDLE OF A PEARL

Despite the cool, pine-scented air in this high mountain valley, and the countless butterflies and birds, Luchon left me disappointed and resentful. The long, dusty trip by carriage and wagon had not been worth it.

Within an hour I had explored the whole place. The spa was half-empty, and most of the visitors were elderly and infirm. There was no one my age, not a single handsome boy in sight.

I returned to the small but luxurious quarters we had taken for the month and threw myself onto my bed. "There's nothing to do here." My mother rolled her eyes. "Why couldn't Sigrun come? It's not fair!"

"You will have plenty to do soon enough. For now, stop pouting and get up." She crossed her arms and watched as I dragged myself to my feet. She had better not laugh at me, I thought darkly. "Come on. Let's get something to eat. The food here is supposed to be delicious."

This turned out to be true. We took one look at the spread of delicacies at the nearest cook-shop, and stepped right up. I lost a little of my resentment.

"Smell the cinnamon in this pastry! And look at the bowls of fruit—it's a cornucopia." Mother chatted boldly with the proprietor as a bored old slave fanned away the few flies that hovered hopefully around. The cook basked obsequiously in the glow of her praise.

"Standards of hygiene," the plump, eager fellow assured us, "are of the very highest and most modern! Offal is disposed of properly of course. And rats? Ha! They are nonexistent! Everything— everything! is cleaned and sluiced with water every night." We believed him. We were paying plenty for exactly what was provided: safety and comfort. No one should run from plague only to drop dead from dysentery or typhus.

When I fell into my bed at last, full of spiced meat and candied apricots, I drew the thin netting around me into a pale, gauzy tent. Far-off music played quietly, but before I could sort out what instruments were playing which melody and counter-melody, and which of those high, warbling tones might be a human voice, I was asleep.

The next day we spent several hours in the baths, wallowing in the spa's milky, steaming water. It was hard to get used to the sulphur stink, but since we'd paid for its health benefits we pretended to welcome it.

My bathing robe wasn't doing much to protect my modesty. Heavy and wet, it clung to my bosom. At least the men had their own set of baths.

I tried my best to ignore the other women and their endless chatter about children, household hints, the sexual practices of foreigners, and other thrilling topics.

Gritting my teeth, I let myself sink up to my nostrils. We were stuck here for a month. Baths, lectures, food, tours of the flower gardens. It was hell. I let myself sink completely.

Another dreary day passed. I actually looked forward to going to bed, for it meant we'd be closer to the day we could leave. But I was rudely awakened that night.

Mother pulled my little tent of mosquito netting aside briskly. "Wake up," she hissed. She was dressed for outside, wearing the baggy harem-style trousers she liked, a plain dark tunic and shawl, and leather boots and gloves.

I blinked moisture into my eyes and peered at her. "But it's still dark."

She gave me the look that always got me moving. Cold, direct, with one eyebrow quirked up. She didn't have to say a word. Another damned lesson. What would she make me do this time? Would the gods of air and darkness be watching, waiting?

"Now, Vara! Hurry up."

Outside, the air was cold and moist. A few birds were already calling with a certain desperation in their shrill voices. I heard a nightingale's trill, and other songs I didn't recognize, and shivered as we left the manicured gardens and started up a narrow dirt trail.

The sky was turning pale lemon in the east, with just enough light to make out where to step. The path quickly became steep and rocky. I was panting by the time we reached a flat spot at the top of a hill.

We settled our bottoms on a cold, hard rock. The brief spurt of excitement I'd felt was reverting to bad temper quickly. It was too foggy to see anything, I was hungry, my foot hurt from stepping on a loose rock, and the clammy air was reminding me of the family crypt. "This is stupid. What are we doing here?"

She gave me a sharp look. "Don't take that tone with me. You're here for a reason."

My stomach grumbled. Mother ignored the small noise, remaining focused on the gradually lightening sky.

Why had I been so happy to come to Ilixion? I missed the city and its life and bustle, no matter its modesty compared to Massalia or Córdoba or even fabled, crumbling Rome. And what if everyone at home was dying of plague right now?

"Stop fidgeting; we'll be here for only a few minutes more."

Well, halleluiah. Perhaps the fog would burn off and we'd see a bear. Maybe it would eat us.

The grey paled, intensifying into whiteness, the light of the rising sun coalescing into a watery silver. There was no horizon, the fog was too thick for that, but there was suddenly a glow spreading through the veil before us. It brightened fast, extending all around us until it seemed we were in the middle of a huge pearl... mysterious, white, glowing.

I shivered, and felt suddenly that we must be very high. Even though we still sat upon solid rock, it was as if we were displayed before the sky on a promontory that pierced the heavens. It wasn't frightening, no more than the minaret had been... at first.

My mother said, "See how the mist glows? Each tiny droplet of water in the air around us contains a bit of the sun. But it will soon be gone. Before it burns away, I want you to try something."

I looked at her, expressing my skepticism with my eyes.

"Look into the mist, feel its texture, its motion. There are currents within it. You can see them. You can move them."

I could see nothing but the eye-dazzling paleness. Not a speck of colour, just white. "How? I can't see any currents."

"Push a little."

Push? How could you push air? Oh.

I pursed my lips and blew. The fog thinned and swirled tantalizingly, and I could hear a sort of thrumming overhead. I hoped my mother knew what she was doing.

I peered ahead with all my might, trying to shove the blinding mist out of the way with the power of thought alone, since breath from my mouth did nothing. A wee hole appeared. With a focused effort I concentrated and *pushed*.

The hole enlarged. Like a smoke ring from an old man's pipe it spread and wobbled, a hazy little window through the fog. I could see the far-off flank of a mountain, still shadowed as the sun rose behind it.

"Very good. Now, I want you to pull the mist to you."

"What? Why? It's cold!"

"Try, Vara."

There was no use in complaining. We'd stay here until Ragna Svobodová saw results. So I pictured the mist as a cloak, and after several minutes gained the prize of a chill film laid on my skin and hair and clothes. I shuddered, yet what was wrong with a pure fine fog sent down by the God of Water? If there was such a being... I reached out an arm—an arm made of blood and bone and mist—and spread my fingers.

I groped with my hands as if testing the air's strength. Mother watched, expressionless, as I peered up at the sky. My mouth opened and I drew in a great gasp of air. Suddenly I could smell everything.

I'm not saying I couldn't smell things before—the pine trees, the lavender and thyme that our footsteps had crushed—but now I could detect every little nuance of scent. Everything in the dirt under my feet, everything growing and dying all around us. There was so much... My nose began to tingle and itch, and soon I was sneezing.

Mother put her arm around me as I wiped my nose on my sleeve. The sun was burning its way through the fog. I couldn't wait to see it go, and before I knew it I leaned a bit with my thoughts and pushed. The last tendrils swirled away and vanished. The air, and my arms and face and clothes, became dry.

Something indicated its approval. Something big.

Something right behind me.

I whipped my head around, but there was nothing to be seen. Still I felt... *attention* upon me. Someone was watching. Some*thing*. My flesh was crawling.

The air was getting hot. A roaring sounded, getting closer. Mother stood and began to look around alertly, her hand on my shoulder.

The heat grew, and the wind picked up. The smell of burning— it was a forest fire! I could see the flames, just on the other side of the nearby trees, and I could hear the squeals and groans of animals and trees cowering before the blowing flames. I grabbed my mother's arm. "We have to run! Now! Now!"

She shook my hand off.

The scorching heat died or veered away. No flames, no roar. Had there really been a fire? The sun was rising into the cool air, yet my nostrils were full of the smell of burning flesh.

A ghostly pale shape burst through the shrubs. Then another. A swarm of them raced toward us. We clung to each other, and I could feel my mother getting ready to shove me down and shield me with her body.

One of the pale shapes hopped onto a boulder, bleating.

We gasped in unison and then began to laugh. Goats! It was only a herd of goats. Curious, they bounced and scampered around us, peering up with their slitted yellow eyes. The goatherd, a skinny, barefoot youth clad in leather pants and a rough-woven vest, followed them, looking very surprised to see two ladies, in tears with laughter, here on his mountain top.

He edged past, gave us a couple of clumsy bows, and hurried after his goats, who had already lost interest and run off seeking their grass and herbs.

The world returned to normal. The phantom smoke vanished, the heat of a non-existent forest fire evaporated, the goats were gone, and I could feel nothing of that *attention* that I'd felt before. Had the Gods been watching, their interest piqued by what I'd done?

This was twice my mother had exposed me to scrutiny. I wanted no more of it.

"Don't look at me that way," she said. "You have to know what you're in for. There's no avoiding it, Vara."

"*You've* managed to avoid it," I muttered.

She tightened her mouth. "I avoided nothing. I was never given the opportunity to use what I had learned. Not that I learned enough... I know my education has been lacking, in many ways, most especially in *da resu* lore. When I was young enough to learn, I paid little attention. When I became old enough to gain wisdom, the opportunity was gone." She paused, observing me with what I knew was frustration. "I've seen what I needed to see. You are a true *da resu*, as strong as any I know of. The Gods are watching you. Next we will try something more difficult."

She made me wallow in mud. There was a marshy place hidden by the trees where no one came—it stank of sulphur, and there were insects—and made me lie in the dirty mess of weeds and muck. "Feel it, Vara! Dig your fingers in, pull it to you. Don't you know we are all dust? We come from dust and back to dust we go."

"This isn't dust, it's mud! How will I ever get clean?"

"Stop complaining. Can you feel your skin drink it all up like wine?"

I hated her with cold passion right then. Something wriggled next to my buttocks, and I shrieked, bursting out of the muddy hollow like a calf from the butcher's arms.

I wiped the muck away as best as I could before it began to soak in, splashing vainly in the warm, murky water that trickled into the marsh from somewhere. Ready to spit with fury, I pulled on my clothes and glared at her. "What good is all this? What am I supposed to be—a spy? An assassin? I won't do it! I won't!"

"You must."

I turned and walked stiffly to the path before she could see my tears of anger. Why was she doing this to me? Was I to be a lonely spirit made of dirt, forever apart from the world of the living? What about her? She was *da resu* too; why wasn't she rolling in the mud? She had a husband, she was a mother, she was mistress of a huge, wealthy villa. I would die never knowing those things.

On the way back to our quarters, the nightingale sang again. It was in a cage swinging from a bracket attached to the stone wall. Trapped and alone, it didn't know enough to stop singing.

By the time we'd been at Ilixion half a month I'd worked up a store of anger at how women and girls were pushed aside, literally, by men and youths who would simply walk over us if we didn't jump out of the way, and figuratively when our words were ignored. I hadn't noticed it as much at home, where most of the people around me were female, or of lower station. It rankled, and I wasn't sure why; it was perfectly normal. Was I getting above my place in life, thinking that a woman might argue with men?

Mentally rehearsing the moves the Theravedan warrior woman had shown me lifted my spirits. A knee in the right spot... How satisfying it would be to see the smug expressions turn to shock and pain. But I knew better than to try.

I'd got more lessons in fighting, but they'd amounted to only two short evenings with a muscular and impatient Saxon female, her brown hair shorn as close as a leper's, who let it be known without saying a word that I was too soft and clumsy to bother with. I tried, I really tried, to handle the dagger and the garrote the way she showed me, but I kept thinking of blood and death and fear. My hands would start to shake, my nerve to fail, and soon she'd have me on the ground with her heavy body on top of mine, her knife touching my skin, and her sneers of derision in my ears. I wasn't cut from warrior's cloth.

Mother paid the woman extra to keep at it. But the Saxon bitch had enough after two nights; she took the money and didn't return.

I really would rather have sulked in my room than attend that evening's philosophical discussion. Nothing but boring grey-beards telling us nothing new.

"Vara," sad my mother, exasperated with my sighs and glares as we dressed to go out, "try to behave yourself. There are musicians coming on once the debaters are done. They just arrived from somewhere I've never heard of. You'll like them."

Our seats were halfway up the array of stone tiers in the hillside that formed the semi-circular theatre. Since this was a high-class place, they were thoughtfully padded with feather-stuffed leather cushions. Long shadows fell across the orchestra area, and torches flared and wavered in the cool breeze of evening.

Two elderly men tottered from behind the skene and arranged themselves upon a cluster of artistically broken classical columns which they used as seats. Each wore a draped white robe, and had a laurel wreath in his hair. I groaned. We'd be suffering through a debate between Seneca the Younger and Plato, a production so old it had more whiskers than they did.

The moment they opened their mouths the oldsters were revealed as youths, and not particularly compelling at rhetoric. The musical troupe couldn't take the stage soon enough. The men spouted platitudes, and were not doing well before a crusty, opinionated, hard-of-hearing audience. I wished they would just shut up.

I yawned, not bothering to hide it behind a hand.

Plato noticed and shot me an evil look. Dared I stick out my tongue? No. I couldn't be bothered.

The chorus of boys warbled shrilly, their high voices eerie as they sang long, wordless tones in a style of music I hadn't heard before. As a background to the men's talk, it was actually more interesting than what they said. The chorus, singing in a minor key, wove their voices skillfully into a wandering motif that made my skin shiver.

The actors yammered on, veering away from philosophy into crude jokes about public figures. Everyone liked this much better.

What we saw next made it all worthwhile.

Chapter Eleven
THE NIGHTINGALE'S TOOTH

With a loud jingling of tambourines and rattling of drums and those weird instruments that are merely a rack of wood thrummed with sticks, the musical troupe stormed the stage. Everyone began to hoot and cheer.

The musicians clustered on one side of the stage and began to play. Two citole players, two men rattling tambourines, and one hugging a big, pear-shaped oud which he immediately began to pluck in an insistent, fast rhythm.

One of the tambourines was flourished by a young man dressed only in a baggy set of dark red trousers slung low on his hips, like the harem-style pants mother sometimes wore. I couldn't tear my eyes away from his oiled chest, strong arms and glimpses of his muscular legs through the thin, clinging fabric. His black hair was clipped short, his face was narrow but handsome, with full lips and high cheekbones. His whole body kept time to the music's beat. He began to chant along with the melody, in words I didn't know. Another language to learn. My hips started twitching in time to the rhythm.

Next the dancers, all men of course, raced in, twirling and

flipping as fast as they could across the stage and back again to start an intricate pattern of legs and arms and flying robes, bells at wrist and ankle jingling.

They were good, but I kept looking back at the tambourine player. Then I saw him wink at me. I glared at him for his impudence and turned my eyes away from him, until, through no fault of my own, my gaze happened to slide back over in his direction. He yawned, and I felt myself flush.

It was Plato, his false grey beard gone. Defiantly I turned away, my head high. Though I risked the odd glance, I never caught him looking at me.

The sun was long gone when the performers bowed their way off stage, catching tossed coins and little bags of candy.

That boy had been so beautiful… How could I look at a boy like that, watch him move, enjoy his flirting, and not imagine more? His strong brown arms around me, his lips on mine, my body so close to his that perhaps with my *da resu* powers I'd draw a little of his substance into my skin…

Was it my fate to die a virgin? It wasn't fair.

Mother linked her arm with mine. "Are you hungry? I think that cook-shop next to the rose garden is open for business."

"No, I'm not." I know I sounded surly.

"Well, I am. It's early yet, and I want something sweet. Come."

Before I knew it we were lined up in front of one of several little shops selling small skewers of spiced meat, fried fish wrapped in flatbread, and an enticing array of sweets. Maybe I was a *little* hungry.

Suddenly Plato stepped boldly up beside us and flourished a low bow.

My mouth dried up. I kept my eyes on my feet, and hoped I didn't smell too much of sweat.

"Beautiful lady," he said to my mother, "you must try the lamb meatballs cooked with raisins and mint." He smacked his lips.

Mother looked down her nose at him. Since he was shorter than she, it was easy. In fact, he was barely taller than I. "Must I?" Her voice was cool yet not completely dismissive.

He grinned, taking in both of us with his lively dark eyes. "You must. And if you and your lovely young sister could find it in your heart—and purse—to buy some for me, I will tell your fortunes."

I didn't know whether to laugh, frown, or call the guards of the watch.

But Mama nodded regally. "So be it."

Soon we had a platter of food delivered to us at a small table where there were only two chairs. Mother and I took them, and Plato obligingly flung himself on the ground beside us, leaning back on his arms and gazing up at us with not the slightest trace of humility in the presence of his betters.

Mother motioned to the platter. "Go ahead, have some food. I hope the fortunes you tell are happy ones."

"Oh, yes, my queen. Always happy."

Soon he was licking his fingers and looking a little less as if he were about to go off in sparks like one of Pada's fireworks. Perhaps it was the unexpected company, but the food tonight seemed more delicious, more hot and spicy, than ever before. Mama's barbaric eating-habits—she had always insisted upon spearing her food with her knife instead of using her fingers like a civilized person—didn't seem to bother Plato.

"Now," she said, "I want our fortunes."

He managed to perform an elaborate bow without standing up, somehow rolling his body in a graceful, athletic move that was fascinating to watch. "First," he said, "we must find a secluded spot where jealous ears will not be listening." His eyes were half-lidded and frankly suggestive. He seemed older than he looked, which might have been eighteen years.

I expected Mother to send him packing, having done her charitable duty to the poor and theatrical, but she rose and led the way toward a small grove of trees with a splashing fountain and a stone bench beside it, obviously placed so the noise of the water would cover conversation. A place for trysts and secrets. Here she settled, motioning me to join her.

Plato crouched beside us on his haunches.

Mother asked him his name.

"I am Eneko Saratxaga of the province of Nafarroa, called Navarre in your language. I am at your service, my queen." The Navarre was a province of the huge, sprawling Muslim Empire, which stretched from south of the Pyrenees, through most of the vast continent of Africa, around the Mediterranean and eastward to the Ganges River. He must be Vasconi, a people renowned for their seafaring, and their stubborn and ferocious fighting ability.

With a nod, Mother repeated his name, her tongue rolling over the strange syllables. "Eneko Saratxaga, we are well met." His name sounded outlandish, perhaps false. I wouldn't even try to say it.

He slid a hot glance my way. My insides gave a strange throb. The feeling disturbed me, but I ignored it. Our fortunes were about to be told. Could I ask him questions, get advice from another realm? Just how much might I ask him without revealing myself as *da resu*?

Mother murmured something into his ear, and he whispered a reply. Eneko Saratxaga's handsome face was suddenly serious.

Mother reached for my hand and leaned close. "Vara, this boy is in my service. He is no mere fortune-teller."

"You know him?"

"I do. Not by sight, but by name and a word he knows to tell me, a secret between your father and myself that we use to make sure of loyalty."

Eneko lowered his eyes and bowed.

"But he's just an actor. How can we trust anything he says?"

"I trust your father. If you do not wish to hear what this boy says, go now to your bed."

We scowled at each other. But I was curious, and excited by the mystery. This, I realized with rush in my blood, was what I longed for during the hot nights and boring days of study and propriety. I wanted secrets and intrigue, passion and danger. "I will stay."

She nodded. "Good." Turning back to Eneko, who had watched our small battle with a straight face, she said, "Tell me what you know, boy."

"In good time. First I give you this, my queen," he said. He pressed something into her hand. Then he looked at me. "And you as well, my princess." His warm hand grasped mine, perhaps for a little longer than necessary, and uncurled my fingers. Suddenly there was a hard object in my palm, the size of the end of my thumb. A triangle of something gleaming black.

"What is this?"

"It is a magical token. A nightingale's tooth."

We both looked at him with suspicion.

"It is said to ward off poison, and to cure snakebite. Do you not know the legend?" He was taking a chance talking of snakes, they being Saraf's symbol.

My mother shook her head. "No. Pray tell us."

He settled back and began in the traditional way. "Once upon a time, the lowly little nightingale familiar to us now was as big as a Roc." He waved an arm, indicating something the size of an ox. "Her glossy brown feathers swept the ground, reflecting the light in jewel tones. She was very unlike the small, drab bird we see today. Also, she had teeth."

"But no bird has teeth."

"Ah, but the nightingale did. Large and sharp they were, as sharp as a lion's."

"What happened to her?"

"She became jealous of other birds who could warble sweetly. With her great size and sharp teeth she could best any other bird in a fight, and so was feared but never loved. She moped and brooded over what she had not, and spurned that which she had. One day she met a genie, who, seeing her jealous nature, offered a trade. Genies," he said in a lowered voice, "are quick to sense a deal. Beware of them, for all they want is to get the better of you."

Mother nodded sagely. She was hanging on his tale as fervently as I was.

Eneko continued, "'Genie', begged the nightingale, 'give me the sweetest voice of all the birds!'

"'What have you to trade?' asked the wily spirit.

"The nightingale thought. She had her beautiful plumage. 'Take my long, glorious feathers in exchange,' she bargained.

"The genie shook his turbaned head, the jewels upon it rattling. 'The peacock has much finer garb. What else have you?'

"The nightingale thought again. She had nothing else. Sadly, she turned away. But then the genie said, 'Wait. I see that you have teeth, very sharp and plentiful.'

"'So I do,' she said. "You may have them, if I may have what I want.'

"'Done,' said the genie, smiling widely.

"At once her teeth fell out to scatter on the ground before her. She felt very odd, but happy, and clacked her new toothless beak a few times. 'At last I will be loved by all for my wonderful song!'

"She tried out her voice. From her throat poured the loveliest melody the world had ever known. The other birds flew down, perched in trees and crept along the ground to be close to her, and to hear her magnificent voice."

Mother drew a long breath. She said, "Ah... the nightingale bested the genie. She got what she wanted."

Eneko cocked his head to one side. "So she thought at first. She sang to any who would listen, and at first all the birds and animals clustered around to hear her. But she became proud, as she had been of her teeth. She began to demand payment, and to hear that lovely voice many birds and animals and even humans paid her in gold coins. For a while she was fat and happy, rich and admired. She demanded more gold, but the coins and listeners stopped coming. She began to shrink, becoming smaller and smaller, her feathers losing their sheen. Everyone was tired of her singing and bragging, and one day a small blackbird, who had always been proud of his own melodious warble, had enough. He began to peck at the nightingale, and buffet her with his wings. 'Be gone!' he trilled. 'No-one wants you here!'

"At one time, before her bargain, the nightingale would have devoured the upstart bird in one savage bite. But she no longer had teeth. She had never really learned to fight, since everyone had been afraid of her. The blackbird easily drove her out of her home, across the mountains and into the desert. There she lived, alone, sad and shrinking until she became the small, drab and toothless bird we know today."

Mother smiled a little, satisfied at the outcome of this morality tale. "Pride doth go before a fall, they say. So the genie bested her after all."

"Yes. Plus, he cleverly gathered the fallen teeth, knowing their value. To this day a nightingale's tooth is a good luck charm, and a powerful warding token."

At this we both looked reverently, if a little nervously, at our small black triangles. These might come in handy against Petru and his chosen god. While Mother slid a gold coin into Eneko Saratxaga's hand I tucked my odd trophy into a pocket tied inside my tunic, planning to ask one of our housemen to drill a hole in it so it could join my Owl and my Eye.

Ah. That was it. I had seen this tooth already. It was when I died. The chain around my blood-soaked neck had held an image of this very shape. Sharp, black; there and yet not-there. Foreboding of something, which I knew at the time was bad. As I'd watched my death I had seen the pain I must be feeling, but I couldn't feel it. Would it really happen? Obviously the lucky tooth had no power against steel.

Mother jogged my knee. "Vara, are you listening? Eneko and I must talk privately now. You may help us by keeping a watch for anyone approaching, no matter how old or frail they might appear."

"Of course."

Rising, I began to pace around the secluded grove. No one was near; I could hear nothing other than the fountain's rattle, normal night sounds and the odd raised voice from the direction of the cook-houses, which were closing up for the night.

What was Eneko Saratxaga telling her? What if he were an agent of Petru, sent to trick my mother? The nightingale's tooth was a bad omen, I feared. But Mother trusted him. But... *That which is handsome on the outside is often ugly underneath...* I kept up my perimeter patrol, ears and eyes sharpened for any sign of eavesdroppers.

Nothing happened. Their whispering voices changed after several long minutes to more normal tones, and mother called me back. She and Eneko stood, and shared a brief clasp of farewell. "May the Sisters guide you, my friend," she said to him. He bowed to us both, but then reached for my hand and brought it to his lips. A mere whisper of heat touched my palm, but it went straight to my heart. And somewhere farther down... Then he vanished into the darkness.

The night turned chill and empty. The wine-like sparkle of Eneko's presence was gone.

He was a spy, so by nature was clever and devious. Everyone important employed spies; it was often the only way to get information. He would have no interest in me, except as a child of his patron.

"Do you want to know what the boy told me?"

"Yes, please." I wanted to know a lot about Eneko Saratxaga.

As we prepared for bed she whispered in my ear. "First, these nightingale teeth are tokens of service, held not only by us but by others who share our cause. Eneko is distributing them to those he and Jameel know. Should you or any one of us need to test a person's truthfulness, simply ask to see the tooth. If they have one, they are safe.

"Also, he told me who is secretly owned by Petru. And what cities and families might be willing to lend arms and men should it come to that, and who has grain and horses to sell. He told me other things, but you do not need to know them."

But I did. I had a taste of intrigue, and I wanted more.

Mother and I settled into bed, and soon I heard her breathing slow and deepen. As silently as I could, I got up, dressed, and slipped out into the night.

I knew where the visiting entertainers were quartered, and after a few heart-pounding minutes I approached the night guard who leaned against a tree idly spinning a twig in his fingers and tossing it into the air. He jumped when I slid up to him and touched him on the arm.

"Mind how you sneak up on a man, missy! You'll get your nose cut off."

I let him huff for a while, trying to look contrite and meek. "My mistress would have the boy called Eneko tell her fortune."

"What? Now?"

Lanterns still burned in the encampment, and I could hear voices. It wasn't very late.

"Now. She will pay him well."

"And what about me?"

I had anticipated this, and had a coin ready. He gave me a smirk and went to fetch Eneko.

He had changed out of his revealing costume, and looked more of a man, less of a boy. Still beautiful. He followed me toward the guest quarters, but once we were in the shadows I took him by the hand.

"Eneko Sara... Sartex..."

"Just call me Eneko. What is it? Your mother summons me?"

I shook my head, suddenly tongue-tied. He must think me a fool, running after him in the night. What did I want, exactly? I wasn't sure. Gently he raised my hand to his lips as he had done before, then said, "What is going on, little bird?"

"I... I can't go back to Perpignan. There's a curse upon me. On my family. If I go back, I'll die. And I'll be the cause of my grandfather's death. You have to help me!"

"But how, my princess?"

"Take me with you!" I blurted out my hastily-contrived plan, begging him to let me join the troupe of performers and travel with them. "I can help you in the work you do for my parents. I understand the danger—really I do!" Since my mother trusted him, I did too. Perhaps we were wrong, but how could I tell? "I've had a vision that I know will come to pass. I have to get away! Then the vision will vanish like a raindrop in the sun, n-no one will die—"

He took me by the shoulders and gave me a shake. I realized I was crying, and clamped my mouth shut. He folded me to his chest and began to murmur soothing words, as if I were a child. Humiliated, I pushed him away.

He pulled me back, and kissed me on the forehead. I longed for him to kiss my lips, but he would be a fool to do so. He knew better.

All I could do was stare at him, trying not to embarrass myself further.

He said, "I would like nothing better than to take you away with me. Do you know how lovely you are? How clever and strong? But no—girls never know what they have until too late."

Again he took me by the shoulders, this time to turn me around and lead me back to my mother. "Be brave, little bird. We will meet again, I know it." He brushed his fingers along my cheek, then he melted away into the darkness.

My mother must have decided to pretend to be asleep, for I heard her shift in her bed and turn over to let me cry in peace.

In the morning, I fully expected that I'd engineered the end of any freedom I might expect. But she said nothing.

If I truly wanted to thwart the vision, I had to be sensible. I had to plan. And I had on hand the perfect instructor in such things: Miss Carolina Marsh.

We left for home ahead of schedule, since Mother had only been waiting for Eneko to show up. Besides, the mountain nights had started to get cold, and the spa was emptying. We were tired of everything that had once been charming. The servants began to pack, our transport wagons and retinue were ordered, and our accounts settled.

I looked back as our little wagon train joined the main road. The pine trees and serried ranks of vines and fruit trees rose like a green wish, a soft and fertile dream of sanctuary.

That was the last time I felt peace and safety, as our fall picnic had been the last time I felt perfect happiness.

I turned to study the road ahead. Looking backwards, Mother had told me, gained one nothing but sorrow and regret.

Chapter Twelve
FOLLOWED BY FLIES

Plague had struck, but had been confined early to an area of decrepit dwellings and rooming-houses in the river Tet's dock district, at the east end of the city. Quarantine had been ruthless and thorough enough to result in only eighty-seven deaths, forty-three of plague and the rest of other causes. Meaning, according to Sigrun who had listened to her father's grumblings, lack of food supplies and normal medical care within the quarantined area, and from fighting over what meagre resources were left there. All because of Petru's harsh standards of prevention and containment.

Sigrun was squarely on Petru's side. "If the sick aren't isolated, they will spread their disease to everyone else."

"I heard that there were some who caught the sickness and lived through it. They became well again. And then Petru sent his soldiers to kill and burn them anyway." The shouting, screams and wailing from the port slum had been heard throughout the city, according to Miss Marsh. The infected areas were still smouldering. Now I knew why the air smelled so bad.

But the plague was over for this year, as the days shortened and the air grew crisp and dry. I turned the conversation to the stylish gown Sigrun was wearing, and the intricate way her blond hair was arranged. New fashions flowed from the seat of Empire in Soissons, and from Barcelona and Granada.

"Don't you think the colour is perfect with my fair complexion?" She puffed the decorative pockets—displayed on the outside of her pale hyacinth skirt to emphasize her wealth—and began to chatter happily about every little thing that had happened while I'd been away. Which of the servants were carrying on love affairs; the revolting messes the new chef from Friesland was trying to foist on everyone; which new recruit was worth watching at sword practice, et cetera.

While she talked I thought of Eneko Saratxaga, who I might never see again. At this melancholy thought I heaved a sigh.

Immediately Sigrun was after me. "What's the matter with you? You're so mopey I can hardly bear to be with you. I missed you, you know. I had nothing to do."

"I'm sorry."

"Is that all you can say?" She leaned close. "So, did you meet any good-looking boys there?"

I opened my mouth, ready to tell her all about Eneko, but I closed it and shrugged instead. "Everybody there was tottering toward the grave. I hated it!"

A look of vindication flashed across her face, instantly replaced with a sympathetic grimace. "Well, it was even worse here. I was ready to scream from boredom."

Why was I reluctant to confide in my friend? Her jealousy and resentment at my mountain spa vacation were understandable. I really couldn't blame her.

We parted ways, she to bustle off to her father's quarters in our villa, ready to queen it over his dinner, ordering the servants about as if they were slaves, and thinking of the slaves as carriers of pestilence, to be killed like rats.

I stood for a while in the hot, sun-slanting hallway between one life and the next. Sigrun sailed away like a ship on the ocean, over the horizon and away on her own course. What course was I on? Was I destined to go friendless through my little, cut-off life, trusting no one?

Sigrun and I had grown up together. We'd had small but thrilling adventures and had shared many secrets. But the secrets I had now could be shared with no one.

The best reason to spend time away from Sigrun was this: she loved Petru Dominus, the Scorpion of Askain. He could do no wrong in her eyes, and in mine he was a murdering brute who was followed by flies.

For now, I had to put it out of my mind. I had a goal: to learn how to become a runaway.

Mother was itching for Papa to come home. She had things to tell him that he needed to know. Their ultimate plan must be to unseat Petru, and either to claim the land for their own, join the immense Muslim Empire, or pledge allegiance to Ludvik and the Huns. But how could they do it? And how long had they been planning this?

Could it be since before I was born? But Petru had not been given these lands until 1232, and by then I'd been almost four. They must have suspected that I would be *da resu*, like my mother. Another thing: there had been a baby boy ahead of me, who died very young. Would he also have been *da resu*?

If he had lived, there'd be no need of me.

That thought made me wonder. Just how many of the *resura* folk could there be? How were they made? Could one ever really know? While waiting for death, we were called *da resu*; after, we were *resura*, inhabiting a spiritual realm, a land of magic that somehow intersected our own. My mind balked at trying to imagine what it would be like to find others like myself. I would find out soon enough.

It took three days of sneaking around to catch Miss Marsh alone. She usually had her servant-boy Akil with her, and though she let him go his own way to a surprising degree, he was meticulously well-behaved and frighteningly observant. He acted more like a slave, with a settled calm about him. Servants sometimes grew disgruntled and decided they could find easier lives elsewhere.

I had asked him once if he enjoyed belonging to Miss Marsh. "It is my life," he had said after a moment of looking at me down his nose, like a supercilious camel. I had gone back to ignoring him.

But I did notice that Akil listened, and he watched. He sat in on Grandfather's lectures and demonstrations, and though he rarely spoke he never wore that typical look of bafflement that suffused the faces of the other students. Of course, an adventuress would never take on a stupid servant.

Thinking of clever people made me recall Eneko much too clearly, and too often.

Where was he now? Was he safe and well? Was he busy charming other lonely girls?

Mother told me that his troupe planned to make their way south to Granada, the Moorish capitol, then double back along the coast of the Mediterranean Sea and north through the sometimes fractious Teyhrite-held territories in the mountains, to Soissons in the spring, where they would enter a competition for presentation at the Hunnic Emperor Ludvik's court. All along, Eneko would keep his ears and eyes open, gathering information to pass to my father via letters written in code. Dispensing nightingale's teeth to those deserving of them.

At last I caught Miss Marsh alone in her little makeshift workroom.

"Let me help you with labelling, Miss Marsh," I suggested. "My handwriting has improved."

I'd tried writing a list of botanical specimens to be sent to the Botanist Royal in Soissons, but she was very fussy about nomenclature and spelling. Many boxes and lists had already been sent to her fellow lecturers at Cambridge, where she planned to return once Petru had lost interest in her.

Sitting primly with quill in hand, I took a breath. "Miss Marsh," I said, "how did you find the courage to run away from your betrothed?"

She was boxing specimens of leaves, flowers and seeds. The air was scented with the dusty tang of dried vegetation. Her thin, scarred little face took on a faraway look. "My, that was so long ago... Dear girl, it was never courage. It was desperation. I was barely more than a children, and had a most distorted idea of what is marriage. I had fears of course." She barked a short laugh. "As it happens, my fears were well founded. My betrothed was lot years older than I, and the first time I meet him, as my parents and brothers watched us, I see him look me over as would a horse he intended to buy... for little as possible."

I blinked in sympathy.

"My pride was hurt." She laughed ruefully. "Though I have innocence, I could tell that he didn't want wife, he wanted sex slave, one who looked much like young boy."

My cheeks were suddenly burning. "A... sex..."

"Slave. Yes. There are many ways to own a human. One is marriage."

All I had seen of marriage was the love between my mother and my father, the respect with which they treated one another.

I remembered my original reason for quizzing Miss Marsh. "So... weren't you afraid you would be caught, brought home and beaten? And forced into marriage anyway?"

"Of course. But I am a long time planning my getaway, you see." She abandoned her box of specimens and hoisted herself to a sitting position on the table, swinging her feet, which were clad in pretty leather sandals embellished with jet buttons, visible for once under the hem of her drab gown. Her toes were long, thin and white as lard. Her orange cat leapt up beside her and she began to stroke it. With her free hand she held up one finger. "First, I needed money if I hoped to get away far enough not to be discovered and bringed... *brought* back. So I stole coins from pockets and purses, also some of my mother's jewellery. I knew she wouldn't miss some of the less... fashion... fash..." She waved a hand.

"Fashionable?"

"Yes. Fashionable things for months." She held up another finger. "Second, I knew that a lad would get more away than a lass." She dimpled at me.

To agree that she had the narrow, flat-chested body of a boy would be rude. I held my tongue.

She laughed, kicking her feet. "Next I took trousers, boots, jacket and hat from old things once worn by my brothers. In attic was satchel and blanket, too. I am all ready to run."

I was soaking this all in. Could she possibly imagine that a pampered, wealthy girl such as I would dream of running away from home?

"Next I await opportunity."

"What sort of opportunity?"

"I know there will be time when no one noticing me gone for a few days. It came at last when my parents and brothers go north to hunting estate." She put a hand to her brow and pretended to swoon.

I understood. "You were sick."

"I stay behind with servants who forget me before carriages one league up the road. I fill my satchel with cheese and bread and go that night."

"Oh, good idea." Cheese was peasant food, but better than turnips.

"Then a lot of walking, some leagues in farmer wagons, and buying passage to the continent. Then more walking."

"Did no one guess that you were a woman?"

"Oh, I think some farmers' wifes look at me sideways, but I get away."

She had been lucky as well as brave. "Do you have a lucky charm, Miss Marsh? I have one—do you see? It's a nightingale's tooth." I felt myself blush with emotion as I displayed my little string of charms.

She took the shiny black tooth between thumb and forefinger and drew it close, showing no interest in my eye or owl, which she'd seen before. She snorted and let it fall. "Very nice. It is to bring luck, eh?" Her face was bland, and I could tell what she was thinking. *Ignorant child, to believe in magic trinkets.*

"So it is said," I returned, equally bland of face. "Will you tell me what it *really* is, Miss Marsh?" Part of me hoped she wouldn't know. Perhaps that superior look would leave her face.

And part of me wanted very much for the tooth, and the story, to be as Eneko had said.

But she had an answer. First she said, "Are you sure you really want to know?"

I nodded.

"Very well." She slid off the table and hauled out a large, flat wooden box from under it. "I was going to not show, as it is horrid thing for a girl to see... but since you want the truth..."

She opened the box and lifted a padded cloth to one side, revealing the bare, gaping, jagged jaw of a huge animal. Despite myself, I drew back and gasped. Its incredible teeth, row upon row of them, were gleaming and wicked as rows of daggers. Could this be... could it possibly be... the jawbone of an ancient, immense nightingale?

Before I had time to embarrass myself, she said, "This," while tenderly stroking the hard arch of bone, "is the jaw of a shark. It is type of fish. When it lived, it was longer than two men. And this is a small one."

She ran a finger along the largest row of triangular white teeth. "The shark has many rows of teeth, which they fall out sometime and sometime. He grows more. Long-ago sharks' teeth fall out, they lie on the sea floor where turn black and into stone, like fossil shells you see in my boxes... What you have, Vara, is fossil shark's tooth."

I bit my lip. Though I hadn't really believed Eneko's tale, I was disturbed that he had given me a good-luck charm that was so awful in its provenance. The mouth of a man-killer.

Could I take it as a compliment? Had he detected a fierceness in me that I wasn't aware of? If so, I still had no evidence of it.

Miss Marsh covered the jawbone up and put it away. "It's good to possess something so rare and exotic. And you can tell people of the nightingale and her tooth if you wish."

"You have heard it?"

"I have heard all sorts of things," she said, with a combination of pride and resignation. Her pale eyes had the height of a hazy grey sky in them, and just as much mystery.

The strange little Briton had told me that her fondest desire was to once again cross the Aetheopian Sea to the vast new southern continent, Terra Torridia, past the busy spice isles and thence south of the equator. She knew it to be teeming with riotous jungles, brown rivers one could not see across, ferocious animals, and native wild men who could kill with their poison breath. She had explored only the very edges of this fascinating land, and panted to return. Her wanderlust might have been part of her nature, or it might merely be due to the money she could make from collecting exotic specimens. The courts and colleges of what was now being called the Old World were mad for such things. I could almost understand it: her lust for the new and strange, and the eagerness of the wealthy and bored for the very same.

But she was stuck in Perpignan. There were worse places, I supposed.

The bells set up temporarily beside the half-constructed Communica started to ring. It was time for prayers and almost time for dinner. I left, and on the way down the stairs to join the parade to the prayer ground, contemplated my own jawbone and its small, blunt teeth.

I stopped at one of the little *miradores*—small, enclosed balconies—that we have high on our outside walls, from which females can look out over the town without being seen in return. It is an old-fashioned Muslim type of architectural detail, and suited me right now. I looked through the screen of carved wood, and ran my fingers along my jaw, up over my temples to the dome of my skull. When I died, my skull would empty of all that I was, and would be placed with all the other skulls within our crypt. There to sit, dry and hollow, for eternity.

When my spirit was freed from my dead body, resurrected so that I became *resura*, I would have a new skull, new heart, limbs and eyes. This body, the one I lived in now, would shrivel, dry up, and turn to nothing but teeth and bones.

For the first time I was truly, deeply, frightened of what was to come.

Chapter Thirteen
THE ONE WHO GOT AWAY

I had to resign myself to the idea of using the particles of matter in the air, earth, and water around me to renew myself after death. Though how I should know the way to form such a complex organism as a human body was a mystery. My mother assured me that it would all become clear at the right moment. That had to do, for now.

She also explained that when I became *resura* I would gain the ability to take three different forms. Whatever I wanted, even animals. This took some of the horror out of my impending death.

I avoided thinking of the implications of this odd talent. When I was among the clouds I loved the idea, and when wallowing in filthy mud I felt sickened by the thought of becoming a body made of dirt and slime. But now, at home in an atmosphere of secrecy and veiled cunning, I loved it. What forms might be best?

Finally I asked my mother for advice.

"That is entirely up to you," she said.

I knew immediately that she was lying.

We were alone in a corner of the garden. It was a lazy afternoon, hot and still. She was sitting on a bench sorting herbs, tossing the elderly or spotty over her shoulder and keeping the fresh and green. I settled beside her and leaned close, so we could whisper without fear of being overheard.

"I will make no suggestions," she muttered distractedly. "You must choose for yourself."

I decided to listen to her words, but not to trust them. She and my father had plans that started before I was born.

She was silent for a while, rubbing her fingers among the fragrant herbs. "Be sure to choose wisely," she said at last.

I made an impatient noise and she glanced at me.

"I'm sorry, Vara. Of course you will choose wisely. So: you must think, observe, imagine. What powers might a *resura* need? Strength? Size? Speed? Think upon your power to command nature's particles, and into what forms you might shape them. Watch people and animals, as many as you can, learn what they can and can't do. Then imagine your soul, your thoughts, inside each one."

A *resura* who was groomed to kill might need to abandon her immortal soul. I took a deep breath and prepared to sift through my meagre knowledge of the animal kingdom.

First I imagined myself as an elephant, the perfect example of strength and size. But no. Too ponderous and ugly. Perhaps a horse, or a gazelle? A gazelle... fast, elegant, with lovely spiky little horns to use like daggers... no again. How could a gazelle move among humans without being killed and eaten? A horse, maybe. But that would most likely be captured, saddled and bent to the whip. So many animals, all with some sort of shortcoming. Crocodile. Deadly and powerful, but could I live as one? In a brackish river, lurking submerged and alone. Hated by all. I didn't want a form that was hateful or ugly.

Then it occurred to me: I had the shape I wore now. My own body. But when I pointed this out to her, she bit her lip. I could feel the tremor that went through her. "No. You may not. It is the one form you must not even think of taking."

"What? But why?"

"It would seem to be the easiest, wouldn't it? The obvious

choice. But this is what I was told: should you take your own form, it will be at the moment of your death. Forever to be bleeding, writhing in pain the way you saw it in your vision. It would be worse than useless, a waste of one of your forms, for you could never employ it."

My clever idea broke like an eggshell. A bitter taste filled my mouth as I realized that my own shape, my own true *self*, would really cease to exist. All along, I'd somehow imagined that I'd rise anew, clean and whole, to sail into a new life.

So, three forms, none of which was my own. If I thought about this too much, I would go mad. I put contemplation away for another time, perhaps never, and let my imagination skip around.

"Could I take a man's form?"

Her brow wrinkled. "Would you want to? You know very little of men."

"But men can do anything. They're strong, brave, respected. And I do know men: my father, my grandfather, our horse-master Tuarek Ajat, and many others..." *Eneko.* "If I had a man's body, I could fight, go anywhere I wanted. No one would make me stay inside, or cover my face, or... obey." A man wouldn't have to flee a mate he didn't love, a fate he didn't want.

A man could say no and make it stick.

I heard her sigh. She threaded her arm around my shoulders and pulled me close. I tucked my head into the crook of her neck.

"No one is ever completely free, my sweet child. Not even your Papa. Nor your friend Miss Carolina Marsh, though she has done a good job of stretching her boundaries. No one, not even a prince or an Emperor, is truly free."

This didn't sound good. "But then what is freedom? Is it meaningless?"

"I think... true freedom comes only upon true death."

I swallowed. "But, to be *resura*..."

"You see the problem. We don't truly die."

To be what I was destined to be: undead, a resurrected soul, I could not gain the ultimate freedom of oblivion. Ever.

For just a moment the emptiness, the hugeness of that fate

billowed in my head like the black anvil of a summer thunderhead.

Defiantly I said, "If I were a fish, or a bird, I could vanish into the sea or the sky. No one could catch me." I could fly above the storm, were I a bird. I lifted my head from her shoulder and looked into her eyes. "One of my forms shall be a bird."

Suddenly my heart contracted. The visions I used to have, which hadn't come to me for a while. I'd almost forgotten the bird, who had been fluttering in panic high above the forests and fields, and who had fallen because it didn't know how to fly. My vision had always ended in a sudden looming blackness, as if something else were about to happen.

Bird. Boy. Woman. Were these to be my forms? Must I choose them? Or did I still have free will?

A bird seemed obvious now. I'd learn to fly, whether I wanted to or not.

"A good choice. But keep thinking upon this, Vara Svobodová. Remember that even a small, insignificant animal... a snake for instance... has power. Remember the asp that Cleopatra used upon her enemies and herself. A snake can find her silent way into a fortress and vanquish a king in his sleep."

And there it was. That's why I had known she was lying.

She didn't want me to choose for myself. She wanted me to be an assassin who would slither into Petru's bed.

And how appropriate. Petru's beloved Saraf, betraying his worshipper with his very own sacred animal. I could do the job, I supposed; but then... well then I'd be a snake forever more. Plus whatever other two forms I chose... but I'd always hold that venomous, legless form as one of my own.

I got up and started to walk away.

"Vara," she called after me, her voice low and urgent. "Wait. Think about it. Once you have set your mind and heart upon a shape, it will start to take over. Then after you die, you'll have no more chances to think again. And perhaps only one chance to, to..."

"To kill?"

She didn't flinch. "Yes. To kill."

A task. A duty... to an idea. To others; not myself. I had no value as I was: just a girl with hopes and plans that were irrelevant. I could find true freedom only after true death. And a *resura* did not truly die. So, I might have great powers, but there were rules and restrictions even more stringent than those binding the living. This bargain that I hadn't made was looking less inviting the more I knew about it. Still, I didn't know enough. I stopped to listen to her.

"Vara, all people must die... but we get around it. Did you hope such a miracle would come without cost?"

I felt cold, even in the heat of late summer. "No... I..."

"The price is obedience. So I was taught. Once we are killed, and then are resurrected, we become enslaved. To the one who killed us. Or to the strongest person nearby when we cross over. Or... to the Gods."

Cornered. Trapped. A soul with nowhere to go but to her knees.

Enslaved to my own murderer. That was easy to understand. But what did she mean by strongest person? Perhaps a king or a general? Petru. And if the Great Gods took me, they would not be easy taskmasters. No good choices there, should I have a choice.

But wait: it was my beloved Pada Josef who would kill me. I had nothing to worry about. Not only was he my executioner, he was obviously the strongest person there at the moment of my death, mentally at any rate. I would gladly obey him.

But he'd been killed too. Right after me. And as far as I knew, his soul was the ordinary kind. Had it fled and left my soul alone with *his* killer? A mere soldier doing what he was ordered? My vision had extended no farther, and had no answers.

Would I be captured by the man who thrust his sword through my grandfather's belly? What if Petru the Scorpion strode in right after my vision ended, and claimed me for his own? Or would a God swoop in and snatch me up like a scrap of meat thrown to hungry dogs? They were out there, waiting. I'd felt them that night on the minaret, and among the Pyrenees clouds. They'd been watching me. Judging, coveting.

My head was spinning from the strange bending of time; what

would be seemed to have already passed.

Yet still I believed it could be changed.

The very next morning there came some interesting news. It spread around the streets of Perpignan with shocking rapidity.

Moping along a sheltered passageway contemplating animals and men, birds and reptiles, I came upon Mama and her father, head-to-head, blonde to grey, whispering heatedly.

She grabbed me as I tried to scuttle past. "Vara, since you will hear this soon anyway, it might as well be from us." She exchanged a glance with her father, who threw up his hands, looking more angry than I'd ever seen him. He turned and strode away.

She said, "News has come, from Massalia. Years ago, Petru took options on several *da resu*. One died of natural causes before the boy could fulfill his destiny."

I opened my mouth, then closed it. The boy who had died of fever.

"Two others," she said, "are still taking instruction from Petru's adepts somewhere in Assyria. I know nothing of their stage of development, health or aptitude." She gnawed her lip for a second. "The fourth was deemed ripe and ready, and was shipped to Massalia five nights ago."

Someone had ridden hard to get the news here so fast. "What happened? Does Lord Petru have his *resura* now?" Were we safe, would Petru have no need to capture me, and would then Pada have no need to kill me? A flare of hope lit in my breast.

"No, he does not."

The flare died. It felt as if my heart had contracted and sunk to the level of my bowels. "But—"

She held up a hand. "All I know is what my spy learned. Don't look so surprised, Vara—of course I have a spy at court. None of his councillors or generals were near Petru and his *da resu*, just two dim-witted guards and a tongueless woman to serve wine and clean up after the deed was done. Petru had the *da resu* kneeling before him. He looked to be a Lokono youth of perhaps fifteen years. Robed in his native loincloth and feathers, bathed and perfumed, bowing low. Petru spoke the words and laid claim to the boy, then with his own hand stabbed him to death." She glanced my way. "The boy died quickly, Vara. He was prepared for his fate."

It didn't matter. He was gone. "Then what happened?"

"From what I deduce, a Great God snatched him away. Right from under Petru's nose." Her lips formed a thin, cold smile.

She drew me to a bench under a tall, glazed window. The light through it was chill and blue, for the weather had turned overnight and the sky was alive with wind-blown clouds and leaves and wheeling birds. We sat and she took my hands in hers. "Petru should have gained his prize. Perhaps the Gods don't like him after all..."

Perhaps they didn't. If we humans knew what the Gods wanted, we could give it to them and be done with it. But they would always want more.

No one is afraid of ordinary gods and prophets. Zeus, Odin, Athena, Jehovah, Allah. They are more like crazy uncles, or wise but absent teachers, or mysterious and irresistible works of art—huge, smooth, painted in jewel colours—that, in another realm, live and play, fight and make up. But never really bother anyone.

The Great Gods of the netherworld frightened me senseless. Though nothing more than shadows and clouds at great height, they were real. I knew it. I had seen them and felt their hot breath on my face. Almost everyone could feel them at certain times. Their power was infectious, unfathomable and undisciplined.

If there was any yet higher power keeping track of their mischief, I saw no evidence of it.

I went to sit at my favourite perch: a window overlooking a glimpse of the wool market. It was quiet now, the few vendors nodding behind their skeins and bales. Then I spied a street-boy creeping up behind a sleepy old woman, obviously intending to steal her lunch, a loaf of bread wrapped in a bit of cloth. Just as his fingers touched the bread she shot out a hand and grabbed him by his skinny wrist.

I couldn't hear the exchange that followed, but it involved shouting and blows. The boy prostrated himself before the old woman, but she paid no attention to his begging and whining. Finally she had her fill of scolding and shoved him away. He scampered off, and the woman bent to pick up her lunch. It was gone.

The boy had snatched it from under her nose while she'd been slapping him. I had to smile. He had nerve and agility, attributes I wished I had.

Could the boy in my first vision be him, or some other urchin just like him? He hadn't been in the city, but somewhere on a lonely road by himself. Weeping with misery. This little fellow was busy cramming his mouth full as he put distance between himself and his victim.

The street boys, of whom there were many, feared no one and went everywhere. They ran in packs, stole food to eat and trinkets to sell. No one controlled them, and they always seemed to have coins for candy. Or could easily steal sweets directly from stupid rich girls.

To be a wild boy... free to run wherever he wanted. It seemed perfect. Mother might not approve, though. Too bad. She must have her own forms, tucked in her brain in case of need.

How far should I go in imagining it? Did the boy have a mother, sisters? I pictured him with no father, easy for me since mine was usually away. Would he fear illness, starvation, slavery? Was he happy or merely feral? I closed my eyes and felt the boy form around me, like a shadow creeping in from all sides. Like dust gathering itself into a shape. As a *resura*, I wouldn't have to worry about injury or starvation, would I? I wouldn't have to worry about being sold as a slave.

For I would already be enslaved. I turned from the window, my heart suddenly heavy.

Chapter Fourteen
THE REEK OF LEMON

Sigrun and I were in one of the smaller private courtyards where warmth from the sun still collected. She was flat on her back on the tiled floor, with her long yellow hair spread in the sun like a fan, reeking of lemon.

Her blonde hair had begun to darken, and the remedy was lemon juice. I was enlisted to anoint her hair with the skin-shrivelling liquid and ward off flies and observers. I understood her vanity, and envied her a bit. My own hair was imperviously black, no matter what I tried.

Sigrun was chatting animatedly about our plans for tomorrow, which included showing off her newly lightened tresses at worship. We had been several times to daytime services at Petru's temporary Communica, wearing our finest robes and veils, and it was rather fun if you ignored the screams of penitents being whipped and concentrated on looking at boys. Sigrun liked it better than I did. But if Eneko had been there...

"Lord Petru says that the more one suffers in this life, the less one will in the afterlife," stated Sigrun. "We should all find ways to suffer."

"I could let one of these wasps sting you," I suggested helpfully.

She sat up, her blue eyes blazing. "See this, you unbeliever!" She pulled down her tunic and turned her back to me. Her pale skin was patterned with thin pink lines.

She didn't seem to be suffering much. "My, those must hurt terribly." I kept my face straight.

"Of course they do! I got Ceta to lay on as hard as she could with a cord of leather, though I had to beat her to make her do it. I plan to work up to the flagrum as soon as I can."

She had to be joking. I almost laughed. But her face was burning with passion. "Sigrun... I'm sorry." What did she want me to say? That I thought she was crazy? She wanted me to admire her pious devotion to the cult of Saraf, and I wasn't going to do it.

I sensed a difficult time approaching in the downward arc of our friendship.

Huffily she lay back down, making a show of groaning and arching her back in pain.

Just then my mother came in, and beckoned me to rise and follow her.

"But, Sigrun and I—"

"Sigrun will be taken care of. Come."

What did she mean by that? "I have no lessons—this is my free time! Why—"

"Hush." Without sparing a glance at Sigrun, she took my arm and hustled me past a couple of our guardsmen who had followed her. I glanced back. Sigrun was clambering to her feet, looking angry and apprehensive as the guards closed in on her.

That was the last I ever saw of my friend.

That evening I accosted my mother as she sat staring at the remnants of our dinner, which neither of us had eaten. Servants were carrying picked-at platters of food back to the kitchen. "What's going on? Where is Sigrun?"

Mother looked at me, and after a pause, said, "Sigrun will not be returning. Neither will her father or brother. The family has been dismissed from our service."

After only a moment's thought I knew exactly what she was going to say. I felt the blood drain from my face, turned and tried to flee, but she jumped up, taking me by the arm and pulling me close. "Vara. It isn't her fault. She's been corrupted by Petru and his insanity. I had to clear out the whole lot of them."

"What do you mean?" But I knew. Sigrun was a spy.

The next day word went round the streets. Sigrun's father had run, with his two children and a couple of slaves, straight to his master. Petru, realizing that his spy family was of no use any more, did the obvious thing: he killed them. He might have taken the time to enjoy it, or he might have thought it no more of an annoyance than finding a broken tool among the rest and throwing it away. Why hadn't Sigrun's foolish father realized what was going to happen, and tried to save his children, if not his own skin? They should have run away from the city, not into the Scorpion's pincers.

After a while I stopped crying and started to think. Mother had been foolish too. She should have kept them, once she knew the truth. Used them to pass false information to Petru. But she hadn't. The betrayal had incensed her, and, I had to admit, perhaps she hadn't trusted me to play my part with Sigrun. She might have kept me in the dark, used me as a channel of misinformation to Petru via my only friend.

Now I had no friend, not that I'd really had one in Sigrun. She had betrayed us all. Yet I cried every night for a long time.

The months turned as they always did.

Winter came. Grain reserves were still high, and the City of Perpignan had enough to sell at a good price to some northern cities, whose stores had run out and whose cabbages had fallen prey to rot. Lord Petru was magnanimous in his aid to the less fortunate, as long as they had gold. Which, of course, they couldn't eat.

At the spring celebration of Venus, which nobody but us seemed to bother with any more, Miss Carolina Marsh presented my parents with a beautifully carved ivory tusk, the like of which no one had ever seen, as thanks for letting her stay with them. It was longer than my father was tall, straight as a spear, with a spiralling pattern embellished with hammered-in gold wire.

Mother hefted it in one hand like a sword, looking like a Valkyrie. "So, this is the fabled horn of a unicorn."

Miss Marsh smiled enigmatically, and winked at me.

Iunius and its summer heat arrived once again. Papa left on his usual extended tour of his trading contacts, intending to start a liaison with a company of Mongols from a place called Tibet. Or so he said publicly.

I turned sixteen that month, and things began to change for me.

Apparently I had become tall, willowy and attractive. Useless to one not in need of enticing male attention. Even my precious memories of Eneko Saratxaga were starting to fade. I hated that most of all.

The biggest change was that I now inhabited the upstairs room, where I would die. I begged not to be sent there, but Mama insisted. "Defiance will only tempt a worse fate."

Was she *trying* to make the vision come true? She and my father were heartless, I told myself, staring up at the rafters where my ghostly self would cling. I had spent the first few nights here waking constantly, alert and panicky, and had tried sneaking out to sleep elsewhere. But mother had found out, made me go back, and after a while I settled in. It's amazing what the human mind can accept.

One night I lay awake, going over in my mind the short, surreptitious lesson I had had that day in close-fighting with a dagger. Mother had hired a lanky, underfed Arab man who, under the lamplight in the cool of a root cellar, had shown me a few things, his eyes holding a calm, disinterested sheen that I found reassuring.

I held the wicked little instrument in my hands now, under the covers, and was testing its point with my thumb. There are many kinds of knives and ways to wield them, depending on what outcome is desired. To kill or merely wound? To humiliate or just warn? All the while avoiding being cut by your own blade, as well as your enemy's.

I was ready to fall asleep when Mother came in like a whirlwind. She didn't waste any time softening the news she'd brought. "Petru suspects us for what we are. He has ordered both of us to present ourselves before him at dawn."

I sat up, feeling a throb in my guts. Petru had been in Perpignan for several weeks, away from his home base of Massalia. Of course he would time it for when my father was away and unable to protect us. "What should we do? Should we run? Can we hide?"

"No! We obey, of course." Her voice was faint, even though since old Kai slept elsewhere now, being unwilling to climb another set of stairs, there was no need to whisper. I'd never heard her so agitated. "He has posted guards around our home, Vara. Even if I thought it was wise to try it, we couldn't escape. We will do as he orders."

"I'm not afraid of Petru." Of course I was afraid of him, but this was a good time for a little bravado.

She grunted, or maybe it was a laugh. "You know I told you that one of your forms should be a snake. A venomous snake."

"I hate snakes. You know that and you don't even care."

She shook her head and put her hands to her temples.

I was tired of my mother's dramatics. "What do you *want* from me?"

"I don't know! Any choice is terrible. If you take a deadly form—a snake, for instance—and your soul is captured by an evil person or a capricious God, he or it will use you to kill."

I understood at last. She thought we were going to die within the next few hours. I put my hands over my ears, but she pulled them down. "We are both in the same predicament, Vara. My forms can kill too—we must prepare ourselves for any opportunity. But...there are men and Gods who love killing, and forcing a slave to do it for them. You might find yourself eternally an assassin."

And what was I supposed to do about that? If it was my fate, then nothing I or anyone did would change it. I tried logic. "As would you, Mother. But you and father want an assassin. What's the difference? Isn't killing a sin no matter what?"

She groaned. "Vara, we don't have time for a discussion of morals and ethics. Of course it's a sin to kill—but perhaps not if done for the right reasons. I would do it, your father and grandfather would do it. Do you understand? Do you have any idea—any at all—" She flung up her hands and spat out an oath.

By now I was out of bed jittering nervously in my bare feet, my dagger still in my hand.

"There's no saving Petru, and no pitying him," she continued. "He loves the evil he spreads, and it's only getting worse. The Gods cluster around him and use him like a puppet. One day he is dull as a tortoise, the next he is a rabid dog again. Jameel and I had thought things were bad before you were born, and were prepared to do what we had to, but that was nothing. We are at war with the devil and he must not be allowed to win."

I kept my mouth shut. Did she want me to become a snake, or not? Was she implying that *she* might kill me in Petru's palace, take a chance that my soul would become hers, and order her snake assassin to kill? But if it fell into the possession of a God, or of Petru...

My long-ago vision had been cruelly incomplete.

More logic. "In my vision I was alive, here at home in this very bed. Petru won't kill us today." And what if I were to kill her, claim *her* soul? Could I doom my mother to sin and guilt?

She stared at me. "But was I in that vision? I know why he suspects us—it's that wicked, Egyptian whore Nebtu that's put ideas in his head. She thinks she's another Cleopatra, but all she has is money. Roman tariffs and tribute, bah! She's got their balls in her hands and loves it." She spat on my floor. Which was better than trembling in fear. "He found out that Nebtu has a *resura* and has been using it for years. It made him look like a fool—and he *is* a fool. He doesn't believe that women can be just as ruthless and venal as men. Apparently someone has finally informed him that he'd met the creature, in its form of a Nubian male dressed up as a king, there to spy for her, flatter him into giving her what she wanted." Her eyes narrowed. "His own *falci* hid her knowledge for years. Hah!"

"His *falci*? What is that?"

"A *falci* is a trained adept, a person—usually a woman—who

can detect the connection between a *resura* and its *alanbir*."

I gritted my teeth. "And what is an *alanbir*?" I wanted to scream.

"The owner of the *resura* soul. Somehow the *falci* can see the link. I don't know." She waved one hand, showing, by an impatient shake of her head, just how frightened she was. "Petru's trusted tattle-tale valued her children over herself. Nebtu had taken the *falci* woman's two boys and was ready to kill them if she didn't obey."

How did my mother know all these things? How many spies did she have?

"Since she used pigeons to send her messages, he's ordered all his own birds killed, the idiot. As if that will stop word from spreading."

I remembered the adoring throngs when Petru had paraded through our city streets. People had tried to touch him or his horse—he hadn't feared any of them, then. Things would be different now. I could imagine his suspicion should a rat-faced peasant or his sweating wife be so audacious now.

Any of them, even one of the horses, might have been *resura*.

I suddenly wondered: what if Petru had friends, supporters who tasked their own *resura* slaves with protecting him? Without one of these *falci* adepts, how could anyone tell?

Mother came to some kind of decision, and turned to me. "What do you know of that automaton your Grandfather has been working on? Is it operating as it should?"

I blinked. *Now* what was she thinking? "I think so. He's been tinkering with it for days. He won't let me look at it."

"I hope he can have it ready by dawn. I hate those evil things—alive but not alive." She bared her teeth. "The damned thing had better work."

"Shall I wake him?"

"No. I'll go to him. Stay here, and dress in your finest clothes." She looked at me hard, and perhaps she read my mind. "Don't even think of bringing that dagger."

Chapter Fifteen
THE AUTOMATON

I could smell my own armpits as we waited for the Scorpion of Askain. The palace was bustling with people; if anyone here ever slept I wasn't sure. There had been no time to bathe, though I'd been allowed to splash some of my mother's orange-blossom perfume on my wrists and feet. We were making a brave show in our most splendid garments and jewels, though what good this would do if Petru intended to kill us, I didn't know.

I squeezed my arms to my sides and tried to slow the frantic beating of my heart. Two of Mama's slaves had carried the automaton into the palace and were now hovering over it. They didn't know anything about it because it was wrapped in heavy cloth to protect it both from damage in transit, and from curious eyes. She'd had slaves instead of servants bring it, in case none of us emerged again. Slaves would have a better chance of surviving than our personal staff.

When we first arrived, we'd been ushered into a little room with no windows and only the door we came in by. Two men, clad in the light, everyday armour of the guard, stood watching, their dark eyes glittering. They could have been twins. The third, a woman of about forty with long grey hair in a thin braid threaded with red cloth, examined us for weapons. She was chained to the chamber's wall, loosely enough that she could easily reach us and force us to bend, lift our garments, spread our legs and so on. She leaned close and sniffed us both one at a time, perhaps to detect hidden poison. This must be Petru's new *falci* woman.

I couldn't tell by her expression what she thought we were; if she suspected or knew we were *da resu*, she would surely tell Petru. We would never get out of here alive. She paid no attention to my mother's huffing and snarls, nor my humiliated whimpering.

Perhaps her powers of detection only worked on those of us who had died and become *resura*, for at last we were summoned to Petru's semi-public chambers. These were a wide, airy suite of rooms, lit now in the pre-dawn by many lanterns and flaring torches, atop a rambling white marble structure built and expanded during the last two hundred years over an extensive stables dating from Roman times. It was said that Petru used these old stables, now far underground, as cells for his prisoners, who never again saw the light of day.

I pictured the layers of life beneath us now, as we stood staring at the view and feigning an air of calm. Through a wide arch we could walk out on a balcony and see over most of the city, for we were almost as high as the old minaret towers that still stood here and there. The ocean wasn't visible from this inland city, but we could see the Tet glitter faintly between dark banks. Dawn's thin lemon light was barely discernible in the east, and points of lamplight from streets and buildings pricked the city's gloom below us. The room was sparsely furnished, white and chill, hung with pale tapestries and floating silks in shades of milk and ice, dotted with bleached rugs and white furs in piles. It looked like the abode of an anemic saint.

On the level below us was the lamp-lit bustle of Petru's government, thick even at this hour with the smell of ink and wax and paper, the metallic tang of coins and bars of silver, the sweat of over a hundred scribes recording taxes, taxes, and more taxes, plus the lists of those who had committed myriad petty and major crimes; the racket of voices and footsteps, the clatter of Chinese adding machines. And this wasn't even the main city. Perpignan was a backwater. The bureaucracy of empire was horrendous.

And on the level below the clatter and talk? Silence, darkness, and the stink of the dungeon. In which we might soon find ourselves, if he didn't kill us outright.

Which was an entirely different problem. I was finding it hard to breathe.

Mother put her arm around my shoulders and hugged me close. "Vara, stand straight. You at least will live through this day, for you have seen it. And I don't fear death. We can get through this, but it's going to take every bit of cunning we have. And perhaps the gift we bring will soften his mood." Her voice was calm and slow, but she started like a rabbit at the sound of someone approaching.

Two of Petru's personal guard entered, stamped their feet and stood to attention, staring at the opposite wall. We bowed low as Petru Dominus stalked in. He looked like a splash of blood on the white skin of this pale, cold room. Our two slaves dropped to their bellies, noses pecking the floor.

Petru's mane of ginger hair was loose as always, his moustache empty of decoration, and his upper body bare but for the binding leather straps of his soldier's harness. The warrior king. A scarlet cloak was clipped to the harness by gold wolf heads, their jaws clasping the rich cloth that hugged his neck. He was shorter than he had appeared when on horseback, less muscular but still a strong, bulky man. He looked ill, his face puffy around sunken eyes that alternately stared and blinked rapidly, as if his own body had forgotten how to operate itself. He padded across the floor to stop an arm's length from us. Sick or not, he was still powerful.

A whiff of something burning came along with him. Something hot and rank, stinging my nostrils. The smell a city got when burning out a nest of plague victims.

He looked at my mother, and his hands twitched and reached, just a little. Then he clasped them behind his back.

That's right, I thought venomously. Don't even think of putting your filthy hands on her. I looked for the flies that followed him, saw none, but heard their buzz in my head.

Behind Petru crept an elderly scribe, to settle at a desk in one corner. He was there to record everything that was said and done, making his secret marks with wax and stylus. Later, if Petru decided to take us before his judicial court, he would have plenty of evidence to use against us. We, of course, would have nothing.

Petru started right in. "You know why you have been summoned here."

Mama simpered and fluttered her hands. I kept a stony expression. She knew what she was doing. "The honour is great, my Lord," she said. "What use can we be to you?"

Petru's eyes were so very blue. As blue as my mother's. Northerners both, with a core of barbarism that might never be tamed. "Sit," he commanded, waving us toward a bare wooden bench. We sat. A slave came in, bearing wine, which she placed upon a small enamelled table and then withdrew, her stride hampered by the chains that linked her ankles. She had the wavy brown hair and olive skin of a high-born Israelite. How had she ended up here? What was her story?

Petru poured us wine in plain silver goblets. Mama sipped hers, so I did too. It was sour but potent, and I could taste the cup's metal. Could the wine be poisoned? Whether it was or not, we must do as Petru demanded, if it be drinking deadly wine or submitting to interrogation. We could fight, but we would lose.

"You are of use simply by being pious and beautiful, Ragna Svobodová, wife of Jameel." He glanced my way. I kept my expression blank, despite my urge to vomit. When he said my father's name, *Jameel*, it made the hairs on my arms stand up. He didn't use Papa's full name; an insult. He didn't just want to taunt us, he was trying to rile us into indiscretion. Hatred surged within me, and a futile satisfaction as I noted that his pretty blue eyes were red-rimmed, and the pupils at their centres were small as pinpricks. It made him look crazy as well as brutal.

Mama set her goblet down. "I regret that my lord Jameel-husband is not in the city, for I am sure he would be of much more use to you."

He turned back to her. "Do you think so? In what way?"

Her voice was cool and soft, almost sweet. "Why, in any way

you desire, my Lord. Does not our family pay its taxes on time and in full, do not we report to you regularly what new trades have been made, and share willingly in the profits? My husband's negotiations with the Bagratuni of Kars have profited us all, have they not?"

"He has opened up that reclusive kingdom, I admit it is so." He gestured to the wall, where dark wood benches, like outcroppings of bedrock, were piled high with furs and supple white leathers. "I have some of their trade goods here." Sprawled across the floor was the entire hide of a lion, which must have been enormous when alive. It too was white, its luxuriant mane the same rich cream as its snarling teeth. An albino, like a rat Grandfather kept in a cage and treated like a pet.

I pictured Petru as an old man, his long ginger hair turned white as snow. Would he like that? I also pictured his back bent and his eyes rheumy with age, his strong legs withered and useless. It occurred to me that as a *resura* I would outlast him; I would see the ravages of time destroy his body and erase even the memory of his proud scars.

The thought gave me strength.

Petru poured himself a cup of wine and swallowed it in one gulp, then poured more. I felt easier about my own, and took another steadying sip.

"When will he return?"

"I do not know, my lord. Sometime before the storms of winter."

"And where is he at this moment?"

Her head was high, and her eyes did not waver from his. "Again, my lord, I do not know."

"Ah, but I do. I know his every move."

The scribe scribbled and tapped away, transforming words into shapes, innocent remarks into stones. Women, not worthy of crucifixion, were generally stoned to death. Petru would have a pile of them ready to throw.

Mother remained silent, staring him down. I didn't know whether to fling myself on the floor and beg him to forgive her and spare our family, or proudly step to her side and attempt to copy her regal glare.

"Our Lord Petru Dominus has Saraf the Burning to see and hear for him," she said at last. "And his serpents to bring the sting of death to the wicked. What need has he of spies?" Was she being sarcastic or diplomatic? He knew we'd uncovered Sigrun as a spy in our very household. And we knew what had happened to her.

Abruptly she turned and gestured imperiously for her slaves, who were huddling in the anteroom feigning deafness.

They hoisted the automaton high, paraded it in and placed it upon an ornate table near the brightest window. The sounds of early morning rose in the warming air and brought the scents of food and smoke and the sluicing water of street cleaners.

The slaves removed the heavy wrappings and backed out. The automaton was an elaborate scene of a bird—a nightingale, which almost made me burst into nervous laughter—escaping the clutches of a civet cat, hopping to a perch and singing a song. The whole construction was made of enamelled bronze, studded with jewels. Each tiny leaf was fashioned of carved jade, the cat's spots were inlaid gold, and so on. Quite a nice present. I had no idea how it worked, though my grandfather had patiently described its operation to me. I prayed that it would function now, and not disgrace us.

It had been primed and set. All mother needed to do was depress a small lever.

After a flirtatious smile at Petru, who did not smile back, she did so. The bird fluttered its metal feathers, the cat opened its mouth and snarled, the bird slid up a tiny wire, opened its little beak and emitted a high-pitched but charming warble. I had been assured by Grandfather that it was based on ordinary principles of mechanics, just like the adding machines, or the huge grain mills and manufactories that supplied food and products of all kinds in our modern civilization. Nothing special about it.

Petru watched it perform, a little smile on his lips. He began absently to rub at his head, tugging at the tangle of ginger that lay in lank waves to his shoulders. He pulled it quite hard, as if he enjoyed the small pain. Then he began to laugh. A laugh that turned to a deep, guttural groan. With one last harsh tug at his locks, he grimaced and blinked as if fighting back pain. But he liked pain, did he not?

My stomach was in my throat—*now the Scorpion will kill us and take our souls*—but then Petru reached out, found another tiny lever, and set the automaton in motion once more. I heard my mother's sharp intake of breath. She hadn't known it had more to offer.

This time the performance was entirely different. The civet cat rose on its hind legs, and an outsized, red-enamelled phallus thrust forth from between its legs. It moved forward on tiny tracks, while the tree opened its carved amber trunk to reveal an ivory maiden with her plump legs open to receive it. Cat and tree-woman began to copulate.

I looked away, shrinking against my mother. She held her head high. I knew she wanted to smash the thing to the ground for betraying us.

Petru bent forward to get a good look. "I saw this once, at a Nawab's palace in Persia years ago. How did your husband acquire it?" He peered close, showing his teeth. "Never mind, I'll keep it." I could only imagine what he thought of her motives. I was having doubts myself. Had she known what the automaton would do? Just how far would my mother go to protect her family?

Petru suddenly dumped his wine on the floor and dropped the cup, and while a slave ran to wipe up the mess, he shouted for coffee. I barely prevented myself from making a face when the bitter stuff was brought in.

He flung himself on the pile of furs, slopping dark droplets around with a fine lack of care, then suddenly seemed to deflate. "You can't understand," he said at last, "how difficult it is to oversee so many different peoples. Difficult, and costly. Each petty tribe has its taboos and rules and traditions. Its own gods. Each wants nothing more than to fight all the rest. It has been so since the days of Abraham."

He looked up, his pale eyes bright but red-veined as if he hadn't slept in days. "And one must know every damned one of those rules."

I noticed that the scribe had stopped recording and sat head down as if in deep thought. Or trying to pretend he wasn't there.

Petru drained his cup and leaned forward, as if confiding in us. "I spent four years in the dungeons of Soissons, you know." I had heard of the Emperor's prison, and how it had recently been scoured out, cleansed and modernized for the benefit of the inmates' souls. Stories went around of the things and people found down there, and what had been done with them. And to them. Petru must have been there in the old days, before the scouring. I squashed down a morsel of pity.

"I was considered a threat by Ludvik's father Zdenek, so he put me where I could do no harm." Suddenly he grinned, baring all his big yellow teeth. "Where I festered like a boil on his ass! Ha! I went in an ignorant youth, and came out a man of conviction. And do you know why?" No longer was he tired and sad. "I heard the word of Saraf." A rapturous look suffused his ruddy face. "Saraf the Burning came to me in visions and taught me the way. And it was not the way of those decadent filth in the capital, may they rot in their own excrement."

It was hard to keep up with his moods, to even hope to placate him.

"I heard the word and felt it too," he said. "In every whipping, in every drowning—they do that even to this day, to cleanse your soul. I heard and I learned." He began to pull his hair again. I don't think he knew he was doing it.

Telling us these things meant he intended our death. We would never leave this room.

He leapt up and strode onto the balcony and back restlessly, then stopped in front of me, his hands firmly clasped behind his back like a boy trying not to grab candy. A waft of his ripe masculine odour came my way, and I felt my forehead grow clammy. *Don't faint. Be strong.*

"Those fools down there think me a god," he said. "But I am only the hands and mouth of my God. I will teach them what true devotion means." He looked at me. "You, pretty girl, are in need of instruction."

Mother jumped up and grasped one of his hands. "My daughter is but a child, who knows nothing. Tell me why you summoned us here today!"

"I would know what you are."

At last. He'd come to the point.

Her gaze slid sideways. A mistake, though she corrected it immediately. Too late. "I am your servant."

"I ask much of my servants." He nodded at one of the dark wood benches nearby, ominous in this pale room. "Would you bare your throat to me upon that fine African ebony?"

"What use could I be with my head on the floor, sire? I could tell you nothing."

His eyes blazed. He made a fist and clubbed her across the face. She dropped to the floor, and I cringed beside her where she lay gasping, but not cowering. I felt a swell of pride in her, and helpless fury toward him.

"I know what you are," he bellowed. "Both of you! Demons both, and better use dead!" He aimed a kick at her, but I managed to deflect it with my hip. I was instantly sorry, for it felt like he'd broken a bone. Mother groaned and spat blood, keeping her eyes down.

I braced myself for another kick, but Petru turned away from us and began stamping around his palatial chamber, like a furious child. He screamed curses and pushed a bust of Augustus off its plinth to crash to the marble floor, and tore down the white-on-white tapestries to trample upon them. *Barbarian.* He couldn't control himself—how could he control a *resura*?

Keep your mouth shut. If either of us defied him, he'd kick us both to death. And take our souls.

I could feel the Gods clustering close, drawn by his fury and his burning heat, ready to seize what they wanted. Suddenly I felt bigger, thicker—how could I explain it? Thick with fear, made stupid with it. Through the opening to the balcony I could see clouds gathering, clotted and grey, lit with brilliant flares that were nothing like lighting.

I wanted to join him in destruction. I wanted to use my teeth and hands to rip everything to shreds. The urge was almost irresistible.

But then he stopped suddenly. He stood still, surrounded by spilled liquid and shards of ancient marble, looking about him as if surprised.

He swayed on his feet. I could hear his breathing; he sounded like an ox in heavy traces. His hands went again to his head, and I could see his arm muscles bulge as he pressed against his temples. He looked around, his eyes wide. "What... what have you done?" Was he talking to himself or to us?

A grinding pressure grew in my own head, as if I was somehow aligned with his emotions. My mouth was open, I was panting, and I felt suddenly as if all the air in the world had been sucked away. I fell to my knees. My head hit the floor. The smell in the air had changed. Instead of the thick smell of burning, it was thin and bitter like rancid beer.

It was the Gods. The Gods were playing with him. With all of us. Damn them.

"Get out," he whispered. I could barely hear him. "Now. Go. Get to your home, and stay there." Suddenly his whole big, burly body slumped as if he had aged twenty years in a hummingbird's wingbeat.

He looked like what he had once been: a solid, steady, ordinary man who merely wanted to improve crop yields. Petru's newly exhausted eyes looked just beyond us, maybe to where we'd be after our deaths. Where he would be. "I will have you back when I am ready. I... I will have you back..."

Unwilling to waste such a miracle, I picked myself up, hauled Mama to her feet, and we limped away as fast as we could. At any moment the Gods would have him in their cruel grasp again. I shot a glance at the elderly scribe, wondering what he made of this strange turn of events, but he had hidden his face behind his hands.

We were led out of the palace by men who had been waiting at the end of a long, cold corridor, and by a different route. We were told to wait at the bottom of a flight of stairs. After a few minutes of nervous speculation, a male slave glided up, took hold of a silken rope and drew a heavy cloth aside. There was an opening in the wall behind it, a window of sorts. On the other side was a small, unadorned room, the size of a storage closet. Within it was a stone tub of water. In the tub was a man, his face the only part of him above water. Lines of pain creased his hollow, whiskery cheeks.

We had a good view into the water. It was tinged pale red, and many long, sinuous shapes moved gently within it. Lampreys. They clung to the man's belly and chest, their hideous sucking mouths clamped tight on his pale flesh. The man's head turned slowly, and when he caught sight of us he began to scream, his eyes rolling white in blackened sockets. With all the pitiful strength of his emaciated body he bucked and thrashed, his chained, bleeding wrists and ankles heaving. The red water churned, but the eels clung tight.

The Gods who rode Petru had planned this. Oh, they were having such sport with us all!

Our slaves crouched on the floor moaning and praying. Mother hauled them up, slapped them into obedience, and in a sad, beaten column we made for home.

Huddled together in her big carved bed, I asked her why Petru hadn't killed us when he had the perfect opportunity.

She laughed, a quite horrible sound, but there was a gleam of defiance in her eyes. "A very good question. Ouch." She rubbed her bruised cheek. "I would trade all the cold wine I drank last summer for some ice now."

I said nothing. My mind was still stunned with our narrow escape, and a creeping horror of snakes and eels made my belly shrink. Petru could have slit our throats. He could have let lampreys eat us to death. No one would have stopped him. He might have had two *resura* in his command. Our luck had been thin. Terribly thin.

I could see my mother's hands shake. "You saw the way he changed. He was in thrall to the Gods who ride him... then he was not. They spat him out like a bit of gristle." She snorted, and burst into harsh laughter. "They were toying with him! Ha! And so we got away."

"We were allowed to escape. For now. But—"

"But when the Gods decide they want more amusement, they will pick him up and chew upon him again."

"If Petru had killed us it would be over, we would know our fate."

"I am not ready for my fate, my dear child."

I needed to ask her a question. A thought I'd had in the darkness of midnight wouldn't let go. "You could kill me. Or Papa could. Then I would belong to you, wouldn't I? I could be your *resura*."

It was a rational solution to some of our problems. Mother and Father wouldn't have to worry about me anymore, and I wouldn't have to fear giving our secret away. A secret which seemed to be out anyway. Sooner or later Petru would kill us. As soon as the Gods wanted it.

She was actually contemplating the idea. I wanted to blurt a denial—*I didn't mean it!*—but managed to hold my tongue. Her eyes were shut tight, and to my amazement tears were leaking from them. Beaten and humiliated by Petru, she hadn't cried; now she did.

"Oh, my dear Vara, I have thought of it!" She let out a sob. "And I have thought of killing myself... but what a sin it would be! Against the one God who loves us all, and against the *da resu* way. And my dear Jameel-husband... oh..." She opened her eyes but began to shake her head back and forth. "I couldn't do that to him! Petru would blame him and would kill him very slowly. I know Jameel would feel the same were he to kill you to try for your soul. Besides, it's just as likely a God would get you anyway." She clutched her sore head. "Worse than Petru. Someday I will castrate that pox-ridden, goat-sucking, dog-eyed, turd-eating..."

"And he's as smelly as a barrel of rotten cod," I put in.

With a shriek of hysterical laughter she grabbed me and gave me the hug of a Novgorod bear. "How could I kill such a one as you? You give me strength. No, I simply couldn't bear it, Vara Svobodová-bint-Jameel. You are too precious to me, and to your father, in your living body, with all your cleverness, your humour, your courage."

Courage? How could she think I had courage? I wanted to vanish into the caves of Cantabria like the Ancient People, invisible souls guarded by their paintings.

"Vara, when we become *resura*, we will be so forever. We will take our forms, and they will not be those we have now. You will never again be the beautiful young woman you are now."

That was too much. I wrapped my arms around her and wailed.

She remained silent until I managed to dry my tears. Then she murmured, "Life is precious, partly because it's so short. Don't look upon this life as a mere waiting period before your transformation to a wondrous new existence. You must not disdain the humanity you have now."

"But I don't want to die. I have no courage."

She sighed deeply. "Nor do I, despite my boasting. But we cannot alter what fate has assigned us. We cannot try to slip out of the bargain, nor alter the rules of the game. That is what I believe."

Forcing a smile, I drew away, drying my eyes with the backs of my wrists. "You're right. If I have no real courage, perhaps I can pretend the false kind."

She smiled back, but her eyes were full of concern. "It will have to do. We'll find a way. When your father gets back..." She bit her lip. "No. We must not turn our problems over to him. He is human, and we... we are not."

I felt my heart give a thump. I hadn't thought of it that way before.

"Go now," she said. "Get some sleep. Woden knows we had little last night. Later we'll have a meal—something nice—and plan a way around Petru Dominus."

I admired her pluck, but I didn't believe it would make any difference. Petru Dominus was like a burl oak lightning-struck and split in two.

The next time he took us and tried for our souls, the Gods might let him do it.

It came down to one thing: I had to remove myself from the game, since I saw no way to win it.

Chapter Sixteen
THE MEANING OF SCARS

Lowering my feet into the cool river water was the most delicious feeling I had ever had in all my life.

The simple relief of pain rippled up my legs all the way to my hair. I almost swooned. Some of my blisters had burst, and now stung sharply, but that was nothing compared to the sheer bliss of sitting still and soaking my rubbed-raw feet. It turned out that Epicurus was right. Pleasure is the absence of pain.

I'd thought I was a strong and active person. Apparently I was wrong. Walking from Perpignan to the ocean-port town at the Tet's mouth was very different from scurrying around our villa in soft slippers, and strolling the marketplace in pretty padded sandals with servants to carry the things I bought.

Wearing the stiff, heavy sandals of a boy was a bad idea. I'd stolen them from Akil, whose arrogant attitude annoyed me to where I felt he deserved whatever he got. When I tried to engage him in conversation, he gave me only cryptic, maddening answers designed to make me feel stupid. I wanted to like him because he was beloved of Miss Marsh, but he made it very hard. He could wheedle new sandals from his mistress, since he was so clever.

If I was clever, I would have stolen a donkey to ride. Too late now.

I sighed. Another thing: binding my breasts so tightly that I could barely breathe was unfortunate... but if I didn't they would give me away.

The water flowed past, uncaring. I flexed my toes and let out a groan. Miss Marsh, damn her pale eyes, had made it all sound daring and fun. I let myself hate her a bit, all I could muster at present, and sank backwards on the sandy shore, leaving my feet in the water. I felt Grandfather's precious gravity pull me down, down toward the centre of the world. A thin screen of reeds, brambles and palm trunks hid me from the road, and I was quite sure my layers of sweat and road dust made me vanish into the dirt.

An intense wave of homesickness swept over me. How could I have imagined I was a self-sacrificing adventuress? I felt ashamed. Even the people I'd walked past had shamed me. They had so little, and were constantly scavenging or trading for just a little bit more of what I would spurn. Grain scattered from an ox's feedbag, twigs fallen from a bundle of firewood on an ass's back.

The old men had watched me pass from their shady benches, eyes glittering as they talked and sipped their tea. The women worked, the children ran and yelled happily, fighting the dogs for bones to chew on. The animals I saw were hobbled, even the goats, who had learned to hop around in their constant search for something edible.

A veiled woman, riding a donkey sidesaddle with her feet almost trailing the ground, had clopped past me as I trudged along, sending me a suspicious glare as she poked her little beast with a sharp twig to make it trot faster.

I should definitely have stolen a donkey.

Sitting up again, I dipped my hands in the water, sluicing it against my hot, dusty face. In these months—high summer—rain fell so rarely that it was never expected, only welcomed, as an exotic stranger bearing gifts would be welcomed. I didn't dare remove the makeshift turban that hid my hair. Last night I had held my dagger against the twisted black rope of hair in my hand, pulled tight and ready to be sliced off at the nape of my neck, but hadn't possessed the fortitude to do it. I was too vain.

All along, while stockpiling food and collecting coins, I prayed for Papa to suddenly arrive home and tell me all was well and we were safe, and let me go back to the way it was before. Instead all I had was the orange cat who insisted on curling up on top of the little pile of belongings I was trying to cram into a satchel. At least the damned cat liked me.

I knew one thing: Papa would get himself in trouble with Petru the moment he learned of our treatment at that monster's hands. *Oh Sisters, keep him far away. Keep him safe.*

My skin itched from sun and dust. I wondered briefly if I could use *da resu* skills to make the particles of dust fly off my clothes and skin, and become clean without benefit of water or scented oil. It should be easy, but I couldn't drum up the strength or interest. Besides, my layers of dirt were a good disguise. I had even rubbed some on my face as a sort of beard, hoping that from a distance it would look like a man's stubble. I made myself replace what I'd just washed off.

A line of wagons rumbled slowly by, the drivers yelling and chattering, so close I could smell the oxen's sweaty hides and dung-spattered legs. I held perfectly still. A dog following the train briefly ran down the bank to drink, sniffed at me, growled, then scrambled back though the spiny underbrush at his master's whistle. They passed and I breathed again.

I might be caught at any moment, found out as a female runaway and either sold into slavery or hustled home quickly for a reward. But if I did escape Petru, and my destiny, what would happen to Mother and Father? Was I doing something very, very foolish?

No. I was not. I saw no other course.

My mother had lost whatever advantage she might have had the moment Petru threatened me. I was afraid of what she might bargain away to protect me.

I was a pawn, small and useless in the game, but capable of bringing down a queen.

I hadn't eaten any of the food I had brought, only lapped water from the river in my cupped hands, having neglected to bring an actual cup. But the bread was hard as rock, the cheese smelled rancid and greasy when I sniffed it.

Also, I was much too conspicuous travelling alone to stop and eat, or to advertise the fact that I might be worth robbing by buying food. Despite the plentiful traffic and the marshals patrolling the roadways, even a young "man" striding along as if with some grand purpose was liable to be accosted and roughed up just for looking different. For casting his gaze too low, or not low enough. I spent a lot of my time diving for cover.

My thoughts turned mutinous. If I were already dead, and in my *resura* existence, I could take my bird form and fly over all this dust and dung and danger. I would never have to return to Perpignan.

But at that image, myself forever wandering alone, I caught my breath in a wave of misery and tried not to sob. I failed.

Night started to creep in as I huddled lamenting my fate, and with it came cooler air, but, oddly, more traffic on the road. Bright moonlight showed more men and fast-moving chariots, fewer families or flocks. I could hear the constant, lugubrious chug of the pumps to the north, and see a glow on the south-east horizon which I knew must be the torch and lamplights of the small port city of Linqua, which was my goal. Since my plan included creeping into the city under cover of darkness, I forced myself to stand. I debated donning the ghastly sandals once more, and decided to pick my way barefoot.

Soon I could smell the ocean. A tang of salt freshened the air, almost making me feel hungry. All day I had observed the many boats plying the river, up and down. Papa had described many of them to me, and I now I could identify some: square-rigged, old-fashioned knar; wallowing cargo cogs; a few lateen-rigged carvels with their rakishly back-swept triangles of sail.

The river was more busy than I had ever seen it, even now as night was falling. Some ships were man-powered, the largest I saw having twenty-five oars on each side. I heard the men grunt and chant, and the drum boom, as they sped past upstream. The ships were on their way up to Perpignan, or on the downstream route to far-off places, loaded with olive oil, wine, grain, cloth, cork, metal, people—everything that could be contained in a crate, barrel or sack, or chained securely to the deck. Some were built especially to transport horses, though I could hear or smell none today.

Many must be carrying instruments of war, for war, my Pada assured me, was not far off.

I'd seen interesting things today, which once would have delighted me. The vast, groaning Archimedes pumps sucking away at the swampland to make more fields, gangs of men and mules carving out channels in the muck, the tiny clusters of dwellings and shops close on the roadway, everyone busy trying to sell whatever they had to sell. Tempted by some sweet pastries dripping with butter and stuffed with walnuts, I had almost tried my talents at acting the boy to buy some, but feared I'd be instantly found out as a female. Stoically, I had walked on.

And I was still walking. How had Miss Carolina Marsh, small and thin, found the nerve to accept rides? Was she courageous, or merely desperate, as she had claimed? Perhaps I wasn't quite desperate enough.

I reached the outskirts of Linqua and found a secluded corner where I hunkered down and made myself munch through some of the vile cheese and lumps of bread. My headache receded, at least. A nearby public fountain quenched my thirst. After scouring the taste of cheese from my teeth with one of my little bundle of siwak twigs, I gobbled a few almonds and sweet, sticky dates as a reward and returned to my corner. I should have brought more of those and tossed the cheese into the river.

Crossing my legs tailor-fashion, I leaned against the still-warm stone wall, feeling somewhat revived. It had taken a while to find a spot that smelled only a little of urine.

But the city had what I needed: ships that travelled the known world.

A world that was getting larger all the time. "We are in a marvellous time, Vara!" I could see my Pada striding up and down, the faithful Saskia following his every move with her sad eyes. "The Vikings and the Vascones led the way, and now everyone is sailing west to the new world. There are schools teaching the ways of the savages there, better to trade with the arrogant bastards. It's marvellous!"

His favourite word.

What now? Hobble my way to the harbour? Try to snatch an hour of sleep? That would be foolish; even in this little corner I was exposed and helpless. My only hope was to complete my plan: buy passage on the first ship heading anywhere. I hoped my little store of coins and trinkets might be enough.

I found my way simply by heading toward the brightest glow. Torches and oil lamps flared everywhere along the waterfront, and smoking braziers where ruddy-skinned men with eagle feathers in their long black hair were cooking food for the workers. The port scene danced in the moving flame, the orange and black of light and shadow adding exotic life to the wharves, cranes, towering piles of bales, boxes, kegs and amphora of oil and wine, lines of animals, crates of squawking birds crammed in till their feathers flew, and countless men. Men of all colours, most young, muscular and sleek with sweat as they worked.

Gawking like a country clod, I was certain this port never slept. Only a few women were to be seen, heavily veiled and hurrying in purposeful directions. Papa had told me that quite a few companies of traders, shipbuilders, merchants and foreign moneylenders were owned and operated by women, though in many countries the women had to employ a front line of suitable males to appease the sensibilities of foreigners, as some cultures were of the opinion that women were foolish and easily cheated.

Hoping I wasn't one such, I was scrutinizing the ships in hopes that one would bear a big banner stating *Welcome all Runaways! Low Rates, Clean Beds*, when a woman caught my eye.

She was different from the rest. For one thing, she wore only a loose robe of fine red silk, her sleek, muscular arms bare and shining under the golden glow of torches. For another, she had no male at her side to guard her. Tall and straight, black as the ebony of Petru's killing bench, she strode along bearing a basket laden with skeins of creamy white wool atop her head.

She was beautiful, and not very old, perhaps twenty-five. Both her ankles bore metal cuffs with a hammered design that looked like words in some strange language. They looked like slave cuffs with the chains removed. Around her neck were ropes of beads, shells and teeth.

The light caught her high cheekbones, and illuminated her one flaw: scars on her cheeks like those borne by Miss Marsh. A phrase from some eastern language I had learned recently came to mind: *The warrior's face shall be fearsome.* That was one translation. Another was: *Let the scars tell of a warrior.* Now I understood what the scars must mean.

What had Miss Marsh done to earn hers?

A line of three girls, small, medium and large, filed behind her, also with baskets on their close-shorn heads. She and her basket towered above the men around her, men who dropped their eyes as she approached, but raised them again to watch her avidly as she moved away.

The girls, probably her daughters, followed obediently, eyes down. One of the men reached out a hand and, quick as a mongoose, grabbed the trailing girl's arm, hauled her close and dug a hand between her legs. He released her almost immediately, snickering, and the girl stumbled away. Her basket of wool dropped to the ground, she caught her balance and let out one shrill scream, like a bird's shriek.

Her mother turned.

The air seemed to shimmer between the woman and the man. I smelled a sudden pungent gust of sea air, cold and salty as winter's ocean. Her black eyes locked with his. A knife appeared in her hand, and before I could see how she did it, the blade flew across the distance between them and pierced the ruffian's heart. She walked close, retrieved her knife and spat upon his twitching form. Then, standing over the corpse, she screamed as her child had done. A seabird's wild cry.

I saw the man's body soften and melt, turn into a puddle and seep away into the cracks between the street-stones. It took only a moment. The man's companions climbed over each other in their efforts to get away. She helped her child settle the wool-basket upon her head once more, and they formed once again into their line and strode off.

Staring, mouth open, I realized what she was: a Kek freewoman. Men and women like her weren't mere ordinary folk who had been released from servitude by a sympathetic master, or who had managed to pay off a slave-bond. The Kek were once slaves—born that way, or captured and sold into slavery—but had done something so miraculous, politically expedient, or courageous as to earn permanent freedom. Rather like a gladiator who'd vanquished an unbeatable foe. What had this woman done?

She had a God on her side. A God of women? Brutal, unforgiving but just. A god who favoured the weak. As the woman and girls turned a corner and vanished, I found my gaze shifting to the drying trickle of greasy water that marked the foolish man's last moment of life.

Perhaps... perhaps for my third *resura* form, I might consider such a one, or a melding of the Kek woman and the Theravedan female who had tried vainly to teach me; the ultimate fighter... surely better than a snake.

Turning at a slight sound, I suddenly found myself on my belly, gasping. Someone had knocked me down. I looked around to shout my anger, but quickly closed my mouth.

Two men leered down at me, both clad only in baggy breeches, their greasy hair in the patterned coils of an imported bound-worker. I'd seen a few in company with the traders who owned them at our villa, making deals as proxy for their bosses far away. Neither slaves, servants nor employees, they had just enough authority to lord it over a child or woman.

Which did they think I was?

If that Kek woman reappeared now, would she come to my aid? But she was gone.

I tried to get to my feet, but the taller of the men pushed me back down with one foot, standing over me and laughing. The shorter one was swinging my satchel tauntingly.

"What is this?" cackled the tall one. "A boy fresh from the hills and ready to pluck!" He poked at me with a toe, and I tried not to shriek. Did I have the nerve to try what I'd learned? He leaned over, peering at me in some confusion, his legs straddling mine. This was too good an opportunity to pass up. I kicked upwards as hard as I could, then scrambled to my feet.

With a thrill of glee I watched the lout curl into a ball around his tender parts. He clutched himself and howled. Tears leaked from his eyes, which were screwed shut. He'd lost interest in me, but the other man let out a curse and lunged for me. At last I remembered my dagger, but as I fumbled for it I was kicked down to my belly again. A string of curse words told me who he was.

He'd left off Latin and started speaking Tamasheq, a north African language which I understood and could speak a little.

"Leave me alone!" I cried in his language as I grovelled on the ground. "Don't touch me or, or—" The man snatched my dagger away and stuck it in his belt, giving me a humiliating slap. The man I'd kicked had recovered enough to emit a few curses in between gasps of pain.

The shorter man narrowed his eyes at me. "What is this? Not a boy, I think." Suddenly he made a grab for my improvised turban and yanked it away. My hair fell free. "Ha! Look at this!"

He took me by one foot and dragged me along the ground for a few feet till I was weeping in pain and fury. He laughed and flipped me onto my back, then he squatted down and gave my breasts a vicious squeeze. The game was up now. Instead of just a beating and robbery, I could expect much worse.

Chapter Seventeen
THE ORANGE CAT

Kicking and screaming did no good. The man I'd hurt particularly enjoyed it, laughing at my attempts at self-defence. They each grabbed a foot and dragged me into the shadows.

"My father will pay you," I howled. "Let me go!"

"Pay for you? Ha! I doubt you even have a father! Now shut up or we'll slit your throat first."

I already knew what that was like. By now I had given up fighting and was planning my revenge, should I live through what I knew would happen next. A horrible thought struck me: what if one of them killed me and captured my soul? I began to fight again, as they prepared to take their pleasure.

Then, with a yowl and a hiss, out of nowhere came a cat. Its ears were laid back and its claws were out as it launched itself at the closest man. A whirlwind of teeth and claws sent blood flying.

I lay gasping like a fish, watching as the cat ripped gashes in one ruffian's face and neck, then leapt nimbly onto the other's head to do the same thing. It became almost comical. If I wasn't in so much pain I'd have jeered at them like a street whore.

The cat was in complete control, leaping easily from each man's grasp, twisting like a ferret to rake at their eyes. An orange cat.

I began to crawl away as fast as I could before the cat got his neck wrung.

It was Miss Marsh's pet, I was sure of it. It had followed me.

With one final banshee yowl, the cat leapt into the darkness, leaving the two men torn and bleeding. Cursing feebly, they staggered off, one supporting the other. They'd forgotten me. Still I crawled for the darkness, only to feel a hand on my neck. I shrieked and rolled away.

"Quiet! It's me, you stupid girl."

I couldn't see who it was through my tears of pain and fear. I only knew I needed to get away.

Again the hand grabbed me by the scruff of the neck, hard, as if I was a pup that needed scolding. "Stay still! Do you know the trouble you've caused?"

The accent gave him away. Akil, Miss Marsh's servant-boy. What in the name of all the saints and stars was he doing here? Had he come after that magnificent cat?

"Don't touch me," I yelped. The hand let go and I dropped to the dust. "No, wait! Don't go!"

"Oh, for the love of—" He took my arm and hauled me upright, growling. I was learning so many new curses this night, I wondered how I would remember them all. "Stand there! Don't move, and don't speak."

I obeyed, not sure whether to stride off in fury or to launch myself at his neck in an embrace. He unwound his turban-cloth from his head and thrust the length of coarse grey linen at me. "Cover yourself with this. Now!"

I did, deciding against pointing out how rough and unpleasant the fabric was. Soon it hid my hair and face and Akil seemed to calm down.

Should I thank him? He was merely a servant...yet he must have followed me here, just as the cat had done...

No. That wasn't it.

I knew what he was. Of course. My heart began to beat faster as I examined him in disbelief. He had to be *resura*; not only did it fit the facts of his and the cat's arrival, it felt right. Somehow I simply knew it, and thinking back to his behaviour at home, around Miss Marsh and others, confirmed my deduction. That damned orange cat had curled up and watched me weep and shiver, gather my courage and my bag of supplies and run from my home. But to challenge him now, while I was in such a vulnerable position, would be foolhardy. What if I was wrong? He was my only ally.

He must have been sent to retrieve me, and I had to convince him not to. In fact, I must convince him to help me escape. I had to get him on my side. This might be difficult, since I had spent the months I'd known him either ignoring him or berating him for ugliness and obstinacy. I bit my lip and looked at Akil with new eyes. To what might he respond?

He had my hand in his and was hauling me away from the wharf-side district, grumbling under his breath.

Yes, he was clever. He had demonstrated his intelligence to my very demanding grandfather. Yes, he was loyal. Had he not been servant to the strange and difficult Miss Carolina Marsh for years? He'd had plenty of opportunity to run away or find other employment.

Akil was stubborn, sly, and had not the proper respect for his betters. And he was so very plain. Completely unpleasing to the eye. Eneko still glowed in my mind, a hot ember that burned higher when I thought of him late at night, alone in my bed.

Why, when he had all of nature to choose from, would a *resura* pick the body of a crippled, pocked mulatto? He could have had the form of the most acclaimed athlete or dancer in the land. He could have been beautiful.

"Any fool can see you are a woman," Akil snapped, yanking me into a dimly-lit eatery full of workers cramming down food and huge amounts of pungent beer as fast as they could, before getting back to their jobs. Some of them took the time to eye us.

Akil shoved me into a corner. "Keep your eyes down and don't say a word. If you want my protection, you had better keep a civil tongue in your head." He scowled, sighed, and finally muttered, "Sorry for this." Then he shouted a few curses and slapped me smartly across the cheek, hard enough to inform any watchers that he was in control of this female.

Tears of anger sprang from my eyes, but I bit my tongue and nodded meekly to indicate my understanding. It would be death or slavery to defy him now. He strode up to the shopkeeper and exchanged a few words with the man, then returned bearing a small satchel the man hauled out of a cupboard. I deduced that Akil had arranged for the storage of useful items. Was this part of his life as *resura*, the foresight to plan for escape? He grabbed my hand, tugging me once again in his wake.

"Where are you taking me?"

"Shut up."

I dug in my heels and began to argue. "You can't talk to me like that—"

He stopped, turned, and slapped me again, much harder than before. "I said, shut up."

He set forth again, not looking back. Stumbling after him over the cobblestones, weeping in earnest at the pain from my bleeding feet, squeezed breasts and bruised pride, I had no choice but to follow.

He led me northwest into a residential quarter, where every window or doorway was dark and closed, though the odd mumble of talk or smell of cooking escaped the sheltering walls. Eventually he seemed satisfied and let us stop for a moment. I could see him fairly well in the light of the moon, which was still up. "Akil," I begged. "I'm sorry! It was the only way—I had to run. I have to keep running! You don't understand." I could never explain to him my predicament.

He surprised me. "I understand very well." I felt a stab of fear. What did he mean? Did he know my secret? His voice had lost its harsh, demanding tone now that we were far from the scene of the crime. "Vara Svobodová bint Jameel... " He said my name slowly, rolling the syllables over his tongue as if they had flavour. He should not call me, his superior, by my name. Should he? "We all have plans and tasks. Secrets and lies."

I let it pass. On one hand, he was my saviour. On the other, he was preventing me from altering fate. If he dragged me home, he would contribute to the deaths of myself, my grandfather, and probably my mother.

I couldn't let him dominate me. Mother had told me I was beautiful, womanly. I had intercepted glances from many a boy and man. Though it was Eneko I pined for, I might possibly bend Akil to my will...

"Stop that."

"Stop what?"

"The way you are looking at me. It's whorish, and I pray to any God who might be listening that you will never become a whore."

At that bit of insolence, I slapped his face, probably as retribution for how he'd treated me, but immediately cringed back for fear of retaliation.

But he merely snorted and shook his head. "Females. I've only met one who was worth more than a copper drachma."

"Akil, listen to me! I can't go home—I can't! If you won't help me get passage out of here, at least pretend you didn't find me and let me go." Couldn't he see how desperate I was? What business was it of his whether I vanished or not?

He stared at me stonily, his good arm crossed over the bad one.

I felt a surge of anger and frustration, and looked him up and down scornfully. "What's the matter with you, anyway? I know what you are. Why do you take the shape of a cripple?"

His lips curled up in a cruel smile. "A cripple in the garb of a slave runs little risk of assault. People look the other way when I shamble by. Perhaps, Vara Svobodová, you should think upon that. Your attempt at disguise did little to help you."

"But—"

"Enough. You are coming home with me. And let me warn you—I may look weak and clumsy, but I am not. You cannot best me and you cannot escape me." He grabbed my arm and began to haul me away.

Limping along in his wake, I cursed under my breath. I didn't want him to turn back into a cat and rip my eyes out. My adventure was at an end. I ground my teeth till my jaw shot with pain.

I had one more question. One born of spite, just to hurt him. "Was it your beloved Miss Marsh who killed you?"

He didn't react, which made me want to hit him. Finally he said, "In a manner of speaking, I suppose she did. Now, be quiet. Another word and I will beat you till you bleed."

We marched along silently for half a league. The bruises and scrapes I'd gained really hurt, but not as much as my feet. It was hard to keep up, and eventually he noticed and stopped walking. When I caught up to him, there on the deserted, midnight road under the faint light of the moon and stars, I saw his expression of disgust. He thought me soft and spoiled.

"It's my feet," I told him, trying not to whimper. "It hurts to walk."

He scoffed. "It'll hurt worse if you're caught again by someone I can't control." I stood snivelling until finally he said. "Sit. I'll take a look."

He removed my sandals—his sandals, actually. "If you're expecting me to produce a carriage for you to ride in... oh." He tried to tug the leather straps out of the mess of seeping, dust-caked scabs.

He stood and sighed. "Stand up." I did so. He bent forward, picked me up with his good arm and slung me over his shoulder. Outraged, I gasped and struggled.

"Hold still."

What choice did I have? He carried me down the bank to the river, dropped me on my bottom at water's edge and began to rinse my feet, working loose the scabs and dirt.

"Thank you," I whispered. I meant it.

"I wish I had some oil. You shouldn't be walking at all, but we have to keep moving."

"I know."

Those men had taken my bag and dagger, but from his satchel he produced a knife and a piece of cloth, which he cut into strips. He bound my now clean, but still bleeding, feet in them, then removed the cloth that hid my hair and cut it in half with his knife. Soon my feet were two shapeless bundles on which I could stand

and walk with relatively little pain. He steadied me as I climbed the bank again and we set off once more.

As we walked in silence, I had time to think, while plaiting my hair and shoving it down the back of my tunic. I should have refused to let him touch me so intimately. I was used to my maid washing and oiling my feet, but to have a boy, even a homely, unpleasant boy, do it felt quite different. But why? My father used to bathe me when I was very young; I had distinct memories of splashing happily in a basin of warm water while he laughed and rubbed a big green lump of Aleppo soap all over me. I loved the warm slipperiness, the musky smell of laurel, the freedom of being naked.

Akil's hands had been as gentle as Papa's. Had he looked at my ankles? Had he found them slender and enticing, for which I should have him beaten? Or had he merely thought of my body as a useless hindrance?

What did a *resura* think of living people?

Slowly we wound down the distance northwest toward Perpignan. "May I ask you a question?"

"If I may choose not to answer," was his reply.

"All right... Akil, what is your third form?"

He laughed. "Can't you guess?"

So, he was an insufferable, over educated, supercilious cripple with a desire to be invisible, and a cat. If I were him, what would I choose for my third form? What would anyone choose if they had the chance?

"Well," I said, considering, "I'm sure it's a bird of some sort. A scrawny chicken. A worm-ridden crow, perhaps."

He laughed again, sounding really amused. My heart lightened a bit, and my feet seemed less painful. "Someday I'll show you," he said. "But not now."

We had covered another league or two when Akil must have tired of having me leaning on his arm and moaning. We turned off the moonlit road, empty now in the smallest hours of the night, to find shelter in a patch of high reeds. He formed a little cave by stamping the stems down and bending the taller ones over our heads. We would be invisible from the road when daylight came.

I sagged into a lump on the ground. It felt so good not to be moving. The whine of an overeager mosquito caught at my tired brain, but I found enough focus to urge it, and its companions, away. My *da resu* powers would probably not repel snakes, however. For comfort, and perhaps to ward off any reptiles that might be present among the reeds, I reached for my necklace, which, thankfully, my attackers had not had time to take. Eye, Owl, and Tooth, all were there working together, I hoped, to provide a level of luck that would see me through the next few days.

It was too dark to see anything, and I had my eyes closed anyway, but I heard Akil rustling about perfecting our hiding place. I felt quite grateful and warm toward him. Then suddenly the air felt different. Something had changed.

I opened my eyes. Blackness. I strained so hard to see that little sparks appeared in my searching eyes. Panic clutched me, but then I began to hear a soft, rising rumble. The purring of a cat.

I think I was about to reach out and pet him, but fortunately I fell asleep before I could do anything so embarrassing.

Chapter Eighteen
A CUPFUL OF INDIFFERENCE

I awoke at dawn, ravenously hungry. Since my satchel with its remaining store of dates and nuts was gone, I looked to Akil to provide for me. He was nowhere to be seen; perhaps he was off catching a mouse to eat. But what about me?

I went to the river to relieve myself and to splash water over my still-dusty face, giving a rueful thought to my complexion. A cacophony of birds chirped, sang and squawked overhead and in the water, and a vast shrill hum of insects joined in the morning song. The rising mist revealed thickening boat traffic. I crept back up the slippery bank, flopped down in our reed-shelter and pulled Akil's satchel toward me.

Just then, as Akil the boy, he returned from wherever he'd gone. He scowled at me. "Did it occur to you to ask permission before rummaging through my possessions?"

"No. Why should it? Do you have something to hide?" There was nothing to eat in there anyway.

He retrieved his satchel from my inquisitive paws and set it aside. "If you're looking for food, I have none. Can't you wait until we're back in Perpignan?"

"I'm hungry! Aren't you?"

He shook his head, whether in negation or disgust I didn't know. "Wait here. I'll get you something." He pushed his way through the screen of reeds and was gone.

Immediately I began to fret. What if he was abandoning me? What if something happened to him and he simply never returned? I sat hugging my knees and nibbling my fingernails until I noticed how filthy they were.

Suddenly there was a commotion of flapping and shrieking overhead. An eagle circled, harried by several small birds and holding something in its beak. It folded its great wings and dropped from the sky to land heavily beside me with a buffeting rush of humid air.

I jumped back. The bird was huge and black, the feathers of its head and neck gleaming gold. Its dark wings bore white flashes, and its feet were tufted with downy white feathers between each sharp black talon.

Awkwardly the splendid creature walked forward, its wings partially open for balance, opened its wicked yellow beak and dropped a chunk of bread at my feet. It looked up at me, cocking its wild hunter's head.

I bent down and took the bread, pretending nothing remarkable had just happened, though my heart had expanded with awe and gratitude. To show how unimpressed I was, I sat, crossed my legs and began to tear off pieces of the gritty peasant loaf and stuff them into my mouth. I was afraid to say anything for fear of breaking the spell.

The eagle, which of course was Akil the Annoying and Ugly, clacked its beak a few times as if laughing, then with a ripping sound like flags in the wind took off straight up and vanished into the sky.

Greedily I finished the bread and wished for more. Akil had counselled me to avoid drinking from the river, since it was filthy with all imaginable trash that made its way into a handy stream of water. I should buy beer or watered wine instead. I hadn't thought about that yesterday, and hoped I wouldn't spend the next few days in a misery of sickness. If I complained to him of thirst, would he fly off to find a wineskin to lay at my feet? Never again would I presume to think of Akil as a servant.

I hoped to make him my friend.

My body ached more that morning than it had last night, but Akil allowed me to lean on his arm, and we made good time once we had said goodbye to our little reed nest. By now I had resigned myself to slinking home in disgrace. I might have to acknowledge that fate was stronger than my will. But the failure of my brave, self-sacrificing, stupid plan still rankled, and it was going to be very difficult to face my mother. For once I was glad Jameel-my-father wasn't there.

Another thing: Petru had ordered us not to try to flee, yet I'd done it. Had he found out? Was my mother being punished for it right now? My heart lurched up and down along with my aching feet.

Akil plodded along silently, showing no signs of changing form, or even of warmth toward me. I glanced at him sideways. His withered arm flopped at his side, and his lame foot dragged. He seemed to be watching the horizon, lost in his own thoughts. This was going to be a very boring few hours. Remarks about the road, the people on it, the sights to be noted on either side, went unanswered. Consequently, I began to pester him with questions.

"When did you die, Akil?"

Nothing.

"Come on, tell me! Your secret is out, you might as well tell me something about yourself."

Heavy sigh. "Oh, very well. It was... let me think... this is the year of Julius 1245, so it was 1238. The third day of Martius."

"How old were you?"

"I was older than time, and young as an egg."

"Akil, I'm serious. Someday... someday I'll tell you why." I knew his secret, so to be fair, he should know mine. I wondered if this followed, or if I just wanted to impress him.

He said, "You don't have to tell me anything. I was in my thirteenth year."

At that moment we had to hustle to the side of the road, onto the dusty, weedy verge among various kinds of shit as two lines of wagons attempted to pass one another. Akil drew my head down onto his shoulder and turned me away, whether to protect me from dust, or from curious or hostile gazes I didn't know. He smelled nothing like the ruffians who had tried to abduct me last night. He smelled like oatcakes and stone dust. And a hint of pine.

I took a good sniff while I had the chance. He didn't smell at all like a person who had been trudging along in the heat, and by now he should stink as much as I did. He didn't smell like a person at all.

As he held me, I started to feel an odd vertigo. Nothing like what I'd felt on the minaret with Mother; more like the sensation of melting, as wax melts. Different bits of wax, candle ends, scrapings... melting into one another to form a soft, seamless mass. It was Akil's magical flesh into which I seemed to be falling, melting, dispersing. It was drawing me in, hungry for substance. I began to feel sick and frightened, though the tension between us— me alive and he *resura*—kept us apart. A thin skin of separation... But I could sense the nearness of danger, the closeness of his strange flesh, a roiling mass of particles that sought order and form, and were willing to take it from anywhere.

The wagons passed, he let go of me, and we moved on. I took a breath and rubbed my arms, which were tingling and itching.

"What's it like, being..." I waved one hand vaguely, not wanting to say *dead*.

"Not as wonderful as I thought it would be, Vara Svobodová."

"But still wonderful." Flesh that was not flesh. A universe inside.

"Considering the alternative, yes."

After that he wouldn't talk for a while, and I was concentrating on imagining what would happen to me when I got home. I would be punished, and I would deserve it, I supposed... though it did seem unfair.

Getting through the city gates would be the hardest part. Akil, of course, could change form and slip inside any time he wanted as long as he knew how to avoid people who liked to throw stones at cats. Fear that he would abandon me, or take the opportunity to gain favour with Petru by turning me in, coursed through me.

My trust in him was put to the test as we drew near the city.

Two marshals at a checkpoint ordered us to stop. When I'd left the city—such a short time ago—I hadn't really noticed the checkpoint, as no one bothered to search a lone boy leaving unless he showed signs of stealth or of wealth. They stopped and searched those who entered, ostensibly for security purposes, but in reality to enforce a gate tax. Basically it was a couple of mounted soldiers and a small holding area of angry, disgruntled folk who obviously had been declined entry, but who refused to give up trying. More soldiers were nearby, ready for action in case it was necessary.

One marshal dismounted and swaggered close, while the other watched. The horses had cropped all the nearby grass, and looked bored and prone to biting. We stood quietly, knowing better than to try to explain, excuse, bluster or demand. Security measures had become more and more harsh as Lord Petru spent more time travelling at random around his territories thinking up new taxes and rituals, and less in his capital of Massalia.

"What's your name, boy?" The marshals addressed Akil, ignoring me. I was just a road-worn, exhausted peasant woman.

"Akil al-Halim."

"Where are you going?"

"Into Perpignan, where my aunt lives," stated Akil.

"And who is this aunt of yours?"

"Fayruz bint Ibrahim al-Halim."

"And what is your business in Perpignan?"

"I bring this cousin, to work as cook's assistant." He shoved me forward.

I dropped my eyes, desperately attempting to look meek, stupid and obedient. And as if I knew how to boil grain or chop vegetables. Which I didn't.

"And then?"

Akil shrugged. "And then I shall return to my parents' home in Linqua." All the while, Akil's voice was low and respectful, and never did he meet the marshal's eyes. At one point he seemed to stumble or lose his balance, for he lightly brushed the marshal's arm and then apologized profusely for his clumsiness, bowing low. "We have had little to eat, kind sir."

The marshal snorted, prodded Akil back with the hilt of his sword and scratched his nose, looking us up and down.

"Let's see what you've got in that satchel, boy." He rummaged for a moment but found nothing worth appropriating. "Very well. You are free to pass." He tossed Akil a small square of something brown. He caught it in his good hand. A biscuit, perhaps? Maybe he'd give it to me to eat. "On your way." He climbed back aboard his steed and the two marshals resumed scrutinizing the road, ignoring us completely. A couple of heavy wagons were approaching; much better sport.

I let out my breath as we hurried away. "Akil, you were perfect! Do you really have an aunt in the city?"

"Of course not. Hurry, before they come to their senses."

"But we are free to pass!"

"So we are, unless the one I didn't manage to touch starts thinking about it."

"What do you mean? Can't we slow down? My feet still hurt."

"No we can't." He hurried toward the gate, through the makeshift camps and dwellings that lay outside the wall.

"Akil, what's that thing he gave you?"

He showed it to me. Just a small square of terracotta with a triangle stamped into it. It meant nothing to me.

"You get one of these if you are cleared to enter. You hand it over to the gatekeeper, and you're in."

"Wouldn't it be easy for someone to make these and enter without permission?"

"The symbols are changed at random, and there are dozens of them. I suppose a really determined forger could do it, but there are easier, if costlier, ways to enter Perpignan."

"What did you mean, about touching the marshal?"

He hesitated, then, probably realizing that without an answer I'd quiz him mercilessly, said, "Merely that there is a bottomless well of indifference in this world, and I drew up a small cupful. It aided him in deciding we were harmless."

"What's that supposed to mean? Akil, you're being much too cryptic."

"And so I shall continue. Will you please, for Allah's sake, shut up?"

I did, for we were at the gates, but I vowed to corner him as soon as we were safe at home and demand answers. A lot of answers.

The token worked, we entered the city, which seemed to have changed not at all during my adventure of barely two days, and were soon at home.

My idiotic hope of sneaking quietly to my rooms, ordering a bath and removing all evidence of my disobedience was immediately dashed.

Mother, Kai and Miss Marsh, who had apparently been keeping vigil from a high balcony, came rushing at us in a flurry of shrieks, sobs and recriminations, all from Kai. Right behind them, though moving more slowly, trundled Pada Josef and his faithful Saskia.

My mother sent me a blistering look and went directly to Akil, took both his hands in hers, kissed them, and said, "I am forever in your debt." She bowed her head before him, then looked up, her eyes brimming with tears, and said, "You shall have a place in our hearts and house forever, and treasure as well, as soon as Jameel-my-husband comes home." This last was said with a catch in her throat that I immediately picked up. What was going on?

He in turn bowed to her. "It is my honour and delight to return your daughter to her home," he muttered gruffly. "I expect no reward."

Carolina Marsh stepped forward and bestowed one of her enthusiastic hugs upon me. "I'm so glad you are back safe," she said. Her voice changed to a hiss in my ear. "Come to me later. We need talking."

Before I could speculate about this, Mother grabbed me for her turn. But instead of a hug I got a hard shaking and an angry glare.

A warrior woman did not praise the gods over the safe return of a runaway daughter.

Akil and Miss Marsh went off to their little room, arms around one another like mother and son. I felt strangely bereft. I had grown to tolerate Akil and even to admire him, though if he was a friend yet I couldn't guess. Perhaps I'd see him later, when I visited Miss Marsh.

Very soon I was upstairs in a tub of water having the filth of the roadway rinsed from my hair and body. My feet had been exclaimed over, carefully washed and anointed with the special medicinal oil that Kai knew how to make. It stank, but I knew it would work. The bruise from Petru's kick had turned a deep purple, but did not hurt much anymore, and perhaps it enjoyed the company of all my new bruises.

At last Mama and I were alone. We sat side by side under a window, and as she combed my hair she began to talk.

"I knew right away when you left, Vara Svobodová bint Jameel. We are linked, you know; I need not tell you how. Perhaps you feel it too."

I bit my lip against the painful tug of her comb. Her hands were rough today, abrupt, and I could feel how cold they were. My hair, which I had been too proud to cut off, hung in damp ripples to my buttocks, and was chilling my shoulders. Did I feel a connection to my mother? Right now I was too tired to care.

"I have known what Akil is for months," she said. "When I realized you had gone, I went to Miss Marsh and begged her help. Akil..." She sighed and put the comb down, took up some scented olive oil and rubbed her palms with it, then ran them down the length of my hair. "Akil knew instantly what to do. And he seemed to know where you were heading."

Of course he had. As a cat, he'd been right there listening to me mutter and moan to myself as I prepared to leave. All the times I'd stroked his orange fur... what had he thought of that? He must have enjoyed it, for the damned beast had purred. It was impertinent trickery, wasn't it? I turned to look at her. "Did you see him change?"

Her face took on the same expression I'd seen on the faces of mystics and preachers, a sort of amazed bemusement. There was joy and fear together; was it rapture? My own Valkyrie mother had seen something that truly impressed her.

"I did. It was like something in a dream...it didn't make sense. There was a... *twisting* in the air, the feeling of a storm coming. I was looking right at him. First he was Akil, the boy—the next he was nothing but mist and darkness. And then he was a great bird, an eagle I think. He vaulted out the window and was away before I could see him clearly."

How I wished I could see him change! I *would* see him do it, someday, no matter how curt, insolent and superior he might be. I'd see it.

I'd be doing it myself someday.

My mind suddenly leapt to my own future. What bird would I choose? An eagle, like Akil? That didn't seem right. Too big, too masculine, and all that rending of flesh. Besides, he would assume I was imitating him and laugh at me.

I imagined all the beautiful birds I had seen. Peacocks, pheasants, multi-coloured parrots. And the useful birds: best among them being the carrier pigeon, who could find her way home across oceans. However, Petru had banned the breeding or keeping of such birds other than his own, and any found were destroyed. In fact, I recalled, he'd recently killed his own flock and was waiting for new chicks to hatch and be trained, ones unsuspected of being *resura*.

None of these birds was what I wanted.

Then I knew. It would be the nightingale, whose symbolic tooth I wore around my neck. There had been one in a cage at the mountain spa, and I had examined it at the time. It hadn't impressed me for looks. A small, insignificant bird, one that could easily go anywhere without notice. Insignificant, but with the soul of an ancient, dagger-toothed shark... I smiled.

Mama put away the oil and drew me close. She was trembling. Perhaps there *was* a connection between us, for, shivering suddenly, I knew that something had put the fear of all the gods into her. Something she wasn't telling me.

"Mother, what is it? What's going on?"

"Vara… it's Eneko Saratxaga. He has been captured."

Chapter Nineteen
THE CATAMITE

"What! When?" I jumped to my feet. Immediately all my blood drained to my feet, making them throb worse than ever. I felt sick. "Where is he?"

"Here. He was brought to the city yesterday, straight to Petru's palace. I heard about it only an hour before you returned."

I knew he would be tortured until anything he knew came out. Petru had no mercy for spies. Look what had happened to Sigrun and her family.

It was already too late for us to run. And I didn't want to. Immediately my mind began to churn with schemes to rescue Eneko, each more ridiculous than the last. Petru Dominus had the weight of centuries behind him, and the massed wiles of rulers determined to punish rebels.

I said, my voice quavering, "If only Papa were here. He could buy Eneko's freedom, couldn't he? Couldn't he do something?" Something miraculous. He was my father.

"You should thank all the Gods that he *isn't* here, Vara. He'd be in chains beside Eneko right now."

Three interminable days later, we got news that Eneko Saratxaga was to be tried within the week, along with other suspected criminals, in the coliseum, in front of the usual crowds that came to watch the spectacle of justice being meted out. The term *justice* meant little. To gain the notoriety of the coliseum you had already been convicted.

This was terribly quick. Usually interest in a public trial was whipped up over weeks, the better to generate profit for the sponsors. Lord Petru must have wrung as much information from him as he wanted and was now ready to make an example of him. What if Eneko was in a tub of bloody water right now, eels sucking out his innards? He'd only have to keep him alive until the trial, the better to set an example with his public death.

I cried myself into sickness, and had to be dosed with herbs to calm me. But the horrid images would not leave my mind.

My mother had managed to send off a cryptically-worded warning to my father, using some convoluted path of messengers. Whether it would get to him was up to the fates. As was what he chose to do with the information. I was forced to accept the very real possibility that we might never see Papa again, for he would be insane to return home now.

At last I remembered I had been invited to visit Miss Marsh, up in her scientific aerie among her precious specimens. To distract myself, I decided to go. Besides, it was time I made a proper thank-you to Akil, and perhaps to worm my way into his affection... The thought that he might help us somehow lurked in my mind. He was a magical being, after all. It was possible he could somehow free Eneko...

I needed to give him a present. What might a *resura* want? Jewels? Inappropriate for me to give him, no matter who or what he was. I owned some very nice pieces of amber and carved ivory, given me by Mama's side of the family, but they were too big, also they were locked away for me to claim upon my wedding day. Which I would never have. Useless, to me as well as to Akil.

Fine clothing? A length of the very best silk for a new turban? Which he rarely wore, preferring to let his wavy black hair be looked upon directly by the gods.

Every boy or man I'd ever encountered loved sweets. Eneko had loved sweets. I bit my lip to force back the tears. I dispatched Kai to Sigrun's and my favourite old sweet-shop, instructing her to buy the most expensive items there.

That afternoon, carrying a beautifully carved box layered with delicacies, I made my way to Miss Marsh's special area, with the thick, sweet scent of vanilla—a spice so new and exotic that hardly anyone had it—filling my nostrils. Akil would love this. He should be somewhere nearby.

Miss Marsh, when I found her, was lying flat on her back with a damp cloth on her forehead. I started to quietly creep away, but she opened her eyes.

"Vara, my dear girl! Do come in." Her eyes were dark-shadowed and sad.

Shyness and a weight of depression overwhelmed me, and I wished now that I hadn't come. "You asked me to come talk with you. Is this a good time?"

"Never mind me, I have only a headache."

I wondered if that was true. Perhaps she was as worried as I. Her position in Perpignan was worse now that our family was in disgrace. If we escaped death or prison, we would be banished, all our remaining wealth confiscated. She'd be wise to escape now.

"May I send for some tea?" I asked politely. "Or some of the medicine that Kai makes? It helps the headache."

She shook her head. "No, no. I wanted to talk with you about Akil."

I felt my eyelashes flutter a bit. Akil. His image popped to mind: homely, aloof, supercilious. Our friendship had gone no further since my return home. The box and its luscious contents seemed like a waste of money. I put it on the floor, and longed for Eneko Saratxaga's brilliant smile, and the gusto with which he would devour the treats. He might even have kissed me, his dark eyes glowing. But he was locked in irons underground. That's why I was here. My sweet-smelling bribe made guilt war with need.

"I... I wanted to thank Akil," I stammered. "And you, Miss

Marsh." But did I really? I might be leagues away in another land by now but for Akil's interference, free of my past and my future.

Or I might be dead at the filthy hands of rapists. I wasn't ready to die, I knew that now, though the time of my vision was coming close.

"I will to tell you about how we came to be... partners."

I took a breath. "Akil told me that it was you who killed him. Is that so?"

She held very still for a moment. "Ah. So you know what he is." Her face wore a look of intense misery. "He must trust you very much. And yes, I killed him. But I didn't mean to."

I waited while she blinked back tears, suddenly regretting my harsh question.

"It has been a long time. Akil and I have been together for... it is now more than eight years. When we met, he was but a child, the most beautiful boy I had ever seen. Strong limbs, auburn curls, a face that was so perfect he could have been a cherub. The family I was lodging with owned him, and they were training him to be a Catamite."

"A Catamite? What's that?" I was still trying to accept the idea of the homely boy I knew having once been beautiful.

"Gods forgive me," she muttered, running her fingers over her scars. "I didn't realize for many months what they were doing to him, nor did I give thought for what might be inside that pretty head of his." She looked up and smiled grimly. "What is a Catamite? Why, nothing more than a young boy trained for sex with men. Many men. A Catamite is a plaything, a slave of the most degraded sort.

"I finally understand when I see my host give him wine, then bring him into the baths with other men. Being small, he soon became tipsy and pliant. I will spare you the details, my dear Vara Svobodová, but he told me years later that he was passed among these men for hours. The worst thing? That often the boy becomes a shameful panderer, seeking gifts and attention in exchange for his body. Worse than any whore."

My hand had gone to my lips. I didn't know what to feel.

Horror. Confusion. And revulsion. How could I look Akil in the eye again?

Tears suddenly spilled down Miss Marsh's weathered cheeks. "But that was not the worst."

I didn't want to hear it, but just then we heard irregular footsteps approaching. Akil, the poor cripple boy with the heart of an eagle. Miss Marsh shut up at last.

He must have seen the guilty looks on our faces. I blushed hotly and looked at the floor. Akil stood for a moment, assessing the situation. Did he and Miss Marsh have secret signals to share information? Perhaps he'd simply been listening from the next room, for he gave a deep sigh and sat himself down cross-legged on his pallet of blankets, the place the orange cat usually occupied. His place.

Finally I was able to meet his eyes, but it took a real effort of will. After what he had done for me, was I about to shun him for his shameful past? What choice did he have, back then? I felt my chin tremble. Miss Marsh found my hand with hers and squeezed it.

"Vara," she murmured, "Akil is a person of many shades. And much light. It is my dear wish that you and he might become friends."

It was my wish too, but were my motives pure? No. I wanted him to save Eneko for me. If Akil could do that, I would love him forever.

Akil, who had met my gaze with a look of shuttered defiance, abruptly turned away. "I don't know if that's possible," he said flatly. "We are too different."

I wanted to claim an equal heritage to his: soon I would be brutally thrust into the same spirit world he inhabited. But I kept my mouth shut. Should I reach for his hand?

No. He would only pull his away.

Remembering, I reached down and handed him the sweets. "I brought you this. A gift of thanks." Politely he opened it and sniffed the box's contents, his nostrils flaring. He shrugged noncommittally, and put it back on the floor.

His tawny eyes drilled into mine. "Shall I tell you what they had planned for me, the little *da resu* boy?"

I shook my head *no*, though I had the horribly prurient desire to find out. I also knew he was going to tell me no matter what. He wanted me to understand the very worst of him, and this, strangely, gave me heart. It was a sign of respect, I thought, a sign that he desired my approval. So much so that he dared jeopardize it with the truth.

"Miss Carolina Marsh is more than a mother to me. Certainly more than the woman who bore and then sold me. My parents couldn't resist the money offered for a *da resu*.

"Can you possibly imagine what was in store for me? I hope not. I would be trained as the fantasy plaything of the depraved. Think of it—after death, as *resura*, I could be male or female, or a combination of both. I could be any sort of animal. There are men who prefer animals, you know." His voice was clipped, harsh. I could barely breathe. "The possibilities were disgusting and varied, and I was trained to set upon the most outrageous forms my masters could think of for my three shapes. I would be auctioned off to the richest, most degenerate man this side of hell."

Miss Marsh spoke up at last. "You see, Vara? Worse than being an ordinary, run-of-the-mill sex slave." She had to stop and blow her nose. "Finally I understood what sort of being he was. In my travels I studied with mystics and scholars, and listened around the campfires of ancient tribes." She touched the scars on her cheek. "There is more strangeliness in this world than you can imagine. But this... to use such a treasure this way... it was evil."

She took a deep breath. "So I stole him. I walked right into the slave quarters where he was being held, past the eunuchs, the women, the ordinary boys and girls, took him by the hand and led him away. I was known as sometime teacher of the brighter servants. It was how I earned a living. I planted, like seed, the idea that the boy would bring more price if he had more to offer besides his body. How to read erotic tales, perhaps.

"I pretended to scolding him because shirk his studies, and led him quickly to my own cubbyhole. No one interfered. No one imagined that I, a small plain woman, might be up to not good. I hushed him, wiped his tears..."

Akil snorted. "You slapped me a few times to shut me up. I was a snivelling brat." He hugged his knees and grinned at her—a frightening sight, with his snaggle teeth and angry eyes.

"You had been trained as brat. A spoiled, frightened, miserable little being. Kept drunk most of the time, you could barely think." She crumpled her sodden handkerchief and looked at me. "I undress him out of his silken robes and find him simple garments of a servant boy. I cut off his long curls and rub ashes onto his pretty skin. And then we walk away."

She had started to look quite sick, and couldn't meet my eyes. "I... I didn't know what would happen next. I swear I didn't know."

"I pray that you would have stolen me anyway," growled Akil.

I had been sitting so still that my feet had gone to sleep. "What happened?" I got up and stamped around to stop the tingling, but kept my eyes on Miss Marsh. "Did... did you kill him then?"

She doubled over and began to weep anew. "Yes. It took three days. I didn't know!"

Appalled, I looked from one to the other. "Three days! What do you mean?"

Akil said, "I'd been fed poison for years, along with the wine. And also the poison's cure. I was told this when I was seven, so I knew what would happen to me if I ran away."

Miss Marsh wailed, "You knew it all along, and never told me."

Akil looked down, frowning.

"He was barely more than child," she continued at last. "When he was deprived of the..." She waved her hand, searching for the word.

"Antidote," I provided.

"Antidote. When he didn't get antidote, he began to die. I didn't know what to do, though we found an empty shepherd hut where to hide. Then I must to watch him suffer, and only could give him water, hold his head. Akil, you never blamed me. Never."

"But," he said, "I could have told you what was happening. I could have returned to that hell-hole and become a freak, degraded beyond sense or redemption. You saved me. I am yours."

His words sent a shiver down my arms. They weren't just dear friends and partners—she was his *alanbir*, the owner of his soul.

She shook off the last of her tears. "And I am yours, as if I were your mother."

Akil's eyes held a dark hurt that even I couldn't miss. Was it because he would never be free? Having a good and kind master still meant that you were a slave. He said, "Perhaps now you understand why I chose this crippled, ugly form, Vara. That at least I managed to do before I died—choose, of my own free will, the three forms I will have forevermore. Miss Marsh counselled me, when she understood what was happening. Those last days of my life were well used. I get no more covetous stares, no more groping hands and lewd suggestions. I am almost completely invisible. And I like it this way."

"You... you aren't invisible to me." I bowed my head and felt my throat closing up. Why had I said that? I felt as though my heart would break. Akil was so strange and so sad. But I could never pity him. He was too strong.

I looked up. Did his eyes look a little warmer?

It was Eneko I loved, of course. Akil was much too aloof and cold. Much too strange. What could I give him? He needed nothing from me, wanted nothing.

And Eneko would soon be dragged before Petru Dominus, the Scorpion of Askain. His glib tongue and charming ways wouldn't get him out of trouble this time.

Akil's fate had been sealed when his soul was captured by a small, kind, weather-beaten woman from far Britannia.

It was Eneko Saratxaga whose fate was in the balance now.

Chapter Twenty
THE SCARLET APRON

I mages of the horrors Akil had suffered coiled like snakes in my brain. My hopeless plan to enlist his help withered. I had no idea what to say to him, and was ashamed to talk with him. I wasn't worthy. His short human life had been so awful.

Why did I persist in ignoring the truth? Gods, kings, and generals with their armies rule us all. It has always been so. Those who kick against their traces are made to suffer.

I started wondering about the concept of age. How did it apply to a *resura*? Akil had died when he was thirteen, eight years ago, and had chosen a human form that seemed to be perhaps nineteen or twenty years old. But was he still that frightened, degraded child inside? I would die within the year, at around sixteen or seventeen, we had estimated. Besides a bird, I had chosen to appear as a woman and as a boy. No, I recalled unhappily, a snake. A snake and two others. But would I remain a girl, at least on the inside?

My time would come soon now, and my nights were often interrupted by sudden, heart-pounding jolts when I was sure that Pada Josef was looming over me. But nothing was ever there. Just the lonely night clinging around me.

Little sleep and no appetite had made me nervous and hollow-eyed, and thinking of Eneko made it worse. Never did I picture him revealing a word against my Mama or Papa, despite whatever torture he might endure.

That shows what a fool I was.

But I had to believe in honour and valour, the ability of a man to withstand anything. Anything, for the sake of honour. If such higher instincts weren't real, then what point was there in anything?

Was there an ultimate God above us, the King of Gods, watching our efforts? Applauding and encouraging them? My Pada had asked why, if such an all-powerful God existed, he couldn't control the others.

Suddenly I found myself weeping. I couldn't stop it, only sop up the tears with my shawl. No one was there to see or hear me, and I admit that I really didn't try to stop. If I got rid of all the tears now, I wouldn't disgrace myself later, when it would be very important to be brave.

My mother wasted a lot of money and influence trying to get Eneko freed. Or bought as a slave and shipped off to the new world across the Aetheopian Sea. Anything. But nothing worked.

"From what you've told me, the lad is strong and resourceful." Grandfather stroked his beard nervously. We were effectively under house arrest, and since people knew we were out of favour, they had begun to shun us. Some of our staff had quit, and there was endless speculation about what might have caused our sudden drop in status.

The day came for the public trials. The travelling courts had been suspended, as Petru liked to mete out justice himself. Also, he suspected the official judges of conspiring against him, and many of them were now being judged. Petru had little interest in mercy.

We dressed in simple clothes, and ordered provisions for what would be a long, hot day. Our servants and guards carried food and water, for us and for themselves in the cheap seats up in the blazing sun, while Mama, Pada Josef and I crowded into a rented litter.

The stuffy, jouncing box stank of mouldy cushions and cat piss, the litter-bearers couldn't get their steps in rhythm, and the floor was sticky. But we didn't want to call attention to ourselves by arriving in our own much nicer Roman style sedan chairs. However, the inside was private and we could talk on the slow, nauseating trek.

It occurred to me that, should things go badly, I might never have another chance to be alone with my family. There was something I wanted to know.

"Mama," I whispered, "Why is it—"

"Vara, speak up. I can't hear you over the din." We were passing along a side avenue near the physicians' quarter, and it had got noisy. And even more smelly. The acrid tang of medicines being boiled and blended seeped through the privacy curtains, and I could hear the characteristic yelps and moans of someone getting a tooth pulled.

I leaned close to her ear. "Why are you still alive? You are *da resu*—why were you never made *resura*?"

Surprisingly, she smiled. She drew the hangings aside briefly to peep around, then shut them against a shaft of hot sunlight. When we passed into the shade of a building, it was as if night had fallen. We all put our heads together.

"I was a gift to your father's family," she said, her voice low. "Part of a plan hatched many years before. I was to belong to them, and to your father particularly, linked by the bond of marriage so that when he killed me I would be less likely to be snatched by a God."

Aghast, I blurted, "*Papa* was to kill you?"

"Obviously he didn't." Again the smile. "The marriage went as planned; what was not anticipated was that we would fall in love. Like the Caliph in the tales of the *One Thousand and One Nights*, Jameel wanted just one more night with me. And I with him. The *resura* forms that had been chosen for me, and that I was locked into, he would not find so appealing... after one night came another, and another. And I became pregnant."

Pada Josef, sagging in his corner, sighed and said, "I knew that you two would be trouble."

"What? Me and Jameel?" Mama grunted. "Of course we were trouble. Like I said, love is for fools."

The litter wobbled as the bearers negotiated a turn, and the light within it changed again. The baby she bore must have been my brother, the one who died.

"It wasn't supposed to happen. I'm sure I was being fed potions to prevent it... they didn't work. Perhaps our love was stronger than their plans. But what a dreadful fuss was made... I was beaten and given abortive, but the baby stuck tight and was born, and lived for six months. He was malformed, sickly... his death was a mercy. But your father bartered a lot of money and influence to keep me alive for that half year... and during that time I became pregnant again. With you. I admit I was secretly very pleased. But that time, Jameel was beaten too."

"Why did being pregnant make a difference?"

"Because no one could know if the unborn child was *da resu* or human. If human, it would be a dreadful sin to kill the innocent babe—Jameel's offspring—along with the mother. If *da resu*... I don't think anyone knew what might happen. An undeveloped soul, completely unformed and malleable... it has been said that such a new, untarnished soul is powerful, controllable only by a Great God. If joined in power with its *resura* mother..." She shook her head. "We did not want to risk the consequences. So yet again we waited for the birth of a child."

I sat with my hands jammed between my knees, gnawing the insides of my cheeks.

Leaning close in that swaying box, she stroked my hair. "That child was you. Your father and I decided that, no matter what anyone might do to us, we wanted our lives to be our own. At least until you grew up."

"And now I am grown up."

"Yes. The time has flown. It has been dangerous, and has led us into many deceptions and schemes that came to nothing. You were barely dry when we left his parents' house in Córdoba and fled to this country, under the protection of my family, who had started to regret their bargain. My father, though he had brokered the deal, was willing to accept my return, and wait for another time to fulfill the bargain. The political situation that had seemed so urgent had changed, and for several years the world was peaceful. It was decided to wait and harvest two fully-trained *resura* at a later date." Her face hardened, and I wondered what secrets she knew, and which of those were secrets no longer. "But Jameel and I have had our lives and our love... and now we must accept the fate that has been ours all along."

I felt a surge of anger. Had my mother given up already? "But it won't be your proper fate! Papa isn't here. You might be taken by that pig, Petru!"

"Hush." She jerked her chin. "He will never take me, or you."

"You can't be sure of that."

She looked away and didn't answer.

Our futures rushed toward us, dark as storm clouds.

The litter stopped and we bumped to the ground. It was time to enter the coliseum.

Perpignan's coliseum is built to hold many thousands of spectators, and has extensive underground passages, cages and holding chambers, and all sorts of machinery to put on shows. Pada Josef told me that he once saw the huge, ancient coliseum in Rome flooded with water to stage a sea battle, but that was long ago during an outburst of generosity by a certain sub-consul whose head later rested on a pike for all the money he had squandered. Rome, hugely indebted to Egypt and clinging to the tattered dignity of age, quickly reverted to its program of austerity. And since the Huns proclaimed to despise the excesses of previous empires, true spectacles anywhere these days were few and far between.

Petru hadn't wasted any gold on today's event. We could tell that it was to be short and brutal. We found our seats at the north end, in the area reserved for our class, and our servants quickly spread out cushions, placed jugs of wine and water for us, and left us. There was no sign of Eneko, though several other men, and a woman, were on display in a ragged, sorry line, and two more were hustled in as we watched. A couple of crosses lay on the sanded floor, ropes and tackle at the ready.

The seats were perhaps one quarter filled with an assortment of citizens. Acrobats and animal-trainers were displaying their talents out on the sand until the real show started, and vendors were circulating among the spectators with trays of food and drink for sale, but no one was paying much attention to them. People talked of war, and of their sons who had been conscripted. Some were proud and boastful. Others kept their mouths shut and merely looked worried and sick.

The air was electric, as if a storm was brewing. People were becoming short tempered, swatting at flies and snarling at one another. Demanding that the executions begin. I looked up at the sky, and there they were: the Gods. Why did they reveal themselves to me? What did I have that they wanted? A soul. What was that worth?

They were as eager for a spectacle as the howling men and women here on Earth. Stirring things, adding heat to the pot. Or perhaps it was only thunderclouds I saw above us.

I looked down, feeling flat and angry. I wanted to smash something.

Suddenly Petru entered his box, which was just below us, and began to peer around him, checking for faces. When he saw ours, there as ordered, his head jerked a bit as if one of his flies had bitten him. He stared for a moment, then looked away.

A scribe began to read out a list of names and crimes. The usual. Thieves, an adulterous woman, two brothers who had apparently conspired to kill their own father (and failed, for the old fool was there begging for their lives), several tax evaders. A whole row of whimpering blasphemers, their bodies covered in red, seeping S-shaped brands. Still no Eneko.

My eyes stung with sweat. Punishments were pronounced and meted out quickly, and the guilty were dragged off, either mercifully dead, or alive but bleeding. Two of the tax evaders turned out to be high-ranking officials, charged also with spying and treachery. Their status was rewarded as they were hoisted up on the crosses, there to hang gasping and twitching as the crowd jeered.

If after two days they were still alive, they would be cut down and allowed to go free. As paupers. Their wives and children wailed and rent their hair. The air had the familiar burning trash smell, and I knew that if I looked up, I'd see vast faces in the clouds. Open, grinning mouths that perhaps were holes into the next world.

A break was called. Petru and his attendants vanished into the building, and fresh sand was raked over the blood on the ground. The clouds grew lower and darker, and even those who would normally relish today's events were looking sick and beaten. Some tried to leave, but somehow couldn't; they hurried to the exit points, but then turned and trudged back to their seats, looking baffled and scared.

Mother eyed her father with concern. He had been coughing more lately, and today, in this heat and horror, looked near death.

His eyes were closed and he began to rock slowly from side to side. I watched him, alarmed, as he began to groan, a deep, frightening sound. "Pada, are you all right?"

Mama grabbed my shoulder. "Look! Petru's coming back."

I realized my cheeks were wet with tears, and quickly wiped them dry. Petru prowled into his ornate box and stood looking down into the arena.

Grandfather was bent over now, muttering into his knees, but I couldn't spare him attention. Not now.

A line of guards marched in, followed by an oxcart pulling a sturdy metal cage. Within the cage was a man, whose chest was cloaked all in red. At first I thought it was a scarlet apron. I was wrong.

It was blood. The man was Eneko Saratxaga.

I recognized him only by his black, curling hair, as his body was much too thin, marked with cuts and bruises. A soldier prodded him out of the cage, and he fell to his knees on the sand. He tried to get up, but was thrust down at spear point.

His tongue had been cut out. I knew this from the way he

choked and spat and bowed his head to clear his throat. Grovelling on the ground like an animal.

Suddenly I found myself crumpled on the stone floor of our tier of the arena, black sparkles obscuring my vision, the cloud faces dripping close. Mama hauled me upright and pinched me mercilessly. "Get up! This is no time to faint!" Tears were streaming down her cheeks, darkening the folds of the veil across her face, and she was muttering curses. I leaned against her, my ears ringing strangely and my nostrils full of that burning stink.

Pada Josef suddenly shot upright as if stung. His eyes rolled back and he began to speak. "The warp is torn. The weft rots. The blood, the blood..." He grabbed his head and whined like a dog. "Everywhere... Oh Sisters, spare our land..."

Petru turned slowly and gave us a Medusa look. Mama pushed her father down and clapped a hand over his mouth. Petru lifted his lip in a little smile. The blood rushed back to my head and my thoughts cleared and narrowed. If I had brought my dagger I would have launched myself straight for him. Watch *him* grovel and bleed, cut out *his* tongue.

Suddenly he hoisted himself over the balcony's edge and dropped to the arena floor. He strode across the sand to Eneko, dagger in hand.

Eneko spat blood and tried to lift himself upright, but was too weak and broken. Petru took him by the hair, bent his head back and with two quick stabs put his eyes out.

The crowd roared its approval, and an echoing thunder came from the sky. Mother and I stood side by side as straight as we could, gazing upon Eneko Saratxaga, he of the sparkling eyes and glib tongue. I heard his laugh and felt again his warm breath on the palm of my hand. Instead of a blinded wreck I saw the lithe, flirting boy of that warm summer evening in the mountains.

Gone, gone forever. My vision started to close in again and I swayed, but Mama wouldn't let me fall.

The hot wind came again, driving the arena's dust up my nostrils. It held the blood and tears of all the poor destroyed souls who had suffered and died here. I could do nothing for Eneko but pity him. Beg his forgiveness for being part of the family that used him and then watched him die.

Petru began to speak. "A man with no eyes can spy no more." A pause. A few ragged cheers greeted his words.

"A man with no tongue can spill no secrets."

Both crosses were already occupied. Eneko wore no chains, and he still had his hands and feet. I knew then what Petru was going to do with Eneko.

He was going to set him free.

Chapter Twenty-One
TOOTHLESS

Miss Marsh and Akil were waiting for us when at last we got home. I unwrapped my shawl from my face and gasped for clean cool air.

My mother strode through the house to the courtyard, stripping off her veil, and splashed her face and arms with water from the fountain. Her father Josef was reclining on a chaise beside it, looking terribly pale. His eyes opened but he didn't move.

"Eneko Saratxaga has been tortured, humiliated and brutalized before the whole city," she stated, her voice thick with anger. "Then that pig Petru released him, barely able to crawl. Now he is somewhere in the city, dying alone."

Miss Marsh drew in a sharp breath and her small blue eyes flashed. I could see in her the wild young girl who had defied her parents, but she could do nothing now. None of us could.

Akil stood like a tree stump, expressionless. Did he not care about anything human any more? Did being *resura* mean you lost all compassion, all connection to the heart and soul? What use was it, this magic after-life?

I shoved him in the chest with both hands. He ignored me. I shoved harder. Was I trying to knock the tree stump over? Make it weep and wail as was right at a time like this? He barely moved, letting me vent my sorrow and anger upon him. "You! You could find him, save him! Why don't you do something?"

But then he gave me a look of such misery and shame that I clapped a hand over my mouth and turned away. Perhaps he had a heart after all.

Pada was trying to stand, but couldn't do it. He coughed and gasped, waving his hands feebly. He was trying to talk and no one was paying attention, until he slowly rolled off the chaise to the floor. A fine spray of red settled next to his mouth on the tiles, and he wiped at it with one hand as if to hide it. Mother sank to her knees beside him and began to weep at last. Akil shuffled away as if he was the ancient one, looking even more the useless cripple. Pity. Hatred. Love. Death.

Was there no longer room in this world for love?

Later, after we had settled Pada Josef in his bed with Saskia attending him, I started to gain a little sanity.

How could I ask Akil to save a man who was as good as dead already? But perhaps he could be induced to attack Petru himself. Revenge might be all we could hope for. But Petru would have any strange animal killed as it approached. His new *falci* sniffers would point the finger, and his archers would shoot anything or anyone unfamiliar, particularly something so fearsome and unnatural as an eagle in the city. He'd have even a little cat slaughtered.

Akil would be captured, like the gryphon I'd seen those years ago. Could he turn to dust and re-form somewhere else? Or would he be held in wire, vainly switching form to try for escape? I could see now that there were rules to the miraculous existence of a *resura*, and I needed to figure them out. I chewed my nails. They might burn him, or encase him in a stone tomb. If I could think of ways, so could Petru.

He would come for my mother and me soon. The Gods would prod him back towards insanity and he would obey their wishes. He would take the bet, gamble for our souls. He would do anything to capture us. My skin crawled. Just how far did the powers of a *resura* extend, when the soul within it was forever chained?

Later, as Mother, Miss Marsh and I made ourselves try to eat something, Akil returned from somewhere and bent to whisper in his *alanbir*'s ear. Miss Marsh nodded, sighed, and dropped the fig she had been tearing open.

"Akil has found that a local Vascone family carried Eneko away," she reported. She looked stern and rather sick. "They will tend his wounds and try to keep him alive. There aren't many Vasconi left. Nor Romani, nor Muslims or Jews. Petru and his Sarafites are getting rid of everyone who doesn't knuckle under."

Mother closed her eyes. I could see her lips moving in a silent prayer.

We were in the smallest dining hall, off the winter kitchen. Smoke from the latest fires in the deserted Jewish quarter penetrated the house, laying a thin film of soot everywhere. Many of our staff and slaves had already vanished, but the few who were left were the good ones, the loyal ones. I prayed we'd be able to care for them and perhaps even pay them, in the coming days. Or perhaps the ones left were the spies. Akil slunk around the perimeter of the room like a cat. A thing that looked human but was not. A cat that wasn't a cat, a bird that was not a bird.

He let his tawny gaze slide across my eyes. He wouldn't look full at me. Our night in the reed nest meant nothing. My feet had barely healed and he had already forgotten our friendship.

Miss Marsh said, without bothering to honey-coat it, "Petru would not have done what he did to the boy unless he'd got what he wanted. I don't blame Eneko, and neither should you. I have seen men tortured, and they all talk, every one of them, unless they are lucky enough to die first." She looked at me with pity in her eyes.

I put my head down on the table and heard myself moaning. My heart was in a giant's hand, being squeezed dry of everything, everything... love, hope, happiness...

A hand on my shoulder made me shudder. Mother had stopped praying and gone back to crying. I pushed her away roughly. Did she regret using Eneko for her own and my father's purposes? Did she feel guilt at the suffering she had caused?

Later, Akil, as cat, crept away again, taking whatever circuitous route he'd found to avoid the guards around our villa and get to Eneko's side. He returned after dark.

As Akil the boy again, he told us what he had learned. "Eneko is alive, but I don't think for long. I could smell the bad blood eating him." Akil looked square at me then, at last. His eyes showed nothing, not even fatigue. "Don't weep for him, Vara Svobodová. He goes to meet his god."

The next morning I gazed morosely out an upstairs window, thinking of the caged nightingale I'd seen in the mountains. It sang when it should have wept. Perhaps when a bird sang, it was really crying. For its mate, for its young eaten by cats, for the nasty, short, little life to which it was doomed. How bitterly the nightingale must regret bartering away her teeth.

I felt my mother approach, or perhaps I simply recognized her footsteps, but suddenly there she was next to me, an ominous presence.

Stubbornly not looking at her, I said, "The God of madness has thrown fire into Petru's mind and burned out his sense."

"Don't pity him," she said. "It's a trap."

"I don't pity him. I fear him as I would a rabid dog."

She glanced sideways at me, and I could suddenly feel something bad coming. It did. "Your father has been kidnapped."

"Kidnapped! What? By whom?"

"Whom do you think? Petru, of course. I received the message just now—Miss Marsh read it to me. *Kidnapped.* Bah. It's a ruse. He thinks I am stupid, wants me to let him *negotiate* for Jameel's freedom. I had to play along for his courier's sake, and replied offering all the money and credit I have in exchange for my husband's life."

"You can't do it! He will take the money and kill him anyway!"

"Of course he will. Whore-mongering bastard, he has my man." She clenched her fists until the bones showed white, and I saw the skeleton that was within us all, waiting for our flesh to be devoured.

"I will find a way to get Jameel-my-husband back," she whispered. "There must be a way."

Later, Akil found me. I was sitting cross-legged under the sheltering branches of a lemon tree, laden with ripe fruit, in a far corner of the kitchen gardens, where I'd hoped I would have some privacy. He folded himself beside me on the stones, which were littered with dried leaves and fallen fruit. The lemon tree needed water. Our villa was already being neglected.

Akil said, "When I found your friend Eneko, and he understood who I was, he tried to tell me something. He took my hand and with his finger drew shapes on my palm."

Oh, Sisters have pity. My throat ached at the thought of his poor groping hands, that once rattled a tambourine under stars he could no longer see. "Do you know what they meant?"

Akil shrugged. He looked the same as always: neutral with an edge of unpleasant arrogance. I was starting to hate him for all he had, even though it wasn't much. Eneko, if he were lucky, would soon die the painful, squalid death of an ordinary human. His soul would flee to the darkness.

"The shapes looked like this." Akil drew his finger across the dusty ground, forming angular lines. Words. I tried to decipher them, then realized that of course it was his native Vasconi. *Mezedez barkaidazu.*

I whispered, "They're words... they mean *please forgive me.*"

I covered my eyes. Eneko was apologizing for betraying us. He had given his life, and all his valour and brilliance had ended in nothing. It was I who should forgive him. I bent over and wept.

And yet... he had given Petru what he wanted. Eneko had

possessed a secret that was worth a life. My father's whereabouts.

Akil unexpectedly placed his good arm around me. He pulled me close and murmured in my ear. "He was delirious. It meant nothing." Had Akil actually been moved to comfort me? How very odd.

I knew how difficult it was for this strange, damaged boy to touch another, even his own *alanbir*. I tried to pull away, but he pulled me tighter. "I wish I had known your Eneko Saratxaga. I would have been proud to call him friend."

I didn't know what I felt about Eneko anymore, and I wanted to ask Akil what he thought of all this. What did this intrigue and pain mean to a ghost in solid form? But Akil could only put up with closeness for so long.

Abruptly he let me go, but not before I again felt that odd and disturbing melding I'd felt on the road from Linqua. Touching Akil was dangerous.

"We should tell my mother. She needs to know."

But Mama was asleep, and I couldn't bring myself to wake her. She would only try to think of some stupid plan to free her husband.

Akil returned to his *alanbir*'s side, and I left the dusty corner to find my Pada, and was surprised to see him up and at work. Coughing fitfully and grey as a rag, he was at one of his big messy desks furiously writing letters, sealing and addressing them, and handing them over to Saskia. She had three already and was waiting for the next. Grandfather knew a lot of clever, interesting and even important men, but I think we all knew none were influential enough to help us now. They were scientists and scholars, and what we needed was lawyers. Or assassins.

I stood beside him, watching the reflected light of candles in the glass vessels set haphazardly here and there. I loved his workroom. It was like entering a different world, one of thought and logic. Hate and war were not necessary; kindness and curiosity were.

And revenge. Revenge was necessary.

I could feel my insides growing hard and cold, like the soft mud of an autumn road firming up against winter. Ice and stone.

He sighed and rubbed at his quill nib with a bit of grimy lint, waving Saskia away. She descended the stairs, clutching the letters to her bosom.

As soon as she'd gone, he beckoned me close. "My balloon, Vara! Remember? It's ready, all it needs is its basket and the fire to heat the air, and it will rise up and carry you and Ragna away!"

At my look of horror, he talked even faster. "You must flee! He has Jameel, he can't have you too." He wrung his hands, panting and wild-eyed. "It will work, I swear it. The silk balloon will rise, and the winds will take you to safety."

It was insane. I could see so many ways it could fail. But all I did was nod and smile, and tell him how clever he was.

Within the hour six soldiers came and confiscated the balloon plus every other scrap of silk they could find, including clothes, and every basket in the villa, small or large. They hauled the whole lot of it out into our forecourt and set it ablaze. The pile burned astonishingly fast, and filled the air with limp, clinging black shreds.

We went down to watch the destruction, morose and sick. No use to object; we could trust no one. All that work, for nothing.

By now I was in the mood to hate everyone, including Eneko. Was I becoming just as bloody-minded as my mother? Already I had assigned my darling to the nether world, and was thinking only of myself and my family, and how I might squeeze the last drops of usefulness from a dying man. I hated my Pada for trying to pacify me, I hated my mother for being beautiful and fierce and utterly helpless, and I hated Akil for being Akil.

Repenting my harsh thoughts, I took my grandfather in my arms. He laid his head on my shoulder, as if in exhaustion. He felt cold, the thin skin moving loosely over his old bones, and his sparse grey beard was trembling.

Mama and I were good for nothing. We were like plunder waiting to be taken, food waiting to be eaten, marble statues waiting to be crumbled to dust and turned into mortar for prison walls. We were no use until we were dead—until then we were a liability.

I wondered where Akil was now. If he was as smart as he thought he was, he was dragging his *alanbir* and anything they could carry away into the shadows, never to return.

Saskia, back from her errand, ran into the smoky courtyard then, crying. She said, "The letters, my lord—The soldiers tore them from my hands. I'm sorry—"

She was nursing one elbow, and my grandfather took her in his arms. "Are you hurt?"

"No, only a little. But—the letters, they will be read!"

"I was a fool to try to send them. It is not your fault."

She wept into his neck, and I knew that she really loved him. "As I tried to slip past the guards, I heard them say that fighting has started in the north. They—they say Petru has taken the warehouses at Toulouse, and is close to gaining two of the biggest mills. He'd have enough flour to feed his whole army... They say he's trying to cut off Ludvik's supply chain before marching north. He can be everywhere at once! H-he can read our minds—" She began to gasp.

"He can do no such thing, my dear." He patted her back, but she only wept harder.

"No one was on the streets but soldiers! They said that all the Imperials have been ejected from the Villa Ventonge with their eyes put out, and the workmen chained to their forges."

The Villa Ventonge was the small fortified city just north of Perpignan, renowned for its production of high-quality sword-steel and armour. Obvious even to me that it he'd want it. Petru had planned well, hoarded his gold and his favours, aligned his forces. It was war, and he had the Gods on his side.

My father had been doing the same thing. But he had failed. He lacked ruthlessness. With no one in his way, Petru would succeed.

We were well trapped now. If we did manage to slip free, we'd find ourselves in the middle of a war. A war fuelled by the Gods. Their evil dripped down upon us sorry little folk on Earth, and drove us mad.

Even Akil was trapped. Though he could fly away, he would never leave his *alanbir*. I didn't think he could do that, even if he wanted to.

None of us would be safe until Petru was dead.

That night, in my bed, I opened my eyes to thin, wavering darkness. Something had awakened me. The air prickled and sang, as if a storm blew close. A man was standing over me.

His face became clear. It was my Pada Josef. He had a knife in his hand.

With a thrill of horror I looked past him to see if my younger self was floating overhead, watching. I wanted to tell her that she must not waste her life in trying to avoid her death. For it was to come, as foreseen. But I saw nothing.

A soft whispering in my ears turned to a roar, as if from many huge throats.

The Gods breathed all around me. I heard them laughing. They laughed at my fear as they fed upon it. I bared my teeth and laid my head back. Whatever came next, I would find the strength for it. Somehow.

My Pada Josef's tears fell hot on my neck. "Vara," he said. "Forgive me."

PART TWO

In a time beyond time, I felt myself shrink and diminish like a droplet of water under the hot sun. A pitiless heat that drove me down and down through dust into darkness, a darkness so deep and gleaming with power that it became all light, every lamp and fire and blazing sunrise I'd ever seen. This—at last—was my time of dying. And of rebirth. And the girl that was Vara was no more, but was something new under the sun.

Chapter Twenty-Two
ALL FROM DUST

The Nightingale took up a shard of stone in her beak.
Knife-sharp, black and wicked as the horn of Abbu, it cut
her tongue.
She welcomed the small pain. Drank her own blood.
And the shard became a tooth within her mouth, and the
tooth multiplied.

Her arms clutched at nothing. At dust, at the air itself. Someone had been holding her, comforting her while she cried. But why? And who? Part of that someone's essence stayed with her, in her skin like ointment. An eerie wind whined around her, and a distant thrumming as if thunder rolled around the world, far off at the edges.

Everything was wrong. Her arms were thin and dirty. Her feet were bare, she saw, planted in the dust of a roadway. But where, and how? There was an old woman, she thought, somewhere... she looked around her. Nothing. Had there really been a grey-haired crone possessed of sad blue eyes? That was wrong too. She looked down at herself. A small body, naked but for a filthy breech-cloth. A street-boy. She wore the body of a street-boy.

She fell to her knees. Her neck sang with the slice of steel, the memory of a knife in the hands of an old man who loved her. Who had killed her, and laughed.

She fell as if from sleep into wakefulness, with a gasp. Changed. Shifted.

She was walking. Dust and sand clogged her eyes and nostrils. She blinked, feeling the residue of tears, and blew out snot onto the road she trod upon. Her eyes cleared. The sun, silvered by low clouds, was still hot enough to make her sweat.

She had been dreaming of a dirty little boy crying for his mother. It was as if she saw him, ahead of her on this road.

The tears, and the memory, evaporated.

Who am I? She looked down at herself once more and saw that she was a woman now, tall, dark as polished walnut, lithe and slender as a willow but strong as an oak. Was she now fifteen or fifty? It didn't matter.

She walked a narrow path bordered on one side by poisonous spurge-olive and dry, spiky juniper bushes, and on the other by a steep drop to a desiccated creek bed. Behind her were fields where skinny goats foraged busily for whatever they could wrest from the rocky soil. Her hammered bronze bangles and cuffs, symbols of her status and freedom, jangled at each step. A weight dragged at her side, and she found it to be a long and very sharp knife in a sturdy sheath, its tang wrapped tightly in well-worn leather. A thin woven cord extended from the handle in a short loop. It was the right size for her wrist. Good, she thought. I have a tooth.

The air was dry and full of the juniper's clean scent.

She knew that the juniper berries could be harvested and sold to midwives and other herbalists. But how did she know it? She could remember no teacher, and no time when she had not been walking along the path... but perhaps there had been an old man who liked to drive facts into her head. Grey-bearded and clever...

The old man had loved her, and taught her all sorts of arcane things which she had assumed were useless. The woman stopped walking, remembering something else. The old man had pressed a knife to her throat.

She clutched her neck, bangles clashing like the sound of distant swords. *I am Vara.* She collapsed and huddled low in the dust, the smell of juniper stinging her nostrils.

Her own dear Pada was there in her eyes, over her in the darkness, a howl of anguish on his lips. *Forgive me...*

The winding, dusty path was rarely used, so she was able to cry alone for a nameless time, remembering.

She changed. Shifted. Fell again, and kept on falling. No—flying, high in the air. She was a bird. Dreaming again, only dreaming. Remembering a vision. But the sky was close, huge and white, above and around her. She *was* a bird. She had wings, and they were beating in perfect rhythm to the flutter of a tiny heart in a tiny brown breast.

In the sky were billowing clouds that made shapes of themselves, faces, buttocks, breasts, oxen and dolphins and men, then dissolved only to form again. Relentless, thick and thunder-full, stroked by lightning.

Wind buffeted her. Updrafts from the pale, baked limestone far below, crosswinds from the ocean that she could see if she turned her head. Her bird vision was very sharp. The horizon lay like the rim of a platter all around her, curling into the grey-blue distance. She was flying east, she could tell this easily because birds had a magic stone in their heads that told them north from south, and let them fly to their mates and children without even the need for stars.

But she had no mate or children. She was empty of love, bereft of family and alone here in the sky.

I am Vara. Her wings knew how to work, at least, though she hadn't always known the art of flight. She had gathered bits of air and cloud and floating dust and made her wings. Her nostrils, edged with the most delicate of hair-like feathers, drew in layered scents from below. Olive groves, thick and warm. Sweet orange trees and grape vines whose gleaming leaves and ripe fruit made her want to plunge into their jewelled branches.

She was a bird, hanging in the middle of the hot dry air.

Panic seized her, and her thrumming heart went cold. She had made a terrible mistake. Her wings suddenly forgot the art of flight.

She fluttered ground-ward, flipping like a leaf, so small and light that the air slowed her, but not so light that she could escape the pull of gravity.

Her wings would not obey her mind. The ground rushed up and she despaired for her life, but suddenly a looming darkness was in the way. She struck it with a gasp of fear and surprise, finding she could cling with her small talons to the crisp, dense blackness. Feathers!

She had landed upon the back of a huge bird. Or perhaps it had flown up to catch her. Had it pitied her? Or was it about to eat her? Panting, she clung to the stiff glossy feathers between the beating wings and rode the huge creature down to land under a pine tree.

A golden head turned and looked at her, its great beak clacking. Feathers ruffled and slid into place as the bird folded its wings and shook her off its back. She hopped down to the needle-carpeted ground.

"Thank you," she said. Her piping, tiny voice sounded ridiculous in the booming air. Everything was so big.

"You are welcome, Vara."

She found herself huddling down in a fluff of her own brown feathers. Vara.

Vara is my name.

Oh gods above, oh heavens pity me. It has come to pass.

I am *resura*.

And somewhere in the city of Perpignan, a man lay dying. The pain would not let go. Every jagged, glutinous swallow, every laborious breath, was a shriek in the everlasting night. His hands would not stop groping away at his own miserable body, trying uselessly to rub sight into sightless eyes and pull words from a tongueless mouth.

Eneko Saratxaga was ready to die. He was willing to take his chances with whatever gods were looking down at him, sipping his pain and gnawing at his regret and sorrow. They loved that sort of meal. He was a banquet for the lying gluttons. If he had ever loved the gods, he did so no longer. He had been sorely mistaken about their benevolence.

He hadn't the strength to turn himself on the thin pallet his keepers had laid him on, days ago. They made desultory efforts to clean and feed him, for which he was not grateful. He knew he was feverish, for delirium had already caught him in its poisoned claws.

It wasn't really a giant scorpion hanging over him, prodding and stinging him until he begged for death. It was only a man inside the hard, spiny skeleton of the desert creature, bearing its cold insect heart instead of a hot human one. Such a devil-spawned creature cared nothing for pain.

It liked pain.

He'd told the scorpion everything he knew. And more.

And when the cat had come and nudged him so insistently with its small cold nose, he had wanted to tell it everything too. But then it wasn't a cat, it was a man, a man who told him that, yes, he would die, and very soon. But he would not die in vain.

Eneko doubted that.

Chapter Twenty-Three
THE MEMORY OF STEEL

The eagle became Akil the cripple, and the little bird—a nightingale who was Vara—became Boy, under the hot sun of midday. She couldn't remember how she did it. The threaded clouds were still there, seen and not-seen; she could feel them as if they were creatures hunting her. Thunder like shouting voices sounded from afar, telling tales she couldn't understand.

Where am I, Akil? she cried. It wasn't her own voice. *Who am I?*

Glimpses of the hillside across from them glittered between the branches they hid behind, and suddenly she knew where she was. The little boy whose body held Vara's mind and soul hugged its knees and made itself look about. *Think. Remember.*

There were workers over there among the olive trees, and they were familiar to her. There was old Emil, his favourite blue hat marking him out. And Luc, and Joan, Luc's only child, who looked very pregnant. Vara felt a throb of homesickness at seeing them, for they were the ones who had presented her with the biggest, most luscious bunches of grapes they could find, the most perfect peaches and apricots when they were at the peak of ripeness. They had smiled on her from their wise, sun-dark faces and laughed as she stuffed her mouth with sweetness.

They were on family land west of the city, above the Red Kite orchard, which was the highest on this south-facing slope. Family tradition gave bird names to their various fields and orchards, so there was Red Kite, Black Kite, Kestrel, Purple Heron, Oystercatcher, and quite a few more. Jameel ibn Hayyan al-Kindi had always said grape vines would be better on Red Kite, instead of the olives, but the venerable trees had been here many hundreds of years and it would be very unwise to even think of cutting them down.

The Gods would be displeased.

The men and women who today beat and combed the trees for their fruit were whipped by soldiers, and were working without rest. All the bird-fields were under Petru's control now, and their bounty was being hauled off to feed his armies.

The cripple Akil and the ragged boy sat hidden in the trees as they watched the guards and the workers. Vara, the little urchin lad, had to turn away. Why did she still feel the wrenching pain of sorrow and pity, now that she was a spirit being? The whole miraculous thing was a cheat. She rubbed her throat.

She had to confess the error she'd made to someone, and Akil was the only one around. Her throat was whole, but her tokens were gone. Eye, Owl and Tooth. Around the neck of a dead girl, they'd most likely been stolen, or burned along with her old body. Or tossed into a mass grave. She'd never know what happened. Her own true self, gone. The horror of it bent her double. All her luck was gone. All the lore and love and history held in those three little things, gone. Her hair, her skin, her eyes and lips. All gone. Everything.

Akil watched impassively as the boy hid his face in his hands, wailing. He waited until Vara, whom he knew was inside that scrawny brown body, recovered a bit and sat up again to stare bleakly at the distance.

He didn't try to comfort her. There was no comfort now.

"Akil," the boy finally said, "I made a terrible mistake. I chose the wrong form."

"This little boy, this street beggar? What is wrong with him?"

"No... I mean that one of my shapes was supposed to be a snake. I'm boy, bird, and woman. I was supposed to be a snake so I could kill Petru. The very first thing I did as a *resura* was stupid and selfish. I've betrayed my family!" Again she bent and sobbed.

And knew that her repentance was false. She had known all along that she would never take the form of a snake. Her dutiful intent to do as her mother wished had been at the front of her mouth, but the stubborn knowledge of what she was going to do crouched in the back of her mind like a bear in a cave. And when the time had come to fulfill her intent, the bear had emerged.

Akil poked at the dust with a stick, making lines and circles. He wished Vara would stop crying so much. It was a waste of time. "What's done is done," he said at last.

She looked up. "Why should you care, anyway? You have an *alanbir* who loves you and will forgive you anything! I have no one." A bitter laugh escaped her, incongruous from the mouth of a child.

"No *alanbir*? No person or God has taken you?" His eyebrows went up. "This is very odd...consider yourself blessed, if you like. At any rate, it's too late to lament now. I can help you, if you wish." He tossed a pebble up and down in his one good hand. "There are many ways to kill a man."

She wiped her cheeks. After a while, she said, "Akil, why wasn't I clever enough to think of a name for myself? I can't be Vara in this body."

Akil glanced down at her, his tawny eyes half-shielded by his thick black eyelashes. It felt strange to her, to be small, for as Vara the girl she had been as tall as Akil. And proud of it, happy to look down benevolently upon those not so blessed. Now she was a child, and with a boy's parts under the breech-cloth too. She hadn't thought of that, before.

Also, she had never noticed the thin wavering above Akil's head, before. It was like a heat shimmer. Sometimes she could see it, against a dark patch of leaves for instance; most of the time it wasn't there. The shimmer seemed to rise into the air like a thread, curving in the wind but always pointing east. Toward Perpignan. Toward his *alanbir*?

She had checked, and there was no shimmering above her own head. She picked up a stick and drew a jagged line in the dust. Then she wiped her small palm across it. The grit and dust didn't stick to her skin unless she willed it to. "I don't need a human name any more. I'm not human, and I never have been. And now I look like a boy, but I am a woman."

Akil said nothing.

Vara contemplated her fate as the shadows of leaves and branches moved across her thin little arms and her bare brown feet. She felt a horrible, welling grief for what she had lost, like hot oil inside her. She must swallow it down before it sickened her.

Akil said, "So, when you awakened as *resura*, you met an old knife sharpener."

She nodded glumly. "I think it was my mother, in one of her forms. She didn't say so, but I... I could tell. She looked at me as if she wanted to stuff words in my head, just as when she was alive."

For of course she was dead now. Petru must have killed Ragna Svobodová by now... did her mother belong to him? How could she tell? The hot oil rose, and she swallowed it down. "She comforted me, and I was about to talk to her and ask her questions, and then suddenly I was someone else. A Moorish woman, walking along a dusty road. Then I was the little bird you saved." The visions that had plagued her before her death. After a pause she said, "What would have happened to me if you hadn't caught me? If I'd fallen to the earth?"

Akil shrugged, tossed his drawing-stick into the bushes, and leaned back. "Nothing, I think. We cannot die."

"I had thought that would be a good thing."

Akil smiled sadly. "You are already learning the way of the *resura* folk."

She snarled and began to beat him with her small fists, but he changed into an orange cat and crept into her skinny little-boy lap, and began to nuzzle her face as she bent weeping with humiliation and fear. "I don't want to learn," she sobbed. "I want to go back! I want to go back!"

Akil kneaded Boy's bare belly with his paws, purring roughly though his tail lashed back and forth in agitation. "Hush," he said. "You cannot go back."

It was odd to hear words from a cat, so strange that she almost laughed. Also, he sounded just like her mother when he said hush. How she hated him! But at the same time she loved him. At least he'd made her stop crying. He sprang off her lap to claw briefly at a tree trunk, shredding off bits of grey bark with his claws, then shifted his form back to human.

Vara couldn't tell how he did it, it was so fast. She blinked and he was there.

Akil settled himself once more on the ground. "I'm sorry you're unhappy and afraid. I'm sorry you couldn't take the form you were assigned."

Dejectedly she hung her head. "I'm afraid of what is to become of me. Who will be my master? I don't understand. Have I been claimed by a man or a God, and just don't know it yet?"

He cocked his head to look at her, and at the air above her head. After a long time he said, "You'd know it if you belonged to a God. For one thing, we wouldn't be sitting here talking." He eyed her calmly, contemplatively. "You would be in such thrall that you could not speak without permission."

She began to chew on her fingernails.

Akil continued, relentlessly. "If a man has caught your soul... I also don't know why you are still here with me. A man would be using you already. A God might bide its time." He shrugged. "When my life shifted into this magic realm, it was obvious to me right away that Carolina Marsh and I were joined." He thought for a while. "I can't describe it... I simply always knew where she was, and how far away. If too far, I felt compelled to reach her, and to listen to everything she said. For a long time I clung to her as if I were drowning, mostly in my cat shape." He snorted, remembering the sick, damaged little being he once was, who had at last found a mother he could love. She had carried him around in her arms as he purred and mewled. He must obey her, but he could also love her.

"It could be that you are a free *resura*."

She stopped fidgeting and sat still. "I didn't know there could be such a thing. Free... I have never really been free. I belong to my parents, my family. My home."

The tears she had shed had vanished, into the air or into her *resura* skin. She looked up at him and, squinting, saw the tiny glimmers above him, the little shreds of sun-glitter that made it appear as though he was attached by an ephemeral thread to something. A puppet-master. A thought, a wish, a command that would make him dance. She tried to keep her breathing steady.

"What does it mean to be free?"

Akil looked away. "I'm the wrong person to ask."

Later Akil changed to an eagle and flew away, and the boy Vara sat hugging her knobby knees trying to imagine what it would feel like to be permanently bound to someone she didn't even know. Or some*thing*. A God. Akil had told her, when she'd still been human and had been relentlessly questioning him, "As I lay dying, Miss Marsh warned me that a God might get me. I said I hoped it would be the God of Ennui, for then it would get bored and leave me alone." She had laughed at his remark, and been rewarded with a slight curve of his lips.

Most people believed that the Great Gods were so unlike people as to be unknowable, and some denied that they even existed, deriding those who claimed to see or feel them, so Vara gave up thinking about them. Instead she tried to remember how to make herself turn into a bird again. How had she done it last time?

She had to find out what had happened after her own death. If the *resura* Knife Woman was indeed Ragna Svobodová, as Vara believed, then to whom did *she* belong? Petru? Some crazy God?

She closed her eyes and tried to concentrate on the *resura* lore her mother had so doggedly driven into her head. It had been dismayingly sparse. "I have these three forms," Vara whispered to her small knobby knees. "I can use them. Boy can run and climb, and steal things, and pass unnoticed almost anywhere. Freewoman can converse and negotiate—men will listen to her, and soldiers will be afraid to kill or imprison her. Either of them could carry poison, and Freewoman has a knife."

She opened her eyes and looked to the sky. "And Bird can fly above everything, and peer in windows, and hop and creep close to anyone she wants. For who will fear a tiny bird?"

But a *falci* adept could sniff out the truth.

A sudden vision of Petru Dominus thrusting her into a stone box and clapping the lid on it made her heart clench. For a moment she was surprised that she even had a heart, but then thought, well, there is nothing to stop a heart from beating in this realm. No one to say I can't have one.

But from where did it come? Did she have red blood, and would it spill if she were cut? To test this, she took a thorn from a nearby acacia tree, and after a moment of hesitation, jabbed it into her smallest finger. It hurt only a little, and a tiny drop of blood welled up.

She smeared it away with her thumb, and wondered. *I can bleed. I can feel. What is the advantage of being dead?*

The advantage was *now I can't be killed anymore.*

But then she had a horrible vision of her throat being slit again, and again, always to heal and always there to be opened once more. And she wondered where her real body was now. Perhaps it lay somewhere, cleaned and dressed properly for burial... perhaps someone had managed to get her earthly remains back from Petru. Most likely not.

She might have been burned. Or dumped in a mass grave with lepers and heathens. Did she really want to find out?

She spent the night under the trees, curled like a dog in a pile of leaves. She had thought she would suffer the long dark hours shivering with cold, but the night air didn't seem to affect her. She didn't even feel hungry. She prodded herself with the acacia thorn now and then, not enough to break the skin, just to prove to herself that she still existed.

One thing she vowed: she would find her necklace and its three tokens. The only thing that would stop her was if it had been burned. But most likely someone had taken it. Stolen it. She would find her necklace and somehow keep it close.

Akil flew back at last, shortly after dawn, landed heavily beside her and did his magic shift to human form. She had clapped a hand over her eyes against the dust his huge wings had kicked up, but peeped between her fingers to watch him change. It was as her mother had said. He became a whirl of darkness, a dizzying centre that sucked her vision down and around, then back again to see his familiar form: the homely cripple.

He didn't seem so homely now that he was her only friend. She reached out her small brown hand for his one good one. His long, strong fingers twined with hers, and suddenly she became very conscious of her flat bare chest, complete with tiny brown nipples. Quickly she let his hand drop. When she'd fixed upon this form, the boy she envisioned had been clad as usual for street-urchins in hot weather: a close-wrapped breech-cloth and nothing else.

That had been another mistake, and Vara vowed to remedy it if she could, though a little boy draped modestly in a shawl would be ridiculous. Right now she was too confused and dispirited to try changing to her Freewoman form. Perhaps her forms could be changed, improved upon... though she'd never regain her true human body.

But this was a stupid thing to worry about now.

"Where have you been, Akil?"

"I went to Miss Marsh," he said. "She called me, but I would have gone to see what was happening anyway."

"Well? Tell me!"

"War is happening, that's what. Petru left the city two nights ago—"

"I don't care about war! Tell me what happened to my mother—tell me of Jameel-my-father!"

"I know only what my *alanbir* told me, and what I could see as first I flew, then crept as a cat into the city. I know nothing of your parents." He looked away from her, frowning as if annoyed, and Vara wanted to slap him. But it would look idiotic for a small urchin boy to strike a man, no matter how petulant he was. Not that anyone was watching.

But, she reasoned, trying to still her urge to scream, she must learn to act the part she resembled. She steadied herself. "What of Miss Marsh? She's my friend as well as your mistress."

When he turned his eyes on her again, with a warmer look, she was surprised at how that meagre comfort lit her spirits, like a beam of sun. How pathetic, she reflected, that I've come to this.

"She has left your villa, along with Miss Saskia and Kai and some others, and found temporary shelter among the Uzmite Sisters. They do not intend to flee unless the fighting washes back from the north and Perpignan is threatened. She will earn her keep with them—and a place for the few relics she managed to carry away— by helping them tend the sick and old."

Vara smiled and clasped her hands together. "Ah! I knew she wouldn't run away. But she's wise to leave our home... and I am relieved to hear that Saskia and Kai are safe."

Her smile faded. Her home was probably being looted right now, though it seemed to matter less than she'd thought it would. You didn't love things, you loved people.

The next question would be very difficult. "What... what happened to my grandfather's body? Do you know?" She couldn't bear to think of the old man, all his learning and wit mashed to nothing by booted feet, and his frail old bones tossed in an unmarked grave. Her body, she knew from the vision, had been taken to Petru, a thought that made her shudder. What he'd done with it she might never know.

He shook his head. "I'm sorry, no. But I overheard Saskia and Kai whispering about pooling their money and buying his body back, should anyone admit to having it. And then seeing to his placement in your family's burial ground."

"Our crypt. We have a crypt." Sorrow was a heavy weight, like stones holding a soul close to those who loved it. Poor old Saskia, how red her eyes must be by now. "He gave his life for mine, Akil. He knew he'd be killed for what he did." Josef must have learned that Petru was after her that very night. And her mother too. Had

Ragna experienced visions of her death too?

She remembered her grandfather's triumphant laugh, which was probably what earned him the sword in his belly, and bared her teeth at the sky and the vicious Gods who dwelt there. Perhaps she really was free. If so, it was Josef, Count von Svobodá who'd assured it.

She didn't want to think of her mother's body. For she was dead now.

Akil let her sit silent for a while, for which she was grateful, but he kept glancing at her. Finally she asked, "What is it? Why do you look at me so?" She should be trying her skill at changing form, trying to fly again.

He dropped his head as if caught peeping through a window, but then he looked directly at her again. For a moment she wondered if he was brave and honest, or merely clever. "You," he said, "the little boy, appear to be about the same age I was when I first met Miss Carolina Marsh. Perhaps nine or ten years old. I was remembering myself as I was then."

"What were you like? Do you remember very much?"

His eyebrows rose in a sort of half-grimace. "Unfortunately I do. I think I don't want to talk about it after all." He looked away. "It's just... you are such an innocent. You know nothing of the world."

At this she bristled. "That's not true! I know all sorts of things—languages, geography..."

"That's not what I mean. You can have a head stuffed with facts and still be as ignorant as a kitten. And as easily swallowed up by the dogs you'll soon find are out there waiting to tear you to bits."

"Well, they can't. I'll fly away. Or I'll be Freewoman—her arms are so strong, she could kill any dog."

"You know when I say dogs, I mean men."

"I don't fear men." That was an outright lie. She feared Petru, and she had feared the two scoundrels who had almost ravaged her. But Freewoman could best the likes of them. The Freemen and Women had gods above them, watching and ready to smite any so foolish as to attack them.

But then she wondered whether that divine protection extended to one who was not really what she seemed. Freewoman was an image that might fool a human, but not a God. Would they punish her for her deception?

And why, now that she was in the realm of the dead, did life seem to be going on as normal? Men picked fruit, other men went to war, ordinary little birds chirped overhead. The ordinary sun beat down, and the grit of dust dragged under her fingers.

Akil saw the look on her face, and instead of baiting her into further displays of the ignorance she so hotly denied, got up and pulled her to her feet. "You had better learn to fly, little bird. I won't carry you anymore."

She felt a shrinking reluctance, remembering her panic when she'd fallen from the sky. To be so high, with only feathers to sustain her... she had thought herself unafraid of heights.

"How should I do it? How did I do it before? I can't remember!" Her teeth chattered as she hopped around in the dappled sunlight, tentatively flapping her arms.

"Stop doing that. It looks stupid." He grabbed her arms and made her stand still. "Just focus. Turn your mind to what you want... close your eyes if it helps. Didn't your mother teach you anything?"

Perhaps not the right things. She focused. A bird. A small, insignificant bird. With the soul of an ancient shark... she started to feel a hollowness inside, and opened her eyes.

Akil scowled at her and she closed them again. The hollowness spread, sucking at her belly like hunger. She started to fall, and flailed her arms uselessly, but kept her eyes shut. The hollow blackness increased from the inside out, and shrank her into a tiny fleck of life crouched on the dusty ground. A bit of chaff tossed from a pan of grain. She opened her eyes. Everything was huge and moving around her, and everywhere she saw danger.

Panic at being so exposed sent her springing upward and in an instant she found herself looking down at the treetops.

She was flying. She let out a squeak, her wings beating raggedly. She managed to flutter down and cling to a branch. Akil was looking up at her, grinning like a fool. Damn him.

She let go of the branch and tried again.

Without the slightest grace, she fluttered in a drunken circle and landed on Akil's shoulder. He looked at her, and grinned, and the size of his big crooked teeth almost made her fall to the earth again. He took her upon his finger and drew her close to place a tiny, careful kiss upon her beak.

She hopped away and found herself Boy again, sprawled on the ground panting.

Akil flopped down beside her and prodded her with a finger as if she were truly a boy, a little brother perhaps.

"Don't touch me, you, you—"

"Unnatural being? Spawn of Loki? What?"

The dirt she lay upon wouldn't even sully her skin, which should be sweaty. She could smell things, like the clean dark pine needles above her, and the coppery dirt under her hands. She could smell Akil too, with his comforting scent of oats and stone dust. She remembered when he'd held her close, on the road home, and how she'd felt the strangeness of his *resura* body. Formed of nothing but dust and air, it wanted to draw her in, use her substance in making his own. It had felt dangerous, seductive, and she knew she must not touch him without awareness of that danger. For her new body would seek to engulf his, just as his did to her.

She should be able to taste things. Last night she had tried chewing on pine needles, which should be astringent and bitter but were not. She'd found some sheep's sorrel, which normally was tangy as a lemon, but even it had no flavor. She wasn't hungry, nor was she tired.

If she were tired, she could sleep, and escape this strange new life for just a while.

What if she could never sleep again?

She bit her tongue to keep from crying. This is what I was born and bred for; I must embrace my life as if it were a treasure brought to me in the hold of a vast ship, across seas filled with eight-armed monsters.

She had done it, though. She had flown, and managed to land.

She knew where she must go next.

His pain seemed to have drained from him into the floor and away. Somewhere below, in the netherworld, a dark God was eating it.

Eneko's thoughts drifted to the girl again, as it did more and more. Guilt, sorrow. A grinding regret. At least the scorpion was leaving him alone.

The cat who turned into a man had come and gone, speaking soft, useless words. Yet he'd been heartened and soothed, momentarily.

What was the girl's name? Daughter to the estimable and rather frightening Ragna Svobodová... how lovely that girl had been. She had liked him, he'd seen it in her eyes and her blushing cheeks. He'd claimed a chaste little kiss from her. He hoped that Valkyrie mother of hers was guarding such a treasure. Vara, that was it. Though his eyes were gone, he still had his memories, supple and gleaming, falling like that girl's raven hair in strands that thinned and drew out into quavering lines of night-dark. The air was moving around him, hot and then cold, and he shivered.

A nightingale was singing, very close. It must be right outside the window. How soothing it was, to hear the little creature; he could almost imagine he was home, where birds sang all the time.

And then the liquid warble was right there, by his ear, as if the nightingale sang for him alone.

He could almost make out words in the song, but they drifted away. He thought of his mother and the songs she loved to sing, and he thought of that black-haired girl in the mountains, and he thought of the sugared almonds his father brought sometimes from the market... The pain wasn't nearly so bad now. He didn't even feel thirsty. And in his eyes were flashes of light, golden and quick, though he thought that couldn't be so, considering his eyes were gone. Then there was no more pain and no more darkness at all, and in his ears was the sweetest song he had ever heard.

And then he fell into soft white light, as if his eyes had grown back and could see the sun sail forth from the mist. He had his tongue and his voice again, and he sang out an answer to the nightingale.

Chapter Twenty-Four
KNIFE WOMAN

Boy sat with his back against the east-facing stone wall below a high balcony open to the elements. He had stopped crying hours ago, but he still sat there, staring at nothing, plucking idly at a crack in the ancient paving stones.

One of the women who had noticed him earlier came by every so often, suggesting that he might like something to eat, or that the streets were not safe and he should find a hiding hole. Her name was Agnes, she had lived in Perpignan all her life and was a widow now eking out a living in a charity-room, and she did not like what had been happening lately. Men and their wars. Children were fair game these days for work in the factories and mills, and one like this would be snatched soon if he didn't look out.

Agnes knew of course that the boy had no home; he was a street-boy, good for nothing. But she was a kind-hearted woman, concerned for such a sad little being, and had even tried to stop her friends from telling the boy too much about what had happened three nights ago.

He crouched, rocking on his skinny little haunches, over the place where the lady had fallen. He was stroking the stone with a finger, and then licking and sniffing it. Very strange. Even stranger was what he said.

"I can smell my mother here."

Agnes's heart had gone cold. It was the very spot... there had been blood spilled from the lady's poor broken head. Nothing now remained. The street had been washed clean. And that woman couldn't have been this boy's mother, for she had obviously been high-born, fair and soft, with her blonde hair streaming free. Perhaps she'd been kind to the boy, given him alms, and he'd remembered her.

An old woman pushing a barrow came along the street, a knife-sharpener by the looks of her tools and implements. A scrawny old vulture, but bright of eye. She stopped before the boy, who after a moment looked up at her. Agnes, who had been about to pull the lad up and drag him home for a bowl of bread and milk, faded back into the shadows.

At the sight of the knife woman, the boy burst into hopeless wailing once more. He jumped up and started to run away, but the old woman, surprisingly fast on her feet, caught his arm and pulled him close to her bosom. There he clung for a long time, while she stroked his curly brown hair.

Agnes, relieved to see that the boy had a protector, crept back to her small dwelling.

Boy helped the old woman push her barrow. The wheel squeaked, just as it had in Vara's vision. They trundled it around a few corners and down narrow streets, away from the cold bulk of Petru's palace. Finally they stopped and hunkered down on the edge of a public water-trough. Vara put her hands into the slow trickle from the aqueduct. She felt the silky coolness, but had no desire to drink. She still wasn't thirsty.

Knife Woman settled herself, arranging her dowdy skirts around her feet. What a pair they were, Boy thought: a withered crone and an underfed child. She should have become an elephant, able to force her way anywhere, trample over men and beasts alike. It would take a long time to force down an elephant, and during that time it could do a lot of damage.

She reached for Knife Woman's hand and held it to her lips. It was gnarled and cold, and had none of her mother's soft flowery smell. This new creature, this Knife Woman, smelled spicy and hard, like the fireworks her Pada had bought. A very odd and rather attractive smell. She couldn't call such a woman Mother. She couldn't tell if Knife Woman was in thrall to a God; surely not to Petru, for here she was free to roam about the city streets.

But perhaps that was all a trick.

"Eneko is dead," Vara said, and rested her cheek on that lumpy old hand.

Knife Woman didn't say anything for a while. Then she said, "There are people who say *it's the will of the gods* when someone dies. And often it is their will. But usually it's the work of man. We can't influence the Great Gods, nor can we get vengeance for the evil they do. But..."

Vara's small chin went up. "But we can get vengeance upon men."

Knife Woman nodded, and sighed deeply.

Vara, still not knowing if she had a real heart within her chest, nevertheless felt something contract in a throb of bitter melancholy. Eneko Saratxaga and Pada Josef might be gone forever into true death, but she and her mother still had means to stick a knife into the heart of evil. They were outside both death and life.

A question came to the front of her mind. But what if the answer was wrong?

"Knife Woman... when Petru had you..."

"When I died?"

"Yes. You changed. Into your new forms. I see one of your bodies now, but what of the others? You must have a deadly shape, a snake perhaps. Why didn't you use it?"

Knife Woman stiffened, then sagged again like the tired old crone she appeared to be. She said, "Do you mean, why didn't I rise from my death on the stones, fly up there like an avenging angel and kill that monster right then and there?" She furrowed her brow. "Let me ask you this: when you awoke in your new form as the street boy, where were you? What were you doing?"

"I... walked a dusty road. I think it was outside the city wall..."

"I found myself in the west quarter, where the fruit market used to be. All was empty, broken. The area was deserted. I was pushing my cart. I looked down and saw my hands..." Her voice choked and stopped. Knife Woman spread her gnarled fingers, the veins high as swollen rivers. "I knew that I was dead. Never again would I be... me."

Never again would she be the woman whom Jameel followed with his dark faun eyes. Gone was her golden hair, her rounded bosom, her silky limbs.

Vara placed her little brown hand into the old wrinkled one. "I'm sorry. I shouldn't have asked. Forgive me." She shuddered, and pushed the memory aside. She let go of her mother's hand, for in it she felt that same seething of particles she'd felt in Akil's body. Dust become blood and bone, air and mist forming eyes and heart and memory. So very strange... "So, some amount of time must have passed."

"It was the rest of that night and day, for evening was falling."

It didn't matter anymore. Any slim chance Ragna Svobodová might have had to spring up from her death and kill Petru was gone now.

"Do you know where my father is?"

Knife Woman closed her eyes. "No." Then she opened them, looking somewhere into a bloody distance. "But I will find out."

After a while Knife Woman got to her feet. She said, "We have much to do." She took up her barrow and begin to push it along the street.

Boy jumped up and ran after her. "Knife Woman! Wait! What are we going to do?"

No reply. She was being ignored, just as any child would be. It had been a stupid form to pick. She should have chosen an imposing, handsome man instead. Everyone hung on their words.

Vara stared resentfully after the crone, who bumped her heavy cart over the stones, muttering to herself. "I have made mistakes. So many mistakes. Oh, how foolish I have been." Vara was afraid for a moment that the old woman was going to cry. Of course not. This was her mother.

Wasn't it? How could she truly know?

Vara trailed after her. Some of Ragna Svobodová's mistakes had been with her own daughter, and she had to bite back sour reminders of how ill-prepared she was.

Perhaps she should trust nothing this *resura* said. Petru might own her. Or a God. She could be a slave, bound forever to an unseen master who sought to trick her.

She stopped walking and felt her mind run in little circles of fear and doubt. This familiarity that Knife Woman displayed might be a lure to gain her trust. She watched the air over the crone's grey head, but could see no indication of that little ripple, as was over Akil. Did it mean that her mother was linked to no one? What if she was not meant to see it? Could a God not cause one to see anything, believe anything?

Too many questions, not enough answers. She closed her eyes and thought about Freewoman. She *decided* to become Freewoman, tall and exotic, and after a few moments of dizziness and that strange hollow feeling at her belly, she did so. She opened her eyes, and felt for the knife in the folds of her silken robe. Still there. Still waiting to be used.

Freewoman hurried after Knife Woman, her long legs covering ground rapidly. The metal cuffs on her ankles chafed and dragged, but they were there forever so she had better get used to them. And to the knife. As that Arab man had tried fruitlessly to teach her, it could be an extension of her arm. In her arm and hand lived the memory, the *knowledge*, of how to kill.

Suppressing a shudder, Vara made herself stride along, head high. Her mother glanced at her sideways, snorted and shook her head, only to walk on stoically. Had she ever suspected her child would take on such a form? A woman, robed loosely in fine silk, dark as a Nubian slave, yet outside the law. Above it. Could she see how useful this form could be?

Together they pushed the cart, knives and tools rattling. The streets, empty due to the strict curfew, were dark. Oil was being requisitioned for the troops. They'd be spotted soon, and ordered off the street. Where would they go? To their own villa? A house full of ghosts.

Vara said, "I went to bed that night and woke in my vision, just as I had seen it. Everything happened as it was foretold." Her own grandfather. For her, an easier death would have been a quick stab to the heart. But she knew her old, sick Pada hadn't the strength. She'd seen how hard it was for butchers to penetrate the rib-wall of a sheep carcass. They had to put their backs into it. There were few options that night, for she had to be killed quickly and thoroughly.

Again she eyed the old woman beside her, and still she could see nothing to indicate thralldom.

Did that mean her mother was another free *resura*? Surely that was unlikely... unless it was due to some attribute of shared blood. I would be wise, Vara told herself, to forego placing my trust in this creature. Until I know more.

Knife Woman said, "My father was with me when Petru's men arrived, that last night of our lives. Neither of us could sleep. I'd gone downstairs just for the sake of useless activity... it was perhaps an hour after midnight. I knew that Petru would try for us that night, if he was going to at all. As a usurper and a rebel, he has a war to run. Things are happening fast. Knowing his own character, he can't risk trusting his generals. He wanted to collect his *resura* slaves to take with him.

"So I kissed my father goodbye, and whispered in his ear. It was time to do what was foreseen those years ago." Vara saw her mother then, in the old woman's expression. "He kissed me on both cheeks, and held me tightly for a moment. The soldiers arrived not long after that and took me to Petru's palace, to that big white room we were in before."

The room with the balcony overlooking the city. Vara nodded, and did not look at the old woman any more. She knew what was going to happen next, and felt the faint twinges of sickness in her belly. Just an echo, as scent was an echo of the taste of food. There were advantages to being *resura*.

"His men held me down while he had his way with me. I had

given up hoping I might bargain or buy my way out of what was coming, that I might get my husband back." Knife Woman glanced at the tall dark woman striding beside her, as if judging the strength of the soul within the unfamiliar body. She seemed to find it adequate, for she continued, her voice still flat and direct. "Though I prayed my soul would fly to Jameel somehow, I knew that I would belong to Petru soon, or to a God. If a God, I hoped it might be one who hated Petru." She barked a laugh. "There must be some. All I could do was concentrate on my own spirit, perhaps to hoard a tiny part of it to myself. Do you understand?"

Vara gulped and nodded.

"He choked me to the point of death, but then, over and over, he stopped and let me breathe. He drew his knife along my skin, just enough to draw blood. He was enjoying himself. I fought of course, I couldn't help it, though I was ready to die and take my chances by that time. I thought that perhaps there would be a moment when I could take one of my new forms—when I could strike him dead. Before I became his helpless slave." Vara could hear Knife Woman grind her teeth. "He told me that he loved me. He told me I was a witch who deserved to burn forever. He wanted me to lash him with his damned whip."

Vara wanted to stop her ears from hearing. But she loved her mother, and her mother needed to tell her this, needed to share the pain. To lessen it just a bit.

"Then he made a mistake. He left me for a moment to get more wine—he'd dismissed his men and killed his slaves so had no one to serve him. I sat up, tried to catch some breath and think of how to escape. Then..." Knife Woman bowed her head, reluctant to go on.

"What happened?"

"Soldiers came in, carrying two bodies. My father's, and yours, my dear child."

"So, you knew he could no longer hurt us. He hadn't captured my soul. Or he'd have been gloating."

Knife Woman nodded. "Petru went mad. Once he saw he'd lost his prize, he was like a berserker. First he killed the men who'd brought you. They stood there and let him. Such is the power he holds. He took your necklace, the one with your special tokens."

But then the old woman smiled. "But I knew that you were safely gone from this realm. Whether you were owned by a God I did not know... but he was distracted long enough for me to run to the balcony and throw myself over." Tears spilled down her thin, withered cheeks. "I had only a heartbeat to think of my darling Jameel, and of you."

Her scent had lingered on the unforgiving stone.

"Now I have an eternity to regret what I've lost."

They stood together, in the shadow of a familiar building: a shop the family had loved to visit. It had the best tea and cakes in the city, though now it was shuttered and dark. Even were it to reopen someday, they'd never eat cakes here again. What would her Papa, if he ever returned—if he still lived—think of this crone who bore Ragna's soul? She had ridden beside him under the sun, urging her horse ever faster. He would never see that wild girl again, nor pull her close in bed.

At last Freewoman asked, "*Did* Petru capture your soul?"

"Am I bound to that monster, you mean?" Knife Woman snorted rudely, then spat on the ground. "He had no luck that night." Her voice changed to a whisper. "No one owns me, child. No God holds my strings. And do you know why?"

Vara shook her head.

"Because none of the Gods wanted me. I could tell. They sniffed and poked and licked, but then they shunned me, and I think it was for taking my own life. Also, because I am too old, too stubborn and too evil to be desired."

"How can you be evil? Mama—"

Knife Woman turned away abruptly. "Hush. Don't call me that. You know nothing of what I can be. Do you have any idea what Jameel and I planned for you?" She covered her mouth with her hand as if to stop the words that might betray a purpose now irrelevant, a betrayal suddenly pointless.

She calmed herself, leaned close again and pushed a finger into Vara's chest. "Know this, my child: no king, no murderer, and no God owns us. We are free *resura*." She crossed her arms over her sagging breasts. "I learned nothing of this possibility, but I believe it must be dangerous. Surely blasphemous, and we may suffer for our freedom, but the fact remains: we have power and we can use it for ourselves."

Once more Knife Woman took up her cart and walked on, the wheel squeaking. Vara hurried in her wake.

"Do you plan to enter his barracks and sharpen swords? Really?"

"Yes."

"But a true sharpener of blades knows the quality of the metal by the sound it makes when it's ground or filed—Kai told me this. Her uncle was one such. It is not easy!"

"It will be for me. I'm but a harmless old woman, earning my bread by her labours. He is gone to war, and has taken that *falci* bitch with him, of course. He is not there to be killed, but I shall certainly glean useful information."

Vara thought about it. As she knew how to balance a vessel on her head, and how to cut a purse and steal food, so Knife Woman must have within her the knowledge she needed.

"You could learn of Jameel."

"Yes. Rumours of him swirl like clouds of flies around a butcher's shop. Each rumour has as much weight as a fly."

"How will you sort one fly from all the rest?"

She who had once been Ragna Svobodová smiled. Her teeth were yellow and crooked, and a few were missing. Vara bit her lips to keep from weeping. Her mother had had strong white teeth, and was missing not a one.

"When I have done it, I will tell you."

Akil went to the house of the Uzmite Sisters, drawn to his *alanbir*. It was where he belonged, and he knew it; not trying to ease the plight of a new-formed *resura*. No matter how lovely and infuriating she had once been.

His guise of homely cripple still served him well. He suspected that no one could fathom any *da resu* planning such a form, when he could have the most magnificent of bodies. He'd seen a few over the years, some strutting proudly in public, most lurking in shadows as if wondering how they had ended up this way. All doing the bidding of a master, but worth it to the vain. So many muscular princes and lithe dancers, so many lions, peacocks, dolphins and stallions. Why choose an ugly shape?

It kept him invisible, and that was what he wanted.

Akil ducked his head under the low stone lintel and entered the small anteroom behind which lay the Sisters' hospital. He could hear groans and coughing from the dim, stuffy rooms where the sick and dying lay. All those left behind when war scooped up the young and healthy. There were pregnant women, babies and children here too, their cries and shrill voices painful to his ears. He tried to ignore the smell.

The pull of his *alanbir* in his mind was greater than his pity for the sick and abandoned here at the once peaceful house of worship. He walked past them to the meagre courtyard, which held tethered goats and penned geese. The goats were being milked by two of the Sisters, bent over their pails in their drab hooded gowns. Everywhere was cluttered and dusty-dry, but fairly clean.

Carolina Marsh was somewhere out of sight arguing with the group's Mother. He could hear her sharp tones prodding the hard exhaustion of the Mother's voice.

The pull lessened as he drew closer. There was a balancing point in his relationship with his *alanbir*; too far and he suffered, too close and he suffocated. He knew the never-ending guilt she lived with, the constant desire to hold him close and weep over what he once was. But she was an intelligent woman, the most intelligent person he had ever met, excepting perhaps for Josef, Count von Svobodá. She would never drive him to madness with futile quests and impossible demands as some *alanbir* did to their *resura*.

Just as he caught sight of her—arguing with the Uzmite Mother over some point of medicine—a tiny bird fluttered to his shoulder. A nightingale. Vara! He hadn't felt her coming. Was it because she was free?

He didn't envy her. The air above her might seem clear, but

above the air was the realm of the Great Gods, and that was thick with purpose. He suspected now that there must be other free *resura*, also that they would hoard their freedom jealously, not calling attention to themselves.

The nightingale began to chatter in his ear, tiny peeping words like pecks, and he brushed her off. She flicked to a perch under an overhang, where once pigeons had nested until they were all killed by Petru's edict, or more recently caught and eaten. She shut up, but he could feel the force of her displeasure shoot from her beady eyes, and tried not to smile. She was a queenly little being, even as a drab brown bird hiding in the shadows.

He looked up at her, conscious of his withered arm. But she'd seen him as an eagle, she knew what he could do. He put a finger to his lips. "Meet me later outside, as Boy. I will bring you in and introduce you to the Sisters as an orphan in need of shelter."

She would have to be satisfied with that. He turned away and continued on to Miss Marsh, whom he took into his arms for a brief hug.

"Oh!" she said as he let go, tucking her sweat-stiffened tunic back into place. "Akil, that was unexpected. Where have you been?"

He let her go. Touching her—touching anyone—was something he didn't know if he enjoyed or not. Memories of touch still gave him waking nightmares. Since his kind did not sleep, his demons followed him in daylight.

"I have been with a friend of ours. A young woman once of the household of a trader and his north-born wife. She sends her best wishes for your continued health." A loud peep sounded from the shadows, and Miss Marsh started as a nightingale suddenly landed upon her shoulder, then fluttered back to its hidden perch.

Miss Marsh put a hand to her throat. He feared she was going to burst into tears, but that was not the sort of thing she did. He relaxed a little, knowing she understood him.

She peered into the rafters, uncertainly. "I know of whom you speak. She was a friend... tell me, Akil, how does she fare? I am sorely lacking in news, and I feared she was dead. In fact I was quite sure of it."

Had Miss Marsh seen Vara Svobodová's body? Would she know where it lay?

But that body was not Vara, not anymore. "She fares well. She has taken a journey into a new realm, and finds herself quite torn in pieces."

She nodded. "Ah... yes. So it was fated." She turned back to the Mother, who had given her attention to a sniffling child tugging at her apron. Akil could see the Mother's attempt to soothe the toddler's fears, but she was obviously tired to the bone, her face as sagging and grey as her habit. She hadn't noticed the bird.

Miss Marsh bowed at the woman, saying, "My former servant, Akil. I need talk with him. Mother... forgive me for my arguing nature. I shall follow your orders." Her brow wrinkled and her eyes grew narrow. "Though still I think—"

Akil stepped forward. "Miss Marsh is called away. Please forgive her, she is needed elsewhere." He took her arm. "Come."

She trotted beside him, waiting until they were out of earshot of the Mother before peppering him with questions. "What happened? Was that my dear Vara? Is she really... like you? Does... does she know her mother is dead?"

He ducked his head once more as they left the crowded shelter. "You can ask her yourself." She was used to his brusqueness, and only tightened her grip on his good arm as he hustled her out to the street.

When the ragged little boy ran up and clasped her around the waist, she almost shoved him away. But then she understood, bent down and took the boy in an embrace. "This is one of your new forms? Oh, my dear child..."

Akil kept watch, trying to look as stupid and harmless as ever. It was a disguise that worked well everywhere. Even Petru's rapacious army would pass him over as useless for fighting or work. And anyway, no one here was the slightest bit interested in a cluster of homeless beggars.

Instead of reentering the Sisters' sanctuary, which though relatively safe was probably the most crowded and clamorous building in the area, they walked to a deserted nook in the market, where once had stood the rolled and stacked ranks of a carpet-seller's wares. Gone now, either prudently removed by the vendor to who-knew-where, or looted. All they needed was a place to talk.

They had just settled into the shade, Akil and Boy squatting on their haunches, Miss Marsh sitting cross-legged like a cobbler, when Knife Woman appeared. She parked her barrow in such a way as to block the view from the street, and groaned to her knees beside the others.

Miss Marsh stared at the old woman for a long moment, then cast a desperate glance at Akil. "Akil, my dear," she whispered, "is this who I think it is?"

Akil in turn glanced at Boy, who hiccuped and wiped his nose. In a quavering voice, the boy Vara said, "Miss Marsh, this... this is Knife Woman." Boy huddled into a ball on the pavement. "I don't know what to say anymore... it's so confusing! I want my mother!"

Knife Woman watched impassively. "Hush. Stop that foolish crying." At this, Boy cried harder.

The old woman turned to Miss Marsh. "It is I, Ragna Svobodová. You need not fear me, for I am owned by no man or God."

Miss Marsh glanced at Akil, who nodded. "It is true," he assured her. "Though I don't understand it. Perhaps a blessing, perhaps not."

Knife Woman shrugged. "Perhaps all our lives are but a dream. Yet, I am glad to see you well and safe, Carolina Marsh. I have been much vexed by worry over my household... what of Saskia Lubodová? What of Kai, and old Eli, and that damned expensive cook I should never have hired, and all the rest?"

At this barrage of questions, Miss Marsh squeezed her eyes shut and became completely still. Akil knew her; this was her way of organizing her thoughts and emotions. He'd often thought she was too emotional, and silently approved of her efforts to accept reality. Though it was in her nature to explore the world and all its truths, she often railed against the obvious. A paradox.

Boy had stopped crying. Knife Woman—Ragna Svobodová—

wore the look of a hawk, her eyes focused piercingly upon Miss Marsh, and her mouth half open, as a hunting bird will do when it is scenting prey.

Ah, he thought. A hawk. Very good. He wondered what her third form might be. He and his *alanbir* had talked about it, Miss Marsh being of the opinion that Ragna Svobodová would do well as a giant python, the strangler snake. She had examined them in her travels, ones that had been killed by tribal hunters in Africa. They grew so huge they could kill a horse with ease. How perfect an end for Petru Dominus, slave of Saraf, to be crushed to death by his own symbol. Akil tucked his withered arm under the good one, rocking gently back and forth on his big splayed feet, and waited.

Miss Marsh finally opened her eyes, obviously trying to keep from weeping too. "Most of the house staff and servants have fled. The cook vanished that very night. Saskia and Kai came here at first, then left the city. They plan on making their way to Kai's old home in the mountains of Cymru, where her sister still lives. You need not to worry, they are clever and stronger than they appear. But, my dear friend, I am so sorry for what has happened. I... I know how you came to die, for everyone knew a noble lady throw herself to death from the palace." She laid a comforting hand on Knife Woman's knee. "Saskia and I were no success to claiming your body, or Josef's. Or Vara's. I am very sorry. I heard that all your earthly remains were take outside city gates to burn along with many other dead." She hung her head for a moment, and her lips trembled. "It is an outrage. People such as you... your bones should to interred with ceremony in your family crypt. I... I was very fond of Josef Svoboda. I don't know what has happened to his spirit, but I hope it is find peace."

At that, Boy looked up, his little snot-streaked face filled with surprise. "I remember! I remember what happened to him!"

Everyone looked at him—a creature whom they had almost forgotten was the girl Vara—and waited for him to elucidate. In the silence, Miss Marsh's stomach grumbled, and she made an impatient noise.

Akil knew he'd soon need to fetch her something to eat, or she would start to suffer. And her suffering would become his. He loved her dearly, but why did she have to be so... human?

Knife Woman beckoned to Boy, who shuffled closer and leaned against her legs. "Well, child—tell us what you know."

The urchin began to speak, and in his voice they could hear Vara's. Her maturity, her sorrow, her love. "I didn't remember it until just now. My Pada... my Grandfather Josef, gave his life to keep my spirit safe, and I belonged to him for a moment." Boy shook his head as if trying to rattle memory back to life. "I felt it, unmistakably. For that moment, before his soul fled, I... encompassed him. Or he held me in his hands... I can't explain it. We were joined, as a leg is joined to a body. I felt safe and warm. Happy, though I knew I was dead. Then he died too... he saw something, or heard a call, I think. And he let me go. Set me free from the bonds of an *alanbir*. The warm hands around me were gone."

Knife Woman let out a sigh and bowed her head.

Boy continued. "I feared Petru's soldiers might somehow capture his soul, even though he was never *da resu*. But when he let go of me, and of life, I felt him shoot past me like a horse running free, or like the hot wind of summer blowing by. It felt..." She stopped again, and moved her hands restlessly. "His spirit... it felt happy. Eager. My Pada Josef saw something ahead of him that he wanted to run to. I couldn't see it, but he knew that was where he wanted to go. Then there was nothing. It was hard for him to kill me. But he did it, and I am grateful."

Akil wondered if her gratitude would last. He closed his eyes and saw the beautiful girl he'd known, whose feet he had washed and bandaged, and felt the faint echo of the sorrow and pity a better man might have felt. But he wasn't a man.

Akil had never known his own father or grandfather. He'd never mourned them or regretted their absence, for he knew they would have done nothing to protect him. They'd have sold him just as fast as his mother had.

But Josef... everyone missed him, revered him. And he was gone into real death, never to return.

He watched Knife Woman and knew she would not let them waste time in mourning. She needed action and purpose. Most of all, she wanted to find her husband. He could see it in her tense movement, her scowl of frustration.

Akil felt a smile tug at the corners of his mouth, and banished it. She might not understand that he was like her: he wanted to kill someone. Not necessarily Petru Dominus. There were other candidates ahead of that man in Akil's memory. But he would do.

Chapter Twenty-Five
THE LITTLE BEARS

Miss Marsh, Vara could see, was fascinated by the *resura*, both her own Akil and the new unfettered souls she found herself allied with. They were so different from ordinary humans.

For instance, the matter of food. Vara watched the woman chew the flat-bread and greasy salted mutton that Akil had scrounged for her and felt no hunger. Not that this meal looked or smelled particularly appetizing. She could barely remember the delight she'd once felt at tucking into a tasty dinner, or selecting sweets at the shops.

And even if she could eat, her little boy body would not grow. It was inconsequential. Weak. She had been stupid to pick this form. Vara indulged in a few moments of bitter regret. She should have been a snake, though the thought of slithering on the ground made her sick. She could have chosen to be a wolf, who could rend flesh. Even a goat, who wore sharp horns, could rip open a belly. Too late now.

Another long, hot afternoon, and the four of them had gathered, as had become their custom, in the deserted nook in the market. They should leave the city, but they needed information. With her skills in high demand now, Knife Woman had found employment at a barracks near the palace, and had spent the day quietly working away among the other craftsmen attending to the soldiers' needs, pretending deafness, until the men grew used to her and understood that she knew her trade. As she had known they would, they stopped paying attention to her and went back to their jokes and games and gossip. She had gambled that Petru would take his *falci* sniffer with him on his campaign, and she had won. No one suspected her.

Much of the talk was about the growing legends of Petru. They were many and varied. He was everywhere at once. He was *resura* himself, and was jealous of all others of his kind. He could turn into the wind and travel faster than a racing camel. He was the son of the God of War, sent to the world to sow strife.

The men nodded at this tale, for there was obviously strife everywhere now, and they shut up for a while. But soon their mouths were flapping again.

Knife Woman learned that the men were ordered to report to the East Gate shortly after sunset that very day, as Lord Petru was expected to arrive. He had quickly conquered the city of Montpelier, up until now the fastest-growing town in the south, killed its ruling family and confiscated everything of value. A load of rich booty was being shipped in. It would need to be sorted, archived, and either sold to buy more war equipment, or hoarded. Some of it would, apparently, be distributed among Petru's loyal troops, which would attract new troops and more loyalty.

"As you can imagine," Knife Woman reported, "there was a lot of speculation about what will be shared. Coins, fine weapons, spices... that sort of thing. I pretended not to hear a thing. They say there's a string of high-born girls coming in, probably the daughters of those he killed, and the most beautiful one will be awarded to the winner of a contest of marksmanship."

Akil grunted and turned away. He knew what happened to beautiful slaves.

With Petru returning to Perpignan so soon, they could not stay in the city. There were too many spies, too many weak-willed folk who would gladly tell whatever they knew or imagined in exchange for safety, or food. And the longer they were stuck here, the less chance they'd have of reaching Jameel before it was too late.

However, they had a small, mundane problem to solve. How were they to get a human woman out of the city?

Vara, Ragna and Akil could simply fly away, but Miss Marsh's corporeal form would be stopped for certain. And Petru Dominus knew her. He would undoubtedly want her for ransom or interrogation, and his men knew that.

Carolina Marsh sat disconsolately, picking shreds of gristle out of her teeth. She was obviously chagrined at her new status as drag upon any plans they might have to find and free Jameel. She said, "Perhaps Akil could pull or push me out in a small cart, hidden beneath something..."

"Like what? Dead bodies?" Knife Woman snorted. "You wouldn't like that, my friend. And everything, no matter how small and rattletrap, is being thoroughly searched. You'd be discovered right away."

"Oh. Yes." She thought some more. "I guess bribes not working these days, not that I have bribe money to give... Why cannot I simply stay here? I be safe, I think. I doubt the Sisters would betray me."

"Can you be sure?" asked Knife Woman. "Don't underestimate a madman's thoroughness. Do you want to put them in danger?"

"But I'm useful here, among sick and old. What could I do to help search for Jameel al-Kindi?"

Boy spoke up. "You're clever, Miss Marsh, and you have a silver tongue. You are an expert in survival, and you speak many languages."

"As do you, my dear Vara. I mean, Boy. You really should think of a name. Mere survival is not what we to seek... and there is another problem. What of my *resura*?" She looked at Akil, who wore a sour look. "Would you return to me each night, after your travels? How far and fast can you fly?"

"Quite far, and quite fast," Akil said. "But eventually the city's guards will notice an eagle swooping in and out, or even a cat creeping along the walls. Some of them are not as stupid as you might hope... their commander has warned them of *resura* folk and what we can do. They'll try to capture me just for sport. Though we can't be killed, we can, unfortunately, be captured. And exist forever caged in stone."

Or in a mesh of wire, recalled Vara. The strange mixed-up creature in the market, that day of the Sisters' feast. It was caught and helpless. Unless a form was physically small enough to slip out of a cage, it was trapped. There were rules to her new existence, and she had better learn them fast.

Miss Marsh nodded reluctantly. "And there is yet one more problem..."

This, thought Vara, was why Akil looked so... cramped. He was caught between two needs: to help his friends, and to serve his *alanbir*. She watched him shift uncomfortably.

"Yes," he whispered. "Our pact. That I will be by your side when you die." He shrugged, a gesture very much like Miss Marsh's own shrugs, Vara noted; offhand, fatalistic. They were bound by much more than love. Each was in thrall to the other, there was really no owner and slave. She had felt that helpless, unquestioning attachment herself, during the few brief moments when Josef had owned her.

Miss Marsh said, "Since I took Akil's life before its time, I owe him mine in exchange. It is my theory that should an *alanbir* order her *resura* to kill her, then obey he must. It's only logical—every order obeyed must be. And once that bond is broken—by wish of the *alanbir*—the *resura* should be free as well, of all obligations and bonds to the living."

Yes, thought Vara. It did make a certain kind of sense. And there was the risk that if another were to kill Miss Marsh—Petru most likely—he might acquire the *resura* soul. Akil, used to a kind and loving master, might very well find himself handed over to a monster.

Or to a God.

Which fate would be worse?

Knife Woman looked shocked. "But... it's unthinkable! How could a *resura* do such a thing?" Vara saw her mother's knobby old fingers form a circle, partially hidden in her lap. Did she imagine the Eye of Uzma would ward off a God?

She knew her mother feared that being free *resura* was somehow terribly wrong, and that they must pay somehow. Vara's instinct was to side with her Pada in his belief that mortals owed nothing to Gods who alternately neglected and tortured them.

"It is just idea," the little Briton said. Her command of the language waxed and waned, Vara noted, depending on her level of distress. "And of course, for Akil to kill me would be resort of the last." Though her voice was conciliatory, her grey eyes retained their cool assurance. She was not, Vara saw, willing to challenge her theory by letting Akil stray far from her side. Nor was she asking to be killed at this very moment.

"So we are back at the problem's gate again," said Knife Woman reluctantly. "And it's the gate that's the problem."

Then Vara, drawing little circles in the dust of the market's pavement, heard Miss Marsh draw in a sharp breath. She looked up to observe a crafty expression stretch those thin, scarred cheeks.

"I think I have an idea. It depends on I do a thing most people cannot."

"Oh? And what is that?" asked Knife Woman.

"Let me think it for a while... I need to gather a few items."

Akil, Boy and Knife Woman looked at each other in puzzlement.

Miss Marsh said, "We agree that I cannot stay here in Perpignan while the rest of you flee? Yes?"

Reluctant nods all around.

"Very well." She clambered to her feet and dusted off her skirts. "I must first make some excuse to the Uzmite Mother. Perhaps a sick family I must attend." Her face and posture told Vara of the joy this woman took from action. She was like a man that way. Direct, courageous, indomitable: she was a woman whom Vara had no doubt would prevail. Her spirits lifted a bit.

Miss Marsh vanished into the streets.

Knife Woman sat, looking pensive. "We are running out of time," she said. "I'm having little luck getting useful information from the soldiers, but I've been thinking of how to do it better." She looked at Boy. Boy, seeing the glint of ice in her eye, wanted suddenly to run.

But Vara, within that little body, sat firm. "And what have you thought of, Knife Woman?"

"A plan that is probably foolish. But it's the only one I can think of. Boy, do you have the courage to get so close to Petru's men that you could smell their sweat?"

Of course she didn't, but if it was her mother's wish, she could and would do it. As a nimble street urchin, she could sneak close to them easily. Boy nodded.

From a net bag hanging on the side of her barrow, Knife Woman pulled out a big handful of sheep's wool. The lanolin-filled wool was used to buff a shine onto armour, leather trappings and sword blades. She teased the handful into two balls, then formed each ball of wool into a sort of nest, two halves of a hollow sphere. "Do you think, as Bird, that you could hide in this ball, perfectly still and soundless?"

At once, Vara regretted her agreement. She'd be a tiny spy, protected only by a fluff of sheep's wool. A cage, and though its walls were soft, still it was a cage, and could be flattened, burned, or ripped open to reveal her. But who else could do it? Her nightingale form was the smallest. After a few moments of trying to think of a way out, Boy got to his feet and said, rather faintly, "Yes. I will do it."

Knife Woman nodded once. "Good."

"But wait," she blurted. "Before I do this, I must ask one thing."

"And what is that?"

"I need to see my home once more." One way or another, she might never glimpse her old life again. It was time to say goodbye, time to stride firmly into her new existence.

Time to stop longing for a past that was dead and gone.

Knife Woman's eyes narrowed. "Very well, but you must be

quick. Akil, you will accompany my daughter. Don't let her linger."

Akil bowed, changed to his cat form, and ran along in the shadows as Bird flitted through the maze of deserted streets to their old neighbourhood

Vara had to steel herself to approach the ornate metal gate at the main entrance to their villa, which hung open as if someone had been trying to pry it off its hinges. A bad sign. Of course the place must have been looted; it looked also like part had been burned.

A fire smouldered fitfully in the courtyard. Scattered evidence of cooking lay everywhere. Empty wine jugs, small bones picked very clean. She recognized broken pieces of their furniture in the fire, scorched and splintered. Vara felt a hot surge of anger. Her home had been vandalized, probably by the very neighbours who had once been friends. But no. Their friends and acquaintances had abandoned them at the first sign of trouble.

She felt a pang of concern for the animals that had once lived sheltered lives within these walls. Amjad was probably safe in someone's hands, as he was valuable. But the other horses, their hawks, their cattle, goats and fowl... all dispersed, stolen. Or killed and eaten. She'd really liked some of those poor creatures, and had watched many of them being born. You grew to love something, even a lowly hen, when you cared for its everyday comfort. Of course, later you killed and ate it... but you showed its tiny spirit gratitude and respect.

Fuming under her breath, she ducked behind a screen of vines and changed to Freewoman. As the stately and untouchable woman, she could spin a believable tale of why she was within the gates of a house not her own, should anyone be watching the place and challenge her. She could claim to represent an insurer, performing an inspection of the property. Akil could be her scribe.

That thought made her wonder what had become of all Papa's extensive staff. His scribes, his lawyers, his translators and accountants. Too valuable to work to death in a slave camp, they might by now be annexed to Petru's government. But perhaps they'd had enough foresight to scatter with whatever they could carry.

Freewoman strode to the villa's main door, then stopped. She couldn't do it. She couldn't go in. The thought of revisiting her once happy home, where murder had been committed only days ago, nauseated her. Her own dried blood, and her grandfather's too, would still be all over her bedchamber. Who would have cleaned it?

Her gleaming brown shoulders sagged. "Let's go, Akil. There's nothing left here, nothing important. We have better things to do."

What she wanted to do was fly as fast as she could to find her father. But fly where? Petru had many prison camps, several palaces with ample slave quarters and dungeons. He owned ships, mills, mines and manufactories. By now, if his attempted coup was going well, he would control many more. Jameel could be held in any of them. Or he might be dead already. If he had no more information to give...

An image of poor bleeding Eneko Saratxaga flashed behind her eyes. She knew something, now, of interview techniques. Seeing the man being eaten alive in the vat of eels had stripped away what remained of her childhood.

Vara knew most of Jameel's trade routes, and the timing of his travels. He'd most likely been apprehended at a port city on the Mediterranean coast of Askain, as soon as he'd made landfall on his way home.

She stopped. Her father was not a trader, he was a warrior. She understood that now, the need for him to be other than what he seemed. Perhaps he hadn't been following his normal routes. In fact, it was unlikely. He could have been travelling anywhere, contacting allies, formulating plans and strategies for the war he'd known was coming.

Petru's men would have been waiting for the best time to pounce, no matter where Jameel was. Then he'd have been locked away until Petru had opportunity to practice his techniques of persuasion. They might have months to find Jameel, or they might have only days. Or they might already be too late. All they could do was listen for loose talk.

Could one little bird, hiding and hoping for good luck, be their only hope?

Her eye was caught by a fragment of charred wood at her feet. She picked it up. Carved into the dark wood was a familiar little figure—a bear cub.

Her hand began to shake. The wood was from her parents' bed. Papa had told her many stories of that little bear and her family. The bears, and the other animals carved into the frame, had wonderful adventures. They travelled the world, they entered into spirited discussions with philosophers and kings, they made friends with exotic animals. Vara had loved those evenings, cuddled between her mother and father, waiting for Papa to say *And now I shall tell you a story...*

She dropped the broken fragment, squared her shoulders and strode away. Akil slouched along in her wake.

Akil could tell that his *alanbir* was pleased with herself.

"What have you got there?" he asked, as they sat on the bottom step of the Minotaur stairs. Named for the hulking beast, which Akil knew must have been *resura*, it was once a favourite gathering place for students and lecturers, prophets and salesmen.

Carolina Marsh had brought a small parcel with her, and handed it to him. He could smell it, something meaty and acidic. His nose wrinkled as he opened it and pulled out the contents. "What under the sun...?"

"It's a pig's bladder. Don't be squeamish, I'm not asking you to eat it."

The rubbery, sagging membrane looked nauseatingly... internal. She took it from him, and Akil wiped his hands on his baggy grey trousers.

He had to close his eyes as she put her lips to a puckered orifice, like a person's navel, and blew into it. He could hear her puffing away lustily as the bladder began to inflate. She let go, grinning at his disgusted expression, and it sagged into flaccidity.

"Can you guess what I want this for?"

Akil refused to play her game. He was annoyed with his *alanbir* and her damned cleverness; with Ragna Svobodová and her relentless desire for revenge; even with Vara. Why had the girl chosen such foolish shapes? A small, helpless bird—idiotic. Had she not realized she would be stuck with these forms forever? And now she was playing spy, tucked in a wad of wool—the most foolish idea he'd ever imagined. He might never see her again.

What did he care about some stupid pig guts?

Miss Marsh clucked her tongue. "Well then, I'll tell you what it's for." She bundled the bladder back into its wrapper and stuffed it into a pocket slung from her leather belt. "But we will wait for Knife Woman. She might have news." After a pause she patted Akil on the knee and said, "Don't worry, Akil. I am sure dear Vara will be all right…"

Vara, as Bird, had to remind herself that she really didn't need to breathe. She could remain as still as death within this soft cocoon and not reveal herself with movement or gasping for air. But she very much wanted to gasp for air. The ghost of her human lungs demanded it.

Knife Woman, using the trembling voice of a harmless crone, had presented the ball of wool to the lead man in Petru's guard as they mounted up. They were meeting their master at the East Gate, as had been ordered, and the man had brushed her off at first. "Take it, young man. It is very fine! Polishes up the armour very well indeed. Just tuck it into your saddlebag… there you are…" She must have dipped into Akil's well of indifference, for the man merely grunted and let her have her way. Vara felt the wool compress around her as it was pushed down into the darkness of the bag. She couldn't hear perfectly, but she could hear enough. If she had needed to breathe, she wouldn't have been able to, for the space was very tight. Then came the men's voices, the clinking of harnesses, the clop of horses' hooves. The shifting echoes as the squad moved along the city streets to the gate. Then the waiting.

A certain rising tension in the air, and the groan and rumble of the gate opening, let her know when Petru approached. Suddenly there were many men nearby, with their horses and mules and dogs. And that familiar, nauseating smell of burning trash.

The little bird squeezed her tiny eyes shut, the better to hear. *Oh Sisters, help me now!*

Vara would know Petru's voice anywhere, but didn't hear it until they were very near the palace. An advantage of being a bird, you knew where you were all the time, as if visible stars wheeled overhead. She could feel the streets and buildings wheel around her like the points of a compass.

The guards halted outside the palace, and performed the ritual of handing over responsibility for their leader to the inside men, preparatory to returning to their barracks.

She despaired of learning anything useful, but then she heard Petru's voice, rough and leaden with fatigue. The Gods, she thought, were driving him hard. She wished they'd kill him. "I stay only one night. Have fresh horses ready at dawn, and send word that more must be waiting at Montpelier, for I will go on to Arles."

"Yes, Sire... Arles? The siege progresses as planned, but..."

"I am going past there, into the mountains." Vara heard him emit a sort of laugh, if a person made of nothing but bone and bile could laugh. "There is a trader there with whom I must talk."

A lance of ice went to her heart. That was it. He must—must!—be referring to her father. How many other important traders could there be? It might be nothing, but it was the only hint they had. They could trail Petru around forever waiting for him to interrogate Jameel, but what good would that do? If they didn't get there ahead of Petru and his instruments of persuasion, Jameel would be doomed.

This was their only chance.

Vara almost shoved her way out of the wool right then, but stopped herself in time. Later, as the horses clopped along, she stealthily forced first her beak, then the beads of her eyes, through the clinging mat of wool. At the next turn, far from the nearest

torchlight, she flitted free, a strand of wool clinging to her tiny
foot.

❧

Akil sat hunkered onto his haunches, waiting. His years of
captivity as a child, with its hours of boredom among the harem
women, and the monotony of the revels he had been forced to
attend, had prepared him for the tedium of waiting. He could
endure it.

Vara had been gone for hours. Knife Woman paced back and
forth, conferring now and then with Miss Marsh. Neither of them
looked happy.

Night was well advanced. They had left the Minotaur stairs for a
secluded alley, knowing that Bird would find them.

Akil was settling into a trance-like state, his mind smoothing
into a blank field, when he was startled by a bird landing on his
shoulder.

Its bright little eyes were inches from his own as it shifted its
wings into place, hopped to the ground and began to stride around
like a small warrior. It was Vara. He felt himself grin, and reached
out a finger to stroke her glistening brown feathers.

But Knife Woman slapped his hand aside. "Don't touch my
daughter. You have no right." He gave her a look, but she stared
him down. Akil dropped his eyes. It was true, he had no right. No
right at all.

The nightingale began to speak. Her words hissed and trembled;
having a sharp beak in place of soft lips hampered speech, as Akil
knew. But her meaning was clear.

"I know where he is." She leapt into the air and beat a quick
circle of the area, scanning with her sharp eyes, then landed beside
them once more, changing immediately to Boy, complete with
tousled hair and grubby loincloth. And a big grin. Akil closed his
eyes for a moment, remembering slender ankles and blistered feet
that needed his touch. She needed nothing from him now. She was
mastering the art of being *resura* very well.

"Where is he?" demanded Knife Woman, grabbing Boy's hand to hold him still.

"I'm not exactly sure, but Petru told his men he was going into the mountains northwest of Arles, leaving at dawn. To *talk* to a trader. He said nothing more, so I don't know exactly where my father may be, but at least we can get close."

Knife Woman's eyes blazed. "It has to be him, and I know where he is! He's in that limestone quarry Petru and his Sarafites took over last year. He is no more than thirty leagues from here."

Boy exclaimed, "They'll work him to death in there! We must go to him at once!"

Knife Woman said, "The mine is no longer active. Only prisoners and guards are there now, I'm sure. But my Jameel could be anywhere within its tunnels and pits."

"We can find him! We can fly overhead and see, or we can bribe the guards—"

Knife Woman held up a hand. Boy shut up, seething with frustration. "We must think of a plan."

Akil looked at his *alanbir* and saw only a look of chagrin on her face. Miss Marsh knew her human limitations. "You must go, now. I will stay here, for I'm much too slow. You three can fly to him. If Jameel al-Kindi is to be found and freed before Petru has a chance to tort—question him, you must act quickly."

Knife Woman shifted back to hawk form, a blur of dust twisting so fast that Akil barely followed it. And he knew how to *see* a *resura*... Ragna Svobodová was frantic with impatience, and the hawk's movement betrayed it. She sprang about from ground to ledge to fountain's lip and back, her beak snapping.

"You shall not stay behind. It is too dangerous. For you, and also for us, should you be captured and made to talk. You said you had a plan to get past these walls. You had best set it in motion, my friend." She spread her wings, gave a great leap, and shot into the air to vanish among the stars.

Chapter Twenty-Six
THE PIG'S BLADDER

The stars were dimmed by a haze of smoke from villages that had been set afire, and the crops and storage barns blazing. Akil could smell it. All was quiet here by the river; even the insects had ceased their rhythmic call. Now and then Akil heard the gentle lapping of the Tet testing its banks with no intent to breach them.

He shifted in the mud, his feet squelching. Though he wasn't bothered by the chilling air, or the damp prickling of reeds, his flesh crawled with disgust at the slime he crouched in. It reminded him of the oil he'd once had to slather upon the naked bellies and buttocks of his masters, and his masters' guests. Might they rot in hell.

"Be still, for goodness' sake, Akil!" Vara was in her Boy shape, small and almost invisible beside him, the little sun-browned body blending well with the riverbank's muck. "Can you feel her?"

He could. Carolina Marsh was somewhere to the north-west, and she was in a state verging on panic. Not an emotion she normally felt, or would willingly acknowledge. Her heart was pounding and her breath was laboured. Now and then he felt her choke.

The three *resura* had flown at random, one at a time, over the walls just after moonset, when the night was darkest. Petru's city marshals were well drilled in vigilance. No one wanted to risk getting shot, even though they couldn't agree on what might happen to their magical bodies, which functioned almost like true flesh and blood. They had flown in different directions, at varied levels, to reunite here, where the water was shallow and slow moving.

Akil grunted as he felt his lungs strain against an urge to gasp for one long clean breath. It was what Miss Marsh was feeling; her fear was scattering her emotions wide. He breathed slowly through his nose, trying to ignore the multiple stinks around him. The very stuff from which he, and the other resura, were made... The skin of his back quivered with the knowledge that at any time, an arrow could pierce it.

But it wasn't his own back that was in jeopardy, it was his *alanbir*'s.

Doing her best to imitate a dead body, she was floating face down on the black current that swept the city of its trash and waste, including the bodies that now, in troubled times, were no longer getting any kind of burial. With luck, the current would carry Carolina Marsh under the city wall to freedom.

Hawk was circling overhead, her sharp eyes alert for signs of movement, whether a body floating on the current, guards patrolling the banks with torches, or late-night prowlers about their secretive business. She was to screech three times quickly for danger, once long and twice fast to alert them to Miss Marsh's approach. Were she to float past them, she'd be caught in the quickening current as the Tet flowed southeast, and might never reach shore.

The hawk cried once long, then twice again fast.

Akil stood, peering into the rippling shadow and starlight that was the river. Boy clung to his withered arm, and he almost shook the small hand away in his eagerness to retrieve his *alanbir*. He bent and began to slap rhythmically at the soft mud, three slaps, a pause, three more. He dared not call out.

Splashing sounded from upstream, accompanied by wheezing

gasps. Akil waded out, at last spotting a dark wet head and flailing arms as his mistress made for shore. She rolled sideways to haul the inflated bladder from her bosom, letting it bob away into the darkness. He saw her teeth gleam as she spat out a long, hollow reed and reached for his hand. Grinning fiercely, she swam to shore to be hauled the last few lengths by Akil and Boy.

She sprawled gasping on dry land while Akil tried to wring water from her clothes and hair.

The hawk landed beside them and became Knife Woman. She began to strip off her friend's sodden clothes. Akil wrung them out thoroughly, glad the night was warm.

Her small leather boots were tied around her neck, for she'd refused to leave them behind, and no corpse would be tossed in the river with perfectly good boots still on. "They were made by the finest cordwainer in Spain and fit me perfectly," she'd explained. "Years of wear are in them still." Miss Marsh had an unfortunate passion for footwear.

Despite the mild air, she began to shiver, her teeth chattering as she suppressed a crow of triumph. "You cannot imagine," she whispered, "how filthy the tunnels in the cloaca are! I put my head up when I knew I was underground, and I was mightily sorry at once. Thank Mithra I could only smell, not see. And I had thought this little city so advanced and sanitary!"

She did smell rather bad, and not only from polluted river water. He must steal a lump of soap for her as soon as possible; the risk of disease was ever-present for humankind. In his former life of ignorance, he'd have prayed to a God to chase away illness. It had been Miss Marsh who informed him that in her opinion, washing was better than praying.

Akil wanted suddenly to shake sense into her. In the city, she'd have a chance for what small comfort it still offered. The Uzmite Sisters would have hidden her. Next she would order him to seek Jameel al-Kindi with the others, and he could not disobey. But if he left her, she'd be utterly alone, with nothing but what she could carry.

"Akil, my darling boy," she said, sounding calmer. "I know that look. You angry are with me. But aren't you also proud of me? Are not you pleased that I possess the swimming, as few people do?" She took Knife Woman's hand and drew it to her cheek. "I learned from naked savages of Terra Torridia, in one of their immense brown rivers. They thought I very odd and funny, particularly when I refused my underclothes to take off."

"You *are* odd and funny," replied the crone impatiently. "Do you feel ready to press on? We must find you shelter as far from the city as possible, before dawn."

"Of course. We all must go, and fast." She struggled back into her damp clothes, assisted by Akil.

Knife Woman led the way, moving with a purposeful stride, faster than Akil had ever seen her cover ground. She had abandoned her cart and all its tools and supplies. Akil had no idea how this worked, and spent the next few hours trying to deduce whether she actually had a real—that is, not magical—knife sharpener's barrow, or if it was a part of her *resura* form. An extension of her old-woman body. But if it were an extension, then it must remain part of her forever more, mustn't it? How could she alter a form she had chosen?

He gave it up, and promised himself to ask her when there was time. There was so much to learn about being what he was, and he feared the others knew even less than he did. He wanted to seek out more of their kind to study. Or even befriend, if that were possible among bound *resura*.

At last Knife Woman stopped. Akil, who had been carrying the exhausted Miss Marsh on his back for the last couple of leagues, saw that they were at a laneway meandering off the side-road they had been following. It was lined with perfectly straight cypress trees, as rigid as soldiers.

"Here we are," said Knife Woman, her crisp, aristocratic diction reminding Akil that within her was Ragna Svobodová, mistress of a huge and sprawling estate and attendant farms, orchards and mills. "I know this farm. The family is part of our Villa's holdings, and tend many of our orchards. The eldest son took over when his father died, and was teaching his younger brothers and sisters the arts of pruning and grafting, even of creating new and sweeter varieties of fruit."

They could smell no smoke, nor see any lamplight. At this time, the start of day, the farm should have been active.

"I hope they are well," murmured Knife Woman. "I had hoped they might shelter you. But if they have fled, I don't blame them."

Akil glanced at Vara, who nodded and changed to Bird. She flitted off, to return in a few minutes with news. "The farm is deserted. Not even a chicken, and the main house is open and empty. It looks as if it's been looted and partially burnt."

Akil saw Knife Woman's face harden. She knew what had happened. Soldiers, like a swarm of locusts, had come upon a peaceful farm, conscripted the men, raped the women, stolen all the food and taken pleasure in destroying what remained.

Dawn light was brightening quickly. They hurried up the lane to spy a small shed, half buried in lush grasses and a flourishing myrtle tree, its scented leaves and white blossoms nodding gently. Petru would have that myrtle cut down and burned for its sacred connections. Saraf didn't like reminders of other gods.

Knife Woman bent and lifted a leather flap that covered a small opening, and peered inside.

"It looks untouched," she said. "This is the house that my tenant Matheus de Grignon built for a family of dwarves who were in his employ. Man and wife, and a child of normal size. The dwarves found better pay in the city once their child had grown tall enough to be useful. For you, my little friend, it should be perfect. Everything is small." She grinned, a flash of teeth. She found a flint and lantern among the abandoned clutter, and soon thin yellow light illuminated the hut.

Miss Marsh sank onto a mouse-eaten, miniature Roman-style lounge and groaned with relief. "I feel quite big in here. Ah, it's so good to lie down... Akil, dear, could you removing my boots, please? They are still damp and must be stuffed with something to dry and hold their shape."

Akil snorted as he bent to her bidding, though there was nothing but dry grass to stuff them with. How could she think of boots at a time like this? Women were hard to understand. At the sight of her dirty, blistered feet, he had to look away. In his hands would always be the feel of Vara Svobodová's smooth, tawny skin, her slender ankles firm and warm. He was glad that Vara hadn't chosen forms too similar to her own human one. He might have looked at her more than he should. "I'll find you some food."

He changed to Eagle and in a matter of minutes was back with a small brown rabbit flopping dead in his talons. Akil the eagle dropped it at his *alanbir*'s feet. She snatched it up admiringly.

"Oh, thank you, my dearest boy. I am so very hungry." She stepped back outside, slapped the soft little carcass onto the ground, pulled out her knife—sharpened by Knife Woman—and commenced to skin and gut it. "I can get a fire going. Now you must fly away to find Jameel al-Kindi. I to stay right here."

Akil spread his wings. Ragna Svobodová was already in the air, circling impatiently over the hut.

The three birds rose, and as Akil looked back towards the rapidly diminishing hut, he observed Miss Marsh standing at the door, skinned rabbit dangling from one hand, gazing upward avidly after them. His eagle eyesight made her scars and her every worried wrinkle visible, but also the hopeful look in her eyes. She would never give up. She had not given up on him, ever, though he had been ready to surrender to despair more than a few times.

He looked ahead to where Hawk's sharp brown wings beat eastward into the rising sun, and quickly caught her up. Nightingale was riding on her mother's back, as she had once sheltered on his.

As they flew, the nightingale conversed with the hawk. Vara knew that they must not rush blindly into a trap, for certainly Petru would have deduced that in their *resura* forms they would try to rescue Jameel al-Kindi. But he couldn't know what forms those were, or that they were free. He probably assumed that, since he didn't possess them, they'd been taken by a God, who presumably had no interest in Jameel. But could he take that chance?

No matter the legends, Petru could not really be everywhere at once, nor did he have enough *falci* adepts to sniff each suspicious being. And he must be quite certain they could not yet know where his captive was.

"With a little luck and planning," stated Hawk, "we should be able to infiltrate the mine and find Jameel-my-husband."

If he's even there, thought Vara, regretting her earlier enthusiasm. What if she was wrong? "How can we do it?"

"It must be you, my dear," said Hawk. "My forms would not pass. Knife sharpeners are not needed at mines. But you, as Boy, may get in, if you are clever and careful."

"I... I will do it. I must do it," said the Nightingale.

"Yes. You must... and you will. I have confidence in your courage."

The girl Vara would have laughed at this, for the one thing she knew she lacked was courage. Her mother had it, Carolina Marsh certainly had it. She didn't quite know about Akil. He might be courageous when it was necessary, or he might merely be logical. If it made sense to rush into danger, he would do it. If it would gain him something to help a girl escape ruffians, he would help. But to rescue a man he barely knew? One who was damned to a lingering death by a tyrant so powerful even the Emperor gave way before him?

That might be too foolish an undertaking.

Of course, his *alanbir* could simply order him to do whatever she wanted. He would have to obey. Wasn't that how it worked? Could Miss Marsh be trusted to do the right thing?

Her little talons, like Hawk's but so much smaller, clung to the hawk's dense brown and white feathers. Her mother's feathers. Vara nerved herself to look down. They were so very high...

But she found that it didn't frighten her; in fact it was thrilling. Was that why she'd not taken the form of a snake? She hated and feared dirt-crawling snakes, but heights were exhilarating.

They were over marshland right now, glittering in the morning light. The scent of water and reeds billowed up on the warming air.

Great drifts of birds congregated on the water and in the air below them, peeling apart and scattering at the sight of two birds of prey. But the hawk and the eagle passed them by, in search of other game.

She looked ahead, the warm, smoky wind buffeting her. She felt the odd sensation of what felt like another set of eyelids flicking down like a shield over her eyes. Were she human now, her eyes would be stinging. Below her lay forests, orchards and vineyards, rivers, towns and roads. The forests were quickly being chopped down, the orchards and vineyards stripped, the towns set ablaze and the roads filled with the men and machinery of war.

I'm glad I'm not a snake, she thought rebelliously. Nor a man, fighting uselessly for a cruel master. I'm glad I'm not still alive, to weep and lament over the destruction of my land.

She clung to her mother. Akil flew at their side. Ahead were the mountains, where prisoners cowered under the whip.

It was late afternoon. Below him as he flew, Akil could hear a relentless thumping: the continuing catapult attack on Arles, on the west bank of the Rhône. He wheeled lower to get a look. Several of the infernal machines surrounded the city, some on land, another two on huge barges in the river. One of Petru's generals would soon capture that stubborn city and its ancient mills, which could grind ten tons of grain a day now that they'd been modernized and expanded. His armies and generals were spread wide, north and east; he'd soon take Soissons and his Emperor's head. Petru had the God of War at his side.

Akil knew he should have listened more carefully to old Josef Svoboda's ramblings and predictions, and the bitter grumbling he'd overheard from Vara's father. Petru Dominus had a heart that burned for revenge, for retribution, for the joy of vanquishing the empire that had tortured and imprisoned him, then banished him to a sleepy corner of a world he wanted to rule. And the Gods loved it. They applauded his ambition; Petru's rise could not have been so fast without their help. On his own, Petru would still be stubbornly designing irrigation systems and trying to gain favour by pious deeds and heavy taxation.

Old Josef had seen the man's life as a carpet, ravelled and stained, its regular pattern twisting into confusion and madness as he was goaded into greater and greater acts of violence and terror.

The birds flew over the broad Rhône, downstream from the barges and the oared swiftboats laden with archers waiting for the catapults to breach the walls, and came to land in a high, whispering pine grove. They'd seen very few people. Those not conscripted for the fighting had mostly fled to the walled cities, or, fearing the very attack happening now, retreated into the hills.

Life, Akil had to admit as he changed to his human form on the pine-needle carpeted ground, was easier without a real human along. Humans got hungry and tired, and asked questions he couldn't answer. The other *resura* fluttered down beside him, changed to forms in which it was easier to talk, and began to plan.

"How will we even get close to the mine?" asked Freewoman, a note of desperation in her melodic voice. "Even such lonely prisons are guarded, especially now."

Knife Woman snorted. "Guarded by mere men, who often are bored or stupid or drunk. We will get by them, never fear."

"What do you mean 'we'? You mean *me*."

Knife Woman regarded Freewoman levelly. "I do mean you, daughter. As Boy, you will easily slip by them. We will make up a story for you."

"Why don't I just fly in as Bird?"

"Because, my dear child, you must question the men there if you have a hope of finding your father. You can't do that as Nightingale. But a small, harmless boy, properly admitted—not miraculously appeared from thin air—will have a chance."

"I hope you're right about the guards," grumbled Freewoman, looking rather sick.

Akil looked away. He knew a lot about guards and how often they were bored, stupid or drunk, or all three at once. It really shouldn't be too hard for a peasant boy to infiltrate the mine. With

Petru not yet in the area, there should be no *falci* to reveal Vara as *resura*.

Yet Vara fretted, constantly asking her mother questions as they worked out a plan. It was only because she feared that her father's chance of freedom rested solely upon her shoulders. Did she feel an allegiance to her father as he did toward his *alanbir*? Did she have no choice but to love him?

Had he, Akil, already forgotten what it was to be human?

He heard rumbling from the sky, and hoped it was just a storm brewing. The humming tension he felt all around might only be the heat building the clouds into thunderheads. But he didn't think so. It was the Great Gods. They loved strife—the stuff of stories and legends that bolstered their pride—and wanted nothing more than to stir up trouble. A happy, healthy populace tending its farms and flocks was boring. Human lives were fodder to them, the pain and fear of death whetting their appetite for more.

Knife Woman said, "We shall need oil. A small amount of any kind—it doesn't matter."

Freewoman wrung her hands. "What do we need oil for? We have no lamp. We aren't going to cook anything." Her voice wobbled. She bit her lip and shut up.

Knife Woman ignored her complaints. "Akil and Vara, go and get some. Now."

"I can do it alone," said Akil grumpily. The last thing he wanted beside him was a whiny, panicky female.

Knife Woman closed her eyes. "Go! Both of you. I need to think."

They could find no oil. Either it had been requisitioned, or was being hoarded by folk in secret places lest it be stolen.

Boy had found himself enjoying the hunt, realizing with pleasure that he had a store of street-urchin lore tucked in his brain, available when he needed it. Giving up on olive oil or butter, he stealthily pilfered a wad of sheep's tallow from a bucket left in a stable, probably to soften the udders of cows which were most likely cooked by now. It was slightly rancid but free of dung or grit, so he smeared some onto a palm leaf and rolled it up tight. Eagle took the smelly parcel in his beak, lifted mightily into the air and beat his way back the way they'd come. Boy changed to Nightingale and followed.

"Ah! That will do very well," stated Knife Woman, surprisingly, as she unrolled the leaf and took an appreciative sniff. "No one will want to relieve you of that, will they?"

She bestowed a feral grin upon Boy, who wondered if the old woman even remembered that her own daughter dwelt within the skinny little ruffian whose hair she tousled. Did she care? Or did she think only of Jameel, and of Petru?

Chapter Twenty-Seven
IN THE MINE

The dust again. Between his toes, and rising in the dry air to cling to his tongue. Lumped with chipped rock and dried dung, it lay on the road to the lonely limestone mine.

Boy trudged up the overgrown track—a back way in—which was barely wide enough for two donkeys to pass one another. He couldn't risk being observed changing from bird to boy, or he would gladly have flown much closer. In a previous life, he—that is, she—would have been puffing hard, and no doubt complaining loudly to anyone who would listen.

But now, Vara's energy seemed to renew itself like a spring, needing no food or rest. And if there were anyone to see or hear Boy—for instance, archers among the rocks—they must never suspect that he was not exactly what he seemed: a ragged peasant on some paltry errand. To enhance the illusion he stopped a couple of times to idly toss a rock at a tree stump. He would have pissed upon a rock, but that was another of the bodily functions he no longer possessed.

At last Boy reached an open area, about halfway up the hill.

He heard noise from the other side of the hill: the sporadic crunch of hammer against rock, the rattle of stones and gravel, the moans and grunts of men and animals. And the frequent crack of a whip. He crept around an outcropping of pale rock and took a peek.

The pit-mine was an immense hole taking half the mountainside, dazzling white under the relentless sun, blocked with thick shadows that at this time of day were lengthening toward the east.

Boy's heart shrivelled at the prospect of searching the vast open space. It would be almost impossible to penetrate without being seen, even as Bird.

Knife Woman had described all this to him, after a quick, high, reconnaissance flight.

"There are workers and guards at the mine, but no stone is being taken out. It's very odd. I'm not sure what they're doing."

Boy muttered a prayer that the story they'd invented would hold up, should he be asked for it. He dared a few more steps, to get a better view, and his brow wrinkled. The limestone was being mined all right, laboriously chipped and split away from serried outcroppings into brick-sized lumps, piled into panniers and onto the backs of mules and men, and was being hauled upward to the rim.

But once there, it was dumped upon the ground, picked up by other men, put in other panniers and carried down again. The guards were passing the time by tossing rocks at the workers. All of it ended up in the pit's very bottom. He squinted. On the other side, over the heat haze and pale, swirling dust, other men and mules were hauling this dumped rock back up again. It was a circle, fed with new rock by the few wretches chained to the fresh stone walls. The futile work of the insane.

Inside Boy's body Vara experienced a wave of sick anger. This was Petru's doing. Another of his crazy projects designed to drive his citizens mad. Their land, their very civilization, was being ruined.

A hand clapped Boy on the shoulder and spun him around to sprawl on the ground. "What are you doing here? I'll put you to work down there if you like." A fat, swarthy man stood over him, digging between his teeth with an ivory pick. "Speak up, or I'll open your guts just to see what's in there."

Boy scrambled backward, barely preventing himself from changing into a bird and flying away in panic. "I—I don't want work," he stammered. "I am here to see my uncle!"

"And who is this uncle?"

Knife Woman had prepared Boy for what to do next, having extended her scouting trip beyond the mine itself to a few of the taverns and shops in the small town below. Her sharp ears had served her well among the few die-hards still in town. She had said, "There are local felons in the mine as well as political prisoners. Here's what you must say—"

"H-his name is Aribert, son of Anglbert. I—I come to oil his feet." Boy cringed obsequiously. There really was an Aribert imprisoned here, and he really did have a nephew. "His sentence is almost over..."

"Ha. No one's sentence is over, boy. No one leaves the mine lest he's dragged out dead."

Boy began to snivel. "Please, I must see him so I can tell my aunt he lives! She is on her deathbed—it is her last wish." He thrust the palm-leaf parcel forward, displaying the greasy mess within. "Let me anoint his aching old feet and tell him his Berthaude will soon meet her maker."

The man drew back, wrinkling his nose in disgust. "Do I know the name of every flea-ridden bastard here? Take that thing out of my face!" Flies were gathering.

The man drew back a foot, ready to kick him. Boy dropped the leaf and flung himself face-first before the guard, clutching the man's ankle with both hands.

Vara thought, desperately, *I can draw up a cup of indifference... Akil did it, somehow. I can do it too...*

The guard cursed and tried to shake Boy off. "Get off me, you little louse!"

"Please, kind sir! I beg you!" The man's hairy ankle was warm in Boy's hands. He could taste the salt of the fat man's sweat right through his fingers, and the thick blood under the skin, and the bones that built his body. The hum of his life was right there—and the tendency of his soul.

His soul was lazy. He really didn't care about this boy and his hell-bound uncle. No one entered this old pit now but thieves and blasphemers, he hadn't been paid in over a month, and his wife was probably bedding her own brother by now.

The boy was less important than a fly. Let him take care of his old uncle.

With one last kick he loosened the boy's grip. "Oh, get on with you. He'll be on the west side of the pit, with the locals." Suddenly he chuckled. "Don't go to the east side, where the sun beats down all afternoon, though."

"Why not?"

"Because that's where the devils are. The really bad ones... they'll cut your heart out and eat it raw." He burst into laughter, turned and strolled away.

Boy grabbed the palm leaf, scrambled up and ran toward the nearest ramp that led down. It had worked! Vara had felt it happen, the draining away of the guard's resolve. What had done it? She doubted that Uzma or Afra had such power. Had a Great God intervened?

In case the guard had retained a shred of vigilance, Boy headed directly for the west quadrant of the pit, clambering downward as fast as he could. The heat rose the lower he went, as if the sun were pooling itself in this bowl of rock and making a soup of stone dust. Yet the heat didn't bother Boy. He should be thirsty, but was not.

A blessing, Vara told herself, holding panic tightly inside. It's a blessing that I'm not human any more. Some tears leaked from her eyes, but dried instantly, and she shed no more.

Boy found the shadowed opening of a tunnel, partly blocked by shattered boulders and overgrown with bushes, and crept inside to wait for darkness.

Akil wheeled high over the mine, his great wings idling as he watched Vara make her way inside. He wanted very badly to be with her right now. But Knife Woman's plan was probably the best. He had devised nothing better.

He circled, wings dipping and turning the air upward. There were many birds of prey in the mountains—hawks, kites, harriers—as well as other eagles. Many of them were in the lowlands now, feasting on the bodies of the dead, but two were in the air nearby, their eyes on him warily. He was the biggest.

He could see the whole layout of the vast pit, including the guards, the columns of men creeping up and down like lines of ants, each with his futile burden. He saw Boy at the feet of a fat man, saw Boy reach out and grasp the man's leg... was Vara imitating his trick? Yes, and it worked. Boy scampered off. Akil felt a surge of pride.

Eagle's attention was caught by a rabbit nibbling its way across a small patch of meadow grass, and felt a lust for it in his tongue, a need to feel it struggling, bleeding and panting as it died clamped in his talons. It was surprisingly hard to take his eyes off it.

He let himself drift sideways on a current of air until the rabbit was out of view.

He hadn't known it would be like this, when Miss Carolina Marsh was counselling him on what forms to pick. Her voice had been the only thing that kept him from succumbing to the pain of the poison working its way through his body... he could live forever as an eagle, taking his pleasure in flight and in killing. But not in eating. The smell of blood was enough.

What would happen to his *resura* soul, once his *alanbir* was dead? Would he become a free *resura*? Free, like Vara Svobodová bint-Jameel.

But he had learned to love. And love was a trap.

He watched Boy descend into the vast pit, the little brown shape winking in and out of sun and shadow, far below. Vara was more brave than she knew. And less free.

The ties of love were as cruel as wire, and cut as deep.

Akil had been feeling the urge to return to his *alanbir* for some time, and had pushed it away. But he could do nothing to help Vara now. He hardened his heart against the desire to walk beside her and protect her against men and Gods, dipped his great wings and wheeled back towards the hut where Miss Marsh sheltered, a flight that would take until dusk to complete.

The scent of myrtle drew him down. A prickly sense of foreboding had plagued him for the last few leagues. He circled down and landed. Something was wrong. He couldn't feel her. Nor smell nor hear any evidence that she was within the hut, or even nearby. But where would she have gone? And why would she leave this shelter? Fear making his senses prickle, he changed to cat and slunk close, wary of an ambush.

If she were dead he would know it. Of that he was completely sure. Cat peeped in the small doorway. Nothing. Carolina Marsh was gone. She wouldn't leave this shelter without good reason. She knew better than follow her *resura* companions into the mountains.

Someone must have taken her. He sat on his haunches, his orange tail lashing. *Think.* There must be signs.

He began to prowl about, inside the hut and around its perimeter. Inside lay a little pile of picked-clean rabbit bones. At least, he thought, she'd had her meal. His *alanbir* did much better on a full stomach. Outside the hut he found what he'd suspected. Hoof-prints of several different horses, and the boot-print of a man in a patch of yielding mud. Half-dry, which told him the boot had been there fairly recently. He changed to Eagle and leapt into the air.

If she was anywhere within a league he'd see her. His eyesight was sharp enough to spot a rabbit at almost that distance... but there was no sign of her. He circled over the road leading west, back to Perpignan. If Petru's men had found her they'd take her directly to him, or to the city to await his pleasure.

Again he circled, higher, sharpening his senses as much as he could. A faint, tell-tale echo of her tickled his inner lodestone, the one attuned to his *alanbir* and to nothing else.

He didn't need eyes to find her. She was heading not west but east, and at a rapid pace. Toward the mine.

Once he had her in his mind, it wasn't long before his powerful wings had him floating high above her. She was on horseback, held in the firm grip of a soldier of Petru's guard. Another three galloped beside them. The horses laboured and foamed as the men whipped them on. Akil felt a moment of complete frustration. There was nothing he could do for her but follow and watch.

In another two leagues they stopped at a waypoint to change horses. Eagle landed behind a screen of bushes and changed to cat, the better to slink close and overhear them.

Crouched behind a stump, he could see that Miss Marsh appeared unhurt. She was hoisted down from the sweat-streaked horse and told to do her business, and quickly. He could feel her emotion—a mix of fear, frustration and outraged dignity. Mostly outraged dignity. She squatted as the men looked on.

"What good is a scrawny old bird like this?" said one.

"Trust me, he'll want her," said the one who appeared to be the leader. "He's had men looking for her in the city. She's wise in the ways of alchemy and science and... and devilish things like that."

"She's a witch?"

"Probably. But it's not for us to test or punish her—he'll want to do it himself. He'll be glad of this prize." The man's voice was full of smug satisfaction. Cat wanted to claw his eyes out.

Akil wondered how the soldiers had found Miss Marsh. Someone must have noted signs of life in the little hut. The fire she'd made... a bad idea. The men, tasked with scouting the countryside for supplies and fresh conscripts, would have investigated.

How could he let Miss Marsh know he was here? She knew already that she was being saved for Petru, and probably wouldn't be harmed by these men. The harm would come later. She had told him that she could feel him as he did her, but only weakly, like a far off melody.

He let out a yowl. It was very cat-like, for indeed he was a cat; but his *alanbir* knew him. They'd worked out a sort of language, used when he was forced to live as a house-pet or mouser in whatever position she'd taken, among other humans. *It's me. I'm here.*

The men looked about, and one of them spotted him and quickly threw a rock. Cat dodged easily and vanished into the weeds.

"Leave it," commanded the leader. "Mount up. We rendezvous with the Scorpion at dawn."

Cat became Eagle and, once the men were out of sight, took to the air. Ragna needed to know what was happening. And somehow, Vara had to be warned. Petru would be at the mine much sooner than they had imagined.

Chapter Twenty-Eight
HALF A MAN

As soon as the sun dipped below the western rim of the vast, terraced pit, Boy left his hiding place, changed to Nightingale and flitted carefully, from shadow to shadow, to the far side, where the worst prisoners were held—Jameel presumably among them.

What if he were already dead? Vara's very soul trembled. What if she had misunderstood the men she'd spied upon from within the wool-ball, and he wasn't even here? And if he *was* here and alive—he might have been driven mad by torture.

If birds could weep, Bird would be weeping.

But then sense took over once more. Petru would not be coming here to interview a dead man. There was still plenty of time to save him.

Bird clung to a thin branch under a dry, rattling screen of leaves. To gain information, Vara had to be in human form. She must ask questions, wheedle depraved prisoners into helping her... She shuddered. Perhaps she should just fly about until she overheard something.

No. She couldn't merely hope for a miracle. She had to act.

Boy materialized out of the dust, which must, Vara imagined, contain morsels and shreds of her vanished Nightingale self as well.

How very odd this was, and yet she did it now without even thinking.

She'd recognize her father's voice, should he still have one. Perhaps she might even smell him. Her nose had gained acuity in her afterlife.

Glancing around, she was about to step away from the bush when she saw a small person awkwardly hunching up the path toward him. It was a boy, half-naked and burnt almost black from the sun, staggering and grunting as he hauled a wooden bucket along.

As the boy drew close, the smell of human waste became overpowering. Vara felt her Boy nose wrinkle in disgust. But a peasant wouldn't care one way or another about the smell of shit, would he? Perhaps this fellow inhabitant of the mine would like some help. Boy stepped onto the path and said, "If I help carry your bucket, will you help me find my uncle?"

The bucket almost spilled. The boy gasped a curse and gave Boy an evil glare. "Where did you come from? Get off, you'll not take my job from me."

"I don't want your job. I want to find my uncle."

"If your uncle is here, I pity him worse than I pity myself."

"But you can go home, can't you? You're not a slave."

"Ha! True. But I have no home. I was training as a joiner, but my father was taken for the fighting and my mother became a whore, so here I am. It's either this or be eaten by Saraf's brood." He glanced upward and made the S sign on his skinny chest.

Boy quickly mimicked him, then reached for the bucket's handle. "They say Petru sees all and Saraf is his slave. But like I said, I'll help you if you'll help me."

"It would help if you had something to eat," was the response, but the shit-hauler's hand joined Vara's and they started up the path.

Boy shrugged. "I can't tell you the last time I had even a crust of stale bread." But Vara knew. It was on the banks of the River Tet, in a shelter of reeds. In her former body she'd eaten better since, but the bread Akil had brought her was the best she'd ever tasted.

Boy's new friend said, "If they didn't keep the prisoners chained where they work, I'd have no job at all. Though why they don't just toss their turds into the pit is beyond me."

"Petru has his reasons, isn't that right?"

The boy grunted noncommittally. "Huh. If there's reason, I can't fathom it. I carry this mess up, someone else carries it down. I get a bowl of barley soup every day, and that's all I care about." Pause. "So who's this uncle of yours?"

Vara, within Boy's labouring body, suddenly felt weak. This was it. She knew she couldn't trust this lad farther than the next bowl of soup, or the next beating. But she had to know.

"Have you seen an Arab man, slender and tall, anywhere? He's called Jameel."

"D'you think I ask their names? I don't care what comes out of their mouths, only their asses."

Boy laughed dutifully. "Ha, ha, of course. But I need to find him... he knows where some money is hidden in a neighbour's stable." He made the universal sign for bribery with his free hand. "It could buy his freedom."

"Money? Your uncle is probably dead by now. Why not give the money to me, I'll tell you anything you want if I can buy my mother back from the whore-house."

Boy nodded vigorously. "I swear I'll give you what I can."

The shit-hauler burst out laughing. "And I'll name my first born son after you. I don't know of any Jameel. But..."

"But what? Help me, and I'll pray that Saraf never learns your name!"

"I might know someone. He's been here forever, and he's very smart. Perhaps he knows your uncle."

Since darkness had fallen and no one seemed to be watching, the boy left his noxious bucket sitting right where someone would surely trip over it, and led Vara down one terrace and several lengths eastward. They stopped before a pile of rags.

The rags emitted a loud snore, and the boy kicked them. "Chaim! Wake up."

"Fuck off, Hubert, you spawn of the devil."

Hubert kicked again, and Chaim sat up, flailing his sinewy arms in an effort to strike his tormentor, who dodged back.

"I brought you a visitor. This is... I don't know his name."

"Well," growled Chaim, "I-don't-know-his-name can fuck off too."

Boy spoke up, keeping his voice as respectful as possible. Also as low as possible, in case of listeners. Sound travelled upward in this echo chamber. "My name doesn't matter. I'm looking for my Uncle Jameel, and I understand you are very wise and might know where he is."

Chaim, who, like everyone else in here, was filthy, sunburnt and bearded, rubbed his eyes and hacked out a gob of phlegm. "It's true, I am very wise. However, if I am so wise, why am I here?" He glared up from his nest of rags among the rocks. "I'll tell you."

Hubert rolled his eyes and sat down. Boy did so too, and silently vowed to listen to every word this man cared to utter, no matter how pitiful and boring, as long as he came up with something useful.

The man arranged his chains around his callused feet and picked up a hammer and chisel, the tools of his trade. "You see these? I spend my days splitting big rocks into little ones, though I used to be the best mason in the district. Oh, the temples and the palaces I built! Everyone knew me. I was paid, and paid well. Now, due to my own greed and stupidity, I am doomed to die in this stinking pit of hell. I am nothing and nobody." He was speaking Hebrew, which Vara could follow quite well. Chaim eyed Boy with calculation. "I still know a lot, but I know nothing of any Jameel." He paused for effect. "But sometimes I hear things..."

Boy sat clenched into a ball at Chaim's feet, digging his fingers into his own skinny brown arms. "He... he is an Arab man, tall, slender... he wears his hair short like a Roman... he is clever and learned..."

"Stop! How the hell should I know who's in here and who isn't? What's in it for me, to know anything? Do I know how to free myself?" All the while he eyed Boy, his deep-set brown eyes more alert than they should be, considering where and what he was.

Boy reached out and patted him on the arm. The kind, gentle touch warmed Chaim's heart. He had been here so long, feeling nothing but the whip... The lad was obviously intelligent, trustworthy. He might know a way to escape this pit...

"Perhaps I know of a man..." Chaim suddenly shot his gaze at Hubert, and switched to Latin. "You! Get back to work. You don't need to know anything."

Hubert scowled at Boy and sat tight. "He said he'd give me money."

"And I will," whispered Boy fervently. Why hadn't Vara had the wit to plan for coins in her *resura* breechcloth? And why hadn't she conjured a Nightingale's tooth, the token which would assure the right people that she was one of them? Tossed away along with her own dead body. Vara cursed her stupidity, not for the first time. "I swear it!"

"Huh. I'll believe it when I see it." But he stood and began to sidle away.

Chaim shot out a hand and grabbed Hubert by the elbow. "You get back to work and don't say a word to anyone! I can send you straight to Petru's snake pit anytime I like." He made a sign with his fist, two fingers out like a snake-head seeking back and forth, right in Hubert's face.

Hubert cringed, jerked himself free and ran off.

Chaim's hand shot out once more and grabbed Boy, hauling him close. Vara stifled a shriek. The man held tighter and hissed, "You seek Jameel? Why? What do you want of him?"

"He... is my uncle. My mother sent me to see him, to oil his feet..."

"Don't lie to me, boy! What is this man to you? Answer me true or I'll break your neck right now."

What should she say? Vara's thoughts whirled. Not the truth, nobody wanted the truth. "I...I work for the family of Jameel al-Kindi. He has been taken for ransom. They seek to know if he lives before sending payment for his return." Vara tried to send that wave of sleepy indifference that had worked before, and thought she saw the old man's eyes start to drift shut. But then Chaim shook himself and focused once more on her. She let out a very honest whimper. "It's true! His lady wife's name is Ragna

Svobodová, and she is very beautiful and kind."

"How do you know this? You're nothing but an outcast of the street. I'll bet all you really know is how to cut a purse, eh?"

"She saved me from a soldier who wanted me for a plaything, and I became her willing slave at that instant. She sent me here."

The man did not let go, but only grunted. Did he believe Vara's story? She could escape him by changing to a bird and flying off, but she sensed that he knew something. "Please, kind sir, tell me where Jameel al-Kindi is."

Chaim let go. He seemed to have used up his store of energy. He sank back against the rock wall, which was cooling now that night was falling.

Vara, in Boy's little body, hoped her fear didn't show.

At last Chaim came to a decision. He prodded Boy's shoulder with the blunt end of his chisel and jerked his head to the left. "He's over there, under that crest of dolomite. There's a hole, narrow and deep... he's in there. Whether he's still alive, I can't tell you."

Boy closed his eyes in a brief prayer, bowed deeply, turned and ran.

Vara, still as Boy, stood biting her lip at the place Chaim had indicated. She could see no hole. The shadows were thick, unrelieved by any lamps or torches, and only meagre stars were showing through a high haze. She started to sniff the air. Her father's scent, while familiar to her, varied as to whether he'd been riding, or had bathed that day, or had been with her mother... Boy raised his small freckled nose and searched for it. But all Vara could smell was stone and sweat, blood and excrement, and that was everywhere.

A cough sounded from somewhere below. "Who's there?" called a voice, low and cracked, but she knew it at once.

Vara almost burst into tears. The voice was her father's, though it was weak and hoarse. The sound of her breath testing the air must have alerted him.

Controlling herself, Vara said, "A... a friend. I would speak with you."

"A friend, here? Well, my young friend, do you have any water?"

Of course! Jameel would be dry as an old bone, stuck in a noxious hole day and night. Boy had forgotten about the thirst that plagued humans. He tried to remember the location of a couple of rain barrels he'd seen up top. "I can find some. Wait!"

"I am going nowhere, whoever you are."

Boy became Bird, flew upwards until she smelled water. There! A cistern catching a trickle from somewhere higher in the hills, probably slimy and mosquito-ridden. Better than nothing, but how to carry it? Bird became Freewoman and suddenly knew what to do. She wore a silk shawl draped over her sleek brown shoulders. Quickly she took it off, tied it in a knot, dipped it in the cistern and swirled it around until it billowed out, forming a little bag of water. She drew it out, dripping. The water would seep out, but the silk she'd created somehow out of dust and thin air was very good, close-woven and almost water-tight. She made her way back, a trail of drips following her. She could see surprisingly well. Clouds had moved in overhead, and were sending a dim light down. She realized what it must be. The city of Arles was on fire, and the flames were reflecting back to earth. It had either been conquered and set to the torch, or burned deliberately by its remaining inhabitants, to keep it from Petru's grasp.

Among the clouds she could see shapes moving. Roiling and twisting in their desire to observe the chaos. The Great Gods were here to enjoy the sport. She looked down again.

"Where are you? I have water."

"In this hole. I can't tell you how to find it, for I was dead to the world when I was put in here. Perhaps I am already dead, and only dreaming... but then why am I so thirsty?"

Freewoman stepped forward in the dark, feeling carefully with one sandalled foot. Edging around a boulder, she almost lost her footing and toppled into the hole. It was a remnant of the old mining operations, now a handy storage place for an enemy of the state. She knelt and peered down, seeing nothing. She lowered the silk bag. "Here," she said. "I can get more."

He caught it, pulled it in, and soon she could hear Jameel greedily sucking the water from the folds of fabric. She could smell him very well now. Under the stinks of man-sweat, urine and blood was the familiar odour of her father's skin and hair, faintly spicy. She sniffed appreciatively. As a *resura*, smells—even repulsive ones—fascinated her. They told her so much.

For one thing, they told her that Jameel-her-father was alive, and not a ghost or spirit there to trick her. And that he had been in this hole for quite some time—time that was almost over. They had at most another day or two to get Jameel out of here, assuming they didn't get caught before Petru even arrived.

"At first I thought you were a boy, but you must be a woman," Jameel said, his voice clearer now. "What is a woman doing in this death-trap?"

"I am a friend, as I said. I have heard of your fight against Petru. I wish to join you."

Jameel laughed. "What, down here? Your fight would be better elsewhere."

Vara, hearing him laugh, had to wait for the grinding pain in her heart to subside before speaking. "No. No, of course not. But I can try to free you."

"What a fine idea, my warrior maiden. But I am down here, and I have little chance of springing out and dashing away."

"I can help you!" She jumped up. "Wait—I'll show you—"

"As I said, I'm not going—*what*?" His voice was startled.

Vara, now Bird, had perched upon his shoulder. Her nightingale eyes could see better in the dark than her human ones, and she could faintly make out the familiar, beloved lines of her father's face. But he was so thin! And filthy, and his beard was unkempt... and, she saw with a jolt of horror, his right eye was now a blackened socket. Nothing but puckered skin and the remnants of dried blood. Immediately she hopped to the other shoulder, and saw with relief that he still had his left eye.

Jameel held up his left hand, and gently took the bird upon his finger. "What is this? Are you the friend who brought me water, and talks to me? Do you know, I thought for a while I had died and was dreaming of my other life. Before the Scorpion got me."

The bird said nothing.

"In my other life I had the most beautiful wife a man could imagine. And a daughter just as lovely. I was a rich man, a proud man. Now look at me, little bird." Jameel croaked a laugh. "What would those two beautiful women think of me now? I shall never see them again..."

Did he mean he'd never see them again because he would die soon? Or because he knew they were dead? Vara was afraid to ask.

Jameel needed to talk, it seemed. He had always been a good talker, as Vara knew well. A good story teller. He asked, "Whom do you represent, you who must be *resura*? Did my friend Diego the Córdoban send you to find me? Or perhaps it was the King of Akvaristan, that old liar... do not trust him, even if he shows you his black tooth..." He began to cough, and tried to suck more water out of the silk.

Jameel began to mutter despondently. "How futile, to plan the death of Gods or men. I am but a mortal, chained to a mountain, sucking water like milk from a teat..."

Her own black tooth was gone, stolen by Petru. Obviously her father didn't realize who she was. Could she tell him? Inform this broken, shackled man that his daughter had passed from the human realm into a nether region he could never more than glimpse? He'd know instantly what it would imply: that he couldn't trust her. His own child might now be the slave of a man or a God, under a compulsion to trick and torment him.

And of course he'd ask: what of your mother? How does she fare? And she would have to tell the truth: his beloved wife was *resura* too.

No, she thought. Later. Later I will tell him everything. Later, Gods willing, he will be reunited with my mother. Surely their love will transcend the limitations of her forms.

She changed to Freewoman beside him, and he only grunted at the sudden shift in her size. From tiny bird to tall, lithe woman—

how did she do it? Perhaps, should Vara and Jameel ever have the chance to sit quietly together and talk, they'd figure it out. But now, Jameel wasn't up to much more than hanging on to existence. Exhaustion and pain lined his face and dulled his wits.

She asked, "Can you climb out of here, do you think? With me to help you?"

In answer, he raised his right arm. It was wrapped in a cloth crusted dark with blood. "My hand is gone." Ah... that's what the smell is, she realized. Not merely piss and shit, but body-rot as well. She almost whimpered like a beaten dog just then, but forced herself to be silent. But then Jameel gestured downward, and her eyes followed. His left foot was shackled to the rock, the right foot was gone. Only a stump remained, with the swollen, twisted look of a wound that had been cauterized in fire. To stop the bleeding; also, to help keep a man alive long enough to interrogate.

She fell to her knees before him. "Your foot, your hand, your eye... he took them all." Her father had been cut in half, left here to rot until his captor deigned to kill him. She wanted to scream, to rail against the Gods. She wanted to find Petru and gouge out his eyes with her own fingers.

If her father sensed her helpless fury, he didn't acknowledge it. He only sighed. "I'll not be leaving here soon."

"We will find a way," she said, her voice thick with pain. "Your fight goes on, but is hopeless without you at its head, Jameel Al-Kindi. There are many who pray for your return to the world of the living."

"For in here," he grunted, "I am dead. Am I not? Yet I hear the pounding of Petru's machines at the walls of Arles, and I smell the smoke. I know what he's doing, even the why of it. The miserable bastard can't help it."

"Don't waste your pity on Petru." Vara was tempted to tell him what Petru had done to Ragna Svobodová, to fire his anger, but held her tongue. "We have to get you out of here."

Jameel's teeth gleamed briefly in a tired smile. "That would be very good."

Chapter Twenty-Nine
THE KNOWLEDGE IN FINGERS

Freewoman left to find something, anything, that could be used to assist Jameel out of his prison-hole. A stick to lean on, a ladder, a rope. She could hoist him up, or push from below... but his leg was chained.

Vara hoped shit-boy wasn't off tattling to his masters in hopes of an extra bowl of soup. Time kept speeding by, faster and faster. She glanced skyward to judge the night's passage, but clouds and smoke obscured the stars. The mine was lit eerily by the burning city's reflected light, and she was able to note things that were almost, but not quite, useful.

Rocks, which she could push into the hole, filling it so Jameel could climb out. But the rocks were either too small to do the job or too large to shift, and besides they'd make a horrid racket clacking into the hole. So far they had been lucky, but someone would eventually notice them. And what if the rocks hit her father? He'd have even less chance to get out.

She tested some of the starved, dry bushes clinging to crevices. Could she weave stems together and form a rope or crude support? But the branches were brittle, and they only snapped between her fingers. And Jameel was still chained.

She thought of Chaim. He had helped her. She was quite sure he knew who Jameel really was. But whose side was he on, Petru's or Jameel's? Could even her own father be sure? She had to ask. She changed to bird and fluttered back into the hole.

Jameel sat leaning against the rough wall, his head sunken onto his chest, but his one eye opened immediately at the touch of the bird's little claws on his wrist. "Ah, you are back. See? I have gone nowhere."

Bird changed to Boy.

"Someday you must tell me how you do that, little one. Someday I will have many questions to ask you..."

Boy hopped from foot to foot. "There is a man called Chaim chained not far from here. He helped me find you. Do you know him? Do you trust him?"

"Ah! He lives. I am glad to hear it. Yes, I trust him."

"So if I find a way to free him and get him to help us, you can swear to his honour?"

Jameel nodded, and his one eye followed avidly as Boy became Bird and flew up and away, a small dark shadow upon the deeper darkness.

Vara had left Ragna Svobodová waiting for word in a hillside cave below the mine. Bird flew to her, only to find the cave empty. But as soon as she alighted on the ground she felt a rush of air as Hawk landed beside her.

"I found him! He's alive, but... but..." She couldn't tell her mother about Jameel's pitiful state. Like so many other things, it would have to wait until later. "He's chained, but I think I know how to free him!"

Hawk let out a high, piercing screech, and spread her wings wide. "He lives! What is your idea, Vara? For I have none."

"You must become Knife Woman again. As Boy, I have knowledge to pick locks, but I have no tool. You must make one for me!"

"I am a knife sharpener, not a forger of metal. How could I do it? I have never seen a lock pick."

"But Boy has used one. My fingers have the feel of it in them—I know how to release the locked shackles of a prisoner."

Knife Woman began to nod as Boy drew with his finger on the old woman's hand, in a curve that would match the needed tool. "Yes. I think I can do it... but I must form my cart once more." A shudder ran through her stooped body. "I thought I would never need it again..." Boy watched as the cumbersome barrow materialized, more slowly than when the *resura* changed their forms. But at last, there it stood, complete with grinding wheel and all the accoutrements necessary for her profession. Knife Woman began to rummage in the cubbies built into the cart, and came up with a metal file as long as her hand. "Will this do?"

"It's too big," stated Boy. "You must grind it down, then form a bend at its tip."

"How is it that we know these things?" Knife Woman's voice was breathless and jittery as she began to pedal away at the mechanism that drove the wheel. She touched the file to it, and sparks began to fly. Boy ran about stepping on them before the grasses could catch fire.

The night was half gone before the pick was shaped to Boy's satisfaction. He held it in his small hands, turning and balancing it. "It's not exactly what I picture in my mind, but I think it will do. The shackles I saw on the prisoners were old, not the latest ones from Germania." How *was* it that the *resura* knew what they knew? One couldn't deny magic, but perhaps one could discuss it, someday.

Boy changed to Bird and attempted to lift the pick with her beak, then her claws. She couldn't. The metal implement must weigh more than her own body. Dismay filled her voice. "It's too heavy! You must grind it smaller!"

But Knife Woman changed to Hawk and plucked it up with her talons. "I am done with waiting." She sprang into the air, flapping mightily against the weight of the metal.

"Come back!" cried Vara, following as fast as her smaller wings could carry her. "We need a plan! Stop!" She couldn't let her mother come upon Jameel in his pitiable state without warning, nor could she let blind recklessness destroy whatever chance they had. "He has been gravely injured! Even without a shackle around his leg, he'll barely be able to move. We need to stop and think!"

Hawk didn't slow, but before they got halfway to the mine, Eagle plummeted out of the night sky, forcing them both to the ground. Hawk screamed angrily but stayed to listen.

"Akil," cried Vara, changing to Boy. "Is Miss Marsh alive?"

But before Akil could reply, Hawk changed, but not into Knife Woman.

In a tawny-gold blur, a huge cat formed. A lioness came into being, snarling as her lithe body shaped itself from air and dust. The little nightingale hopped backward in sudden panic. Her mother's third form, at last. It was not what she expected. Vara had become sure that her mother had chosen the form of a fierce male warrior, capable of besting a fellow warrior like Petru in battle. Not this long, sleek cat whose tail was lashing like one of Petru's whips.

But she remembered something Miss Marsh had told her, while they catalogued specimens. *The lioness is the hunter in the lion family. The male, despite his virile mane and large size, watches from the shadows as his mate takes down her kill...*

Bird became Freewoman, and stepped forward with her arms outstretched and soothing words on her tongue. The lioness roared, and Vara stood completely still. "Mother," she whispered. "It's me, Vara."

The lioness splayed her claws. "Do not test me, daughter!" The lioness's teeth gleamed ivory-gold under the sky's ruddy light. "Nothing but talk! Talk, talk! Useless! I want to find my man. I want to kill Petru. Is that hard to understand?"

"You think it will be easy? We have to make a plan!"

"There's no time." Lioness lashed out a paw at Freewoman, but drew back her wicked claws just in time.

Vara flinched, but recovered. "Boy and Freewoman will release him. *He* will do the planning. It is not for us to decide the tactics of war, Mother."

Lioness crouched over her fore-paws, lowered her great golden head and groaned. Vara watched her, understanding that, whether she wanted to or not, she must now take the lead. Her mother was too terrified of her husband's plight to think. Jameel needed to be freed.

She changed to Nightingale and hopped close to the lioness's head, shrinking under the hot breath and the teeth. Every Bird instinct shouted for her to fly away. "Mother, be Hawk. Now. We will fly to my father. Take up the lock-pick and follow me. Akil, you too. The guards are lazy and corrupt. We can get to the mine without being seen."

Akil held up a hand. "Wait—listen to me. Miss Marsh has been taken captive." Quickly he explained what had happened. "She's safe for now. But I saw that they are driving their horses to exhaustion and will join Petru soon. All will arrive here within hours."

Lioness groaned again. "Carolina Marsh, captured? Oh sweet Uzma, now we have another human to rescue." The big cat lashed her tail, but changed to Hawk. She and Nightingale took off.

Vara thanked whatever God was on their side—if any—that Petru thought this hidden prison needed little guarding. And why not? Anyone opposing him was either dead or in chains. And who would imagine that a prize like Jameel would be sequestered here, far from Petru's headquarters?

Hawk, following Nightingale, settled to the ground and dropped the pick at the hole's entrance. Boy materialized, grabbed it and immediately clambered down.

Jameel, who had been asleep, came awake with a gasp. "Is it you, my changeling friend?"

"Yes. Hold still." Boy took the bent sliver of metal and inserted it into the shackle's lock, and in a few moments of twisting and prodding had it open. The knowledge within his fingers had worked. The cruel metal clamp fell free, and Jameel rubbed his bruised-black ankle with his one good hand. He tried to stand up and could not. Boy hauled him to his feet. "Another friend is joining us... watch out!"

The orange cat leapt down and immediately became Akil. The prison hole was becoming crowded.

Jameel's eye opened wide. "Ah! You!" Then he sent a long, sad look at Boy but said nothing. He knows, thought Vara with a hard twisting in her chest. He knows it's me. But Jameel said only, "Akil, my friend, I await your kind assistance."

Together Boy and Akil shoved Jameel up and out of the narrow pit, as Knife Woman hauled on his one good arm from above. With a stifled moan of pain, Jameel at last reached the surface. Knife Woman stepped back into the shadows as Jameel rolled to a sitting position and looked about. His face was grey, even in the false dawn of reflected firelight. "I never thought to leave that hole alive. But we are still within the mine."

Boy said, "True. But I can release Chaim as I released you. I should have done so first—but..." But Vara had forgotten everything but her father's plight. "He can help us! But if he is traitorous and raises the alarm..."

"He won't. I trust him. It was in trying to rescue Chaim and some others that I found myself taken, in a trap. But now perhaps the trapped may become the trapper..." He was panting, feverish and exhausted, but he was still in command. Vara's heart swelled, and she had to restrain herself from flinging herself at her father and huddling against his chest, as she had long ago when she was a child frightened by imaginary spirits. Real ones were easier to face, somehow.

"Shall I release him now, Pa—now, Jameel al-Kindi?"

He squinted up at her. "Wait, just a moment, if you please, little one. There was another here just now, a grey-haired woman..."

Boy hung his head. "It is no one, and she has gone now, and she was never here—"

Jameel held up his good hand. "Stop. We must have no deception among us. It is a waste of precious time." He looked about him, and found the strength to raise his voice above a whisper. "Woman! Come forth!"

And out of the darkness stepped Knife Woman. Tears were

streaming down her withered cheeks. She dropped to her knees beside Jameel and after a long shared moment of staring at one another, she took up his good hand and placed a kiss on it. Jameel let out a groan that was almost, but not quite, a lament. As if his heart had shifted within him to find a lower place among his bowels. His shrunken form seemed to shrivel even more.

Vara, aghast at how far her once vital, beautiful parents had sunk, wanted to look away but could not.

Knife Woman reached for his other hand—the one that was no longer there—and after a moment of reluctance Jameel let her take the bandage-wrapped stump and clutch it to her breast. "Jameel-my-husband. You are alive."

"And you are dead, Ragna Svobodová, my wife."

"I am *resura*," she whispered. "My time as one of the living is over."

"And yet you are among us, and by my side. Will you stay with me, and fight beside me, and be my dearest heart?"

At this Ragna crumpled to the ground. He stroked her coarse grey hair, and after a while she composed herself. With an expression of fierce determination, she gazed at her husband, and seemed all at once to put the past out of her mind.

Vara watched, unable to speak, as the two of them agreed, wordlessly, never again to weep for what was lost.

Turning to Vara, Jameel said, "And you, my child... it is you, my Vara-Varisha, is it not?" She nodded. He said, "Free Chaim and bring him here. Be quiet about it."

Chapter Thirty
HOW BATTLES WORK

Chaim was awake, lying flat on his back on the bare stone ledge, staring up at the orange-red of the clouds. He started when Boy stepped out of the shadows. "You again," he grunted. "Did you find him?"

Boy nodded, took the pick from the folds of his breechcloth and started in on the man's shackles. Chaim sat up, rubbed a hand across his face and through his straggling black beard as the shackles loosened, and for a moment sat still, as if his bonds were still there.

Then, with a popping of joints, he climbed to his feet and took a few experimental steps. "Ah! Free. But for how long? I won't ask who you are, boy, for I might not like the answer... I fear that things are not going well, out there." He staggered a bit, then caught his balance and straightened.

Boy took the man's arm to steady him. "You are right. Come with me. Jameel is out of the hole and must speak with you."

Her mother had once, long ago, explained to her how battles worked. Her father refused to talk of such things to a daughter, at which injustice Vara had silently railed. But Ragna Svobodová turned out to know quite a bit about the art of war.

"First of all," she had said, "understand that the best laid plans and strategies will crumble and fall once battle has been engaged."

"But why bother to make plans, if they are sure to fail?"

"Ah, but they won't truly fail if you have enough of them. Never rely on just one plan of action, no matter how sure it may seem, or how many times you have drilled your men in its execution. As Horace wrote, 'To have begun is half the job—be both bold and sensible.'"

"What does that mean?"

"To me, it means that any action is better than none, and that one must be not only brave, but also clever. To have the sense to watch, and learn, and be ready to turn as quickly as Amjad can turn. To wheel about and take advantage of your enemy's mistake."

"But what if my enemy makes no mistakes?"

"Your enemy will always make mistakes. You must be ready to see them."

Vara remembered how she had felt when she had uttered the next, inevitable words: *But we will make mistakes too.* Her mother had nodded. "Of course we will." Then she had sighed, pausing for a moment in her wifely task of sorting linens into those that should be cleaned and mended, those that should be folded and stored away, and those that should be let go to charity. "It is unlikely that you will ever be called upon to fight a battle, my dear child. But I do enjoy talking of such things, don't you?"

And she had. She and her mother were alike that way. It had seemed exciting, dangerous, full of meaning. Much more interesting than household duties. But since that day, back when Vara and Ragna had been human, the world had changed.

Under the lurid, smoke-hazed sky above the mountains east of the burning city of Arles, Vara prayed they would make no mistakes.

Jameel al-Kindi drank an amazing amount of water. Akil watched the man come to life as Freewoman carried another dripping bag for him to suck upon. Also, he tore ravenously at the dove Eagle had caught, after Freewoman had ripped the feathered skin from the small bird and pulled the tender breast meat off for him. Jameel wiped his hand and mouth on the damp folds of Freewoman's silk robe, which absorbed the bloody stains readily. It too was *resura* in nature; another mystery for them to contemplate should any of them remain alive, or with their souls still free, after this night.

Akil sighed. Chances were great that Vara would lose her father in the next few hours, in a second, more permanent way. Jameel would vanish into the Netherworld, beyond the view of human or *resura*, and Vara would grieve and rage against fate. But it was not fate, it was human weakness and Godly desire. Quite similar to fate, in that these things were impossible to change.

But, he thought, there had to be hope. Akil had given up hope in his years in the seraglio, but it had found him again in the unlikely form of Miss Carolina Marsh. He could feel her drawing closer, and experienced along with her the odd combination of exhaustion and anger that kept her from despairing.

But as she drew near, so did Petru Dominus, the Scorpion of Askain. Plus the fighting men accompanying him.

Jameel, Knife-woman and Chaim had their heads together. If anyone had a chance against the coming slaughter, it was them. Though he knew nothing of Chaim, Akil sensed an intelligence and strength within the man. Vara, as Boy, had whispered to him that he'd seemed honest and true to her, when she had earlier touched him. His mind was strong enough to withstand the blandishments of a wily *resura*, in other words.

They seemed to have finished their palaver. Chaim got to his feet and melted away into the darkness, Boy padding along by his side, lock-pick in hand.

Jameel beckoned Akil closer. "Akil, my friend... I would be pleased to refresh myself in conversation with you, but alas, we have no time at present."

Akil shrugged. "Another day, Jameel al-Kindi. How may I be of service to you?"

"You can tell me how your *alanbir* fares. Is she injured?"

"I can feel only her emotions, and they are... mixed. She is not hurt, other than her pride."

"Does she draw close?"

"Yes. And quickly. At this moment she is no doubt planning escape."

Jameel nodded. "Ah. I have great respect for that woman. But you understand what is at stake in this war. If there comes a time when she must *not* escape, but stay and fight, do you think she would do so?"

Akil raised his head proudly and looked straight at Jameel's ravaged face. "My *alanbir* would give her life for a cause that is just. And yours is just."

But then, thought Akil, what will become of me? Could he, without a master alive in this world, remain in the fight himself? He would wish to, but might find himself in thrall to a new *alanbir*. Or one of the Gods who clustered overhead, hungering for the blood that soon would flow. He could feel them leaning close.

Jameel said, "You must find her. Try to locate Petru as well. When you do, report to me. I must know how much time we have."

Akil nodded, and as cat crept stealthily to the highest point of the mine, then became eagle. He glanced back as he circled away to the southwest. So far, the prison-mine was quiet, locked in darkness and in iron shackles. A few torches burned near the main gate, that was all. No one moved down there but Chaim and Boy, who were busy releasing certain men, and making sure that certain others were silenced. It didn't matter how.

He turned his great wicked head to the south, where his *alanbir*'s pull was the strongest, and flew to her.

Unfortunately all he could do was circle above her in frustration as dawn crept ever closer. None of his forms could go unnoticed, certainly not with the *falci* there, so he soared at a height that made him a mere speck against the hazy orange sky. His eagle eyesight was remarkable, so far beyond any human's that it was almost godlike. However, it meant he could see what was coming only too clearly.

Petru and his extensive contingent of men, horses and supplies must have travelled at speed all night, for now the two groups—Petru's large one, and the four who had captured Miss Marsh—had converged at the base of the mountain road leading to the mine. He counted a total of forty men. They had dismounted and were tending to their animals, checking their tack and weapons, quickly pissing, gulping ale and swallowing their rations.

Akil could hear the neighing and groans of the sweating animals, and the fast, slangy Turkic of shouted commands. The only thing that might slow them was the steep switchbacks that wound back and forth between limestone outcroppings and scrubby pines. He calculated that they would arrive at the mine's gates shortly after sunup.

He spotted Miss Marsh, huddled eyes downcast at Petru's feet. He and his personal guard were questioning her. Akil couldn't hear their words, but could imagine what she was saying. Or perhaps not. Was she attempting her dim but earnest ploy? That wouldn't work for long with a man like Petru—he would soon torture her into revealing whatever she could. Yet a show of defiance would be worse. Petru's *falci* woman clambered out of the wagon in which she rode, tottered over and bent to give the little Briton a thorough sniffing. Akil saw her shake her head, extract a strip of dried meat from her sleeve and begin to gnaw it. Miss Marsh turned her head away.

Though Akil knew that his *alanbir* would not intentionally tell Petru anything that might assist him, he also knew she understood what happened to everyone eventually. "They all talk," she had said. "Every one of them." Not only poor lost Eneko. She would do it too.

The men had other concerns right now. Fresh horses were

brought up and saddled. Petru, who was moving in a strangely mechanical way, as if his joints hurt, climbed aboard a big black who snorted and chewed its bit. The man was being pushed relentlessly, whether by his own will or that of a God, Akil did not know. Probably the animals were being pushed too, beyond their endurance, for reasons the creatures couldn't understand.

Petru kicked his horse close to Miss Marsh and gestured for one of his men to toss her up to him. He settled her firmly before him. Akil clacked his eagle beak as Miss Marsh clung to the horse's mane. Clever bastard. A human shield, to augment the breastplate he wore. Even god-addled, the man was wary enough to purchase more insurance against an arrow.

The whole lot of them started up the winding road, Petru prudently letting six of his men precede him and the rest cover his back.

Akil wheeled away toward the south, in case anyone was watching him, then doubled back to the mine once out of human eye-view.

Dawn was a rising glow in the east, and the mine's overseers were waking up. Soon it would be noticed that things were not as they should be. Vara thought herself afraid, but then realized it was actually a wild sort of joy. The horrid hours of anticipation and worry were over at last.

They would fight and win—or fight and die. What did it matter? The hereafter was a mystery to everyone, even one such as she. The idea of clinging desperately to life had become an unfortunate delusion. Was she becoming as cynical as Akil?

That might be a good thing.

They had a goal: isolate Petru and kill him. Any soldiers who got in the way would die too. An ambitious but simple plan whose only advantage was that of surprise. They'd needed to eliminate the possibility that some prisoners might call a warning; these men had been killed or gagged, she didn't care which.

Yes, she was becoming more like Akil, and like Miss Marsh. Bloody-minded, logical, ruthless.

The person she was most like, Vara realized, was her mother. She smiled, though it was a chastening revelation. There had been a time when she'd thought her mother foolish, old-fashioned.

She shifted position, longing for the waiting to be over.

Jameel had instructed each of them to take their most formidable shape, in her case that of Freewoman. Not terribly fearsome. If she could go back to the time before her death and choose again, she'd choose something with fangs and claws, not a mere short-bladed knife.

The weight of the knife against her thigh troubled her. She wished that as Boy she could carry it, but when she shifted form it vanished along with the rest of her woman's body and clothing. If Boy had to fight he would have to improvise. He had used the lock pick, why not a dagger? He could steal one, perhaps. But the lock pick had vanished when Ragna changed form. And as Nightingale? Well—she had bartered away her teeth.

The loyal men hidden among the rocks, ledges and rubble piles of the vast mine were armed only with what implements they'd been using to dig or smash stone, though a few had improvised short spears from broken barrow handles. Vara had to admit that they were all most likely going to die. Except for herself, her mother, and Akil—and all of them would be cast into a lottery of who, or *what*, could capture their souls.

I would rather die.

A ghostly shape jumped down from a rock to land beside her. Shit-boy. Her heart settled. His teeth flashed in a grin as he crouched beside her in the half-light, leaning close.

"I saw you," he whispered into her ear. "I saw you do it! You can change from boy to woman! You are magical!"

The little wretch reached out a stinking paw to touch her, and Freewoman slapped his hand aside. What was she going to do with this annoying child?

"Yes," she hissed. "I am magical—and I can send you straight to the mouth of Saraf if I want, so you'd better be quiet and not try anything stupid."

"Who, me—stupid? Do you think I wish to anger one who has godly power? No! I would serve you."

Vara gazed through the eyes of Freewoman, who, she'd noted, saw colours differently. Everything seemed more intense, reds in particular. She saw, as the light brightened, that Hubert's faded breechcloth had once been red. Had his mother given it to him, wrapped it tenderly around her son's skinny hips? She looked at his filthy, starved face. If they got through this alive, she should try to find the boy's mother. Perhaps she'd give up whoring if the war was over.

"Hubert, will you swear your loyalty to me, and to my master, Jameel al-Kindi?"

Shit-boy nodded vigorously. "I will! I swear it!"

"Because if you betray us, I can kill you in more ways than Saraf or Petru ever imagined."

The little rascal bowed and made obeisance to her, as if she were a queen. Freewoman reached out a hand and grasped his shoulder. He flinched, but did not try to run. Through his skin she felt his fear, and his hope, and his grinding hunger. She nudged a little with her mind... *tell the truth, boy...*

"I will serve you," he repeated. It was true. He meant what he said, at least for now.

"Very well, Hubert. You are under my protection." She wished she could get the boy something to eat, for it would go far to ensure his allegiance. "When this is over and we escape, I shall conjure you a feast fit for a Sultan."

Hubert's eyes fairly glowed. What use he could be? Not much less than anyone else here, she supposed.

"Hubert, you know this mine well?"

The boy nodded. "Oh, I do! I know many things! For instance, I know of a secret way from the southwest terraces into a cave."

"A cave?" That could be useful, should they need to retreat. And be trapped inside it. Not good. Retreat was not part of the plan.

"And I have heard that the cave has cracks and tunnels leading out onto the mountainside. When the winter rains come, the water comes rushing out, and joins the stream that serves our village."

"You have heard this?" A secret escape route. Could these cracks and tunnels accommodate a man? It seemed too good to be true. "Why have you not taken this way out?"

The boy shrugged. "There's nothing for me out there. My home is burned to the ground. Everyone I know is gone. Here there is work and food, and I don't have to fight."

Vara suspected that the cracks and tunnels were the product of Hubert's imagination. He was trying to please her. "Hubert, find a place to—"

But then the air changed. The scent of the lavender and sage that clung to the rocky crevices around them changed to the familiar stink of burning waste.

Petru had arrived.

Chapter Thirty-One
THE GODS CARE NOT
FOR JUSTICE

A kil had pointed out that should Miss Marsh die, he might be suborned to the other side. Jameel had seen the danger, and ordered Akil to free her if he could possibly do it. This was complicated by the fact that she was clasped in the arms of their enemy.

"Do your best," Jameel muttered from his position propped against a square chunk of rough stone. Akil smelled the bad blood sickening him, felt the heat of fever. Jameel saw his concern, and waved him off. "Go! Signal when you succeed."

When. Not *if*. The man was half-dead, and yet he thought and acted as a general. "Eagle will shriek twice when she is free," Akil said, then vanished into the shadows.

As the orange cat, he sprang up upon a narrow ledge overlooking the mine's entrance, the one spot he'd found that was out of view of the mine's guards. Were he a man, he'd be seen, but as cat he could flatten himself against the rock. If only he could prevent his tail from lashing. In all the years Akil had been *resura*, he had rarely become excited by anything. Or interested enough to pursue a calling of his own, as his *alanbir* pursued hers—that of exploring the world and collecting its mysterious treasures. He had despaired of vaulting himself out of the slough of boredom and lethargy in which he'd found himself. Conscious, yes; aware, yes. Grateful for a second chance? Of course. Truly alive? No.

Akil believed he had never really felt alive.

But should he not seek a mission, a calling into which he could pour his intellect? He had been gifted with a second level of being. It would be a shame to waste it. But nothing in this world of pain and treachery had ever engaged his sustained interest.

Until now.

The love he felt for Vara Svobodová bint Jameel had opened a door in his heart that he hadn't known he possessed. He loved Carolina Marsh as he might have loved a mother. And that was a source of comfort and sustenance to him.

But the door between himself and others had been built of hatred, locked with the disgust he'd garnered from his years of captivity among degenerates. It had opened for Vara, and for her alone. He had never expected to love a mere human, not in the way a man truly loved and desired a woman. He had liked Vara when she was a girl travelling through the world of the living. She was clever, beautiful and kind. Also lazy, impulsive and rather clumsy. He smiled. She was not perfect, nor ever would be.

It was part of her charm, he reflected cynically. Was that why he longed to protect her? Was that when friendship had become love? He'd felt the essence of what made her unique among beings when he'd held her in his arms. It had been a revelation to him. Her heart was pure. She abhorred liars, loved animals and children, adored her parents. She had always thought of herself as too thin, too plain, too ignorant to be worthy of much respect. How wrong she was. Never had he touched another *resura* in such a sustained way; never had he realized the powerful urge to meld that roiled within his being. It was completely unlike the sexual joining he'd experienced, and hated, when he was human.

He thought she had felt it too, but he might be wrong. Was it love they felt, or merely an irresistible desire to meld, as two drops of water would become one? Could he continue his days knowing she at best merely tolerated him?

Cat willed his tail to be still. And his mind to focus.

His whiskers bristled at the scent of men and horses. Six mounted men preceded their master. He must wait, not waste his moment of surprise on mere underlings.

The men passed below the orange cat's quivering whiskers. Then Petru on the big black. Carolina Marsh sagged limply before him in the saddle, as if half-dead from exhaustion. Akil knew by the prickling of her mind that she was feigning a swoon. Every muscle in her strong, small body was straining for action.

A hail of rocks suddenly clattered down onto the soldiers, clanging against metal armour and thudding on unprotected flesh. Hubert in particular had remarkable aim. As the soldiers looked for targets, Petru reined in his horse, which reared and tried to circle. He drew his sword and glared about. Had his grip on Miss Marsh loosened?

The sun was fully up now, but a thick, oily shadow fell from the roiling sky and laid itself across Akil's cat body. His fur sparked and his *resura* flesh recoiled. The hand of a God, taunting him. *Little Cat, what do you plan?*

Leave us alone. Find your sport elsewhere.

He hissed and prepared to jump as Petru backed his horse toward the ledge. He had been manoeuvred there—and as was his habit, he wore a light leather helmet and only decorative armour Such was his arrogance. Something Akil had confirmed earlier from overhead.

Cat sprang for Petru's head, yowling as he clawed for the man's eyes.

But the Hun was a brilliant horseman, and he still had Miss Marsh clamped under his elbow. Suddenly she screamed and went limp as if struck by a rock, and when Petru tried to dislodge the cat, she slithered to the ground headfirst. Akil saw her roll away from the horse's pounding feet. Petru had lost his human shield. Cat sank his teeth into Petru's neck, levering himself forward to claw the man's eyes, but suddenly felt himself digging at air.

Someone had grabbed his tail and was swinging him in a circle.

He felt an explosion of pain and darkness, then in a spinning of dust and choking smoke he found himself high overhead, as Eagle. He was looking down on a scene so tiny that it looked almost comical.

The inevitable had happened: he'd been killed in one of his forms. *So this is what death means for me now.* His first death, years ago, had been much more painful and prolonged.

He knew he'd clawed Petru's eyes. He'd felt them tear open; certainly he'd blinded the man. Yet Petru sat his horse as if he'd been born there, expertly turning it this way and that as he shouted orders. Eagle swooped as low as he dared, and saw Petru's face. It was dripping blood, the eyes ravaged and surely sightless, yet it was obvious he could do whatever passed for seeing, when a God was riding you.

Eagle plummeted to the earth in a swirl of darkness, grew legs, and fell the last few feet to Miss Marsh's side. Akil scrambled forward and dragged his *alanbir* into shelter. She bared her teeth, cradling one arm and gasping. "How fares the fight?"

"Yet to be seen," he said. As Eagle again, he shot into the air and screamed twice.

Vara saw an arrow fly past Hubert's bare belly. Saw him turn and run.

She paid no more attention to him. There was no time. Hubert would find a way to survive. She might yet serve him the feast she'd promised.

Freewoman flattened herself into a patch of shadow, ready to catch a soldier off guard. No luck so far. But then she heard two screams from overhead. Ah! Miss Marsh was free. Alive or dead? It didn't matter, not now.

Vara felt a ripple pass along her spine. Her lips drew back into something not a smile. This mad scene of noise and blood and pounding animals should have her in a huddled heap begging for her mother. At one time, it would have. But she was Freewoman now. And Freewoman knew how to fight.

The memories roiled in her veins. When Vara had picked this form, admiring its stately beauty and ferocious will, she gained all that it contained. Magical memories, knowledge baked into her muscles as wheat flour is baked into a loaf. Time upon time, Freewoman—whatever she was, if she had ever been a real person—had been forced to fight for her life. Most people left beings such as she a wide berth, but there was always someone, usually a man, who wanted to bring her down. Freewoman knew what the cord on her knife was for. It was there to loop around her wrist, so that when the knife became slippery with blood she wouldn't drop it.

I will never drop it. This knife is my claw, my tooth. A tooth that can never be tricked or bartered away.

One of their loyal men, scarecrow-thin and missing a hand, ran past her as if he'd been scalded. Behind him came a mounted soldier, focused so intently on his target that he did not notice the dark, still woman. As he passed, Freewoman stepped out of the shadows and slapped his horse's rump. *Snake,* she thought. *Coiled and hissing...* The horse dug in its forefeet, stopped in its tracks and sent its rider overhead to the ground. Freewoman leapt onto the gasping man, and with her blade found a sliver of belly below the stiff leather armour The knife seemed to know its way into a man's guts. And out again. Her hand understood just how to turn her wrist to wipe blood off the blade as she pulled it from the dying man's flesh. Vara watched, appalled but unrepentant.

This is for my father. My mother. This is for Eneko. She whirled away, letting the spooked horse plunge past her, and sought the next belly.

She killed three more men in this way before she died the first time.

The humans were slaughtering one another. Akil couldn't tell who was winning, and had no time to figure it out.

He changed from man to eagle to cat and back again over and over, doing as much damage as he could. In his human form he managed once to get close to Petru, but the man's bloody eye-pits swung his way like the portals of hell, and in an instant he'd swung his heavy blade and severed Akil's good arm at the elbow. Petru, forgetting such a minor adversary at once, kicked his horse away to find the next victim.

Akil cradled the bleeding stump of his arm, appalled. How could he regain his form? Didn't he have to die first? The pain was intense... but only for a moment. He watched, fascinated and appalled, as his arm grew back in a flurry of dust and blood. Was this regeneration a curse or a blessing? To be killed or maimed, over and over... it might be hell indeed. The severed limb lay on the ground. It twitched, shuddered as if it were burning, then sank into the dirt like water.

The stench of blood and spilled guts was thick in the air, the screams and groans of men and horses clawed at his ears. Miss Marsh could be discovered and killed at any moment. A death most permanent. Fear for her safety clotted his reactions, forced his attention away from the business of killing.

Sudden motion near the mine's supply shed caught his eye. Freewoman, not a trace of Vara's softness in her, leapt from the sparse cover of a cedar tree to stab at a dismounted soldier sprinting by. But she was too slow. The soldier saw her, and with one slash of his short sword, cut her belly open. She fell, clutching herself, a look of surprise on her face. The soldier ran on, oblivious.

Akil, transfixed in horror, watched as Freewoman became a puff of smoke writhing in the air like a silk shawl in the wind. Nothing was left of her.

He stumbled forward, forgetting about Miss Marsh, Jameel, their battle—then stopped when she suddenly materialized as Boy, halfway along one of the limestone galleries. Boy shrieked in anger, changed to Nightingale.

She flew to him, became Boy again. "Akil! Did that soldier see me change?"

He must have a heart because it had started to beat again. "No.

He thinks you're dead. We need to find Jameel. If he has died—"

"He lives. I saw him a minute ago." Boy crouched, a coiled little spring staring into some distance Akil couldn't fathom. Boy said, "We can't win, not like this."

"We must regroup. Plan. Find a better way—"

"What better way? Can you think of anything? We have nothing but starving prisoners throwing rocks, throwing their lives away. For what?"

"Our cause is just! We can't falter now, Vara—"

"Our cause? You're a fool, Akil. We are all fools. How can we vanquish a monster, a-a monstrous puppet driven by Gods—"

But then she stopped. Was silent. She held up a hand, as if to prevent herself or him from talking.

She looked at him, appraising. Judging. In a hard flight of dust-motes, Boy rose, swirled, and became Freewoman, standing tall with her knife in her hand. Not caring if anyone saw. A braided cord connected the knife to her wrist. "Come to me," she said. Commanded. She reached for him.

Something had changed in Vara, not her body. Her inner self. By the look on Freewoman's face, it was not good. Instinctively he drew away.

She caught his good hand, pulled him close. "Akil. My dear friend. My... my love. There's something—a, a thing I want to try. Trust me, Akil! Can you simply trust me now?"

He looked into Freewoman's night-dark eyes. Saw the strength there. He let her pull him in and wrap him in her arms.

Chapter Thirty-Two
THE NIGHTINGALE

Vara knew what she must do. The feel of Akil's *resura* body throbbed in hers.

We can't win this war by fighting like humans.

Had she said it aloud, or merely understood it, deep in her soul?

How Akil hated to be touched! His past haunted him still. "Closer, Akil! Don't let go." He obeyed her, twitching in her arms. She felt the churning presence of all the myriad particles of which his magical body was made. "Do you remember when you held me on the road home from Linqua? Our bodies tried to meld into one. So odd and disturbing, but I was tempted to let myself melt into you, as candle wax melts. Or as wine and water mingle in a pitcher... Oh, I can't explain it!"

He answered, his voice muffled against her neck. The soft, tight curls of her hair cushioned his cheek. "I remember very well. You were human then, but your *da resu* nature glowed in you like a flame. We could have melded... and my body would have eaten yours alive. Devoured every speck of your substance without mercy. That is why, my sweet Vara, I so rarely touch you. But now..."

"But now. Yes! We are both *resura*. Nothing can stop us. Not gods, not soldiers, not hate or fear..."

"Not love."

Love. She knew he felt it too. Not just the bond of the dangers they'd braved, the chances taken, the battles still ahead of them. He loved her. She could feel it. And she loved him. Poor, crippled, clever Akil the slave-boy.

She pushed her fingers into his tangled brown hair. Felt the shape of his skull. The skull beneath the skin. He sighed and trembled. The strange internal roiling grew, insistent and irresistible.

It was too much. And it was not enough.

She pushed him away. "We need my mother."

"Ah," he said, understanding. "She won't be far from Jameel."

She wasn't. The lioness paced around her mate, who held Chaim's head cradled in his arms. Chaim, Akil could instantly see, was dead. Jameel mourned him as was proper, but this was not the time for such earthly rituals; they needed to fight.

Akil had the sudden premonition that what Vara had in mind might go terribly wrong. He also knew there was no way to stop her. Nor should he.

Vara, as Freewoman, dropped to her knees beside her father. "We will mourn Chaim later. Father, please forgive me for what I am about to do." She dropped a fast kiss on his head. Before Jameel could respond, she jumped up and dug her long dark fingers into Lioness's fur, pulling the great tawny head around.

Lioness snarled and struck, her claws barely missing Freewoman's belly.

"You can't kill me, Mother. Don't waste time. Akil! Come to us now."

Akil, ignoring his urge to stop and think, stepped into Vara's arms and dug his own fingers into Ragna Svobodová's hide. The creature panted and twisted under their hands. Ragna, mad with thwarted blood-lust, was unable to shift to another form. Vara pulled them both close. "Trust me," she said.

Akil hung on tight. He at least had an idea of what Vara might do; Ragna did not.

He could feel it starting already.

He closed his eyes. In his travels with Carolina Marsh, he had seen what a vortex could do. There was a stretch along the vast brown river in the Terra Torridia where no boatman would be foolish enough to venture. He'd never seen the legendary Charybdis, in the Strait of Messina, but knew it could suck a trireme down in heartbeats without a trace.

He was in such a vortex now.

Vara knew she didn't need to breathe. Her bodies only did it out of a stubborn refusal to admit they weren't alive any more. *Yet I do live. I love. I fear. I am confused and timid when I must be clearheaded and brave.*

Oh Sisters—what am I doing? Help me now!

She could feel Akil and her mother breathing as she did, hear the deep thunder of their dust-born hearts. They knew it too: *we are not among the living.* Yet their spirits refused to surrender that last and final bridge to what once was. And would never be again.

With the sensation of growing, or swelling, she felt the melding start. Once started it must not stop. She could not let the others grow fearful and break away. The fur and flesh under her hands writhed and tossed like grain fields in a tempest.

They knew what must be done. They trusted her.

Vara let herself go. Let her *self* go.

And felt the other *resura* flow into her, into each other as water from three vessels pours into one greater vessel. One too small to hold it all. The vessel burst.

The strange substance that was the melded *resura* threatened to shoot away like the fireworks her Pada Josef had loved so much, to spend its force uselessly against the sky. She could not let that happen. The last vestiges of her magical body had vanished; she had only her mind to gather the force the three had become.

She saw Akil's love for her, saw his damaged soul, saw in her mother the cold realization that her husband would die soon.

No. Accept their sadness and pain later. *Now we fight.*

Take the claws and fangs of the lioness, the stubborn strength and weapons of the knife woman. Pull in the talons and rending beaks of the eagle and the hawk. Gather the fighting knowledge of the Moorish woman, the wiles of the street boy. Take it all. Grow huge and fierce.

And gather the teeth the Nightingale had lost.

Akil felt himself torn to shreds, and less than shreds. The particles—*atoms*—that Josef Svobodá thought were the minuscule building blocks of everything. He became a mass of swirling atoms, substance without form. Matter without pattern. And then Akil saw the God. Felt it form around him. A new God, one whose mind reached into his and commanded him to obey.

And obey he did. Akil and Ragna clung to one another as Vara expanded, encompassing them in her new-found power. It was like riding the hottest updraft Eagle could imagine. He let it take him, and rejoiced.

The other Gods noticed the new-born one. Reared back like startled horses, and watched from their sky palaces as she grew and strengthened.

The new God was angry and vengeful, and she would not be reined in by those who merely sought sport and disruption. She knew what she wanted.

The Nightingale, small and insignificant no more, rose up, and up, and up, and spread her wings. And the wings were mighty and wide, and drew power from her fellow *resura* and from the dust and air and smoke and blood all around her. In an instant she was the size of a battle elephant, her wings like two great glistening sails buffeting the air. And her beak—

Her beak was like the prow of a ship, and was lined with a thousand teeth. Her wings drove gusts of wind before her as she sought her prey. Among the screaming, grovelling men it was hard to see the one she wanted... The men's souls, like soot-blackened curtains, drifted around their flailing bodies as the other Gods looked down.

They wanted to see what she could do, before daring to meddle.

She saw the soldiers' battle fever vanish as they beheld her. Some abased themselves, begging for mercy. Others dropped their weapons and ran. Those that held their ground she bit in half and spat away. At last only one remained. A man on horseback, barely controlling his screaming animal, his eyes dripping blood.

As the eyes of one she had loved dripped red, in an arena not too long ago.

Petru Dominus, the Scorpion of Askain. At her mercy.

She had no mercy.

He turned his blind eyes up to her, leaning back in the saddle to see the height of her. He bared his teeth and lifted his sword, a puny effort, but she acknowledged his spirit. It was only God-given, though; was he to be pitied? She lowered her sleek head, its gleaming feathers reflecting the lurid firelight from Arles, her great black eyes glittering. She looked into his face, saw the pain, smelled the rot, heard the gasps of his labouring lungs. The man should be long dead, yet the Gods still drove him.

"I will set you free," she said to him. "I will show you mercy."

He slashed at her, his horse bucking in panic under him.

She lowered her head. Opened her beak. And with one snap of her jaws she crushed him, felt the hot blood spurt and let Eagle savour it. Let Lioness drink it. Delicately she bit his arms off and let Ragna Svobodová, whose soul rode within her, rejoice that the hands that once gripped her neck were no more.

As life fled from Petru Dominus, the Scorpion of Askain, his Gods fled too. Or did they simply jump off as a rider abandons a dying horse? No longer of use.

The air reverberated like a beaten drum, battering Nightingale's ears and buffeting her wings. She blinked, revelling in the wind that blew the stink away.

The sudden wind died, and its absence, and the departure of the Gods, left the air empty. It was as if a violent summer storm had blown through in an instant and washed the sky clean. The remaining soldiers, and their horses, collapsed to the ground, exhausted or dead.

The Nightingale launched her huge body into the air, flew high and beheld the scene of bloody carnage. Unaware of the change in their fortunes, men still fought and died, and cities and farms still burned. But the fever had broken.

One by one, as if touched by expanding ripples in a pond, soldiers all over Askain felt the air change, looked about themselves in horror, dropped their weapons and fell to the ground to sleep where they lay.

Even the birds and insects settled to rest. Nightingale soared, and those few souls who remained awake dropped to their knees, pointed to the sky as she circled overhead, and marvelled at the thunder of her passage.

Within her breast and brain rode the souls of Akil and of Ragna Svobodová. Ragna could think only of Jameel, half dead in the mine. Akil felt the relentless pull of his *alanbir*.

Nightingale, ignoring their pain, flew wide and far, observing what lay below. The mine pit looked tiny. Such a small arena for such a decisive battle. Her great body cast a shadow that, when it touched a man, caused his heart to expand in awe and fear.

She drank their worship, as Eagle and Lioness had drunk Petru's blood. It tasted good.

Chapter Thirty-Three
AFTERMATH

Akil stopped what he was doing. Just stopped and closed his eyes and became thankful.

He thanked the sun for warming his shoulders, which did not need to be warmed. Yet the sun was generous enough to do it anyway. He thanked the aqueduct system, repaired now, that once again fed clean water to the fountains of Perpignan. He thanked the lemon tree for drinking the water he poured onto it, and for the enthusiasm it showed in producing blossoms.

The lemon tree was the one under which he'd tried to comfort Vara so long ago, when she had been a human railing against the brutality of kings and Gods. He understood her doomed love for the valiant Eneko. From everything he'd learned, the man had been admirable, brave and loyal. He was gone, to wherever humans went when they died. So much death. The most regrettable, from Akil's point of view, being that of Josef Svobodá.

Akil sprinkled his bucket's remaining drops of water onto the ground, for the Gods. *May you cherish and keep Josef Svobodá and Eneko Saratxaga, for they are as brilliant stars in the heavens.*

The Gods did not deserve such souls within their ranks.

He felt Vara approaching. She liked to check on the lemon tree too. It was a symbol, perhaps, of her family's resurgence. She wore her tall, stately, Moorish woman shape. He'd decided that it was much like what Vara might have been, had she lived to grow older than—what? Seventeen years? The same height, the same flashing dark eyes and soft, tight curls. This woman was more muscular, narrower of hip, and much more confident in her ways. Her silken robes were crimson, not the ochres and browns the living, human Vara had preferred.

But much of Vara remained in this woman. As it did in Boy. Not so much in Bird, which might be because Vara had become reluctant to take its shape.

Was it because it brought back memories of the huge, toothed Nightingale she'd become, which had vanquished an army?

No matter how much he coaxed her to join him in the air, she had done it only rarely, and afterward retreated into her own thoughts. He hadn't asked her for over a month.

Akil had feared at the time that the huge Nightingale would never let them go. That he and Ragna Svobodová would be forever locked within the immense bird's iridescent breast, riding with her like worms in a dog's belly. They had stayed melded, cruising the air above the battle, for what seemed like hours.

Vara came to stand beside him. He smelled the cinnamon warmth of her, and let his hand touch hers, but only lightly. He wanted more, but knew she cherished being her singular self. After a few moments she said, "Akil, Jameel al-Kindi asks that you join him. Without his usual staff, he can't keep up with the accounts and records. Even with Miss Marsh and her orphan girls busy at adding columns of numbers." She smiled. "He really does enjoy your company, Akil, and your cleverness."

Akil found that he was perhaps too pleased at these words of praise. Or kindness. Jameel al-Kindi was pressed for time these days, and Akil was eager for work to occupy his mind.

Jameel had been forced into leadership, since almost every other person capable of command and governance had either been killed or had fled the country. Despite his mutilation, he displayed none of the heartache and regrets that his wife suffered, and had found the mental strength to take up the reins of government even while his physical strength lagged.

Ragna, however, spent much of her time as Lioness, sleeping in the sunny courtyard of their home. Jameel had to coax and cajole her to work with him, and she would snarl as he tried to revive her spirits.

Akil thought he understood how Gods were made: *resura* that grew so strong that they simply engulfed any weaker souls they encountered, fattened upon them and used their incorporeal mass as fodder. As Vara had done. Had Vara sucked the spirit out of her own mother?

Was Ragna a weaker soul? What did weakness mean, when the youngest and most innocent among them could attain godhood? And yet Vara had spat out their souls, relinquished their bodies. Set them free.

He plucked a fragrant blossom from the lemon tree and held it to his nose. Then he passed it to Vara. "I am happy to serve Jameel al-Kindi however he desires."

Freewoman's full lips formed a smile that was not reflected in her eyes. "He is lucky to have such a friend as you, Akil. As am I."

He had to be satisfied with that. Akil left Vara and the lemon tree and went to Jameel.

After the battle, before they left the pit mine, the immense Nightingale had performed one last task.

She instructed Miss Marsh, Hubert, and a couple of other survivors to secure Jameel's weak and crippled body to her back, using strips of cloth torn from robes and turbans. Akil and Ragna, their essences still trapped within the huge bird's body, could only watch through her eyes.

She launched herself off the edge of the pit, spread her wings and flew, barely clearing the southwest rim of stone. All of them prayed to whatever Gods they still believed in that Jameel would survive the trip.

They had arrived in Perpignan in an astonishingly short time,

Nightingale's wings cleaving the air in a track straight as an arrow's. She landed with a great billowing of dust and shrieking of people in the square where once Vara and her friend Sigrun had marvelled at a lesser god.

The square cleared out remarkably fast. Not many people were left in the city to run from the sudden arrival of a fearsome, toothed bird, but Akil hoped the Uzmite Sisters still remained and had the resources to tend to Jameel. Seeing through Nightingale's eyes, he noted the destruction in the once rich and well-managed city. Even though the war was over, it would take many years to restore the city's and the nation's prosperity and peace. How much easier it is, he reflected, to destroy than to build.

There was no one to assist Jameel in climbing down from Nightingale's back. Akil observed with pity and admiration as the man fumbled at his cloth bonds, tearing them with his teeth until they loosened and he slid to the ground. As he lay panting next to the Nightingale's feathered shoulder, the huge bird shrank, roiling like a smouldering fire as she diminished and separated. The three individual *resura* emerged as if staggering out of a collapsing building.

Akil found himself sprawled on the plaza's filthy stones, the aftermath of war. He smelled the blood, the urine and offal that would not be washed away until the rains came. Boy tumbled to the ground, his eyes wide and half-mad. Knife Woman appeared in a swirl of dust, her barrow beside her.

She ran to Jameel, kissed him, and yelled at Akil to help load him into the barrow. "The Sisters are not far. Don't leave me until he is safe!" She began to dump the barrow's contents onto the ground, where they would probably, Akil surmised, vanish when she changed form again. He lifted the groaning man into the barrow.

Without a backward look, Ragna picked up the handles and hustled away with her precious cargo.

Akil looked at Boy. The child stood very still, sometimes glancing about as if trying to orient himself. Akil suspected that Vara's experience had changed her forever. He took Boy's hand and said, "Forgive me, my dear friend. I must—*must*—go now to my *alanbir*. Do you understand? I have no choice."

Boy said, "I would rather you stayed here with me, Akil. When I was Nightingale, I cherished the feel of you within me as I fought and flew."

Akil dropped Boy's hand, took his Eagle form and snapped his beak with impatience. What would Vara do? Was he truly free?

For a moment, Boy's face shrank into a scowl, but then some instinct toward logic took over. "Go," said Boy at last. "But come back... when you can."

Back at the mine, Akil and Hubert caught the few uninjured horses they could find and gave them water and grain. The next day, Hubert, Miss Marsh and Jameel's two remaining men rode down the long winding trail from the mine toward Perpignan. Eagle scouted ahead for the best routes around still-burning villages, bridges that had been blocked or destroyed, and the dangerous packs of humans foraging for what food they could find or steal.

It took five days and four nights, as no one was in very good shape. Half-starved, beaten and dazed, Hubert and the men with them could barely manage the odd half-hearted quip to show their spirits still lived in their exhausted bodies. Miss Marsh exhibited her usual stoicism, minus the wry humour Akil had come to love.

The humans were hungry, and there were only so many rabbits and quail Eagle could procure. Every field they passed had been thoroughly plundered of its turnips and cabbages. The two men left the second night, taking their horses and vanishing into the darkness. Their homes and families called; Akil did not blame them.

The city's gates were much easier to get through this time. No tale of non-existent aunties was needed, no biscuit-tiles were demanded. One jittery soldier eyed them as they passed through the arched doorway's shadow, the once-proud white crest atop his helmet cut prudently short. He had hammered Saraf's S on his breastplate into obscurity. Deeming them harmless, he went back to scraping mould off a quarter-round of cheese.

They went first to the house of the Uzmite Sisters.

Miss Marsh brushed dirt and road-dust from her skirt, and despite exhaustion straightened into an attitude of command as she approached.

The Uzmite Mother stepped forth. "Ah. You." She eyed the fierce-eyed little woman who had once worked beside her among the ill and elderly. No love had been lost between them. Everyone in the city was hungry and dirty, no one had time to hear tales of hardship.

"Yes, it is me. I'm hard to kill. Tell me—an old woman with an injured man came to you a few days ago. We must see them."

"They are gone," the Mother informed them coldly. "That old besom with the cart insisted that once her man was out of danger they'd find a better place. She had a tall Kek woman with her too." The Mother provided a theatrical shiver and waited for an explanation, but got none. She snorted. "Claimed she knew a noblewoman who'd take them in."

This meant, Akil surmised, that they'd gone to their villa, or what was left of it. He nodded, thanked the woman and left.

And now here they all were, camping like vagrants in the wreckage of their old home.

One day Akil and Vara decided to visit the scene of Ragna's death. Ragna herself would not go.

"Let Petru's palace rot. I don't care who loots and burns it. There is nothing I want from that cursed place." Lioness lowered her big, square, golden head to her paws and went back to sleep.

So the two of them, as Orange Cat and Nightingale, crept and fluttered their way through streets and squares beginning once again to fill with workers, merchants, traders, and war-battered soldiers looking for honest employment. Petru's palace was guarded only by a scattering of Emperor Ludvik's men, hastily sent to protect what remained of anything valuable. Since there wasn't much, they were spending their time gambling.

Cat and Bird slipped past them and climbed to the big white room. It was littered with shards of what was once ancient statuary, drifting with dust and soot in the unfettered breeze. The albino lion skin was gone. The bench and chairs, tables and wine cups, all gone. Vara became her tall, dark self and walked to the balcony. After one quick glance down to the street where her mother had died, she stood for a long time, gripping the rail and staring up at the sky.

Akil wondered if she was cursing the Gods. Or was she seeking admission to their ranks?

If we meld again, I will know her heart.

He was tempted to force it. Two things stopped him: first, that it would be a violation of her person and her soul, already stretched thin among her forms, and easily torn. Second, that he would regret it. Her power verged toward Godhood, and she could very well consume him.

At last she lowered her gaze and turned back to him.

She seemed to listen as he told her something he and Josef Svobodá had discussed, eons ago. "It is said that the gryphons, centaurs, mer-folk and so on are melded *resura* who were unable to separate and have gone mad. Also that free *resura* can take in the lost souls of other, weaker *resura* and gain their knowledge and experiences. Thus, over the decades and possibly centuries, they turn into Gods. Some benevolent and merciful, some cruel and insane. Will the good eventually overthrow the evil? Perhaps we will know, one day."

"Perhaps." Distracted again, she began to prowl the room, as if looking for something. "Akil... I smell my mother."

Akil knew better than to doubt her.

She turned abruptly and walked to a corner where a drift of broken things had ended up, and nudged it with the toe of her sandal, in case of vermin. Then she reached down and pulled at the edge of a bit of cloth that became a shawl as it rose, expanding and revealing its soft colours. "This is my mother's. She must have worn it, that last time... that last night."

The night she and Vara died.

Something fell from the shawl's folds and clattered to the marble floor. Freewoman gasped. She dropped to her knees and picked up a necklace. Three small tokens—eye and owl and tooth—dangled from it and caught the light.

She cried for a while. She held the shawl to her face, smelled its perfume, still Ragna's special scent. Akil took the necklace from her hand and affixed the clasp around her neck. Ragna's last act had been to retrieve her daughter's treasure from her tormentor. Her fingers went to it, touching each little token. Was she thinking of Eneko?

"Akil," she said at last, "when Nightingale killed Petru I tasted his blood, but also his mind. His mind was like a broken pitcher, shattered and leaking. But there were memories, still fresh. One of them..." She sighed, for she hadn't seen the present in those memories. "We must go and see for ourselves."

She reached for his hand, but he didn't take it. Probably not a good idea to touch her.

"Come," she said. "We must go to the lower levels."

They changed to smaller forms to creep past a cluster of Imperial scribes arguing over a spilled shelf of scrolls half-crushed by trampling feet. Down again, until the air was thick with darkness and the increasing stench of death. Akil stopped to listen. "There are animals still alive down here!"

"There must be. I can hear and smell them. Petru's brood mares, some prize bulls perhaps. Animals no one has been brave enough to steal. Or eat."

"Ah. We can set them free," he said. "Or call them ours."

"Yes. Our family has dominion now over Petru's former holdings. Commanding a magical, giant war-bird works wonders, even if it's just a rumour." A rumour corroborated by the many who had seen it fly. That bird might never be seen again, but its threat had power. "I'm hoping to find something better than breeding stock."

In human form again, they stepped over pools of urine and seepage from the walls, heaps of manure and rotting straw, and made their way past the empty cattle stalls to the horse stables. An air-well let down a thin wash of reflected daylight, illuminating several stalls. All empty. They continued along the row of ornately gated enclosures, peering into each one. At last they reached the end. Vara was ready to admit that Petru's fractured memory of a certain captive had been false, when a big, amber-maned head thrust over the railing to gaze at them. Its dark eyes glittered in the gloom, and it snorted, then began to kick and whinny.

Akil's face lit with joy. "Amjad. It's Amjad!"

To her own surprise, Vara burst into tears.

The hubbub of Amjad's reclamation died down. He was half starved, wild with thirst, but in only a few days was much improved and beginning to be troublesome. Jameel spent much of his time in the stables, close to the steed he loved.

Miss Marsh, tasked by Ragna with imposing order on chaos, had hired two girls from the Uzmite refuge, with the intention of teaching them to read and do sums as well as work as servants. Cataloguing the family's remaining possessions wouldn't take long; everything of value had been looted. Her best find so far had been an enamelled silver platter that someone had hidden among musty horse blankets in the stables.

Ragna, as Knife Woman, came to her one day, a scrap of parchment in her hand. "Here! Read this to me if you please." Professing not to see any value in learning to read, nevertheless she must hold her head high when in the presence of one who could.

Miss Marsh accepted it, cleared her throat and began to read. "It is I, Saskia Lubodová. To the family of the late Josef Svobodá, of the City of Perpignan, northwest quarter. Know this: I and my dear companion Kai are well and safe at the house of the Uzmites not ten leagues from the City of Bordeaux. My sister, whom I hoped to find, has married a Spaniard and gone with him to Cordoba. Kai and I spend our time with the Sisters cultivating vegetables as well as a colony of rabbits for sale, and in prayer and other good works. We shall not return to Perpignan, but will pray for the health and safety of our land and people."

She handed the letter back, smiling faintly. She and Saskia had got on well. "It is good news."

Knife Woman bit her lips and blinked very fast. Then she passed it back to Miss Marsh. "You will add this to our inventory of belongings. I will only lose it."

The threads of life began to weave straighter and clearer. People still wept over graves, but life went on. Ragna slowly emerged from her sorrow at the loss of her beautiful human form, and at her husband's terrible mutilation. Jameel, defying his limitations, was learning to ride again, using a specially made saddle to accommodate his handicaps. When he rode Amjad around the city streets and plazas, men and women bowed before him and called out blessings.

Sometimes, causing much consternation, a lioness padded alongside them, gazing about her at the people who stared back. It was rumoured that Jameel had captured and tamed her, and that she was now his faithful bodyguard. Jameel al-Kindi's horse Amjad did not shy or buck in the presence of the big cat. It was observed, in fact, that the lioness and the horse touched their muzzles to one another at times, as if they were friends.

One afternoon, Vara sat with her mother and father in the courtyard, which had been fitted out with scavenged tables, chairs, and an old bed serving as a lounge big enough for two. Jameel and Lioness reclined upon it. Her great tawny head was in his lap, and with his one good hand he stroked her neck and played with her ears as she stretched. Hubert stood behind them, eating dates and fanning Jameel with a palm frond.

Vara remembered with sad fondness how her mother had taught herself to purr like a cat, something she would do when in a particularly soft or amorous mood. Jameel had loved it; it was an audible token of the love they had for each other. Vara had never really thought about it until now. She had been told that lions did not purr as small house-cats did, but perhaps this was believed simply because no man or woman had ever been near a lion or lioness who was in the mood to do it. Perhaps they had a private life, into which noisy, destructive humans were not admitted.

Vara kept mostly to her Moorish Woman form these days, and had informed the family that they were to refer to her as Vara. It had taken a few days for them all to accept that this was really her; though they had adventured together, everyone seemed to imagine she was a different person now. In fact, not a person at all.

But it was simply her outward appearance. What was inside remained the same. Did it not? And her mother was still her mother, was she not?

Lioness—Ragna—rolled onto her back and allowed Jameel to tickle her belly. She huffed and grumbled a bit, snuffling gently at Jameel's fingers, but then Vara's ears pricked up. Had the grumbling softened? Yes. The deep, rough vibration from Lioness's chest smoothed, became rhythmic... became a purr.

Vara, reluctant to impinge on their pleasure, smiled a little, and bent her head again to lists of farm records. It seemed that conditions were still very bad, but were slowly improving as folk returned to their small holdings and began to plant again, and to search for surviving livestock that had scattered into the hills and forests. Emperor Ludvik, severely frightened and outraged at the recent unrest, had washed his hands of it all and delegated rule to Jameel al-Kindi, and was staying safely in Soissons. Wise of him.

Vara's eyes were on the lists, but her thoughts were elsewhere. They dwelt on Akil.

Akil had become her closest friend. The memory of his touch, and of their melding during battle, was hot within her. She closed her eyes. *I will not weep for what I must not have.*

She must never meld with another *resura*. She was not destined to be a God. She did not want to be one. She knew, now, that madness lay along that path.

But just then Akil, as if summoned by her thoughts, came into the courtyard and settled himself cross-legged at her feet. He didn't look at her, but his good hand slid across the cool stone of the courtyard's floor and encircled her ankle. Just for a moment.

Evening was falling. A nightingale began to sing, somewhere in the city close by.

It is said that once a year, under a full moon, an immense bird flies over the city of Perpignan. Her wings create the wind, and her eyes light the stars.
She is seen by few, and is gone by morning.

The End

Sally McBride's short stories and novellas have appeared in *Asimov's*, *Amazing*, *Fantasy & Science Fiction*, *Realms of Fantasy*, *Northern Frights*, *Tesseracts*, *On Spec*, and many more magazines, anthologies and best-of collections. "The Fragrance of Orchids" (*Asimov's*) won Canada's Aurora Award and received Hugo and Nebula nominations. She has taught fiction writing and edited speculative fiction, co-publishing the magazine *TransVersions*. Her previous novels include *Indigo Time* (Five Rivers Publishing) and *Water, Circle, Moon* (Masque Books). Born and raised in Canada, Sally divides her time between Toronto and the mountains of Idaho where she enjoys skiing and hiking with her husband. She has several works in progress.

CPSIA information can be obtained
at www.ICGtesting.com
Printed in the USA
LVHW041917271222
735800LV00003B/77